Agrico

Celtic Fervour Series
Book 4

Nancy Jardine

Ocelot Press

Copyright © 2018 by Nancy Jardine

Cover Artwork: Karen Barrett

Editor: Stephanie Patterson

Agricola's Bane

All rights reserved. No part of this book may be stored, shared, copied, transmitted or reproduced in any way without the express written permission from the author, except for brief quotations used for promotion, or in reviews. This is a work of fiction. Names, characters, places, and incidents are used fictitiously.

First Edition *Nancy Jardine with Ocelot Press 2018*

"The entire series is set firmly among the very best of early Romano British novels."
Helen Hollick 'Discovering Diamond Reviews.

Find Nancy Jardine online: www.nancyjardineauthor.com
Join Nancy Jardine on Facebook
https://www.facebook.com/NancyJardinewrites
Follow Nancy Jardine's blog:
https://nancyjardine.blogspot.co.uk/
Nancy loves to hear from her readers and can be contacted at nan_jar@btinternet.com or via her blog and website.

Dedication

I dedicate this book to the many ordinary people who, through no fault of their own, find themselves in a refugee situation, or living in harsh circumstances under which usurping governments or ruthless rulers oversee them in a callously brutal way. History provides us with too many of these contemptible situations over millennia; though I fear mankind has not learned sufficient lessons from these historical events to prevent this from still happening in contemporary times.

Acknowledgements

I give hearty thanks to the people who have given me advice during the preparation of this first edition, especially to those authors associated with Ocelot Press. My endless gratitude goes to my editor Stephanie Paterson whose excellent suggestions for changes were very welcome during edits, and whose superb editing skills have polished this story to a shine as dazzling as the lorica segmentata (breastplate armour) worn by the senior officers who appear in Agricola's Bane.

To my husband of many years - immense love always and enduring thanks for the numerous cups of coffee and meals that appeared in front of me as I wrote this novel. I'm quite happy for my cooking skills to continue to deteriorate, though my Roman soldiers and Celtic Warriors are never going to be allowed to let their blades rust!

About the author

Nancy Jardine's interest in all historical periods never wanes, the era of the Ancient Roman invasion of northern Britain continuing to be a particular obsession. Those barbarians (according to the Romans) who lived beyond the Roman Empire's boundaries left many secrets that have still to be unravelled and she hopes, in due course, to find out about a lot more of them.

When not researching, or engaged in various writing tasks, Nancy is a fair weather gardener and a regular grandchild minder. The 'castle' country of Aberdeenshire, Scotland, is a fabulous place to live – there are thousands of years of history on the doorstep and fabulous places for intrepid young explorers to investigate (Nancy included).

As a member of an Aberdeenshire Crafters group, she regularly visits local venues where signed paperback versions of her novels are available for purchase. This direct contact is an excellent way to gain bookings for author presentations across Aberdeenshire which are tailor made for each group she visits. Some prefer information about her writing life and her novels; while others are hungry for a taste of the Ancient Roman invasions of their local environment.

Since retiring from primary teaching in 2011, eight novels have been published, the ninth being worked on, as well as occasional input added to a couple of Victorian based manuscripts.

Nancy is a member of the Historical Novel Society; the Romantic Novelists Association; the Scottish Association of Writers, the Federation of Writers Scotland and the Alliance of Independent Authors.

Agricola's Bane

Characters in Agricola's Bane

A – *General Gnaeus Iulius Agricola*; Aila of Finhaven (Venicones)
B – Beathan of Garrigill (Brigante); Brennus of Garrigill (Brigante)
C – Calum of SrathBogie (Taexali); Colm of Ceann Druimin (Caledon); Conchar of Finhaven (Venicones)
D – Derwi (Taexali captive); Donnachadh (Taexali at Baile Mheadhain); Dhoughall of Dunrelugas (Vacomagi)
E – Enya of Garrigill (Brigante)
F – Feargus of Monymusk (Taexali); Fingal of Wichach (Taexali); Fionnah wife of Gabrond (Brigante); *Titus Sicinia Flavus* (junior tribune)
G – Gabrond of Garrigill (Brigante); Garth of Culbeuchly (Vacomagi); Gilie of Tap O'Noth (Taexali)
H – *Manius Helva* (Tungrian)
I – Ineda wife of Brennus (Brigante)
L – *Quintus Laterensus* (speculatores leader); *Lentulus* (Agricola's junior scribe); *Gaius Salvius Liberalis* (Britannic Judicial Legate); *Crispus Gellius Libo* (Agricola's secretary); Lorcan of Garrigill (Brigante); Lulach of Ceann Druimin (Caledon)
M – Mharaidh of Ceann Druimin (Caledon)
N – Nara of Tarras/Garrigill (Selgovae); Nith of Tarras (Selgovae); Nhiall of the Laich (Vacomagi); Nathrach of Caladar (Vacomagi)
R – Ruoridh of Garrigill (Brigante); *Marcius Rufinus* (allectus special courier); Raghnall of Tap O'Noth (Taexali)
S – Seaghan of An Cuan Moireach (Vacomagi)
T – Torren of Tap O'Noth (Taexali); Torquil of Dunrelugas (Vacomagi)

A.D. 84 Southern Locations in Agricola's Bane

A.D. 84 Local Locations in Agricola's Bane

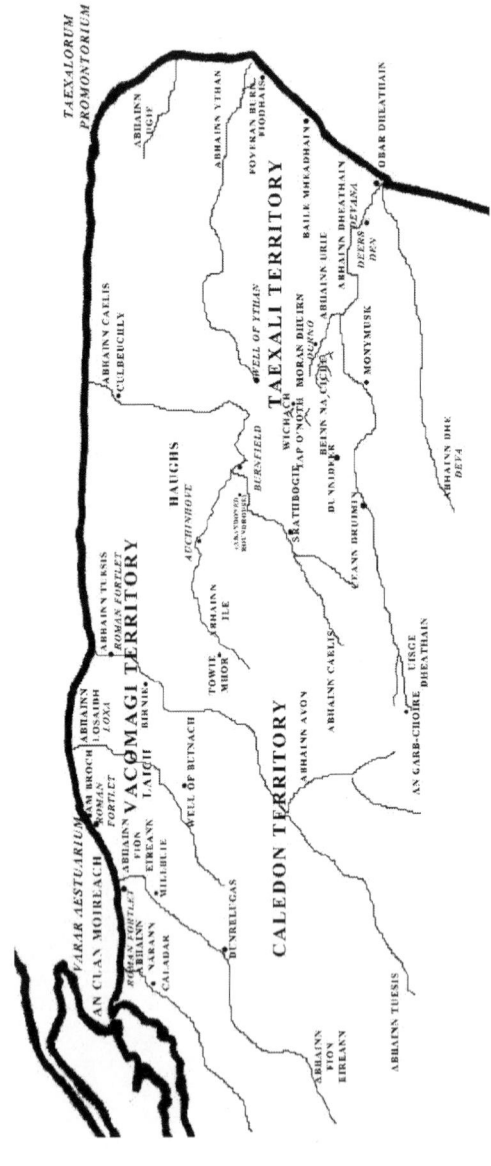

Chapter One

Glenlaff Woods, Caledon Territory

"*Arddhu?* I fear you are not a happy god."

Enya's disgruntled whisper might be unworthy thinking, but the local forest god seemed to favour no one.

A deep chill, accompanied by a squally wind, had descended after dawn causing a last cascade of colourful leaf-drop to glide down from the birches. The burnished butterfly-flutters might have been appealing had the day been a fair one but *Arddhu* demonstrated his anger at the bloody deeds of the warriors in his precious territory.

"Ouu…ouu…ouu…ouu…"

Down the slope from where she took cover, the thundering of capercaillie alarm in the undergrowth of the forest was followed by the strident tapping of a woodpecker.

"Tchik…tchik…"

The double woodpecker call repeated itself.

Two of them!

Her insides fluttered as she pressed her back closer to the damp tree trunk, her teeth clenched tight together to suppress the urge to rant. Her eyes pressed so wide she feared they might pop out of their sockets. After pulling the edges of her bratt tighter across her freezing cheeks for more protection, she sneaked her head round to peer down the hill. They had not been the truest of capercaillie or woodpecker calls. Colm of Ceann Druimin and Nith of Tarras, members of her scouting patrol, had issued their warnings. Two Roman soldiers were in the vicinity.

She had not encountered any of the Roman invaders since the disastrous battle fought at Beinn na Ciche, but she sincerely hoped the otherworld was ready and waiting for the ones she aimed to dispatch there. Slithering sideways to the shelter of the next bole, there was a pause while she drew breath, her life-force thumping in her chest, ears strained for further cautioning.

She snatched a glance down the steep incline, though still saw nothing human. A side-to-side check, and another to the hillside above her, revealed no signs of the enemy, either, before she pressed her back onto the trunk. Why would two of the Roman turds have separated from their companions? It had been drummed into her that the smallest fighting unit rarely separated. Except if they were the ones Uncle Lorcan called *exploratores.* Those scouts evaluated the territory in advance of the *legion*s and often worked alone, or in small groups. She hitched in another large gulp of air when a new thought occurred.

Could they be *speculatores*? She loathed them even more.

She bit back on her imaginings, her head shivering when she squeezed her eyelids tight to dispel the foolish notion, the new-falling sleet not helping at all. Surely, the Roman General Agricola could not possibly be long enough in Taexali lands to be sending out those Uncle Brennus named *speculatores.* Those men were spies. They infiltrated the local tribes to gain information to send back to their Roman commanders.

The faintest of rustling sounds set her senses on alert. Her torso rigid, she filtered out low trickles of melted sleet dripping from nearby foliage, but something else disturbed the intense serenity of the forest. She curled her fist around her long-bladed knife, little by little withdrawing the weapon from its leather sheath and set it alongside her thigh, before twisting around to peer down the slope. Juniper branches trembled a few paces away.

Enya's breath trapped in her throat. Inching her knee around the tree trunk, she prepared herself for attack. The sudden flurry of a mistle thrush taking off from the spiny needles had her trembling with relief, though she continued to watch the bush for longer moments, just to be sure there was nothing more that had disturbed the bird.

Feeling truly brave was not yet a customary emotion that came to her, even if what she showed to others seemed coldly fearless. Since the carnage of battle against the Roman armies on the foothills of Beinn na Ciche, she awoke each new day with strengthening resolve.

Somehow she would overcome her qualms and set out to find her missing brother and cousin, and she would fight against the Roman usurpers with her last breath to achieve it.

"Tchik...tchik..." More repetitions came, reminding her to be vigilant.

She swallowed down the spit she wanted to blast onto the leaves below her feet, but such a gesture of contempt might be too noisy. Her thinking ran on full-pelt though her gaze continued to assess around. Many *speculatores* were Celtic born before they had joined the Roman auxiliary units, but they were now in the thrall of the Romans who rewarded their tribes by absorbing their land into the Roman Empire. Another bile-laden grimace was forced down her throat. Imposed conscription to the Roman army seemed a poor reward for those subsumed tribes.

If Lorcan and Brennus of Garrigill were correct, she would never have to face that fate. A dry laugh was suppressed. Dull-witted Romans! Many female warriors fought just as ferociously as the males of their tribe. The Romans enslaved captive women, or used them so ill before they mangled them into the ground, but she would never let that happen to her.

A twinge of doubt crossed her mind. Brennus' new hearth-wife, Ineda, had not wanted to be captured many seasons ago, yet Brennus had been powerless to stop it, even though he was one of the tallest and strongest warriors she had ever met.

She snatched a peep down the slope. A light sleet fell in the pale-grey gloom, though the leaf-drop had ceased, the early morning wind having died away. The sight below meant it was difficult to focus on particular markers in the way her Uncle Lorcan had taught her. One tree merged into another where the stronger white flakes clung, but she knew that somewhere down there were two Roman soldiers, blending into that murkiness.

It was in the hands of the forest god *Arddhu* who would be revealed first.

Ròmanach buachar each! If she met one of these horse-shit *speculatores*, she would throttle him with her bare hands.

"Tchik…tchik…tchik…"

When the new series of woodpecker taps echoed around, followed by the deeply-croaked repeated kraa of a crow – the pause between each series of kraas being unnaturally long – she made a desperate plea. She vowed to *Scathach,* teacher of warrior women, to give her strength to rid the forest of the foe, and to help her avenge what Rome was doing to her family.

Having checked that the fourth member of her band, Feargus of Monymusk, was still close by, she blew on her freezing fingers before she curved her hands around her partly open mouth and sent her answering crossbill call.

"Choop…choop…choop…"

Her rapid series of choops acknowledged there were now three enemy auxiliaries skulking around. Hunkering down behind the trunk, she shook off the icy layer from her bratt, and then slapped the ends of the sodden wool back over her shoulders. Her fingers were numb and clumsy as she tucked in wayward strands that had escaped her plaited hair. The measure was poor protection for her chittering body, the freezing rain stinging her cheeks like she imagined a branding tine would do, though she had yet to experience that. Such happy celebrations to acknowledge her recently gained warrior-status had been delayed, and were likely to be deferred for a long while.

The slightest slip of slushy leaves sparked her attention, but she quickly re-sheathed her partly drawn knife, her gaze tracking the movements made alongside her tree.

The soft nudge at her shoulder had her rising again to create more room for Feargus of Monymusk, his sidling-in right next to her not unexpected since each of them was set to guard the other. Restrained exasperation clouded the light-grey glance he darted her way, before he reassured himself that all was well in the near vicinity and turned back towards her.

The low-heat emanating from his body was welcome warmth after a few moments, or perhaps it was just that he sheltered her from the elements on one side. She doubted he would snuggle as close to Nith or Colm, unless he had no other option, but presently she took comfort from his thin frame and made no objection to the close contact.

It was an age till he whispered, during which her shaky breathing seemed loud in the absence of natural forest noises, the woodland inhabitants warm and tight under cover, unlike she was. Only humans were foolish enough to be out in such unpleasant weather.

"Vengeance must be harnessed, yet again, Enya. If Nith can only see three of them, then we must hold back an attack. More of them will be close by, though we have not yet spied them."

Feargus' deep voice was the merest flight of wind tickling at her ear, his fledgling red chin-whiskers an itch she had learned to bear. She was becoming used to the young warrior who was only older than she was by a few seasons. He had been her constant lookout companion during her last two days on surveillance duty.

Enya avidly scanned the surroundings on her side and down the slope, her response mouthed rather than actually heard. "What is happening? I neither see Nith, nor any of these Romans, yet his call came up clearly enough."

"Have you spied Colm down there?"

Feargus sounded casual yet she guessed he was probably as anxious as she was about the fourth and youngest member of their patrol.

Colm of Ceann Druimin was the only one bred in the area, but he had the least experience of Roman conquest, having been at the rear of the battlegrounds at Beinn na Ciche. He had not confronted any of the ferocious Tungrian or Batavian forces of Agricola. In fact, he had barely encountered any Romans at all.

"Nay," she replied. "Those Roman auxiliaries must still be at some distance. Nith has to be making use of Colm's local knowledge of the dips and pitfalls of these woods."

Enya felt the censure in eyes and tone when Feargus grunted before sidling away. "Cease your fretting. Nith of Tarras needs no advice about forest surveying."

She could not prevent the compressing of her lips. "True enough, but the foolish man should not be out scouting yet. His battle wounds remain raw and this relentless chill will have his breathing rattling like the drumming of warrior fingers at the feast of Beltane, but will he listen to me?"

Feargus' disapproval continued though his tone held a hint of admiration. "Even I know well enough by now that Nith will not be constrained to take rest. His blood vengeance still lingers too high for that."

Enya was vexed that her foolish friend from the Selgovae hillfort of Tarras would undo the careful tending he had received at sunrise from her Aunt Nara. Nith was a hardy young man, his unshakable persistence in seeking Roman retribution an enviable trait, but ten nights were not sufficient for full-healing of the deep chest lacerations he had received. And the loss of his brother under a Roman *gladius* cut much more deeply than his external wounds. He was heart-sore, had become solitary, and consoling him was not presently in her powers. She wanted so much to have her non-blood brother back, but that Nith had fled, leaving a gaunt and changed shell of the man who meant so much to her and her kin.

Her teeth clattered together when she answered. "N…Nith has not trekked this far from Tarras to succumb to the infernal early winter that you have here in Taexali lands."

Feargus' wide grin broke some of the strain, his head shake a denial which resulted in droplets of sleet to spatter from his bristly chin hair. "This is Caledon territory, and these hills are different from my Taexali eastern flatlands. Yet even here in the Caledon forests, early sleet like this does not usually fall till closer to our shortest day. Our gods send a message to those who skirmish around them."

Enya huffed, a small quiet agreement. "It would be good to know who of us that the gods punish the most. Is the disfavour mainly for my fellow Brigantes to reflect on, or is it directed at our invading Roman destroyers? Perhaps if you pray harder to your local gods, whoever they may be our plight will be alleviated?"

The softest of chuckles escaped Feargus' lips, his eyes twinkling with mirth when they met hers.

"Praying to my Taexali gods would not be the answer."

Enya liked that he could smile, because for the most part since they had met he had been sad to the bone.

"Though these parts do not lie so far from my Monymusk Taexali territory, the folk hereabouts have their own deities. It may be the *Cailleach Bheur* we need to pray to, but I do not have words strong enough to pacify the blue hag. Chief Lulach of Ceann Druimin is the one who knows all across his land." His whispers came slowly as his gaze continued an ever-alert dart.

A tight smile broke free before Enya peeped around the tree for a quick survey herself. Her gaze whipping back to Feargus, she answered, "Chief Lulach may have given my displaced Brigante kin the shelter of his valley, but I dread the man's barbed tongue."

Feargus' nod was slight. "Aye. Your folk have suffered dearly at the hands of the Roman bane for much longer than my fellow Taexali tribespeople have. I doubt there are many Selgovae survivors from those that you lived amongst for part of your life."

Enya stared at him. "How can you possibly know that about us?"

Feargus grinned, the glance that came her way an affectionate one she found herself responding to. "I pay heed around the night-fires. People from far afield are always interesting to learn about. I am eager to know more of the Garrigill Brigantes, and the Tarras Selgovae, who have trekked so far from their homes."

Enya poked her head around the tree, needing to break free of a connection she was enjoying, yet was not sure where she wished it to lead to. "Aye. The continual tramp northwards has me wearied. My kin have had no home to call our own for too many of my fourteen summers, but I did not realise we were so gossiped about at the firesides."

Doubt raised Feargus' eyebrows, his grin gone. "You have come from a great distance and have knowledge of many Celtic tribes, most of whom were nameless to me. My people of Monymusk rarely left the sight of The Mither Tap at Beinn na Ciche."

After another quick survey she nudged Feargus who was backed onto the tree trunk for support, his eyes closed. "Have you never ventured far before Agricola's Roman invasion?"

Light sleet dappled his pale-red eyelashes but his lids remained closed when he answered, his trust in her surveying obvious to her. "No more than the trek of a day to the waters of the coast. My mother came from Baile Mheadhain."

"Nay!" Enya's gasp was louder than she intended. Her clutch at his arm startled her even more than him when his arm stiffened to stone. "Agricola's fleet are beached there."

Chapter Two

Glenlaff Woods, Caledon Territory

Feargus' eyes bled a glistening he could not seem to prevent. "I fear greatly for my mother's kin. Your uncle, the one named Brennus, told me that captives have already been shipped away to be sold as slaves of the Roman Empire. I dread what I might find, but the only way to know for sure is to go there."

Enya ignored the hitch in his voice. He was a proud young warrior. She still had many of her relatives around her, but Feargus sounded like he had none left.

Opening his eyes, his gaze slipped to the trees alongside them. "My father's people were farmers at Monymusk. I seem to have neither kinfolk nor fields to tend, since the Romans encircle them. Or my people are like your brother and cousin: lost to me for now, until I find them again."

"I hate those shite of *Araun*!" Enya's feelings erupted. The searches after the battle had found no trace of her brother or cousin, dead or alive. "I hate what those Romans have done to people who just want to be left alone to live their lives in their own way."

Feargus exhaled noisily though his open mouth. "While the Roman General Agricola occupies our lands, my fellow Taexali are displaced people, just like you Brigante are. We must all rely on our Caledon mountain neighbours to give us succour, and tender us the hand of friendship."

"Aye. Those of us who wish for no Romanisation of our daily ways need to stand strong together. That is why my Brigante kin travelled so far north before the battle raged at Beinn na Ciche. During my later growing years, we had hoped that our move to Selgovae territory, to my Aunt Nara's birthplace at Tarras, would bring us safety from Roman domination. But we were so wrong, Feargus. General Agricola still continues his northern invasions."

"Is that when you first met Nith?"

Enya nodded. A skip to her breathing came unbidden. "Nith and my aunt share a distant bloodline. He is like family to me now, as was his older brother Esk." Much as she tried to remain unaffected, her voice wobbled. "Esk was slain at Beinn na Ciche. It tears Nith apart, though he could do nothing to prevent his brother from making a last charge into those bastard Batavians."

Feargus' finger pointing skywards drew Enya's clouded gaze aloft. "Daylight wanes now. More Romans than those three may be scouring the area, but I do not believe they will come any closer. Your Uncle Brennus told me the invaders return to their turf walls before dark fully descends, as they do at their encampment of the many fists."

"Moran Dhuirn." After yet another survey down into the valley, her answer was a continued snarled spit. "That camp place was well named by Calgach. I wish that there were no fists at all to be seen brandishing those bright swords and shields at Moran Dhuirn – but it is not so."

"General Agricola leaving so many of his troops there seems to be puzzling the elders back at Ceann Druimin." Feargus' statement had her turn back to him again.

She felt deep resentful anger over Roman domination roil over her. She was hardly ever free of it. "That confuses everyone who has had past dealings with Agricola. I detest that man!"

Feargus swung his body round to face her. The reassuring rubs at her elbows were a welcome surprise, though not easy with his spear still in his grip. It was the first time he had given her physical sympathy, along with a softening of his expression.

"As do we all, Enya, but for now we should ready ourselves to head back to the hearths of Ceann Druimin." After a hesitant, embarrassed smile he gently withdrew his hands. He nodded up towards the forest edge before he slipped away to the next large ash tree, then over to better cover behind a wider oak.

A rush of pure disgust of the Roman enemy had Enya snapping the soggy debris beneath her leather-clad feet as she hobbled to a nearby mature pine, the moss linings now too damp to be effective in maintaining warmth for her ice-nipped toes. Behind the pine's shelter, she dipped her trembling head against the fissured bark, fearing her exhausted woodsman skills would be hazardous. Tiredness and anger-laced frustration were no excuse when the tiniest lack of attention could mean death to her fellow-warriors.

She knelt down on one knee finding a balance point, her woollen braccae sodden around her legs. The softest of plops hit the wet tree roots beneath her, melted hail trickling down from her chin. After a long interval, her breathing shallow to suppress the complaints her aching body wanted to scream out, she heard Feargus begin a new bird call. One designed to find out what was happening below.

"Treeil...treeil..."

The high-low trill of his crested tit cry was answered by a thudding capercaillie flutter from Colm, the heavy bird clattering coming from much closer than before. Colm's repeated calls now rang near the sleet-speckled rusty leaves of the blaeberry bushes way down to her right, beyond which was an even deeper glen.

Enya's spirits lifted when a flash of deep brown was visible, though if it was Nith he was still quite far off. The desperate urge to see Nith safe was hard to fathom. Her brother, Ruoridh, often annoyed her, but Nith irritated her even more. Why that should make her smile was unfathomable.

When some truly thunderous flapping of capercaillie wings rent the air, her warrior hackles rose. Nith's strident crow-cry sent small birds to rise from their shelter in a flutter of distress when a clash of metal on metal clanged all around the forest.

Fear fled in an instant, an exhilaration of the hunt replacing it.

Enya took to her heels down the slope after Feargus, skittering and slithering her way through the saplings and around the more mature trees towards the denser glade below. More crow calls came from Nith but none of the capercaillie. It was bellowing human cries that rent the glen.

Colm was being set upon!

Before her long knife was even drawn from its sheath, Feargus launched himself around a thick clump of blaeberry bushes. His spear hurtled through the air before thudding into the lower body of a Roman soldier with such force it knocked the man sideways. The tip entering just below the chain mail meant more chance of it disabling the man entirely. The Roman's gurgling cry was of astonishment as well as agony.

A flash of dull metal to her left alerted her.

Enya's spear did not miss its mark either when it thumped a second soldier to the ground, a man who had bent towards the prone body of Colm. Sheer hatred was in her triumphant call when she saw the enemy struggle to rise.

"Free yourself from my spear, you horse dung!"

Feargus pursued a third soldier who had turned tail and had run off. Devoid of his spear, he was too far away to brandish his other blade but the Roman had no chance of escape. A whup, whup, whup rent the air as Feargus' long knife found its mark after spiralling across the intervening space, hilt, tip, hilt, tip, hilt, tip – the solid hilt accurately finding its mark between the soldier's shoulders. Feargus was upon the felled man before the victim could summon the strength to climb to his feet. Enya had no need to watch Feargus as he hacked at the man's legs, before the last slashes with his knife were made.

When Enya reached Colm, the soldier she had poled to the ground squealed and bleated as he squirmed to free his upper arm from the entrapment, his attempt to break the shaft unsuccessful. Frantically swinging it in her direction, the young auxiliary whirled and bucked to avoid the slashes of her blade. As she raised her long knife anew, the end of the spear walloped against her jaw, the impact splintering the tip, the sudden pain excruciating. The blow was not sound enough to knock her over, but the jarring sent the man sprawling. Landing heavily on his side, he yelped when the pole cracked asunder, the spear tip still stuck firmly in his upper arm. Forcing him onto his front with one well aimed boot roll, Enya clipped away the shallow helmet neck-guard with her knife.

She had him at her mercy but she would give him none.

Striking repeatedly at the freed flesh with her long blade, which was not much shorter than the Roman's *gladius*, a white hot rage engulfed her. Blood spattered and bone cracked.

Would her Celtic lands never be free of the Roman scum? The next cut was for Ruoridh. Another hack was for her cousin, Beathan, and more for Feargus' dead kin from Monymusk. Her blade continued a repetitious slashing. Her brother would be found or avenged. Either way, she vowed to remove as many of the Roman usurpers as she could.

"Enya!"

Fergus' noisy reprimand eventually penetrated her frenzy. Lowering her blade she stared at him, the thudding inside her chest almost engulfing her.

It was his palms cradling her shoulders and his soft voice at her ear that reminded her to breathe properly. "Enough. He will trouble Colm no longer."

Shaking off her battle-rage, Enya forced away the tears that pooled and hovered on her lashes. The sleet-dappled undergrowth around her ran crimson around the fallen bodies. Gulping down some deep breaths, she eased herself away and bent to wipe her knife blood-free on the grasses nearby, forcing an unnatural unconcern. "Is Colm badly hurt?"

"Nay. He stirs already." He pointed to a rapidly swelling lump on Colm's forehead. "It looks as though he has been winded by that Roman's shield boss. Between us, we will get him back to Chief Lulach."

"Nith!" The thought of his safety had her jumping back up to her feet to frantically scan around. "Where is he?"

"Over here."

Enya swivelled in the direction the voice was coming from, sheer relief replacing her battle-lust.

"That was a deed well done!" Nith's praise sounded fulsome but his expression did not match.

There was a downturn to his lip that Enya could not fail to notice, his crackle of words and harsh breathing drawing even more of her attention. His stare moved from her face to Feargus, something annoying him. Ignoring his strange glances, she was so pleased to see he had no new injuries.

Nith looked around the littered area. "Your spears and blades have rung no mercy. That makes three Romans less to trouble us." He broke off to gain a hard-won breath, his fingers roaming to massage his upper chest. "This trio were blundering around further down Glenlaff Woods. I startled them into flight, but they spied Colm before I caught up with them."

Enya stared at the bodies, their spilt blood and torn flesh splattering the ground as Nith turned them over. From having been in fighting-frenzy just moments before, she now felt only a sense of relief. Nith was safe, if not perfectly sound. Otherwise, the strangest of calms had descended. Dispassion. She did not see the mangled bodies as men, or as Roman soldiers; she viewed the remnants only as an eliminated potential harm to her family.

Nith and Feargus began to strip them of useful metal. The pile of helmets, knives and belts grew, but it was not the easiest job when it came to her supporting a slithering body before they rippled off the chainmail. The combination of blood, light sleet and her freezing fingers extended the task.

"None of them are enlisted long enough to have the trappings of medals and special ornamentation." Nith grunted as he and Feargus pulled the mail shirt free of another dead body.

"Could they have been deserting from their unit?"

Feargus' question seemed like a fair enough one, though Enya doubted it. The tie to the Roman Empire was too strong for recruits to break, retribution to their kin being a feared burden borne by tribesmen newly subjugated by the Roman Emperor.

"Thanks be to *Arddhu*!"

Further oaths came from Colm as he struggled to rise, making Enya smirk as she collected the Roman javelins, Feargus having lifted the *gladii*.

Nith stretched out a free hand to help Colm to his feet. "Can you walk unaided back to Ceann Druimin?"

Colm fingered the huge swelling at his temple. "Aye. Though, those strange spears might make me steadier on my feet."

Enya held out her javelin clutch, her derisive spit a direct hit on the face of one of the dead auxiliaries. "They call them *pila*. You are welcome to them."

Colm gave the Roman shield that lay close by a vicious kick before reaching for the *pila*. Pointing to the boss he growled, "That lump of metal came at me like a bolt from *Taranis*."

"Take these, Enya, and tell me what you think." Nith passed her the helmets to carry, before he grasped two of the mail shirts and hefted them over his shoulder, suppressing a hiss of agony as they slapped against his wounds. Feargus had lifted the other shirt.

Tucking two of the helmets under her armpit she examined the third. "This is like the skull-fits that the cavalry use. But why were these men on foot, if they were mounted scouts?"

"Exactly so, Enya. There were no signs of stray horses in the woods."

Nith set a grim pace out of the trees, looking askance at Colm. "That soldier was a lot taller than you. You need Brennus of Garrigill to teach you ways of surviving an attack from an opponent with a higher reach, while you are still in your growing phase."

Enya's flashed grin was short-lived, the stretching at her chin a throbbing sting. With no free hands, any exploration of her wound would need to wait till later. She bit back on an errant yelp.

Nith had tried very hard not to mention that Colm was a small warrior, something the young lad had railed about. It was not unusual for a youth to continue to grow after maturity, though she doubted that would happen to Colm. His father was not typical of the tall reddish-haired Caledons that she had met. Stocky, brown eyed and dark-pelted described well the family of Chief Lulach of Ceann Druimin.

Chapter Three

Moran Dhuirn Roman Camp, Taexali Territory

"On your feet!"

Only the last word was properly heard when the shrill command jolted Beathan out of a fragile sleep and straight into the horror of his surroundings. Unable to prevent the shivers that overwhelmed him he squeezed his arms tighter to his chest, to hold his cloak in place. The yanking of the shackle at each aching wrist told him well enough what the rest of the missed instructions might mean.

His clutching fingers at his elbows could no longer keep in any of the mean heat when they were prised away in opposite directions, the length of chain tethering each man to the next being only a short stretch. Warriors to either side of him uncurled their legs and forced their protesting bodies to a standing position, leaving him no option but to do likewise. Swivelling onto his knees, he looked around to work out what was amiss, since the Roman guards had left him and his wretched companions sitting on the freezing mud for the last long while, the first rays of a pinkish-hue sent by the god *Lugh* having lightened the gloom some time ago.

"Get up!" The commands issued came from someone out of uniform.

Beathan looked closely at the man while he struggled from knees to standing, his legs stiff and awkward from the cold ground, his neighbour, Derwi, almost dragging him back down again when the chain on the other end pulled sideward.

The person who strode past him, and continued along the row, looked no different from his own kin. The tunic, cloak and braccae were not much different from his; the whiskers at the man's top lip the mark of a tribesman.

Beathan bent his head, his drained question not really meant to be answered. "A traitorous native scout?"

Derwi had good hearing. "Aye, I think so. Or perhaps he is the other kind who pretends to be our friend." His words were soft; the snort at the end loud.

The swift return of the scout shut Beathan's lips tight, the man's threat truly menacing. Heavy brows glowered over malevolent eyes, which only twitched after a very long ogling of his neighbour. The curling of the scout's fist around the handgrip of the long sword he bore was not really necessary since Beathan already felt terrified.

"Face front. Not a whisper from anyone."

Beathan gulped. Even the man's teeth were predatory as he paced along a few more captives.

"Do you hear?"

The line had already learned to only nod at such times. Beathan stared ahead biting down his feelings when the scout returned to halt in front him, his intent look a long and penetrating one before the man strode off again. He had only time enough to decide that perhaps the warrior was one of the infiltrators, rather than just a normal scout, when the next worry began.

The clanking of different metals and approaching voices were drowned out by the incomprehensible growled-malice spouting from the senior soldier who strode up the line towards him, a wooden vine rod whipping forward at every opportunity to thwack the nearest unfortunate victim. Auxiliaries under the superior soldier's command who paced alongside him urged Beathan and his fellow captives to stand free of the next tribesman, some of whom had been unable to get to their feet without support.

For once, he almost wished his father's brother, Brennus, had not taught him about the ranks of the Roman army. Compelled to fulfil orders coming from a lowly scout was bad enough, but seeing the precisely-trimmed horsehair brush, bristling out from ear to ear across the top of the helmet, stop in front of him, meant its wearer was of *centurion* status. The glittering decorations adorning the man's chest armour were a further indication to Beathan that the soldier had been long in post in the Roman Army.

More shivers wracked him. He was sure the attendance of this senior soldier could not bring good news. He tried hard not to flinch when the wooden tip of the *centurion*'s mark of office poked him in the shoulder and forced him to straighten up. Intimidating dark eyes peered up at him when Beathan stretched his back and lifted his chin.

He had no idea what language the *centurion* spoke when the man berated him, but he was sure none of it was Latin; and it was not like the common language of the Celtic tribes. He had heard many different variations of that during the long moons of fleeing Roman domination, but this tongue was different. One of the soldiers under the *centurion*'s command, most likely the man his Uncle Brennus called the *optio* – who commanded a half-century – responded in similar fast-spat tones. But Beathan could tell nothing from it. The nods between them as they talked made it seem as if they were sometimes in agreement, though he discerned little from their expressions and gestures during the rest of their conference.

After one last spiteful sideward glare the *centurion* moved along to his neighbour. Out of the side of his eye, Beathan knew only partial relief when he realised the treatment of the next captive was similar. Without incurring the wrath of the attending guards, he watched as each tribesman, in turn, was assessed by the *centurion*. Small in stature the officer might have been, but he was not small in influence. Every other man in his captive line was on the receiving end of that vicious vine rod.

"Stand still!" The scout repeatedly made his own way up and down the line behind the *centurion* and his soldiers.

The inspection was never ending. Beathan could think of no reason for it, but every now and then over the last few days since his capture, warriors alongside him had been unchained, and taken away. Sometimes it was those who had serious injuries from the recent battle, but at other times it seemed to be random. When the guards were close by, the captives were not permitted to speak, so anyone raising objections was not the target. He doubted many of his tribesmen would, or could. The smallest attempts to speak meant a ferocious fist to the gut, or one that knocked a man off his feet. His own swollen cheekbone and split-lip were the results of him not obeying a command quickly enough.

Moran Dhuirn! Many fists. There were plenty of available fists around this Roman camp and all of them happily used. Beathan had heard some tribesmen call the Roman camp Moran Dhuirn even before the confrontation at Beinn na Ciche, Agricola's troops having set it up the day prior to the battle.

Another guard moved on past him. He dared an attempt to open his mouth – not to cry foul of those many fists, but more to feel the progress of his recovery. His lip still smarted, but the dull ache of his cheekbone was a lot more bearable than when he had received the blow a couple of days before.

When there was no soldier directly in front of him, the Roman camp lay spread out before his gaze. Close by, there was a large space that had been left cleared between two long rows of leather tents. Neatly placed, there were too many to easily count, but – he already knew that – each tent would accommodate a *contubernium* group of soldiers. That was two hands worth of men who often formed a bond of loyalty amongst themselves that was like the kinship of his family, the Garrigill Brigantes.

At the far end of the wide walking-space, he could see the high turf wall that marked the camp boundary. The excavated earth from the dug ditch had been piled up and then re-covered with the removed turf. The spikes of wood set into the raised turf mound made it an almost impassable barrier to scale. Impaling hazards would have been strategically placed in the ditches – Uncle Brennus had mentioned that as well – since the camp had been established for more than a se'nnight.

Between the last tents in the row and the camp perimeter he could see men walking mules along the space, having just entered the camp through an opening in the wall. The laden carts pulled by the beasts were filled high with what looked like brush-wood. Other men moved around the camp walkways, most of them with a destination in mind from the speed they moved at. Some soldiers knelt at the openings of tents in the struggling sunlight which slowly warmed the cold morning.

After being a captive for some days, the sight of the camp around him was not unfamiliar, yet something was different. Two men down the nearest row were heaving up the contents of their insides, quite spectacularly and with such force the vomit was splashing back up from the ground. One was uniformed, the other only wearing a tunic to the knees having just groped his way outside. The uniformed one looked to be on duty near the gateway at the far end but was incapable of doing a good job of it. Beathan had seen plenty of men empty their stomach after drinking too much small-beer, and though still a youth he had had enough experiences himself, but that this should happen in Agricola's camp seemed strange.

He felt a grinning satisfaction at their discomfort though it was fleeting. It was not usual to feel grateful about seeing a man empty good food from his belly, but the situation he was in was far from normal.

Beathan shivered again. The early weak winter-sun was now gone behind sleet-filled cloud cover, the first light flakes ominously fluttering down around him. He was not used to being in situations he had absolutely no control over. Sometimes his father, Lorcan, or his mother, Nara, laid down punishments if he had done something regrettable, but he could always improve the circumstances by learning how not to err in future. His chin slipped down, his brows knotting in his attempt to stall the threatening tears. The shame of capture forced his shoulders to fall as well, but his brief moment of guilt did not last.

He whipped his head back up again when the *centurion* returned to stride up and down the long line, the man's underlings a step behind muttering commands he could only guess at.

"Keep your heads up!"

The native scout made his command well-understood by thumping every other man at the shoulder as he went past. Beathan waited for the blow, only exhaling when the scout passed by. Down one of the pathways were the high tents he knew would belong to the senior officers of the *legion*. Coming around from the corner of one of them was a huddle of some five or six soldiers. Beathan did not even try to suppress his alarm.

"By *Taranis*, help us all! That soldier in the front looks even more important than the *centurion*."

Derwi agreed. "Aye, I fear so, Beathan. That moulded chest armour would have taken a skilled smith a very long time to fashion."

The group walking towards them was led by someone of medium height. The soldier wore no metal helmet, just the cloth cap that was worn beneath one sat tight to his ears. What marked him out as being important was the imperious set to the man's chin and the way the group trod in his wake. Derwi was right about the highly polished chest armour because it snuggled tight and was sculpted as though the wearer's chest was bare. The dark-red hue of the soldier's cloak was similar to others he had seen in the camp, worn by senior soldiers, but this one was the kind of super-fine weave his mother strove to create but could never produce. Delicate and soft, the man's cloak fell almost to the ground.

"How high is his command?" His words whispered but he was petrified. His gut churned, yet the strangest exhilaration tingled from top-to-toe.

The figure of authority stopped at the far end of the captive line and listened to what the *centurion* had to report, responding quickly with an obvious nod. The first man's chain was uncoupled. The captive was then shoved away by the one Beathan thought to be the *optio* to form a new line behind the senior officers.

Though too far off to hear what they said, Beathan prayed softly to his mother's goddess *Rhianna*, an increasing anxiety hastening his words as the group skipped along past a few captives before again halting.

"Give me strength, *Rhianna*. Let me live to be the warrior you told my mother I would become. I have nothing here to give you but my life. Let me be worthy of you."

Derwi's determined encouragement came to him in growled tones. "Beathan, listen to me. You are young yet, but fear not. You are already a warrior and worthy of the goddess. Your family have made you a proud opponent. Do not fail them."

By the time the group got closer to him, a few faint words heard meant that Beathan was sure he knew the officer's identity, his fear gone past the stage of making his body shudder and shake. Though he stood frozen, his mind whirled. Was this the greatness his mother's goddess had prophesied for him even before his birth? How could the goddess *Rhianna* want him to be standing in front of the supreme enemy of his family, save that of the Emperor of Rome himself?

His father, Lorcan, had led his kin northwards to avoid the clutches of this man's influence: to evade being forced to follow this Roman officer's dictates. His extended family had tramped north and north again many times, and for many long moons, to shun the habits of Rome.

How could the goddess want him to be in this position?

He understood some of the Latin words spoken before a captive, a few men down the chain from him, was removed but by then it was too late to pray any more. He was the next to receive the special singling out when General Agricola, the Governor of Britannia and the Commander of all Britannic *Legions*, came to a halt in front of him.

Beathan felt astute dark-brown eyes trail from his head to his toes, the man's height not much different from his own. There was no obvious malice of the scout; nevertheless, earnest features regarded him in silence, for many moments.

"Him, too. He was young for battle, but is well old-enough for the slavery I intend for him."

"This stripling, General Agricola?" The *centurion* sounded unsure though he nodded to the *optio* who came forward with the iron tool that unclipped the manacle at Beathan's wrist.

Chapter Four

*Ceann Druimin, Caledon Territory
– Chief Lulach's Roundhouse*

"Find yourself a place."

Nith's nod acknowledged Chief Lulach's command before his gaze swept the area. He recognised some of the crushed-in throng, in the dim roundhouse, as being from Ceann Druimin, people he had already talked to since his arrival at the village some nights past, though there were other faces he had never seen before. Seeking refuge, just like he did, or were they messengers? He hoped they were the latter.

Lulach stood opposite the entrance door. In the centre, was a low-burning fire which emitted a gentle heat. The space between the smouldering logs and the seated row of elders, on low stools or flat timbers of wood set up on slices of tree trunks, was just wide enough for the chief to pad along, yet narrow enough for the fire's heat to be felt by the nearest weary bones.

Most people ranged in behind: sitting cross-legged on the bracken-strewn beaten earth floor; hunkering down; or they stood squashed in at the back. Following Enya, he squeezed into the backmost row of people who propped themselves against the chest-height inner wall between the sleeping booths, Feargus and a slightly swaying Colm trailing after him.

Feargus immediately joined Colm who slithered down to sit on one of the curtained-off mattresses, both clearly preferring to be off their feet. He had had experience of similar head swellings, and knew how disorienting Colm's would be. A rest would do the lad no harm.

After allowing the chain mail to clank onto the pile dumped by Feargus, he remained standing, wanting to see the faces of all who were present. Enya obviously did, too, because after she let the helmets slide to the floor, she daubed herself against him like a well-loved wolfhound, as snug as the mud and straw clabber that clad the shoulder height wall behind him.

When he took a good look around, it was testament to the confrontation that had happened just ten days ago. Various scabbed wounds were still apparent on the faces, arms and chests of those convened, and the purple, blue, and greenish skin-hues were not battle decoration – though all were definitely battle earned. Nothing he could see was seriously debilitating: it was the inner scars on the gaunt faces that he knew told a different story.

He wondered if he looked as rootless and demoralised as they did. The way he was feeling, he probably appeared to them as even worse.

Lulach's tone lightened. "Displaced tribes people, and new visitors – you will always be assured of a welcome at Ceann Druimin."

A low murmur of thanks came from the people Nith did not recognise.

The chief continued. "My women will bring in some meagre fare, but till then, let us share our news. No one need stand, but speak up clearly and ensure you are heard by all of us."

Enya's whisper was a disheartened tickle at his ear. "Nith. This may be more of the bad than of good. Perhaps that spawn of *Araun* is on the move again?"

Momentarily closing his eyes, he suppressed a sigh. Just the thought of venturing beyond the outer edges of Lulach's domain on patrols, and going closer to the Roman camp of many fists at Moran Dhuirn, or to Agricola's newest Roman camp further north, increased his exhaustion. He desperately wanted to kill every single one of the Roman scavengers, but the deep wounds at his upper-chest throbbed more than they should after nights of healing time, and they sucked out his liveliness. Yet, those hurts were of no consequence compared to the roiling resentment that still churned inside him.

"Stay alert, Nith! I want to hear that we are going to march against the scum very soon, and not be distracted by your snores." The hiss up to his chin made him open his eyes again.

Enya. He suppressed the urge to smirk. She was growing to be such an odd young woman: one moment so protective, at others incomprehensibly aggressive.

Of late, she confused him out of foster-brotherly complacency so much. Since the battlegrounds of Beinn na Ciche, he did not know what to call his feelings. Swallowing the new passions she stirred, one glance down at her pinched face and snappy eyes meant he could not disagree with her reasoning about what kind of information they might receive.

Pressed so close in the squeeze of bodies, he could feel the chill of her bare wrist. Like his own, her clothes were sodden. She would get no warmth from them for some time, but gaining information about the Roman enemy had been more important than seeking out dry garments on their return to Ceann Druimin.

Her jaw swelling was substantial, though he was glad to see the cut under her chin no longer bled. The wounded area was rapidly discolouring, but she had made no moans about it.

He gave her credit for her tenacity. After what had just happened to Colm, deeper Roman infiltration into Caledon hills was potentially disastrous to all of those currently harbouring in the higher lands. Resisting the urge to pull her lean body even closer into the crook of his arm, to share some of his own heat with her, he concentrated on Chief Lulach's words.

A spark of anticipation flared. Lingering longer than he needed to at Ceann Druimin, while his main task in life remained unfulfilled, was not his intention. Failure sat ill on him, and it rankled…so badly, it was hard to swallow the spit down.

"Those newly arrived stand briefly and be seen!" Chief Lulach ordered.

Three men rose to their feet and declared who they were.

The lilting voice of the first echoed around the room. "I bring news from An Garbh-choire where some of my Caledon brothers gather by the rough fording of the burn."

After an acknowledgement from Lulach he sat down, leaving the other newcomers to introduce themselves.

"My name is Raghnall," the next visitor declared, slapping his chest once, before he indicated his companion with an outstretched palm. "And this is Torren. We come to you from Tap O'Noth, of the eastern Taexali flatlands."

After Lulach bid them be seated, his next command fully reclaimed Nith's attention. "The Brigantes amongst us show yourselves by raising a hand."

The Garrigill brothers – Lorcan, Gabrond and Brennus – were mentioned in turn by Lulach, as were their womenfolk who were ranged around the fireside.

When Nith pressed Enya in front of him, to confirm her also as a warrior from the hillfort of Garrigill, Lulach caught his movement. He found he, too, became the momentary centre of attention after Enya had been acknowledged, though he was never fond of being singled out.

The chief's voice rang clear. "Nith is of Selgovae blood from the hillfort of Tarras. He came with our Brigante friends, to join Calgach in battle. These far-flung tribespeople have endured much under the hands of Rome for many long winters. This gives them the best knowledge of any of us gathered here." The chief's widespread hand swung about, taking in the whole room. "The rest of us gathered here are Taexali of the nearby Garioch vale, and my Caledons of Ceann Druimin."

Nith was relieved when Lulach's gaze returned to the Taexali pair from Tap O'Noth, the chief's finger pointing to one of them. "The place where you take refuge is closest to General Agricola's camps. What news do you bring us of those Agricolan bastards?"

The chief plonked himself down on his slightly higher stool as Raghnall of Tap O'Noth answered, the man's voice hampered by recent bruising at his mouth, one cheek and jaw still puffy and swollen.

"Our friends in hiding near Dunnideer warned us that a small Roman detachment was headed towards the Caledon hills. This was mid-morning. We soon dealt with it."

Nith thought the warrior's words were full of bragging confidence, yet the man was not quite meeting the eye of the chief.

"Ha!" A satisfied grunt came from Lulach, the slap of his palm to his thigh a confirmation of pleasure matching the gleam in his dark brown eyes. "This is the kind of news we all want to hear of. No matter the tribe, we must continue to work together. I only have the right to speak for myself and my kin, but I will not make any treaty willingly with Rome. I would rather be trussed up like the braying mules those Romans use to cart their goods."

"Aye, overloaded with stolen barley while we of the Taexali starve!"

Nith had heard the man rant out of turn ever since he had come to Ceann Druimin. In fact, the old man did nothing but bluster all the time. However, if the Romans intended to eat the local hulled barley, it would perhaps mean that they were short of their own grain supplies. He relished that thought, a momentary smirk breaking free. Brennus had told him many a time that Roman soldiers hated a wild-barley ration. For them it reeked far too much of punishment. It would be a just end to it, if the Roman usurpers had problems digesting the wild crops he had grown used to eating in the territories of northern Britannia.

He sent a quick prayer to *Anugh,* the earth goddess – to let their Roman turds be a terrible trial to pass, and uncomfortably smelly.

Lulach had no tolerance for time wasted, his hand raised for silence. "Enough! We surely will need to tighten our belts, but knowing we still have the possibility of being alive during the coming winter moons is more important to discuss right now. We fled the battlefield to live another day, and to fight in another way, but that means keeping abreast of the usurpers' movements." He turned back to the Tap O'Noth messengers. "How many Romans were in this patrol?"

Raghnall of Tap O'Noth held up both hands. "Ten." He closed them into fists, and then having looked at his friend for agreement, he popped up one thumb. "And perhaps one more man, judging from the amount of horses they had."

Nipping nails at his elbow made Nith look aside. Enya's troubled gaze silently questioned her wide forehead rumpling. She was probably thinking, like he was, that eleven was an odd number to a patrol, and that the three they had killed earlier had maybe come from their detachment. He patted her fingers with his free hand, and left them there to reassure her, indicating with a twist of his head that they should pay attention to what was being discussed.

Lorcan of Garrigill entered the conversation after a terse nod from Lulach. "Did you gain any inkling of why this very small patrol was in your area?"

A head shake indicated Raghnall's uncertainty. "Perhaps they sought how many of us keep watch. The Roman General, Agricola, has sent out auxiliary groups every new dawn, to scour the land since the confrontation at Beinn na Ciche. Though we do not yet know how, we think he has knowledge of where some of us shelter, even when we move to a different site each night."

Nith knew that would probably be true. The Roman Empire had particularly nasty methods of extracting information from captives. He had heard about plenty of that during his long trek north.

Lorcan prodded for more information. "Have you seen larger groups of Romans near Tap O'Noth?"

"Nay." Raghnall's gaze swept the room as though he sought an errant thought. "Though, when the days have been fair, from the heights of Tap O'Noth, we have watched the dark shadows of *cohorts* of Roman infantry snaking around the distant Taexali low hills, and valley floors."

"Do these large patrols always go back to their camp?" Lorcan asked.

Raghnall's shoulders hunched up. "Maybe, when the dusk is too advanced for seeing clearly, but I have not witnessed any return myself."

"Could those you killed earlier have been Roman *venatores* on the hunt, headed for woods near Dunnideer?" Lorcan of Garrigill looked to the man for confirmation.

Nith had an idea of the frustrations that Lorcan might be feeling. Neither he, nor any of his Brigante friends, had been long enough in Taexali territory to have personal experience of the terrain mentioned.

Raghnall drew a frown at Lorcan's words, but it quickly vanished. "None broke ranks to kill animals on purpose, to fill bellies. They maintained a strict ride towards the Caledon hills. We had sufficient warning to position ourselves near the glen opening, by the ancient stone circle at Upper Ord, and we ambushed them there, with help from warriors of Dunnideer."

Chief Lulach's impatience boiled over. "Did you kill them all?"

Raghnall shrugged, a flash of pain suppressed when the skin stretched over his wounded cheeks. "They scattered into the nearby woods. When the slain were counted, we judged that some had escaped."

"How many?" Lulach roared, jumping up to his feet.

Enya's fingers slipping from his grip left a cold spot at Nith's elbow, her palm resting on her stomach to quell the growl he could hear rumbling from beneath. Her quick smile belied the seriousness of the talk. He nudged her to pay more heed, but she instead grabbed his hand and used it instead of her own to rub her empty innards, her eyes a disrespectful twinkle. He whipped his hand away knowing Enya was grinning, but ignoring her was the best he could muster.

She was unaware of what her amusement, and touch, did to him.

The warmth of the fire and the close knit bodies were gradually heating up wet clothing, as well as the overpowering odours of hard-worked flesh. The fragrance of drying herbs hanging from the beams above made no impact on the blood, sweat and muck around, but Enya's fingers squirming under his arm burned as hot as the embers he dropped his gaze to.

Pulling his concentration back to Lulach, Nith noticed the chief's anxiety. When he looked around the now almost steaming room, many other faces showed a similar apprehension.

"Seven were slain." Raghnall's words were full of umbrage.

"And what of their horses?" Lulach changed tack as he padded around the fireside, on seeing the defensive response he had provoked.

Nith felt the beginnings of a grin break free. He had not known the chief very long, but the man always quizzed visitors about horses.

"At least one galloped back the way they had come from, but we rounded up the rest."

Torren of Tap O'Noth, unscathed compared to his friend, added more of the account. "One horse injured during the skirmish was put out of its misery. We brought you two good mounts to add to your stocks here at Ceann Druimin, and have shared the remainder with those around Dunnideer."

Lulach smiled for the first time in an age, his large teeth seeming predatory in his weather-beaten leathery face. "They are well received. Be assured that they will be used against the Romans with pleasure." An after thought appeared to occur to the chief, wiping away the remnants of the satisfied smirk. "Nith!"

He jolted to attention when Lulach barked from across the fireside, Enya stiffening away from him.

"You were patrolling near Glenlaff. Did you encounter any Romans?"

"Aye, we did."

Chapter Five

*Ceann Druimin, Caledon Territory
– Chief Lulach's Roundhouse*

"Those bastards were in Glenlaff Woods?" Chief Lulach was outraged.

The horrified reaction Nith's answer produced held no surprise to him, because no Roman soldiers had yet come so close to Ceann Druimin.

"Did you kill them?" The question was immediately followed by a belated bawl as the chief gawped around. "In the name of the god *Arddhu,* where is my son Colm?"

Colm struggled to his feet, using the low cot as a support, Feargus springing up on Colm's other side. Nith felt the inspection of all eyes in the room when they settled on his bedraggled group.

Lulach stared at Colm and Enya, relief that his son had returned clear in his expression as the chief sat back down with a thud. "You two have a tale to tell but, since you are both standing, it can wait till later. How many attacked you, Nith?"

"Three, but the deadly strikes came from the blades of Feargus and Enya," he answered, making sure they got the tribute before he turned towards the Tap O'Noth men. "I have no experience of how far those Romans would have needed to travel from the stone circle you mention, to where we were in Glenlaff woods. Could they have been from the same unit?"

Lulach pursed his lips, his tone derisory. "Easily! My warriors cover the distance in a short time. It is merely a stone's throw."

Rumbles of agreement echoed around.

Lorcan of Garrigill asked a new question. "Were they experienced soldiers?"

"Not so much. They blundered around like a panicked boar that had lost its sense of smell."

His chest wounds smarted when he reached down to the pile of metal at his feet, the space around him tightly packed. Enya helped, though, by passing up the chain mail and helmets to show their gains one by one, her own rumble of discomfort making him feel a sudden guilt when one of the helmets clanked against her chin.

"Colm has already dumped their Roman *pila* in the weapon stack over by the door, and Feargus brought back their *gladii*." He pointed with his free hand, while he let the last of the helmets clank back down to the floor from his other. "The spoils for re-using are minimal, but worth lugging back here. From the way those auxiliaries stumbled around the forest, they lacked knowledge of their purpose."

A terse nod and grunt of thanks from the chief acknowledged the plunder, but Lulach's next words held a fury that Nith could see on other faces around the room. "If you only killed three, then another one could still be traipsing around in our forests!"

Nith's answer was blunt. "Aye, it would seem so, but none of my patrol saw any more than those three."

Lulach bellowed to the guard at his door, "Have men ready to scour Glenlaff Woods come the new dawn!" He swivelled round to Lorcan of Garrigill. "You know the Roman ways. Tell us what Agricola will do now?"

Nith watched his friend do what he did so well.

Lorcan's slight pause ensured all around the room really listened. "I used to believe that Roman Army strategies rarely varied, but what Agricola does now in these northern lands is different from what has been done before on southern territories. One certain thing is that Agricola hates to lose any of his men. Retribution is bound to follow."

Lulach growled as he sat forward on his stool. "Why does Agricola still maintain that many fisted camp of his? What makes him keep soldiers at Moran Dhuirn so long after the battle when he has moved the bulk of his *legions* further north?"

Nith had already asked Lorcan the same question. He knew Lorcan well enough that the man could raise people to frenzy with just a few words, but that was not what the chief of Ceann Druimin presently needed.

Lorcan's deep tones rang clear, steady and calming. "He waits for the same thing as he waited for on the day after our rout at Beinn na Ciche."

"That is never going to happen!" Lulach's outburst was somewhere between complaint and derision. The chief turned to another of the new faces and singled out the Caledon visitor with a pointed finger. "You have come to us from Calgach's hillfort?"

Nith could only see the back of the man's disordered tawny hair, but the answer came clear enough.

"An Garbh-choire is no more than a hamlet by the upper Uisge Dheathain but that is where I have come from. And the news is not good. Calgach will not see many more sunrises. For nights, he has been drifting in and out of the grip of high fever, one leg mangled and festering from his fall beneath the wheels of a battle chariot, though the spear wound to his shoulder, which sent him over the side of his chariot, would heal if the gods willed that he lives on."

The warrior paused, to allow the sighs of sympathy and encouragement to roll around, but Nith guessed it was more to ensure everyone in the room really understood the update when the man eventually continued. "But the injuries to Calgach's leg mean he would never lead us again into new skirmishes."

Lulach shook his head forlornly. "You bring us the direst news."

"Who will step up now? Who is there to rally to, to repel the Roman scum from our lands?" The withered crone's terrified cry was lost in the tumult that followed.

One of Lulach's fiercest warriors stood up to confront the last speaker, his temper fit to blast the fire to smouldering ashes as he spat across it. "You were not even there, old woman. You have no understanding of how these Romans fight."

The chief sought to calm the anger around his house, his command directed at his friend. "Aye. And we will, but bickering amongst ourselves will do nothing to achieve that. Our right for our tribes to remain free of the yolk of Rome is only worth having, if we learn how to defend it. Sit down and think on the problems we face. Are you staring at death like Calgach is this very moment?"

"Nay, I am not." The Ceann Druimin warrior slid back to his seat, his anger only slightly drained by the mulish look on his face.

Nith could see that the deep regret about Calgach, which he felt right down to his gut, was shared by those on the opposite side of the fire. He had no personal knowledge of Calgach, but the charismatic leader had brought together many tribes and small clanholds to confront the Roman General Agricola, when no one else had been willing and able to take up the task.

Nith felt Enya tug hard at his tunic, her bothered gaze imploring. Her question at his ear was the tiniest murmur spat through clenched teeth. "Can we believe this Caledon? He has no one to verify his story."

He feared Enya was becoming too obsessed that strangers were not trustworthy. His terse nudge and caution to silence was designed to shush her fears, but the expression of rejected hurt on her face bothered him when she huffed her shoulder away.

Before speaking, Lulach looked up to where the central roof-beams were lashed together as though sending a heartfelt prayer. "Then Calgach will not approach the Moran Dhuirn camp, nor Agricola's new one near the Ythan River, to make treaties with Rome." His swift glare at the Caledon messenger was as abrupt as his thunderous words. "I hope Calgach does not think to send someone else to capitulate to the *diùbhadh*? To make a Roman version of peace like my Brigante friends have warned me about? Their version of peace is one in which we do all the work. The scum afterwards remove the fruits of our efforts from us and call them taxes to belong to their Roman Empire? All of that to ensure that we remain friends with our neighbours!"

The wave of enmity that circled the room was so palpable Nith felt it pass his shoulder blades to seep through the wall behind him, like a soft wind.

The Caledon's stuttered reply was full of affront. "Nay! Not Calgach, nor anyone else to speak for all of the tribes who rallied to his leadership."

Nith watched Lorcan of Garrigill's grim nod in response to the Caledon.

"That is what makes the aftermath of this battle continue to be different from what has gone before in southern Britannia." Lorcan was pragmatic.

Nith admired Chief Lulach's expression. It was with neither shame nor amusement when the man spoke. "Agricola cannot make the usual peace treaties because most of the survivors from the tribes have fled to Caledon territory."

"Does he think us cowards because we retreated from his unassailable battle formations, to live another night?" The response came from the Caledon messenger.

Nith was glad of Lorcan's honesty, because it could influence the chief's next decisions.

"Agricola may think what he will of us, but that matters little." The initial spike in Lorcan's tone dipped again as he continued. "Throughout Britannia, after many battles, the conquered leader has been there to swear allegiance to Rome, before the dead have even been removed from the field."

Raghnall of Tap O'Noth interrupted, his head bobbing in agreement. "Our slain were mostly secreted away in the early morning mists, though the Roman scavengers had by then removed all of their trappings of battle."

"So it was for many of us when we went to claim our kin in the morning haar," Lulach added. Exasperation grew as he threaded his fingers through his disorderly dark locks, and scratched through his tuggy side braids. "But none of that tells me what that shite does now."

"He weasels out information." Lorcan's eyes flared.

Nith admired that his friend's motivation was eventually re-emerging. Like most around him, the outcome of the battle had sapped their spirits. He wished he could summon some of the same renewed fire, but the effort felt too great. He needed a very long, unbroken sleep before that might happen. He squeezed his eyelids tight to clear away the smoke from the guttering fire that nipped and prickled, and forced himself to concentrate better.

"What information does that turd take so much time to gather?" Lulach was increasingly exasperated, his fingers now restless on the fire iron that created billowing sparks to fly up towards the rafters as he poked and prodded his end of the dwindling flames, having added more damp wood from the small pile at his side.

Lorcan of Garrigill was so good at keeping calm when it was needed. Nith wanted some of the trait because it would maybe still his own inner temper.

"Lulach, we have already discussed that Agricola needs the spokesperson for all of the northern tribes to capitulate, and swear allegiance to Rome," said Lorcan.

Nith tasted both the disgust and twisted satisfaction that rumbled around the room.

Lorcan continued. "He needs to conquer the largest tribal stronghold for each tribe, because he will expect the high chief to impose the new Roman rule. From there, he will expect that Ard Righ to ensure that the tribes continue to adhere to Roman domination, and assimilate Roman ways into their daily life by adopting Roman laws and customs. From each tribal stronghold, the Roman Empire will expect to collect the future payments, call them taxes if you will, that the emperor will demand of the people."

Nith knew that was typical Roman policy, but it might be new information to some of the people attending.

Raghnall of Tap O'Noth interrupted his anger high enough to raise the roof beams. "We have no Taexali high king like the Venicones have an Ard Righ, and the Taexali chief of the largest village was slain at Obar Dheathain, days before the confrontation at Beinn na Ciche."

"Aye, that is true." Lorcan's wry response startled some of the company, his twinkling-eyed smile not easy to understand, though Nith had now worked out how his friend viewed that knowledge. Lorcan continued, his tone now persuasive. "I believe Agricola will have been told well before our battlegrounds at Beinn na Ciche that the Taexali only have small villages and hamlets, but he now spends this time proving it. His communications to the Emperor Domitian will have to be based on accurate knowledge, otherwise his esteem goes down in the senate. Mistakes over what the Romans can seize from these lands cannot be tolerated and neither can General Agricola afford to exaggerate what he can claim in taxes from here. These northern territories hold many challenges for the Roman usurper."

Another warrior Nith recognised from Ceann Druimin piped up, harking back to Lorcan's initial words. "Many nights have passed since our failed confrontation. Agricola cannot know where Calgach is, or he would already have captured him."

Nith felt the puff of Enya's soft grunt against his neck when she tilted into him, as though unable to prevent herself, her vitality spent. When he snaked his arm around her shoulders to keep her upright, the brief smile of gratitude from her weary grey eyes almost made him fail to hear Lorcan's words. Her growth from child to woman, since they had come to Caledon lands, was now something it seemed he could not ignore. He shook off the awareness and looked away. Tiredness gave a man too many fancies.

He had loved her as a foster-sister for many seasons, and could do so again.

Lorcan continued. "Aye, that may be so, but I have had nights now to think over Agricola's actions. He has laid aside the capitulation of the tribes to focus on other objectives. You are familiar with your mountain terrain that is to the west, and to the north of Beinn na Ciche. Agricola is not. He spends time seeking knowledge of all of the secrets those territories hold. You are not his captives…"

"Neither will we be!"

The room erupted, almost everyone vying to outshout the other.

"We will kill the Roman scum, and even ourselves, rather than they take us!"

Lorcan broke off speaking on hearing the livid comments that flew around the room. He waited till the outcry faded before continuing. "I mean that he cannot get the information from the lips of the tribal chiefs, because he does not have them in his clutches. Reliance on his own men to provide the confirmation he needs is all he presently has. That is a much slower process, hence his delay in moving from Moran Dhuirn to his current camp at this gorse river that you name the Ythan."

"Would he trust our words?" Lulach's tone denied it.

"If you had capitulated to Rome, and made treaties with him, he would act on the information provided by you…" Again, a heated rumble around the fireside indicted the disruptive mood of the gathering. "…but Agricola is a very astute general; he would also prove it for himself."

"We must tell him nothing!"

The clamour increased as more voices vented their fury.

Nith felt his own blood whip around as Enya's frame became even more rigid against him. It was as though she could no longer contain her ire. Her whispers stabbed up at his earlobe.

"Why do our elders sit around railing at this injustice night after night, yet do nothing? They must get out there and rid us of Agricola's scum!"

Reaching for her tightly curled fist, he grasped it close to his chest, ignoring the new ache to his wound caused by the impact. "We will. But tonight, Enya, we listen." Holding her hand firmly in place, he paid more attention to Lorcan's words.

"Details from local captives make the process of Roman settlement quicker to achieve, but since Agricola does not have that from you, he is adapting his normal procedures." Lorcan's explanation rang clear around the room, squelching the lingering dissenting mutters. "Taxes due to Rome are not always paid in visible grain supplies, or slaves. He hunts out every source of wealth that can be extracted by Rome, and for the use of Rome."

One of Lulach's elders could not hold his snippy tongue. "Then, he will find little! Display of shining metals, the likes of which we have seen decorating those Roman legionaries on the battle field, is rare in our tribes. He will search long and hard to find those treasures in Caledon territory."

More outcries erupted, the responses ringing around the room.

"Our livestock and fields are our wealth."

"You mean they used to be our wealth."

Nith felt the antipathy that flared from one tribesman to the other was unmerited, though he could not discount the facts as the irate man continued. "Agricola's presence across our lands has already ruined our stocks for seasons to come."

Another disgruntled warrior took up the complaint. "With the amount of dead and wounded on the battlefield, some farms will have no able men left to till the fields even when we do return to them."

Someone in front of Nith held a different opinion. "Perhaps we should capitulate. We are never going to free ourselves from those Roman aggressors."

That provoked his neighbour to rise to his feet, elbow pulled back to lay fists in retaliation.

"Stop that, and sit down." Lulach's roar had others separating the warriors before the fight escalated. "Brawls amongst us will achieve nothing."

The female entreaty that followed was surprisingly strident for one so old. "I cannot understand what else Agricola can steal from us."

"Nith! What do you think?" Lulach's question startled more than Enya. Many heads swivelled in his direction.

Enya eased away before he answered, leaving a chill at his neck that was again…uncomfortable. He cleared his throat, casting off the pressure of her leaning. "Like Lorcan, I cannot fathom Agricola's thinking. The Roman general could already have sent the great strength of his *legions* to find Calgach. He has not, but do not think your mountains are a deterrent. He is used to upland campaigning having done that many times during his time as the *legate* in command of the *Legio XX*. Your mountains would be no harder to invade than others he has already fought in, but I do not know why he does not send his men deep into the peaks. He is generally unwilling for many of his troops to die in ambushes, yet he sent out a small patrol to their deaths today. Their purpose had to be something different."

"Did Agricola send out a tiny patrol because he is so confident that he will find little resistance from those of us who survive?" Lulach's question raised the resentment anew.

The first of an onslaught of huffed shouts came from around the company. "Can he be toying with his own troops? Using them as a lure to draw us out?"

Lorcan calmed the last comment from the incensed warrior with a raised palm. "Perhaps, though it may also be that in his overconfidence Agricola is willing to risk some of his men. He has formidable sources to pluck units from. The *Legio II Adiutrix* is a fairly new *legion*."

Nith felt all eyes swivel towards him as they followed Lorcan's pointing finger.

"The *Legio II Adiutrix* was formed the summer that my niece, Enya, was born." Lorcan's gaze rested on her for a moment.

Enya's tiny recoil trembled Nith's arm as the crowd assessed her age. He was not surprised really, because although she displayed the maturity of a well-grown woman, at times she could look so young.

Lorcan continued. "Higher recognition from scouting attempts will do that new *legion* no harm. Nevertheless, their youngest auxiliary troops are easily replaceable. Agricola can request more recruits from recently subdued Celtic tribes across the empire whenever he needs them."

"Ha! If they are young they will be easy prey." The derisory words came from one of the Ceann Druimin warriors.

An alarming clamour near the roundhouse low entrance door created a collective hush to descend before all eyes swivelled towards the commotion, menace in everyone's posture as they sprang to their feet.

Nith felt Enya shove him hard along the wall in her haste.

"Hurry!"

Chapter Six

Ceann Druimin, Caledon Territory
– Chief Lulach's Roundhouse

"Ready yourselves!" Chief Lulach's bawl as he leapt up almost toppled the framework of the roundhouse. His stool flying back onto the spread herbs and brackens was a dull thud, but Nith felt every ear must hear each crack of the dry rushes.

"Nay! No one attacks." The red-faced sentry at the door stuttered an explanation. "There is no need for alarm. No Romans attack. I am sorry. My spear… It was careless of me."

The general movement towards the door ceased as quickly as it had begun.

The uproar that had shaken everyone's wellbeing had been the miserable young warrior's spear dislodging the overfilled metal basket at the side of the door. Those nearest the mess hastened to restore order to the weapon stash when they realised that it was not a warning of enemy attack.

As Enya sidled back to her former space, Nith thought Lulach's glare could set a fire alight, though it was also evident that relief had set in around the room just as swiftly as alarm had. The assembled company resumed their place, as the chief's volume decreased to a manageable level. "If there is no enemy at my door, lad, just tell me why you are here."

"More visitors have arrived."

"Then why did you not already bid them enter?" Lulach's exasperation was voiced through clenched teeth, along with an abrupt hand signal as he sat back down. "And before the wrath of the god *Taranis,* as well as more of my own, descends upon you, go and learn how to handle your spear!"

Nith watched the wily leader assess the couple that his guards allowed through the entryway. They had satisfied the scrutiny of Lulach's outer watch, but had not sidled in like he and Enya had done, so that probably meant no familiarity with Ceann Druimin.

Enya's shudder next to him had nothing to do with any draft brought in by the latest visitors. He snaked his arm around her waist and pulled her close, to give her reassurance. Her head rested comfortably on his shoulder, her hands sneaking into his as they came to rest at her front. Maybe too comfortably, but he was not about to let her go again. She was so close he felt it when her breathing evened back to a normal level.

He was less sure of that happening with his own.

"Join us. Take time to settle in and become aware of our discussion." Lulach made no further moves of hospitality as he switched back to the topic being discussed, pointing imperiously to a warrior at the back of the room. "Continue."

The man re-started the conversation as though no dramatic interruption had taken place. "It will be easy to slaughter new recruits, as your patrol has done today, Nith."

Nith noted the mixed expressions across the fireside when they looked his way, Enya clearly too comfortable to move aside, though she straightened up enough to support her own head. Some people appeared elated with the idea of slaying Roman recruits, yet others showed disgust that young men, some of them forced to fight for Rome, were so expendable.

He chose his words carefully, his intent to calm the tempers as Lulach gestured for the newcomers to come closer to him, sufficient space on a bench having been cleared for them.

"After this skirmish, today, Agricola will send out at least a *century*, with another one to ensure the safety of their arses."

From the low rumble around the room it was clear that was not good news.

The elder seated next to Lulach was appalled. "Ambushing above eight twenties of men would be unworkable, unless we have plenty of warning to gather sufficient warriors."

A disgruntled whinge rippled from tribesman to tribesman. Lulach joined the murky mood by lobbing a couple of logs onto the glowing embers, sending an angry shower of fiery orange-red sparks aloft. "Nith? Would torturing captives be a way for Agricola to extract information?" The question created a new kind of tension around the room.

"Aye, if they are local enough." Nith copied his friend Lorcan's strategies. "Though, many of those Agricola took after the battle would have come from further afield. Their knowledge of distant territory could be useful to Agricola, but he will have to establish safe routes to reach the places mentioned. I doubt he will send his *legions* into any of the mountain passes, till he knows more of the hazards his men could encounter."

Nith watched as the chief turned back to Lorcan. "What other ways has he extracted information from southern tribespeople?"

Lorcan propped his elbows on his knees, but Nith knew the position was determined rather than defeatist. "After capitulation to Rome, fortlets and watch towers sprang up over the landscape to monitor obedience."

"That is exactly what happened a few seasons ago on our territory!" The outburst came from the female who had recently entered the roundhouse.

"Now is a good time for you to tell us who you are." Though Lulach spoke directly to the woman, it was clear that his inquiry was for both newcomers.

"I am Aila from the old stone fortress at Finhaven." The woman then turned to her companion. "And this is Conchar, one of my most trusted warriors. We are northern Venicones, though we bring news from our Ard Righ's hillfort by the Abhainn Tatha."

Lulach offered his full hospitality as was the custom although it was now belated. "New information is very welcome. We have heard little of your tribespeople since our gatherings before the confrontation at Beinn na Ciche, but take time to rest first." The chief then turned back to Lorcan of Garrigill.

Nith did not know Lulach well enough to know if that was a gentle reprimand after the woman's interruption, though he hazarded a guess. He suppressed a tired yawn.

Enya gave him a terse nudge with her hip. "Stay awake and pay attention to Lorcan."

It was quite uncanny. Nith grunted. Enya sometimes knew him too well, but his offended glare only made her grin.

Lorcan continued as though no interruption had taken place. "Guard towers and fortlets prevent free access around the territories."

Conchar of Finhaven spat at the rushes. "Aye, we have lost contact with many of our Caledon brothers. The Roman soldiers who patrol the passes stop our movement back and forth into the mountains. The only way we could reach here undetected meant our journey was three times longer than it need have been."

"You have our sympathy." Brennus of Garrigill's deep rumble joined the conversation. "Cutting off a warrior from his fellows is another means of sapping the strength of the tribes. The Romans use many methods to destroy those they seek to conquer."

Seated on one of the timber planks, Brennus' lofty height meant he was head and shoulders above most of those seated alongside him.

Again Aila of Finhaven intervened, her words a resentful whip. "They gawk as we reap our harvests. And then we have little to show when they seize most of it, and take it to their forts. Of course, as payment, they promise us the strength of their numbers if our neighbours attack." Aila broke off to look around, her words a denial. "Phah! As you see, we much prefer to sit here amicably with you."

Nith's immediate compassion went to the woman. He himself had seen the invasion of the Venicones happen the previous summer, but he sensed that Enya was not so convinced.

Her whisper up to his ear was rattled. "How can we know they speak true, and have not fallen foul of the Roman chains? Perhaps Agricola sent them here."

Once again he feared Enya was too mistrusting, though her elbow jab at his ribs was enough for him to pay good attention to the Venicones, and listen to what they had to contribute. The couple's trek to Lulach's Caledon village would have been hazardous.

Brennus of Garrigill continued. "You tell it well, but many local people become cowed and resentful of their domination, and this leads to unwise decisions and unguarded statements. The Roman patrols pass on even the tiniest pieces of information to their next level of command – from an *optio* who controls a half century of soldiers, to the *centurions*, and on up to the highest layers. Physical torture and flogging of any tribespeople who resist can also mean they learn things we would rather not share with Rome."

A warrior Nith had got to know from Ceann Druimin interrupted. "Will similar treatment come to our local tribes if they return soon to their homes?"

Brennus exhaled, loudly, before his lopsided gaze pinpointed the warrior. "The Roman way is to subdue the tribes peacefully…"

A howl of denial rippled around the room, vocal hostility coming from the newly arrived Venicones, but Brennus immediately forestalled any further comments. "Nay! I mean that they suppress the tribes without major confrontation, when they are able, using the sheer strength of their oppressive numbers."

Nith watched Brennus' one-good-eyed gaze fall upon the Venicones as he continued to explain himself.

"That is what they did on your territory. I deny none of the small successful skirmishes your people organised to thwart them, but it was an impossible task when you were faced with the sheer numbers in Agricola's *legions*. I was not far off and knew it happened. And now, I am sure, if your local Venicones give any resistance, Agricola metes out a very harsh punishment?"

Conchar of Finhaven's head nodded. "Aye, he has not stopped dealing out retribution since his troops first set their hob-nailed feet on our soil."

Aila inclined her head towards the chief. "You do as they demand in your village or suffer dire consequences."

Lulach's impatient hand gestures hurried her on.

"Our situation worsened after the battle at Beinn na Ciche," she added.

"I have not yet heard of this." Lulach's stare around the fireside was intended to confirm that no other person present had heard of it either.

"My tribespeople are now all powerless." Aila of Finhaven's anxiety was picked up by many of those around the fireside.

Lulach's squeal was worthy of an irate wild boar. "Are you saying that even the northern Venicones tribes have officially capitulated? Is this the news you bring to us?"

"Agricola did not send all of his troops north to fight at Beinn na Ciche. He left enough of them on our territory to round up our warriors when they returned to their homes after the battle. Those who resisted capture suffered the sting of the *gladius* and are gone to the otherworld. The most able warriors, some of those personally known to me, have been trussed up and chained along with a number of our women and older children. They have been dragged off as slaves. Our Ard Righ, Trune of the Abhainn Tatha, had no way of preventing their removal. He chose to die rather than be taken at the whim of the Roman Governor."

Nith felt the breath punch out of him as he looked over to the stricken faces across the fireside, the news having a similar impact on Lorcan and the other Garrigill Brigantes.

"Then Agricola was not in the Moran Dhuirn camp all the time we thought him to be?" Lulach sounded devastated with the notion he had been tricked.

"Agricola was there." Aila of Finhaven was quick to answer her voice rising to ring around the room. "It was a senior *tribune* of the *Legio XX* who carted off the most important northern Venicones elders who answered to Trune – the few who had not yet officially capitulated to Rome. The *tribune* hauled them to the Moran Dhuirn camp where they were forced to declare obedience to Agricola. Those of us who remain on Venicones lands must now till the soil as Rome decrees, or we die."

"Nay!" Enya's soft weep cut Nith to the bone.

Her grip around his arm, and her head sinking into his shoulder betrayed her anguish. Grief that he felt, and that he knew was shared by all of the Garrigill clan. Chief Trune had given the Garrigill refugees succour in days gone past, but he had also been a good friend.

He gathered her in a tight embrace, her arms snaking around his waist. Snug. Comforting. And another sentiment he did not quite want to acknowledge.

"Then what are we to do?" The wail came from Mharaidh, one of Lulach's elders. Her despair ripped at the hearts of those seated around her, people who had no experience yet of the oppression of Roman domination on their soil. "How can we prevent Agricola from doing the same to us?"

Mharaidh's unexpected clutch at her breast, and horrified gulps and gasps, had more than Nith's eyes upon her. When she toppled forward from the bench, her wild-eyed yowl to the goddess *Aarfen* was followed by the dull thud of her slump onto the fire's edges.

"Mharaidh!"

The cries of alarm that now rippled round the room were different from before, but more heartrending. Many hands nearby reached out and grabbed the old one back from the dangerous blaze. Frantic flapping doused the fiery crackling around Mharaidh's head, and open palms put out the beginnings of flames at her woollen bratt, a reek of acrid flesh permeating the roundhouse. When those nearest turned the old woman over and laid her flat on her back, their howls of grief were picked up by the rest of the company. Nith could barely peek over the straining people in front of him, Enya almost crawling up his body to peer even more. When Ineda and Nara rounded the fireside to tend her, he knew old Mharaidh would get the best of attention.

"Look at what that oppressor Agricola does to us!" Cries of blame echoed around, and low murmurs of discontent rumbled within many conversations.

"How does she fare?"

Nith watched Nara reach over to speak to Lulach. At his nod, the chief bid two of his warriors lift up the prone woman. Without fuss, they carried the slack body carefully out of the roundhouse, Mharaidh's head hanging back, her reddened chin exposed and her lifeless eyes wide-open. Nara, and another that Nith knew to be the herb-woman of the village, followed after them.

Whispers and prayers to various gods and goddesses rippled around the room.

Lulach eventually called for order, padding his way around the fireside, tension emanating from his flexed upper arm muscles as he shoved back his wayward side braids. He deliberately slowed at the spot where Mharaidh had toppled, his gaze at the flames both reflective and incensed.

"Has she already gone to the other world?" The tribeswoman posing the question spoke into the hush that had eventually descended.

Lulach raised his head, his manner the saddest Nith had ever heard from the chief. "It seems her goddess has claimed her, but if not yet her time, then I am confident her needs will be seen to."

Moving round to Lorcan of Garrigill, the chief's tone turned to unforgiving. "I will not sit back and let Agricola kill more of my people. We must make our own pathway through life, and even choose death according to the will of our own gods and goddesses, not the will of Rome. Help us to find a way!"

From his seated position, Lorcan calmly regarded the furious chief. Nith knew most of his friend's expressions and the one on Lorcan's face held a hint of amazement.

"Lulach, you demand much, but I assure you we have not been powerless since the aftermath of the battle," Lorcan said.

Lulach stomped back to his seat on noticing the many heads trying to glance around him. "We have done nothing but lick our bloody wounds for ten nights!" the chief shouted to the wooden beams above him. "I call that spineless."

Nith wondered what bemused Lorcan.

He also felt he had not done enough after the battle, except patrol the local countryside.

"I, too, have licked my wounds like a frenzied cur for nights, but I see things more clearly now." Lorcan's gaze travelled slowly around to include everyone. "When we followed the *carnyx* call to retreat on the foothills of Beinn na Ciche, we chose life. We could not defeat Agricola then...but we have affected his decision making ever since."

Conchar of Finhaven's voice rose sufficiently to gain attention. "How can that be?"

"The attack of this Roman patrol today is not the only ambush since our retreat from Beinn na Ciche. You have already had reports of other incidents."

"Aye, but only a few!" Lulach still needed to be convinced.

Nith now understood the glimmer in Lorcan's eyes.

"That is true, Lulach. However, a gorse bush has many prickles, and if all of the tribes collectively pluck each one and embed it in Agricola's side, it will cause him immense irritation."

Chief Lulach scratched at his chin growth. "You mean, if we all seize every possible opportunity to thwart him?"

"Are you saying we could still trump him?" Conchar of Finhaven sounded incredulous.

Brennus of Garrigill's loud chortles jumped him into the conversation. "The tribes of the north, are nothing like any he has ever encountered before."

Lulach turned back to Lorcan. "What more do you know of Agricola and his tendencies?"

Lorcan lurched to his feet before stepping down the gap between the fire and seated tribespeople. When he stopped his voice rang clear. "Ineda is the one to tell us more about General Agricola. She has the greatest experience of him."

The gasp that rolled around the room from the newcomers seemed almost damning. Nith watched Ineda dip her chin, a wild defiance etched across her tight cheeks.

Clamped next to him, Enya perked up her voice forceful and compelling. "Ineda knows many useful things, and we all should listen to her."

Lorcan instantly quelled any lingering distrust with the raising of his hand. "Make no mistake. Ineda's knowledge of the enemy is something we can use to our advantage."

"Do not believe a thing that woman says. She must be a traitor! How else can she know so many Roman things?" The Ceann Druimin warrior in front of Nith had voiced such doubts before, but not with such malice.

"Be still," Lulach warned. "We have no need to hear your poor opinions of everyone, and everything."

The man thrust his way out of the gathering, almost trampling Nith in the process. When he reached the doorway, he was not quite done, no matter what his chief had ordered. "Those Romans will not halt for you, Lulach of Ceann Druimin, and no matter how many nights and how many times you discuss ways to thwart them, they will have us grovelling at their feet all too soon." His voice rose even more when his shaking arm pointed at Ineda. "And she will be the cause of it!"

Chapter Seven

Baile Mheadhain, Taexali Territory

"Faster!"

Beathan wished he could go so fast he would be well out of range of the Roman auxiliary who strode past him with enviable long steps: unfettered steps as the man prodded and poked here and there with the tip of his *pilum*.

Darting a glance backwards, he quelled the trembling at his lip as the sight of Beinn na Ciche was lost to him – again – hidden by the hillock he had just skittered down. He had never felt so alone, yet he was surrounded by fellow tribespeople, all of them looking as wretched as he was feeling, if the dejection on their faces was anything to judge by. Misery abounded so much he could spit out a burn full. Though, in truth, what dripped to the ling below his feet was old blood that he had lipped away from the lacerations made by the rough iron manacle at his wrist, and the fresher trickles that came from recent stings of the lash to his face.

He wanted so much to block out the dull glints of the linked-chain armour, and the wicked shouts of the Roman auxiliaries who kept the slave line in order. The only way to momentarily escape the horror of his situation was to close his eyes, but that also led to torment.

Why had his deities deserted him?

His mother, Nara, had so often instilled in him that her goddess *Rhianna* had specially chosen him at birth. She was convinced that he had been singled out from other men, and that his purpose would be revealed at a time of the goddess' choosing. Did his mother now know that he had been selected by Agricola for questioning?

Was his mother dead? Abandoned by *Rhianna*? Had he been captured because Nara had not survived the battlegrounds of Beinn na Ciche? A silent keening ripped inside him. What of the fate of his father and his uncles? They had all been much nearer the front battle-lines than he had been.

The shivers that made his neck tighten were not only caused by the biting wind that nipped at his bare skin, and there was plenty of that, it was more that the slave line now had not a single bratt among it, their cloaks ripped from them before they started this demoralising trek. From his knowledge of the Roman Army, exposure could take many forms.

"Go faster!"

"Go faster!" Derwi mimicked from behind, his undertone meant for Beathan's ears alone. "Free me from these bindings, *a mhic an uilc!* and I will be gone from here as fast as one of *Taranis'* thunderclaps!"

"No talking!"

The tail of the whip slicing at the back of Beathan's leg kinked his stride, his faltering causing Derwi to crash into him, though the jolt of the chain from both front and behind pulled them apart quickly enough, their feet staggering back into the relentless rhythm again.

"Spineless, clumsy weakling, you think yourself a special warrior? Ha! The *Legio II Adiutrix* will show you just how special you are, all of you!" Crowing cackles accompanied more idle cracks of the vicious whip as the guard moved on down the line, the warning clear in the common language of the tribes.

Beathan dared a look at the auxiliary's expression as the man passed by, knowing he would see gloating and sneering satisfaction.

"Pay him no heed, Beathan," Derwi urged. "Never let vermin like that know your weaknesses."

He bit down on his lip. Each new stretch of his already frigid lower leg was now a jabbing sting. Ignoring the blood trickling into his foot bindings, he made a solemn vow to a goddess he knew of, but had never given much observance to.

He had nothing to offer her, but surely she would know his plight and accept that he would give offering when he could?

"*Andarta?* You are revered for helping us to overcome our enemies. Give me strength to overcome mine. It may not be this night, but please heed me?"

Since he had been taken captive, he had sent pleas to all the gods and goddesses that he knew of, yet he remained chained to the man in front and the man behind. Had his tribal deities all abandoned him because he was not yet a man, and had not the strength they all favoured?

As Beathan tripped and slipped down the slope, he did not see the heathers and tussocky brushwood beneath him, nor was he careful of the weary and bowed prisoner stumbling in front of him, fresh weals leaking from the man's arm.

The bloody trail renewed scenes of the recent carnage of battle, filling Beathan's inner vision.

From his position well up the hillside of The Mither Tap, the triumphant Celtic chariot display had turned to total disaster when Governor Agricola's Roman auxiliaries swept around the amassed Celts. The shouts of Calgach's initial success became horrific wails of pain when Agricola's auxiliaries hacked down the tribesmen at the bottom of the slope beneath him, each one fighting against a wall of battering shields, all of them trampling over the bloody and mangled bodies of the fallen, horses and chariots included. The sounds and ghastly stenches of despairing slaughter wafted up the hill to him like furious waves of a tempestuous high-tide.

He scrunched his eyes tight to make the horrific sights disappear.

Stumbling over a large boulder, the yanking at his wrists turned his remembered terror to genuine yowls of agony as his knees hit tangled roots.

A reek around him was real, but it came from the soiled and bloodied captives he was chained to. Scrambling back up he continued to totter as the line skidded down the last part of the hillside.

His eyes beseeched upwards to the god *Taranis* of the skies, who skulked behind ominous dark clouds. If pitched battle against those Roman fighting walls of tightly-fitting shields was not the way to overpower the forces of the Roman emperor Domitian, what was? By *Taranis*, tell him what was?

His family had taught him many things, but they really knew naught. No strategies worked to banish these conquering invaders from Britannia. Since he had been a small boy, his family had been evading Roman domination, but nothing in his past had ever been as terrible as what he now faced.

He had allowed himself to be captured!

"Move."

Bending his head, the flesh at his cheeks scrunched up to hide the humiliation he would not allow the *Ceigean Ròmanach* to see.

When the rapid stab of the *pilum* came at his side with regular ferocity, he absorbed the words he wanted to shriek. His tunic was already shredded, providing little cover for the fiercely-sharp jabbing of the spear. Each new wound was tiny, barely drawing blood, but was shameful. He knew it was intended to be that way nevertheless despaired that he could do nothing about it.

"Walk!"

Understanding the Latin commands well enough, any belief he had harboured about a great destiny being laid before him frizzled away.

He had failed his mother, his tribe and his gods.

Two fat tears he could not suppress dripped to the ground. Blinking furiously to wipe clear the sting, he gulped a large breath and exhaled. It was his fault that Ruoridh, was dead. His last sight of his older cousin was when they had been set upon by the *contubernium* group of Batavian auxiliaries who scoured the woods at the back of Beinn na Ciche, in the deep haar of the morning after the battle.

The slamming down of the Roman shield boss at his temple was a recall he could not lay aside. He remembered the helpless sensation he had found himself in when he closed his eyes to sleep.

Each morning of his captivity, when his slave line was roused with jabbing kicks, came the awful remembrance of Ruoridh lying face down alongside him in a pool of blood before he had felt himself being ripped away, feet first, by two of the auxiliaries. It had taken the Romans no more than a few steps before the haar had sucked away the image of Ruoridh being flipped over by the last auxiliary of the detail, the man's *spatha* held high in a two fisted grip and ready to plunge.

"Move on!"

Beathan ducked away from the metal tip of the spear, cursing his Roman enemy tenfold but refused to look at his persecutor.

How could he have been so foolhardy? Ruoridh had been his best friend.

Was slavery his condemnation for thinking only of his own safety when he had insisted they head towards the north, rather than go west out of the woods like Ruoridh had wanted?

Question after question consumed him as his line trudged across flatter ground made slippery by the recent icy rain. Would his father ever forgive him for letting his foolish temper get the better of him when the Roman swine had interrogated him at the Roman encampment across the valley from The Mither Tap? When the guards had laid into him, he had tried so hard to stay silent, to not say anything that might betray his clan, but he was proud of his Brigante heritage and could not keep that fact hidden. Inner tears stung even more.

"Aiee! *Aarfen?* Free me from that stinging whip." The weak pleas of the man in front of him jolted Beathan's errant thoughts into order and made him think of the present.

He concentrated on bits of his body that did not hurt. They were few, but at least the swelling at his jaw was less bothersome than before.

If *Aarfen* was guiding his fate instead of *Rhianna,* or even *Andarta,* then perhaps it would be *Aarfen* who continued to watch over him? That notion brought a strange sort of comfort. Maybe it was not fitting that *Rhianna* watched over both his mother and him? *Aarfen* was almost as powerful a goddess, so perhaps she should be his personal guiding deity?

Pulling up his chin to the glowering sky, his brows knotted.

"*Aarfen*? Undeserving or otherwise, my future is yours to command. Please aid me through this trial? It was foolish of me to tell Agricola's guards that I am a Garrigill Brigante."

"Beathan," Derwi interrupted his plea. "When that *centurion* commanded his men to set their fists to your face and stomach in Agricola's tent, you were robbed of any choice. Warriors who refused to answer them are all now dead."

He whipped his head back to glimpse Derwi's face, relieved to see support rather than condemnation. "They seem to think that me being a Brigante is important, Derwi – but I wish I knew why."

He had no idea if that was the reason he had been selected from the huddle of captives to join this particular line of prisoners. Derwi was the chief of his Taexali hamlet while he was only barely out of boyhood.

"Look ahead, Beathan. An appeal to *Morimaru* might guarantee you a better future." Derwi's words sounded ominously disrespectful.

Not far away, Beathan could just make out the realm of the sea god *Morimaru* below him. Snow-filled clouds loomed heavily over the water that would be used to transport him in the opposite direction from his Garrigill kin.

A Roman camp had been constructed down near the shoreline, though much smaller than at Moran Dhuirn. It was still an ominous sight, yet the greater threat was the little huddle of ship masts that bobbed up and down behind the rows and rows of tents.

One of those ships could carry him far away.

Inadvertently shuffling into the slumping warrior in front of him, Beathan's hands curved round his neighbour's elbows, a painful manoeuvre when the manacle around his wrist crunched against his bruised bones. Blood from many lash-wounds trickled through his fingers, so much that he was surprised that the man had even been able to walk at all the long last while.

"Halt!"

The command was issued by a mounted Roman rider, the *decurion* in charge of the cavalrymen accompanying the line of prisoners.

Beathan did not care who gave the order, crested helmet or not, it was a welcome one if they were to have some respite from the gruelling march. Dispirited by his inability to do anything but obey orders, he bore the full weight of his neighbour.

"Sit!"

A resounding sound of clanking chains masked the noises of relief around him as the line of people slumped to the ground; Derwi's chain wrenching him almost off the warrior in front's elbows. When he righted himself, he urged his neighbour to the freezing earth. Squirming down, he attempted to relax his aching muscles.

"My thanks, Beathan the Brigante." The man in front's thready whisper was given with the weakest of pats to his leg.

"Rest. There is no cure for you save your inner strength. Garner it well. I will wake you when it is time." Beathan's words were automatic. He knew he copied his mother, Nara, when she was using her healer-tones. Though, he truly was not sure if he would wake at all if he himself fell asleep.

"Aye. You are a good la…"

His neighbour was already drifting. Or dead.

Chapter Eight

*Ceann Druimin, Caledon Territory
– Chief Lulach's Roundhouse*

"Tell us, Ineda. Does Agricola always obey the orders of the Emperor of Rome?"

Lulach's question was not what Nith had expected. There was a smaller crowd in the chief's roundhouse than the previous night, but still plenty to keep the conversation going.

The day had been one of severe frustration. The clear dawn had given way almost immediately to intermittent sleet showers. He had gone on patrol with Enya and six other guards, back to the woods of Glenlaff, to scour the area, but they had had to abandon the search when heavier snowfall settled in, all tracks having become obliterated.

He was less exhausted, but he could not be sure about Enya. She leant back against the roundhouse wall alongside him, as taut as one of the strings of Brennus' clarsach. Having tripped, over a partially-hidden log under the snow cover in Glenlaff woods, she had grumbled and growled at him. The wound at her jaw had opened up again, bleeding more than it had the previous day, but she had rebuffed all of his attempts to help staunch the blood.

He had given up on being brotherly to her, praying to the god *Arddhu* that he should not be partnering her again come the morrow. Her attitude might have been because Feargus and Colm had been dispatched to check along the waters of the Abhainn Dheathan, but he did not want to linger on that thought. Whether, or not, she preferred to patrol with Feargus – rather than him – he did not know, or care, but something clearly had made her mood dark.

When she was in such a snappy temper, he preferred to be on the other side of the roundhouse, but his present place tucked in next to her was the best space available to him when he joined the talk.

"Agricola is not the only one around here who barks out orders." Enya's low snarl was likely only meant for him, but he decided to ignore it.

As before, Ineda was seated beside Brennus across the fireside from where he and Enya lounged against the low wall. Nith watched the Brigante woman's serious glance survey those present before she spoke.

"All Governors of Britannia must obey the emperor's orders, or they lose credibility with the senate in Rome."

A distrustful outburst erupted from one of Lulach's chief elders. "Lorcan of Garrigill told us that the Governor of Britannia only has to obey the emperor. Now you say he answers to this senate? Who should we believe?"

Lulach waved down the question, his frustration evident as he tossed some logs onto the waning flames. "Heed better, Dubh! You must have been asleep again. The senate is like my council of elders. We discuss a situation, and sometimes you make me change my mind about some ruling, or other."

"Hah!" Lulach's hearth-wife chortled from her lower stool, her shoulder playfully nudging him, even though the situation was solemn. "That rarely happens with you."

Lulach's deliberate stare made no difference to his woman's smirk.

Nith felt a tightness inside that he wanted to banish. During the long seasons of trekking before the recent battle, he had been impervious to such displays of affectionate companionship. Though now past his twentieth summer, the bonding with one female had never been an issue to spend thought on, since he had never stayed long enough in any place to acquire a hearth to share with anyone. That had not been for him, nor for his brother, Esk.

He jerked his head towards the roof beams to banish the aching grief he still felt at the loss of his brother, blaming the sudden moisture at his eyes on the damp logs that Lulach had just added to the fire. If he had learned anything from the futile battle at Beinn na Ciche, it was that nothing was constant. Every day still alive was a precious one, and not to be squandered.

Settling down at one shared hearth now held a great appeal, with a good woman at his side to nudge and love him, blessed with the goddess *Brighid*'s gifts of mutual love and respect.

He dropped his chin to stare instead at the bent head of the warrior immediately in front of him. Becoming mawkish was never productive. He needed to shake off his disposition and concentrate on the immediate dangers besetting those all around the room.

The soft fingers soothing his tightly coiled fist made his weakness turn to embarrassment. Knowing it was Enya's sisterly comfort somehow humiliated even more. He flicked her fingers away as she had done to him earlier that day, and tightened his stance, summoning enough strength to stare down at her. Her present reassurance was not welcome. "Pay attention to Ineda," he growled.

He was met with one of Enya's best defiant glares. "You are the one with the poor concentration."

"How long will Agricola remain here?" Lulach asked.

Ineda laughed a little at the question. "I cannot give that answer. This is now Agricola's seventh summer of campaigning."

"I suppose he must be answering well to his emperor and senate?"

Ineda winced before agreeing with Lulach. "Aye, to Roman eyes. Almost everything he knows about military campaigning has been learned in Britannia."

"What makes a governor's task different from commanding an army of Rome?"

Ineda looked to the roof beams before answering. Nith took her gesture to be gathering strength to explain it well to those who were new to the ways of Rome. He found her a woman to admire, her inner strength not a trait given to everyone.

His thoughts wandered to the girl alongside him who was doing her best to ignore him. Enya also possessed an admirable strength of character, but she was still young. He dreaded to think what Enya would be like when reached Ineda's age: a nipping shrew as a hearth-wife, though never a dull one. The notion made him grin which earned him a poke in the side.

"Pay attention!" Enya nagged. "The talk is serious."

Looking down at her rattled expression, he nodded, wondering why he was even more amused by her. "So are my thoughts, Enya of Garrigill."

Her harrumphing and questioning glare set him to focus on what was being discussed.

Ineda's gaze spanned the room. "All major decisions rest on the shoulders of the governor – military and civic."

"Civic?" The cackle of the elder was followed by a phlegmy spit into the fire. "No one has explained this properly. What does this mean for us here at Ceann Druimin?"

A rumble of discord began, but Ineda quickly sought to soothe it.

"As Governor of Britannia, Agricola can move any of the troops whenever he chooses to maintain order. All military decisions are his, except when the emperor sends special instructions."

"Aye. We saw that at Beinn na Ciche when Agricola sent in those ravaging Batavians and Tungrians!"

"We will have no more interruptions!" Lulach gestured the man to be silent. Nith felt the impatience seeping from the chief, the tightness of the man's face daunting. "Speak, Ineda, and tell us of his civic arrangements for it seems likely we should now fear them more than a sword thrust."

Nith watched as Ineda made eye contact with the old man whose sneering expression demanded more details; as though she spoke of things she knew little about.

"As governor, Agricola oversees how the laws of Rome are adhered to by every person in Roman-dominated Britannia. The governor rules over all disputes among the people..."

"How can that be possible? A chief cannot rule more than his own little clan."

A flurry of denials rang around the room.

Nith almost intervened, but Ineda was good at calming tempers, turning her attention back to the chief.

"Lulach, you rule your people differently from Balbithan of the Taexali."

"You mean I am too soft in my decision making?" Lulach was abrasive.

"Nay." Ineda's soft laugh lightened the air. "The opposite holds. The punishments you set are severe, in comparison."

Lulach seemed happier which made Nith chuckle as well, considering what was being discussed.

"Ineda is a commendable woman to be speaking so to the chief," he whispered.

Enya clearly did not hold his same opinion of Ineda's appeal. The elbow nudge at his waist accompanied an ungainly grunt. "He is the worst-tempered chief I have ever known with the poorest judgements. Just like some other people in this room."

Whatever Enya had intended, his mirth increased, her glower making him smile even more before she deliberately set a greater distance between them.

"Pay attention," she nagged.

"I am paying attention, Enya. Too much." He caught and held her irritated gaze for a few moments before he forced himself to concentrate on the conversation around the fireside.

"I am harsher now than before battle at Beinn na Ciche," Lulach boasted. "No one can be allowed to endanger us."

Ineda's hand gesture mollified. "I agree, Lulach, you must keep your people safe. That is our Celtic way. Roman law is much more rigid. After new territory is conquered, Rome sets the same rules and laws of punishment that apply across their empire."

"How do they make these rules work?"

Ineda settled her gaze on Lulach. "Are you the only tribal chief at this gathering?"

"Aye, but what has that to do with this matter?"

She acknowledged him with a nod. "Your word is law in your territory, so long as you remain free of the shackles of Rome. After treaties are made with Rome, a chief loses his ability to make all of his own choices. He must respect the laws forced upon him, just as much as any person of his tribe."

"Pah!" The rheumy old woman was scathing. "You may think you have knowledge to share with us, Ineda of the Brigantes, but how can this General Agricola know what a chief does? We are scattered too far and wide in the Caledon hills for him to know if we obey him or not."

Nith had encountered a similar attitude at many of the villages he had visited on his long trek northwards and knew how difficult it was to make resistant people understand. He decided it was time to intervene, to give Ineda his support. "After capitulation to Agricola," he said, "it is unlikely that you will dwell in your small mountain villages. You will probably be herded into larger settlements along with any surviving livestock, because that makes it easier for Rome to control everyone and everything."

"Will Agricola round us up, and force us from our homes to live and worship like playthings of Rome?"

Nith intervened again. "Aye. Be sure that he will. Agricola will make certain a Caledon or Taexali leader is chosen who will hold fast to Roman rule and will be responsible for paying all of the tribal dues to Rome."

Ineda added, "Agricola has experience of how to make their system work fairly throughout the empire."

At Nith's side Enya erupted. "How can anything about domination be fair?"

The question was so significant a hush descended for a moment.

Nith wished he had an answer.

"How can Agricola monitor this civic progress of Britannia's far southern territories, while he campaigns in the north?" Lulach looked pensive.

Nith approved of Ineda's complimentary smile. "That is a good question, Lulach. A special judicial legate came to Britannia to help Agricola maintain civic and political order."

A female elder, who had grumbled the evening before, interrupted anew. "I suppose you will tell us that you can also name this man?"

"Gaius Salvius Liberalis was the judicial legate when I was in Votadini territory three summers ago. If he has been recalled to Rome, then he may have been replaced by another."

"Will Agricola ever be satisfied?" Enya's angry words rang out louder than her fist-thump at the wall beside him, just missing his lower arm. Nith groped for her tense fingers and cradled them in his own, not convinced it would soothe her in her present sulk, but it was worth trying.

Ineda's expression was grim. "Agricola is relentless about extending the Roman Empire's boundaries, a plan that has not changed since he became governor under Emperor Vespasian and afterwards Titus. Now he plays to the tune of Domitian."

Nith heard the rancour in the voice of the elder. "That does not mean that we should have to play his tune as well."

Ineda's brief laugh broke some of the tension around the room. "Nay, and we will not – if we work out how to continue to play our own. Unlike former Governors of Britannia, Agricola really believes that rules should apply to all across occupied territories with no exceptions."

Nith was not surprised at the wheeze around the room. He knew enough about Ineda to know she was not defending Agricola, but some around the room clearly thought she was.

Enya allowed his soothing gesture of her clenched fist, but would not be silenced. "I see little that is just since those damned Roman invaders stepped off their ships."

"Wait, Enya!" Ineda called back the growling audience. "Hear me. Agricola loves to bleed dry any newly-occupied Roman territory, but that takes time."

"Then we must stop him!" Nith felt every one of Enya's furious words ripple through him – flesh, bone and all – and not just because she was back to being daubed as close to him as the wall he was leaning on.

Nith watched Chief Lulach's expression grow even grimmer, the man's next words showing degrees of despair, defeat, and a desperate urge to change the conversation.

"Why does Agricola, and his Roman scum, not retreat to the southern wooden fortresses during the winter moons?"

Ineda's answer was firm when she turned her focus back to the chief. "The winter season will not prevent Agricola from imposing his demands on the tribes, if he chooses to remain in Taexali territory. He paid little heed to poor weather during past campaigns. Though what he does here in the north may very well depend on what is happening elsewhere in Britannia. He controls all with an iron fist, but we have rebellious southern Celtic brothers who sometimes give him cause to move his troops at short notice – across land, and on the sea."

Someone near the front interrupted. "His patrols scour our territory, but they do not march from Taexali lands. The invaders poured onto our shores from Agricola's ships."

Nith nudged Enya realising the man had probably been introduced before his own arrival at the gathering. "Who is he?" he whispered in her ear.

Enya drew her head away. "He is Garth, a Vacomagi."

Nith squared his shoulders. He knew so little of the lands that lay further north.

Garth explaining that he came from Culbeuchly – where the Abhainn Caelis flowed out to the waters of the sea god *Morimaru* – and that his companion, Nathrach, came from a little further west, meant little to Nith. He vowed, once again, to find out more about the areas. He spoke up before any other questions could be asked.

"Have your Vacomagi villages surrendered?"

Chapter Nine

*Ceann Druimin, Caledon Territory
– Chief Lulach's Roundhouse*

"The Vacomagi cannot have surrendered!" Enya's blurt came almost at the same time as Nith's own question. He caught and held her fervent gaze, willing her to remain calm.

Garth of Culbeuchly replied, sounding quite desperate. "Large patrols from Roman ships swarmed our coastline. They slaughtered any who challenged them, though very few have done that."

Nith thanked Garth for his honesty, all the while aware that Enya was slumping against him. "Some of your warriors fought valiantly under Calgach's orders at Beinn na Ciche."

His arm encircled Enya's drooping shoulders and drew her in.

A soft denial came from someone in front of him. He had tried to be circumspect since the lack of Vacomagi at Beinn na Ciche had been a bone of contention for many Caledon warriors.

Enya's words had calmed by the time she raised her head to speak again, though he could feel her inner turmoil through their contact, the flesh under his fingers a tense, tight knot. "Have any of your local chiefs made treaties with Rome?" she asked.

Garth looked uncomfortable. "No official treaties had been agreed when I left, but many of our coastal people do not see the Roman Empire as something to be feared. The ships of Agricola's fleet have beached on our shores before now."

Nith felt Enya bristling again and, in truth, he also had difficulty believing Garth's words.

Looks of doubt warred with direct hostility around the room.

Ineda clarified the purpose of the Roman marine patrols. "Agricola's fleet sailed the eastern shoreline two summers ago, disembarking only to take on fresh water. They noted where tribal villages lay close to the beaches, though I was told they had no orders to subdue any territory at that time. Agricola will now want knowledge of Taexali and Vacomagi countryside from sea to interior. His full *legions* will not be tramping over moorlands, or sticky bogs, without knowing of ways to cross poor ground. And he will want to ensure no native attack."

Lulach became even more agitated, shoving escaped strands of hair from his side braids behind his ears. "What makes that man so compelled to conquer us?"

Ineda drew back the attention of the gathering. "Do not underestimate Agricola. He is neither reckless, nor is he insane but he is a strong advocate of establishing new tactics where they are needed to get his own way. Believe me, he is very practised at reacting to, and dealing with, unexpected situations."

Nith watched as Ineda broke off speaking to point to him. He shrugged off the discomfiture.

"Nith was correct earlier," Ineda said. "General Agricola wants to know all of the wealth your lands can bring him."

"Would he take everything we hold precious in life?" Lulach's aiming of a small log was perfect as it plopped onto the centre of the dwindling fire, sending sparks up into the air rather than onto the feet of those sat around its edges.

A clamour of alarm spread around the room as every possible source was questioned.

"Does Agricola seek our sites of iron-slick bogs? Extraction of iron from them is a great skill of our smiths, but they do not produce any more than is needed for our own weapons, or tools. We re-use, or exchange with other tribes, when we have a need. Will he demand everything?" The elder looked around the throng, as though mystified by his own question.

Lulach deferred to Nith. "You know more of this than I do."

Nith gave the best explanation he could. "The Romans have a huge appetite for metals. Across the whole Roman Empire, new recruits need supplies of armour, tools and weapons. Soldiers of Rome serve their emperor for twenty-five years, and over that time they need replacements for broken, or lost, equipment. A constant supply of metal is essential."

He halted till he was satisfied that the rapt faces wanted more.

Enya took the opportunity to wriggle out of his clutch and leaned back into her own wall space, his dropped arm feeling momentarily useless. Catching Lorcan's intrigued gaze from the far side of the fire, he cleared his throat before resuming, glad that the heat he felt rising in his neck would be masked in the dimness around the outer wall of the roundhouse.

"In the southern areas of Britannia, rocks yield iron, lead, tin and other ores I cannot name," he continued. "After smelting of the rock is done, bars of metal are formed. Those bars are sent across the Roman Empire to be fashioned into tools and weapons where they are needed."

"What has that to do with us?" The question that rang angrily around the room came from one of the younger Ceann Druimin warriors.

Nith patiently explained. "Agricola intends his troops to remain in this area for a very long time, therefore he will seek local supplies. Less transportation of metals over long distances means fewer goods lost to local ambushes."

There was a hint of optimism in the smirks that Nith saw dotted around the room that cheered him, just the tiniest soar from the gloom that the people had found themselves in.

"Then we must keep attacking his supplies!" Enya's defence of his words were vehement.

"How can we find out when these wagons are due?"

Alongside him, Enya had no intentions of calming the mood, her words hostile. "We can organise raiding parties, but we have to do even more than that to thwart Agricola's progress. We must find all of his weaknesses and destroy him. Send him forth from our lands, like he has done to our enslaved tribespeople!"

Nith grasped her tense fist that itched to pull forth the long knife at her belt. He held on, scrabbling for something less distressing to talk about. "Are there sources of ores on your lands, Lulach?" he asked, coming back to the subject of valuable produce.

Frustration gripped Lulach as he got up to pad back and forth, the man's mouth contorted, his neck and arm muscles clenching. "If you mean iron-laced bogs, then there are plenty of them. If you mean rocks from which iron can be smelted, some of the hill tribes are aware of such lodes, but my smiths use none of those."

Lulach stopped when one of his elders spat into the conversation. "The working of rocks takes greater strength and perseverance."

Another voice piped up. "If you were the one knee-deep in sucking bogs, you would not feel so lightly about the hard work involved!"

More voices joined the fray.

"Enough!" Lulach's bellow calmed the roundhouse. He slumped back down onto his now creaking stool. "We have no time to argue whether bog, or rock, is best. Nith? What can we do?"

Next to him, Nith felt Enya bristle. Where she summoned her fire from he did not know, but he continued to hold her hand tight to his own.

"We must learn exactly where Agricola's troops are sent, and prevent him from destroying our people," she shouted. "Remaining hidden in the Caledon hills will not achieve that. Most of all, we must know the fate of his captives. I am not the only one here who has kin unaccounted for."

Her outburst had the roundhouse ringing with support…and even more questions.

Garth of Culbeuchly piped up. "Roman patrols march over our damp flatlands right now, but those who still live there do not yet understand what the Romans will do to them."

Lulach jumped to his feet again, as though the stool he had been sitting on had been set alight. "Do any of them intend to attack the Romans?"

Garth was quick to answer. "Not that I know of, but defending our territory is as impossible a task as it is for you!"

"Did your warriors all return to their villages after the battle at Beinn na Ciche?"

"Some came limping back to their families and farmsteads." Garth's words were careful.

The room almost erupted, many voices scathing and others malicious. Cries rang around, berating the visitors for daring to come and tell them of such cowardice.

"Hold back your fiery-spite," Lulach roared, "till these men tell us all we need to know. They have not been forced here at spear-point to talk to us."

Quiet descended under Lulach's ferocious scowl.

"You can see that my people need to hear how you two personally stand regarding Roman invaders." Lulach sent another fierce glare around the room to ensure all obeyed him.

Nith could see that Garth was calming agitated breaths, his chest rising and falling more slowly each time he exhaled.

"There are other Vacomagi, like the two of us, who joined those battle-ready at Beinn na Ciche. We resisted the yoke of Rome. However, that means we cannot easily return to our own homes knowing that our families might be colluding with Rome, and who might now regard us as traitors. There are places where we congregate and take cover at night, though we keep a look out for Roman movements during the daylight hours."

Nith felt Enya's nudge and easily guessed her expression.

He wished he could quell her fears but had no answer for her.

A bustle at the entryway heralded the arrival of women bearing empty wooden bowls. And behind them were others who carried in large cauldrons of tempting broth, the smell of it tantalisingly wafting around.

Lulach ruffled his fingers through his side braids, snagging the wiry hair almost off his scalp. "Soon we will tighten our belts, but for now we will eat since we still have food for our bellies. Afterwards, we will thank our gods and goddesses that we still live to thwart Agricola and his Roman scum!"

A muted cheer momentarily lifted the spirits of all present. When the room quietened, Lulach had even more to say. "After we eat, Brennus of Garrigill can chase away our gloom for the time being."

"That I can do." Brennus' smile was tinged with a sadness he could not quite hide.

Nith felt his own smile hard to form. It took little to encourage Brennus. His friend had learned many songs and stories – some happy, some laments – but others would be just perfect for their present situation.

"We have not had music, or song, in this house for many a night. We are not feasting, but your clarsach will bring us comfort.

Nith's stomach growled in appreciation of the fine smells gently pervading the room. Starvation would be averted for another day.

Enya's flat palm patted his stomach. "This night your growls are greater than mine, my friend, but you know that my rumbles always last longer than yours."

His empty-belly was forgotten as he drifted into her gaze. Her bad temper had flown. A hint of her twinkling-banter filled him in an entirely different fashion, yet being only her friend was no longer good enough.

Chapter Ten

SrathBogie, Taexali Territory

"How many of them are on the move?"

The young boy who burst into the roundhouse, in a flurry of agitation, was sure of his information, but Ruoridh was not certain it was what he wanted to hear. Taking his time, he put down the whetstone that he was sharpening the knife on, the stretching at his upper arm wound making a grunt impossible to mask. Forcing himself to sound calm, since the boy was already ill-at-ease, he repeated his words. "How many?"

"A legion?" Calum's bony shoulders rose in a gesture of doubt, his palms opening out to pat off the sleet layer from his tunic and checked braccae, his feet-stomp designed to clear the lingering white from his foot bindings. "Perhaps even more than that? I have no idea. But old Brynn, who is up on Knockandy Hill, says the column is never ending."

"Are they marching this way?" Ruoridh reached for another log to toss onto the smouldering fire while he absorbed the information, and worked out what he should do, having realised that if Calum had brought real alarm, then he would be hearing the older village members already uprooting themselves. The small roundhouse he was in belonged to Calum's mother, the woman who had given him shelter when he had been dragged into her village, weak as a baby from blood loss.

"Nay. Brynn says they are headed up the Abhainn Urie."

Ruoridh had no reason to doubt young Calum, but it never paid to be lax. Not with so many Romans marauding around. His father and uncles had taught him that. He reached for the battered sword that lay nearby, thinking of what he had at-hand to defend himself, yet knowing that his recent sharpening of the nicked blade was the best that he would ever be able to do. He slipped it into the worn leather scabbard that Calum's mother had managed to find for it. "And who was it who told Brynn?"

"He says the news came from Fingal, one of the warriors keeping watch up by the ancient cairn at Wichach."

"From Wichach?" Ruoridh smiled. It was definitely the first upturn of his lips that day, for there was not really so much to find humour in. He sank the knife he had just sharpened into a leather pouch, right to its simple bone hilt. Who the knife and sword had originally belonged to was unknown, but his need was greater than the warrior who lay dead beside them when he and Beathan were fleeing the carnage at Beinn na Ciche. His father, Gabrond, had given him his own long knife many seasons ago, when he had become a man, but going to battle with only a knife was not the same as the security of continuing to fight the Roman scourge with a proper long blade. A notched sword was better than none.

"Aye, old Brynn was certain."

The news Calum brought would be reliable, he felt sure of that, though the numbers on the move could be difficult to assess. For those Taexali warriors, who had never experienced Roman columns on the march, even one *cohort* of soldiers would seem like an endless line, never mind ten times that if a whole legion really was on the move.

"Was it Fingal who brought you here to my mother? After the Roman soldier tried to kill you?"

At eight summers gone, young Calum was greedy for every bloody battle-detail. Ruoridh now knew the names of the warriors of Wichach who had helped him, after he had been attacked by the Roman patrol that bore off his cousin Beathan, but he had yet to properly meet his rescuers. "I am told it was." He moved over to make room for the young lad when Calum sidled on to the low bench. "And I will heartily thank Fingal, when I meet him."

"Tell me again how that Roman shite felled you, Ruoridh?"

Ruoridh ignored the boy's choice of words. "You have heard the tale so many times, you should be able to relate it yourself."

Calum grinned. "Aye. I can. You were just sauntering around the woods, enjoying the heat sent down from *Lugh*…"

"Enough of that prattle!" His instinctive nudge that sent Calum sprawling cost him dearly. He drew his arm across his chest, and tentatively massaged his wound.

Calum ignored him and clambered up onto the bench again, continuing with the proper story. "You had already managed to kill one of the Romans, but another came at you from behind?"

"I was too busy finishing off the first one to realise the other was right at my back." The whetstone was used to sharpen both of his own knives that he always carried in his waist pouch which, to his great relief, he still had after the battle.

"He used his shield to butt you from behind?" Calum was a stickler for detail.

"Aye, but the blow from his auxiliary wooden *clipeus* did not hurt nearly as much as the *spatha* hacking at my head and shoulder."

"*Spatha?* What does that mean?"

"Some Roman auxiliaries do not use the stabbing *gladius*. Some have a longer sword more like ours, and they call it a *spatha.*"

Reaching sideways he stretched out a strand of the boy's damp hair, and then flicked up the small blade that he had just sharpened, to test it. Calum barely flinched when it glinted near his cheek.

Ruoridh stared at the trust on the lad's face. He had only known the boy a small number of nights, yet the innocent faith that radiated there was humbling. Satisfied the knife was keen enough, he sheathed it and set to work on the last item.

Calum jumped off the bench to do some imaginary sword slashes, before snatching up his small wooden practice sword that sat in the iron basket near the entryway of the roundhouse. Returning his way, the boy pretended a serious hack at his wounded head, a movement that came just a little too close for him to feel comfortable about.

"My mother says that tribesmen have the hardest heads of all, and the silliest notions that they can think so." Calum scrunched up his button of a nose and drew a few deeper breaths as he continued to slice his way around the room. "She says the strangest of things, most of the time."

Ruoridh's harsh laugh echoed up to the stout timbers holding up the conical roof. "You'll come to understand her when you've grown a bit more. I, for one, am glad of my hard head, and of your mother's tender care of it. I doubt I would be speaking with you now, if I had been left to the ministrations of Fingal, or any of his fellow warriors. I am so heartened that they dragged me from the battlefields, and all the way here to your mother, because I fear they do not have the same healing skills as she has."

With his forefinger, he indicated the area just above his right ear where the *spatha* had sheared off a chunk of his long hair, as well as a slice of his scalp. The wound was scabbing over well enough, but it was sensitive to the shifting air when outside. His head had bled like a stuck pig, but it was his upper arm that ended up with the deeper wound from the *spatha's* continued down stroke.

"What made that soldier not use his sword again to finish you off? I mean his *spatha*."

In the full innocence of a child, Calum's questions reminded him a little too well of what had happened.

"First, it was the Roman's shield that winded me. It set me off balance, and when the auxiliary followed with the slice at my head, that blow stunned me to my knees. The next thump of his *clipeus* sent me sprawling. The last I recall was his hobnailed boot rolling me over. At first, I thought the yowl I was hearing in my head was my own cry, but now I realise it was the squeal of a distant Roman *cornu* calling for a retreat of the troops."

Calum's eyes were wide and his voice hushed. "*Arddhu,* the forest god, protected you. He made that Roman leave you alive."

Now, able to reflect on the attack, Ruoridh knew the repeated call of the *cornu* caused the Roman auxiliary to rush away before double-checking that he really was dead.

If the men from Wichach had not found him moaning and groaning some time later, he might well have been embracing those warriors recently gone to the otherworld. However, it seemed that *Arddhu* had declared that it was not his time, which meant he had more work to do to thwart the usurping invaders.

Reminiscing got him no further forward, so he shook off the memories and rose to his full height. He would never match the loftiness of Brennus, but before the recent battle at Beinn na Ciche he was already standing shoulder to shoulder with his father Gabrond and Uncle Lorcan. Arraying himself with his makeshift sword belt and waist pouches, he afterwards drew on the rough cloak that had been provided by Calum's mother, since his own had been shredded on the battlefield. Pinning the worn material in place with the simple iron pin that came with the bratt, and drawing up the wool over his head, he urged the lad out of the roundhouse.

"Find your mother. Tell her that I thank her for her hospitality, and all that she has done to keep me alive, but that I need to leave now to find out more of these movements of Agricola."

Calum's fist at the bratt cloth stayed him a moment longer, the boy's expression fearful yet also wistful. "Where are you headed?"

"Wichach."

"But that may take you closer to Roman patrols!" The panic was evident as Calum jumped ahead to waylay him.

"I realise that, but tell your mother that I will do nothing rash to ruin her good healing. I will decide what to do after I speak to the warriors of Wichach. I can no longer remain here doing nothing."

"I want to come with you." Young Calum's plea was so full of eagerness it was tempting to agree, but Ruoridh knew it would be far too dangerous a journey for one so young, and not to be undertaken if it could be avoided.

"Nay, you must bide here and guard your mother." He put responsibility on the lad's shoulders as a distraction, though in truth the boy was the only one around who could do it. "You are the only able warrior here, Calum. Your elders, and your mother, rely on you. Do not forget that I may need you to be a messenger in the days to come, so ensure that you do not fail them."

He could see that the boy was torn between the momentous task awarded to him, and his need for company, but the boy's next pleas went completely unheeded. "You are not yet healed."

"I do well enough, young Calum. The nights in your mother's care has restored plenty of my strength."

That Calum was lonely, there being no other youngsters left in the village, could not be his concern; he had to move on. His purpose had become clearer the more he had pondered it. "Look after your mother. But go to safety with her in the Caledon hills, if any Romans approach here. I know she feels her duty is to tend the old ones, as she is doing right now, but she should flee and save herself if Rome threatens you all directly."

"I give you my word."

Seeing the resignation on the boy's face, Ruoridh sought to cheer him before he left.

"I know you will. I have one last request of you? Since I have no sense of place around here, how do I get to Wichach?"

Calum's grin and subsequent giggles were followed by the lad dragging on his bratt, after which he took him past the furthest roundhouse of the hamlet. The boy's finger pointed, the sleet having let up momentarily to leave a sky lightened enough for long sight. "Look yonder. That over there is Knockandy Hill. Head straight to the lower slopes where you will reach the long cairn of the ancients. If you look northwards from the cairn, you will see an eight-stone circle of our forefathers." A number of other instructions followed on quickly, including boggy areas to avoid, Calum declaring proudly that he knew the landscape well. "The sun will be high in the sky by the time you ford the Malsach Burn, though seeing the sun on such a squally day as today may be difficult. But fear not, long before then the warriors at Wichach will have been tracking your movements!"

The hike to Wichach took no time at all, Calum's landmarks easy to follow. Cover was fairly simple to find, nonetheless, he was relieved that he saw no signs of any Roman patrols on his route. The young lad had been correct in that some young warriors from Wichach confronted him first, their interrogation of his intentions thorough before they would let him go on any further across their territory. Distrust was a common look across their expressions. Even when he mentioned seeking out Fingal, it barely changed their chariness and hesitation.

He heaved a deep inward sigh. There had been so many situations during his growing years when he had experienced a similar desperate distrust that came with the aftermath of a Roman invasion. Everyone and everything was suspect, until proven otherwise.

The three guards questioning him were only a few summers older than he was. As he answered even more about his background and reasons for moving around Taexali territory, he wondered who had instructed them to be so effectively wary.

Their reluctance to escort him to the summit of Wichach Hill eventually waned and he followed in their wake as they scampered up the hill.

"Aye, they are on the march again." Fingal clarified after welcoming him, glad to see that his efforts to keep him alive had not been in vain.

"Did you spy them from here?" Ruoridh asked.

From the Hill of Wichach, Ruoridh saw there was a reasonable view of the closest farmed field-strips and scrub land, but it was not as wide-reaching as the outlook would have been from the summit of The Mither Tap, the tops of Beinn na Ciche soaring much higher above the valley floors than Wichach. The undulating landscape prevented him from seeing where the bulk of the Roman armies might presently be, though he wondered if clearer skies might make that an easier task.

"Nay." Fingal was dismissive. "I bided last night with the warriors at Tap O'Noth, where it is a good deal higher than here. From there, you can see over towards the glens at Foudland."

"So you saw them all move from their camp?"

"Nay, I suspect only some are forging northwards, forward troops bent on a particular purpose. I waited only long enough at Tap O'Noth to see the first of the column snake its way around the pass. It was better that I brought back the news here to Wichach."

"Does no one watch them now?"

Fingal nodded. "Warriors still monitor up at Tap O'Noth, but the sleet showers will have hampered their vision. Someone will return to us here at Wichach by nightfall, with further news."

"Where do you think Agricola might be going?" His question to Fingal showed his lack of knowledge of the area.

"If the Roman column continues the direction they were headed in, they will soon reach the Taexali and Vacomagi border." Fingal's raucous laugh surprised him.

Ruoridh wondered what might be amusing. "How will they tell that?" He was certain he would not know unless someone gave him the correct information.

"The Caelis will halt their progress."

"How can you be sure?" Ruoridh did not know what Fingal referred to.

Fingal laughed again. "Where they are headed, the Abhainn Caelis is too wide to jump the flow. It will surely slow them."

He understood now. Unfortunately, he had to dispel the notion that a mere river course would prevent the Roman army from progressing. "Those canny Romans can cross the widest of rivers easily enough. It might halt them for a short time but rushing water is no obstacle to them."

Fingal clearly did not believe him, his expression bemused. "The water is too deep to easily wade across."

"That will not stop them."

Fingal's snort of derision deafened him, but he plodded on regardless.

"If the gap is too wide to set planks across it, they source enough tree trunks to make hollowed-out flat-bottomed barges. When enough are ready to lie alongside each other, they strap them together." He used his hands, setting his thumbs close together to help Fingal understand. "When that is done, and the vessels are set onto the water, they step across planks of wood that straddle the centres of the barges. It is wobbly, for sure, since the boats sway a little, but in no time their whole column will be across that river."

"You have seen them do this?" He had now gained Fingal's full attention.

"Not me, but my Uncle Brennus certainly has."

"Where would this have been?"

For the next while Ruoridh explained his Brigante birth, and the trek his family had been on for the bulk of his life. Fingal in turn gave him information on the Caelis, the river border between Vacomagi and Taexali territory.

"I did not realise that Calum's village by SrathBogie was so close to Vacomagi territory."

"Aye, it is close for sure. The Vacomagi of the hills claim the land on the far side of the water."

Fingal was deliberately confusing him. Highly amused by his ignorance, the young man's grin was wide-stretched across his cheeks till Fingal eventually stopped guffawing. "It is no surprise if you do not know of it. Bide here a bit longer, and you will learn all of the burns and rivers around these parts."

He refused to be daunted by Fingal's mirth. "Tell me of this Caelis."

"SrathBogie water flows through the pass near Calum's roundhouse and a few twists later it merges into the larger Abhainn Caelis."

"What makes this Caelis river so important for it to be used as a tribal boundary?"

Fingal's glint showed appreciation of the question. "The Caelis goes from strength to strength, many other springs and burns feeding into it, till it eventually reaches the northern sands. That makes it a very important stretch of water."

He understood now about the Caelis, but had another question. "Why did you drag me to Calum's mother? Was there no-one here at Wichach to help me?"

Fingal put down his whittling knife, seemingly happy with his rudely carved horse, yet regretful of his answer. "Before the battlegrounds of Beinn na Ciche, the able of the northern Taexali congregated to the south of the Mither Tap, much like your Brigante kin did. Now, the Taexali who survived the battle remain hidden in Caledon territory. Calum's mother was the only younger woman left in this area that we knew of, one who would be able to tend your wounds. The old healers still alive hereabouts know what needs to be done, Ruoridh, but have no strength left to do it themselves."

"My thanks go to you all for keeping me alive."

Fingal reached for another block of ash wood, readying his knife after scanning the area, dismissive that he had done anything of particular note. "Those of us who still breathe need to look out for each other."

"Aye, that is definitely true." Now came the time for him to learn more of the lands being tramped on by the Roman *legions*. "Are the Vacomagi and Taexali friendly with each other?" Ruoridh was interested to know.

Fingal guffawed. "Were the Brigantes friendly with their neighbours, if they ran off with their animals?"

Ruoridh's smile felt odd, to be laughing at such dire times. "I hardly know. By the time I was aware of tribal raids, we all had to unite against the Romans. They are a formidable enemy."

"They are that. If I were not tasked to watch for Roman movements from Tap O'Noth, or from Wichach, I would be trailing those marauding Roman predators to see what they do next. We need to find a way to expel them from our lands."

Ruoridh sighed deeply. Someone like Fingal would be useful to have alongside. His family had hoped so much that the huge gathering of local warriors would have defeated Agricola, yet the gods had not willed it so. "I should be heading into Caledon territory to discover who of my kin has survived, but my greater urge is to follow those Roman pigs and learn what Agricola plans next. Do you know of any local warriors who are already doing this?"

Fingal looked surprised. "Nay. Beyond sending word of Roman movements to some Caledon chiefs, we have only been guarding our own territory."

Ruoridh felt the man's keen gaze assessing him for the truth of his intentions.

"If you follow the *legions*, and decide that you know what Agricola plans for our lands, what will you do then?" Fingal asked.

Ruoridh explained the courier system that Brennus had set up to send information amongst the tribes of Brigantia. "And before the battle at Beinn na Ciche, there was a good communication arrangement set up in Venicones, and southern Taexali territories. We need to have that here, as well."

"We do, already." Fingal's chuckle was followed by a wry pull of his lip. "Though, I suppose only in small parts between Tap O'Noth and a couple of Caledon chiefs."

Ruoridh returned the smile. "Every bit helps, but we need to have more extensive communication between the Taexali, the Vacomagi, the Caledons and any other northern tribes I know nothing about, yet."

"Must you travel alone to do this surveying?" Fingal's expressive gaze was inquiring.

"Nay!" Ruoridh's answer was immediate. "Someone to guard my back would be preferable, but I do not want to linger hereabouts till I can persuade anyone foolhardy enough to join me."

Fingal's dry laugh reached out to him. "Remain a short while longer, till I have a word or two with the warriors of Wichach. I may know of just the very person to accompany you."

Chapter Eleven

Well of Ythan Roman Camp, Taexali Territory

"Ten? And you only tell me now?"

General Gnaeus Iulius Agricola found a warped satisfaction when the inept junior *tribune* of the *Legio II Adiutrix* fought to maintain his composure. He was as close as a whisker to the young man's jaw, so it was no surprise that the answer returned as a jittery croak.

"Yes, sir, though in total there are eleven men missing." Titus Sicinia Flavus' words were so rushed they were almost indistinct.

Agricola went towards the *carbonarius,* the burner situated a step or two from his tent. Alternately rubbing his nails on his palms and opening his fists, he spread his fingers wide near its weak flames. Angling his body, he stared at the young officer whose very presence riled him every time he had to speak to him. And that had to be frequently, because he could not trust the youth to make sound judgements on his own. The legion the young *tribune* served in would mutiny if Titus Sicinia Flavus issued unreasonable orders, and insubordination of the ranks had to be avoided at all costs.

The weakling should never have been pushed into legionary service at all, but who was he to disobey a direct order from his Emperor Domitian? Rich patronage and full coffers offered to causes the emperor approved of greased far too many palms back in Rome. It was just one more of the myriad of corrupt practices across the Roman Empire that he abhorred.

The return of his senior *tribune* of the *Legio II Adiutrix* could not come soon enough.

He waited for more information, but the officer remained mute, the little tick at his cheek a testimony to the young man's unease. A pause heightened till the junior *tribune* flinched under his determined scrutiny.

Without making direct eye contact, a response eventually slipped free from Flavus. "We have had no communication from the patrol since they left two days ago, sir. We believe they must have been ambushed."

Removing his hands from the feeble heat, Agricola clamped them against his belly, pinioning his cloak in place with his thumbs. He strode back to the irritating *tribune*. "We believe? Who is the 'we' who believe this, *Tribune* Flavus? What gives you any proof that this could be the case?"

Flavus looked discomfited as well he should by his spat questions. The young man was too inclined to listen to the naysayers in the *Legio II Adiutrix*. Much speculation and grumbling was now going on during the aftermath of the recent pitched-battle with the infuriating Caledons, and their tribal allies. Agricola knew his troops were on edge and restless, their stay at the camp near the Well of Ythan longer than he had initially intended, even though they had only been there a matter of days. At times, he felt just as cantankerous as they were, but his reasons differed, and his causes were many.

Complete military conquest of the whole of Britannia was the tantalising objective he was now sorely tempted to throw to the northern winds, since it was proving to bring no tangible rewards. He needed substantial vindication, results that would impress his restive emperor, and the even greedier Roman Senate. He needed them to officially authorise a further campaign trek to the northernmost tip of Britannia, which was still many *milles passus* from his present camp, though he would do it without their approval if he had to. Satisfying his far-off and increasingly irrational Emperor Domitian was proving to be as impossible as maintaining regular contact with Rome, and the winter had not even properly set in, yet. On the other hand, the irregularity of decrees arriving from Rome had meant it was possible for him to forge on this far north in Britannia already.

Pulling his concentration back to the matter at hand, he prompted the hapless junior *tribune*. "You have proof?"

"*Centurion* Rubr..." Flavus' impulsive stutter ground to an immediate halt before he dropped his chin to stare at the ground, the reddening at his neck a shade warmer looking than the *carbonarius*.

Agricola fought to check his temper. If the gormless youth meant Rubrius Mucius, he already suspected the *centurion* of the Fifth *Cohort* of the *Legio II Adiutrix* as being too good at rumour mongering. Maintaining a settled atmosphere amongst all of the troops who surrounded him was essential: total loyalty was paramount across all levels of command in every legion. His grunt of dissatisfaction was misinterpreted by Flavus whose apologies continued as ineffective as they were pointless.

"I mean...sorry, sir. You said to inform you of all developments so we... I...thought you would want..."

His held-up palm stopped the exasperating flow. Not missing the aggrieved flash that flickered across the *tribune*'s eyes, he strode back to the *carbonarius*, this time to keep his feet from freezing.

Used to immediate capitulation by vanquished tribes, he was aware that many of his long-serving soldiers were resentful, their expectations unfulfilled in these barren northern lands. Traditionally, the spoils of war were immediately mopped up; rewards promised to all ranks; with the opportunity to do some pilfering along the way – after which the *legions* moved on to a new conquest. On the route from their last temporary site, across the endless shallow valleys and rolling low hills of Taexali territory, the paltry villages they encountered were mostly abandoned, and had clearly never held any riches of note anyway. A further tramp northwards on the campaign trail might stifle his troops' inclination to bicker over the lack of amenities and spoils, but he was not quite ready to move on.

The goddess *Felicitas* had abandoned him. His expectation of battle success and that of the goddess apparently did not match.

Shivers beset him, but at least some warmth was eventually returning to his toes where they rested almost directly below the feeble heat of the burner. Twisting round, he caught the attention of his personal guard who stood just paces away. Reluctantly withdrawing one hand from his cloak, it took only a couple of wordless finger-flicks at the brazier to indicate that it should be tended to, even though there were no charcoal supplies to add to it. The sappy sparking-wood that was to hand was useless, but it was that or nothing. The unvarying dampness of the day did not help to keep the burner alight either.

He turned back to the hapless Flavus. "You just told me that you think that whole patrol has been attacked, and are probably all dead?"

"Sir." A jittery nod followed the bald answer.

Agricola almost smirked. The young man might actually be learning that a simple answer served him better.

Whatever the junior *tribune*'s mistakes, he vowed not to lose any more men under his command and definitely no more of his valuable horses. *Jupiter*'s arse! It was easier for him to replace men than horses. Some prayers to the goddess *Epona* were also in order, since the Taexali were even more poorly stocked with mounts than their Venicones neighbours had been. He had welcomed any pathetically squat creature that came to him, though he should be long used to the fact that the indigenous tribes favoured shorter-legged animals, even though they were generally taller men.

He turned back to deal with the junior *tribune* once more. "What is your reasoning for this assessment?"

Flavus' throat moved awkwardly before his answer came, his flickering eyelids unable to mask his agitation. "The patrol had orders to venture into the nearest mountain pass. They were to assess the terrain with the ore specialist, and his assistants, but they have not come back. One of the horses was found wandering by a stream not far from our camp, but there was no sign of its rider."

Agricola breathed deeply through his nose, and then exhaled slowly before replying. Keeping a rein on his temper was nigh impossible in the face of the young man's naïve stupidity. "You have made the assumption the detail was definitely ambushed because one mount found its way back?"

"Yes, sir. It still carried the mining engineer's tools."

Jupiter's balls and everything associated! He momentarily studied the mushy ground under his boots, forcing himself towards a calm he did not feel. He had been tasked with personally bringing this particular boy to competence. Flavus' uncle and patron, in the senate in Rome, wielded much clout. Even though he detested the system, Agricola could not see a way to escape the repercussions of ignoring the demand to ensure the boy matured during his tenure as junior *tribune*, though it was proving to be a wearisome year.

"Which minerals expert?"

"Sir, it was Vibius Malleollus Ligustus."

"Malleollus Ligustus!"

Agricola glared down the *Via Praetoria*, forcing his expression to not betray his extreme displeasure. In the name of all the gods! This idiot *tribune* was telling him that one of his best mining engineers had been sent out with only one basic patrol group to guard him. His back teeth clamped together. How had that been allowed to happen?

"And what in *Bonus Eventus*' name did you do about this loss?" He whipped his head up again.

Flavus was now visibly sweating, a trickle running down each moist temple. A fleeting memory came to Agricola of being a rattled junior *tribune* of the *Legio II Augusta*, when he was serving in Governor Paulinus' staff. He, too, had weathered through some trying times when he had angered his superior, but his recollection was that he had never been so slow to grasp what needed to be done.

The young *tribune*'s gulp before answering him was suppressed, though still audible. "Another patrol was sent out after we found the beast, to seek traces of them."

"On whose orders?" he prompted, wanting the update finally concluded. He had to prevent all unauthorised movement of local warriors: on the plains; on the low rise hills; and in and out of the blasted Caledon mountains.

Building stone roads for his troops to monitor the barbarians would be an engineer's delight, so long as he did not lose his best experts!

"Mine, sir."

"Did that happen before, or after, you consulted with the *Praefectus Castrorum* about the size of your rescue patrol?"

The *tribune*'s aghast flinch at his venomous question told him what he needed to know.

"I... No, sir."

Down at the camp entry, the indistinct sight of an *eques* hurriedly dismounting from a well-lathered horse distracted him. As he drew in a calming lungful of air, he watched the horse being whisked away after the messenger removed his belongings, the man's purposeful long stride towards him the only encouraging sign he had seen for the last long while. His personal guard halting the messenger's approach was also noted. They were alert to his orders that all new correspondence and messages were to be brought directly to him. His directive meant a disgruntled senior *tribune* of the *Legio XX*, the man normally enjoying a scrutiny of all correspondence first, but regardless of peeved officers, he needed the whole process to pick up a pace.

Dispatches from the south were arriving too slowly, and with the current situation in Rome it was poor a circumstance to find himself in. Reports from local reconnaissance forays were irregular, and many of those were overdue, causing him a more immediate worry in addition to being a severe nuisance. Sluggish messaging was one of his reasons for lingering in the present camp, though that cause was only one of many.

He took note of other movements around the camp, some of them purposeful, but others looking less so. In the murky distance, an *optio* challenged one of the soldiers under his command, walking around the *tironis* while spouting forth about the raw recruit's lax care of sword sharpening. The scene spurred on Agricola's own decision making.

"Crispus!" he bawled, turning back in time to see Flavus dodge aside to allow his secretary to emerge from the closed tent flaps. "All *centurions* of the *Legio II Adiutrix* are to report to me, immediately."

As expected, his secretary's terse 'Sir!' was all that was needed to have his command acknowledged, before Crispus scurried back into the tent, in turn, calling to his junior clerk to send for the required *centurions*.

"Wait here!" Agricola's barked-out order to Flavus was met with the reaction he expected from the inept young man. No amount of training had so far given Flavus the common sense he needed to take on the role of *tribune*, even at the most junior level. Indecision made the young officer's acknowledgement a rigid one.

As he strode down the *Via Praetoria*, needing to stretch his legs, Agricola grunted a silent reminder to pay more obeisance to the ever active god *Mercurius* who seemed to constantly play tricks. He would have to make special pleas later that night, to ensure that the whole system of messaging and supplies flowed more freely while his protracted stay in the north continued. And he maybe also needed to send a few prayers to *Clementia,* for continued tolerance and forgiveness of Flavus' ineptitude.

Striding past the rows of erected tents, he acknowledged the salutes of men who were not on duty, but who hunkered down at their tent openings, cleaning kit and sharpening weapons. Others huddled around small fires playing *tali,* some extremely adept at catching the knucklebones on the back of their hand. Snuggling his fingers deeper into his woollen cloak, he was aware that their pinched faces were due to restricted firewood and the poor quality of their clothing. Standard issue, adequate in warm climes across the Empire, was useless for remote frontier areas. Much as he might desire it, he was unable to issue the chequered woollen cloth that kept the Caledons warm. The damned barbarians of Caledonia barely produced enough cloth for themselves!

How the local tribes could be so uncivilised was almost inconceivable. So far, reports had indicated that regular trading of goods had never been established in northern Caledonia. They bartered, but no coin changed hands. How was he to inform the senate back in Rome about that, and be believed?

About half way down the *Via Praetoria* he stopped to acknowledge another dispatcher's salute, one whose arrival he must have missed. He pointed to the pile in the man's hands. "Where are they from?"

"Our last camp, sir."

Accepting the wax tablets, he dismissed the soldier. Skimming through the reports took no time at all. There was only a handful, and all contained routine matters, general information for Crispus' legionary record keeping.

Disappointingly, none of that was what made him linger outside.

Tucking them under his cloak, he wheeled around and strode towards his tent to offload the communications before speaking to the *eques*. Heaving a groan of inevitability, Flavus remained exactly as he had left him. His thoughts back to the missing patrol, he contemplated who had sent out the minerals expert.

"General Agricola?"

He turned back on hearing his name, the saluting *eques* bearing a pile of wooden boards inexpertly wrapped in a cloth, to protect them from the elements.

"Where have these come from?"

"Pinnata Castra, sir."

He acknowledged the man's exhaustion, realising that the soldier had jogged up the *Via Praetoria* to catch up with him.

"Did you stop at our last camp?"

The rider nodded. "Only long enough to learn that you were here, sir, and to rest my horse."

The arrival of his junior scribe from the direction of his tent was a timely one, though Agricola knew it would have been at Crispus' behest.

"Deal with these, Lentulus." He passed over the wax tablets from the Durno camp and accepted the wooden boards from the latest dispatcher, a flash of something he had heard recently bringing forth a fleeting upward-turn to his lips. One of the enraged captives, taken after the confrontation, had called his last temporary camp site Moran Dhuirn. When translated, he was told it meant many fists. Durno was a good enough name.

Dismissing the dispatcher, the first proper smile for a long while broke the freeze at his cheeks as he uncovered the pile. Keeping the one that had cheered him, he handed Lentulus the others. "Crispus can deal with those."

Lentulus cradled wax and wood gingerly. Dropped onto wet muddy ground would be as harmful to wax messages as to the flimsier wood, if one smudged and the writing on the other disintegrated into a soggy mess.

A measured pace gave Agricola time to absorb the document again as he continued back to his tent, with Lentulus in his wake.

The smile became a grin. Emperor Domitian should be appreciative that the Venicones territory was fully under control now and that it could sustain good farming yields, so long as some effort was put in to drain more of the marshy flatlands that lay between the mountain passes and the waters of the Mare Germanicum – though he knew the emperor probably would not be. It was reassuring to have some positive news during this ominous campaign into the northern reaches of Caledonia.

"Tell Crispus to reply immediately." Popping the wooden board onto Lentulus' stack, he waved the scribe off. "Wait! Give me that board from the *Praefectus Castrorum* of Pinnata Castra first."

Lentulus looked down at his precarious burden, the momentary hesitation making Agricola harrumph.

"Stay still," he ordered, lifting each board from the top of the pile to read them. Deftly removing the one he wanted, he waved Lentulus away.

As he read the missive about the walls of the *valetudinarium* at Pinnata Castra being finished, it was a sardonic snort that came first before a grim slant to his lips acknowledged that the hospital building might be occupied sooner than he had originally anticipated. He read on. The most important interior buildings of the fortress were taking shape. It would be a while before the whole of the north of Britannia was subdued and settled: a while till the new legionary supply fortress at Pinnata Castra would have its full complement of troops, and its permanent higher-ranking staff. The area for the senior living quarters would be built in due course.

He lifted his gaze from the report and stared down the slushy *Via Principalis,* an inner glow at odds with the dismal scene in front of him. Curbing the urge to call for a horse, to ride off and see what would be his most important fortification in the north, he instead slapped the wooden boards shut. The other side of the congratulatory Venicones coin was the disappointment of the Caledon territories. Reconnaissance updates from *exploratores* during the previous two summer seasons had advised that there was little to be easily gained from the highlands, but he still needed to confirm it.

Extending the boundary of the Roman Empire was his ultimate objective, but the acquisition of worthwhile revenue from new territory won over was essential for his reputation, and for continued occupation. He had to make it worth the huge effort of subduing.

How in *Jupiter*'s name would he achieve regular taxation from terrain that was settled in such an unstructured way? Since he had no local tribal leader, the person he put in place would have to be chosen from some other southern tribe, but that strategy was unlikely to be profitable since not being local tended to cause festering resentment, and the last thing he wanted was to create circumstances where bribery and corruption could flourish. He could not condone anything that would be detrimental to the Empire's profits.

An *optio* ordering his men along on the *vallum*, down by the empty area near the eastern camp gate, disturbed his thoughts. The file of soldiers in the distance halted for a brief moment to allow carts piled-high with firewood to be trundled on to the storage area. In between him and the carts, the drenched leather of hundreds of neatly erected tents now glistened with newly-falling sleet. In the name of *Tempestas*! Why did the goddess send him such blighted conditions?

Disgusted with his treatment, he yanked the neck opening of his cloak up over his head, realising he was a bit late to keep his hair dry. His camp was highly organised. His men were well-disciplined, governed by military rules, but how was he to maintain a structured *civitas* in the wilds of Caledon territory? He gave the board a good shake before he stuffed it under his cloak.

Marching the whole of his assembled armies into Caledon territory was easily feasible but, if all it achieved was a general subjugation of any survivors, what would be gained by that? It would take a lot more than the spoils of a few sheepskins to make it all worthwhile.

He had expected the humiliating defeat of the recent battle to have totally sapped the spirits of the Caledon allies, but that was not proving to be so. The irregular reports he had received during the previous few days detailed a number of petty raids and retaliations near the mountain passes. It was inconceivable behaviour from cowards who had fled the field of direct confrontation with Rome. He drew a bitter breath through his nostrils before heading back to the waiting junior *tribune*.

"Lentulus!" He tossed the board to the scribe when the man emerged around the tent flap. "Well caught! Put it on my desk."

Noticing that Flavus was shivering, he gestured him towards the *carbonarius*. "None of that patrol returned, Flavus? Not even a messenger?"

"No, sir."

"Then perhaps they have gone deeper into the mountains, even though what the goddess sends us has not been in their favour." He swiped his mouth and nose free of the stinging droplets of sleet before holding his hands out to the flames.

The circumstances sent by the goddess *Tempestas* were so unpredictable here in northern Britannia.

"They did not plan to do that, sir." Flavus sounded quite sure.

Agricola did not even try to prevent deep sarcasm from creeping in to his reply. "Sometimes plans change, Flavus. The men are well-trained to adapt to whatever the gods send!"

The hurt squirming of Flavus' lips set him to stride about again. Agricola observed the *tribune* over his curled fingers, while his short sharp-breaths warmed the tips. Changing and adapting plans was a daily occurrence. He had too many concerns to occupy his thoughts, and no time to be bothered with one small detachment being late. Though, of course, the confirmed loss of one of his best mining specialist…and maybe at the whim of *Mercurius* more than two handfuls of mounts…was something he ought to be informed about. Barbarian's balls! He would cut them off when he caught the culprits.

His foray into Taexali territory had been conducted in a light manner, to cover the ground quickly, but hopes of acquiring new equine stock had been well and truly dashed. By *Annonaria*'s bountiful breasts and *Fortuna*'s stinking virtues! What he had done to incur the disfavour of the dual-role goddess? Perhaps ordering the two *cohorts* of the *Legio IX* out of his current Well of Ythan camp the previous day had been hasty, given the way the days had turned out? His shiver of anxiety brought forth the regulatory response from Flavus.

"Sir?"

The boy worried about a patrol of eleven men. He had ordered out a thousand.

He shook off his pessimistic thoughts on realising that the sleet had again abated, and that the grey above him was a shade lighter. Perhaps cursing *Fortuna* was the answer?

"Think positively, Flavus."

"Yes, sir."

Titus Sicinia Flavus was probably incapable of any useful thought, the response given being no more than a learned reaction.

News of the *Legio IX* cohorts' success would come soon. Their task was simple: aid the mariner auxiliaries who had berthed along the coastline to quell any native Vacomagi unrest. Early information had indicted that treaties would be signed without much bloodshed, though better still none at all.

The approach of a *capsarius*, an assistant he assigned to the senior *medicus* of the *Legio IX*, interrupted the conversation.

"This top one gives the latest names and the numbers of those now able to move on from our last camp at Durno, sir." The medical orderly handed over a single board.

"And those?" Agricola indicated the bundle of wooden boards still in the soldier's hands.

"These are the details of the dead, and the others who cannot move on yet."

"In the name of *Aesculapius*! What still ails them?"

Chapter Twelve

Well of Ythan Roman Camp, Taexali Territory

"Still so many?" Agricola barked at the medical assistant.

Accepting the pile of wooden boards, a swift look brought more than a flare of exasperation that such a large number could still be unfit to move on. Sickness and belly gripes were commonplace, but he had rarely known so many men to vomit their throats red-raw in such a prolonged fashion, day after day, and empty their other ends at the same rate. It was an inconvenience he certainly had not planned for. The fairness of the divine *Aequitas* was escaping him.

"Crispus!" His growl had the desired effect, his secretary appearing with stylus in hand. "Is the senior *tribune* of the *Legio IX* still at the last encampment?"

Crispus managed the deference needed, along with a quick scrutiny of the tablet Agricola passed into his hands. "Yes, but his most junior *tribune* is currently here, sir. Should this be sent to him?"

There was enough in the question to make Agricola reflect a moment. "Yes. He needs to reorganise his forward troops for my next two camps. The men listed here," he indicated the numbers on all but the top board, "will not be joining him. Send them south to Pinnata Castra. The ablest will join me at my next northern camp."

Crispus' flash of misgiving was immediately wiped away.

"Yes, Crispus. There is little doubt that we will lose some along the route." It was highly likely, since the last time he saw the ailing they could barely breathe.

Crispus nodded, but lingered before turning away.

That enquiring look on his secretary's face was the special one that irritated him, but also nudged him into action more times than he could count. "Ensure that the *medicus* at Durno gets whatever he needs to improve the health of those sick, before they undertake the trek. I want everyone left in that vomit-and-excrement infested camp to march out in two days: as many as possible to come north, and the others south."

Crispus' eyebrow-raised expression doubted it would be possible to issue recuperative rations, given that there probably were none to be had, but Agricola knew his secretary would send on the instructions as efficiently as he always did.

He uncovered his curled fists and held them over the now fast-burning flames of the *carbonarius,* the last addition of wood providing a temporary blaze. Looking over it towards the despondent Flavus, he growled at the young soldier who remained at attention. "Come closer, *tribune*. This heat will not last long. You are not dismissed, but you freezing like marble on the spot will bring neither of us results."

"Sir!" Relief at changing his position flickered as Flavus obeyed the order, coming to stand near the brazier, but not close enough to gain full benefit from it. The boy was too craven to stand right next to him.

He waited till he had Flavus' entire attention, the boy's light-brown eyes both weary and wary. "Plans constantly change, Flavus. You must always be prepared to revise your strategies, but remember they need to be made on sound judgements."

He was conscious of saying one thing and doing another as his fledgling-officer mutely nodded. He berated himself, because some recent decisions he had made lately had not been sound, after all. Leaving his heavy baggage wagons at Pinnata Castra, thinking they would not be needed for the duration of a short sharp northern capitulation, had been premature. He had not counted on an unplanned malady holding back the forward movement of so many of his infantry.

"And sound judgements can be affected by unforeseen circumstances."

Flavus nodded as though understanding the exchange, but Agricola knew otherwise.

His heavy artillery equipment remaining in Pinnata Castra was not the problem, since the cowardly locals were clearly reluctant to face his amassed forces again, his well-trusted *speculatores* reporting no huge, menacing gatherings at all. Small groups of tribesmen were banding together. He expected that, but no new overall leadership had been declared within the Caledon allies who had chosen to skulk in the mountains.

"Knowing what your enemy plans is never enough."

Again there was a mute nod and that was probably best. Any words uttered by Flavus were bound to be the wrong ones.

"Think through every action you make, because the result always matters. Think of yourself stroking a stubborn mule into movement to pull a wagon full of vital provisions out of muddy ruts, and getting a resulting kick that breaks your leg in two pieces, Flavus."

Agricola grunted. Not having heavy wagons available now was a grim mistake. The sickest men could have already been sent south from Durno, with those in recovery transported northwards. Rescinding his earlier orders, and requesting wagons to make the journey to him from Pinnata Castra some days ago had been galling, but now the goddess *Fortuna* played coy with him because none of the expected transport had arrived, the weather pathetic for moving vehicles.

He looked across at the gormless expression on Flavus' face.

Though, perhaps *Fortuna* was actually favouring him in a strange way, because he certainly would not want the local tribes to get wind of the fact that so many of his troops were debilitated, via information they acquired through carelessness. Aware that Flavus was staring, he snarled. "Sound judgements sometimes take deliberation, Flavus, but others are best when instinctive."

Weary of the conversation, he looked towards the eastern gate. Dusk descended, so the likelihood of many further arrivals was slim. Travelling in the dark was not part of his orders, and certainly not for the food supplies that were being transported. They were too essential to chance an assault by the cowardly natives who lacked the temerity to attack in full daylight.

"What goes on along there?" His question was rhetorical, but Flavus was too literal to have caught on to his vocal musings.

"The soldier looks to be wounded, sir."

Setting off down towards the man, he indicated Flavus should follow. Half-way there, he took in the scene. Two men shouldered a badly-bleeding third soldier, the thigh wound grave. A fair way behind them another group carried a prostrate body – a dead soldier from the lolling of the head off the side of the flat plank of wood.

"How did this happen?" His shout brought the exhausted men to a halt.

The *decanus* of the eight-man unit answered. "An accident, sir. It happened on a slight rise near the woods where we were cutting firewood. The cart broke free of the mule traces, and rolled over the men who supported it from the rear. The slushy tracks out there are impossible for the hooves to get traction on."

He pointed to the second group of bearers. "Is he dead?"

"His leg bone snapped when the wheel ran over him, but he was still alive when we set off back to the camp."

"Find out who was responsible!"

"Sir." The *decanus* saluted but indicated he had more to say, and to show him. The man rummaged into a full bag that dangled from his belt and produced a bundle of leather traces.

Agricola took the proffered bindings and studied them closely.

"Deliberately cut?" Agricola shook the slashed harnesses in front of the decanus.

"I believe so, sir."

"*Jupiter*'s balls!" His fury would not be contained. "Did you hack at any of those devious natives while you were out there?"

The *decanus* flinched. "No, sir. None of us saw any tribesmen. The carts had to be left at the edge of the woods while we gathered wood further in, so they could have sneaked up then."

"In the name of—" He halted, realising he was using *Jupiter*'s name too unthinkingly. "Was no one left guarding the mules?"

"Yes, sir, one man was. The only time he left them was to check a disturbance in nearby bushes, but he found nothing there."

"Yet someone managed to slice those traces."

The *decanus* flinched again, the set to his chin determined yet still mindful of his position. "I vouch wholeheartedly for my men, sir. None of us made those cuts. We would never do anything that would endanger the rest of us, or cause us to have to extra duty cover if anybody was hurt."

Agricola believed the *decanus* of the *Legio XX*. It was unthinkable for any soldier to sabotage in this way. Dismissing the men, he needed to hear no more. He turned about and headed back to his tent knowing the injured men would be seen by the *medicus*. Accidents happened, but losing men on wood cutting details to stealthy native attacks was inexcusable.

Grunts punctuated every pace as he stomped back to the brazier that had lost some of its recent ferocity. Unlike the way his own insides were churning. Turning his gaze back to Flavus who had trotted after him, his words were venomous. "What would you judge that incident to be, Flavus? An unfortunate accident that was not preventable? Perhaps a stealthy attack, undertaken by a lone native? Or was it a small band of Taexali warriors who had been watching that detail collecting our necessary firewood and who took a furtive opportunity?"

As expected, Flavus stuttered an answer, the young man stunned to be even asked for an opinion. "I… It surely was not done by any of our men, sir."

Unfortunately, Flavus did not sound too sure. But Agricola was. He stopped just inside the overhang at his tent opening, ignoring the fact that Flavus stood in the flurry of sleet that continued to whiten all around them.

"Not only are those damned natives of northern Britannia good at petty skirmishes and underhand disruption like this, Flavus, they are also skilled at herb lore. I cannot rule out the possibility that they caused the sickness at our Durno camp. As well as hundreds of our men affected, did you know that many of our horses also had an affliction?"

Flavus almost looked too terrified of the concept to answer him. "But our mules seemed healthy enough."

He suppressed a smirk. If the junior *tribune* was a mule, his task might be easier. "Flavus, mules have more sense than horses, or men. If mules have the tiniest suspicion that something will threaten their wellbeing, they steer well clear. They would starve themselves rather than gorge on contaminated food or water. Our pack animals need no pampering, unlike those still-ailing men back at Durno who cause me to remake my plans yet again."

The troops left at his previous camp would soon, if not already, be basking in the luxury of some decent food in their bellies that had been transported up from the south. Whereas he would have to placate the bulk currently with him that their meagre remains would have to suffice for yet another day.

The gate at the end of the *Via Praetoria* again drew his gaze, like it had been doing all day and was the reason he remained outside in the clawing cold, and now in more sleet that was turning to heavier snow, making the ground a squishy mess for trundling over.

Maybe as well as being good at herb lore these sly natives were more successful at pleading with their own gods and goddesses? He had no name for their local goddess of snow, but she was doing too well at cloaking the land with her white flakes.

Jupiter's judgements! Nothing normal was happening on this present campaign. He had expected to appropriate grain and livestock well before now from the Taexali, to feed his men as they progressed northwards. But the barbarian menace had reaped their fields and had carted most of the crops, and their livestock, off into the mountains when they had rallied for battle. He had not anticipated that.

Agricola expelled a long, slow breath. Seven summers of campaigning in Britannia were becoming tedious. Some days all he wanted was to shed the responsibility of being the Governor of Britannia and Commander of its four permanent *legions*, in addition to all of his extra auxiliary *vexillationes*. Settling down in one place, with no military duties at all, sounded so appealing. Some place where the sun shone brightly. He might even come to know his wife a lot better than through the papyrus they had had to make do with throughout most of their more than twenty years' worth of marriage. The exceptions to that being all-too-brief interludes.

He sighed again. He had spent more time with Domitia when he had been Consul of Aquitania. That now seemed long ago, his time in Britannia constantly on campaign, and no place to be accompanied by a wife.

As weighty snowflakes fluttered down in front of his eyes, they blanketed the military surroundings into the delicate hush that accompanies a complete winter-white. A strange warmth suffused him, fleeting memories of another bright place filling him – a location that was far from the lands of the Taexali.

He disregarded a request from Crispus, and instead flapped his cloak-clad arm at Flavus. "See to whatever he wants."

The sound of a minor dispute going on behind him, he ignored. He instead allowed the snowflakes to rest on his closed eyelids and retreated into pleasant recall.

'Do you not hanker after the concord that Pax extols here?' Domitia's idle, contrary, question often replayed in his head, sometimes at the strangest of times, like this present one. It always held him to a certain frustrated ransom.

He had contemplated her earnest, comely face. But though he was in total agreement with her sentiments, his answer had given nothing away that could be overheard, or misunderstood, as they strolled around the gardens of the *Templum Pacis*. The white marble columns of the recently built temple portico in Rome had twinkled in the winter sunlight, even more so than the numerous statues and fountain decorations that lay dotted here and there around the gardens: riches that had been purloined from Vespasian's newly-subdued territory in Judea.

Domitia had been well-aware that returning to Rome, laden down with the treasures of Jerusalem, had indeed been an immense triumph for Vespasian, the *Forum Vespasiani* having been constructed using the wealth acquired during Vespasian's campaign.

Though Domitia had mentioned nothing, she knew that her husband's eventual return to Rome, after a successful, final campaign in Britannia, would not find him laden with statues, or dripping with golden artefacts. Her time spent in various fortresses in southern Britannia, earlier on in their marriage, had given her ample knowledge of the dearth of spoils he would accumulate from northern Britannia. To her credit, she had never seemed too perturbed about it. Their time spent together was always amiable – and at times a lot more than just amiable.

But dwelling on coupling with his wife, or indeed any of their pleasurable pursuits, was time spent unproductively. Aware that the snow no longer flecked his cheeks, he opened his eyes and gave thanks to his own snow goddess *Chione* for its short duration. He did not even try to prevent the shiver of apprehension that followed the calm interlude. So many things in life were short. That last visit to Rome had been congenial, if brief. It was the aftermath that had had unexpected consequences. He forced down the pangs of sorrow that still sneaked up on him. A protracted absence from his wife now was hardly likely to produce a replacement for their recently-dead son, a child that had come late in their marriage.

Domitia was younger than he was by a number of years, but the likelihood of her birthing more babes grew less as each year passed. He could lay no blame at her feet for the death of their baby, but facing his still grieving wife was something that would have to wait for a bit longer, because having her with him in this unpredictable, hostile territory was not something he would contemplate. The gutless tribes were presently in hiding, but he had no way of knowing how long that situation might last, and their furtive little attacks were growing tedious.

Had his fortress at Pinnata Castra been completed, then Domitia and the other legates' families could have been installed there. It was not so far from his present camp, but Pinnata Castra was still too vulnerable in its unfinished state.

Jove's thunderbolt! He was back to thinking about his dwindling resources. Curses flashed through his head, castigating Emperor Domitian for starving him of the troops he needed to complete these northern campaigns. After another inhalation through his freezing nose he willed his thoughts to still. Again biting down his frustration, he set his focus down the *Via Praetoria*.

It was heartening, at least, that the *allectus* now approaching looked happy to be back in camp, the courier having arrived in the last rays of dusk.

After returning the specially-assigned courier's salutation, Agricola asked some general questions, the *allectus* having been individually chosen near the beginning of his northern campaigns. Discreet and trustworthy, the courier had regularly ridden the length of Britannia, delivering and taking forward sensitive communication.

Agricola accepted the new scroll handed to him. On seeing it was the seal of Gaius Salvius Liberalis, he tapped the end of the scroll a few times on his palm. It was heavy which probably meant an inner scroll. Thanking his courier, he stepped away a few paces as he broke open the wax. A quick read of his judicial legate's information had him taking quick indrawn breaths before he opened the inner letter. The obsequious salutations were as expected, but as he read on his temper flared.

"*Jupiter*'s thunderbolt! He will not have them!"

He shouted to no one in particular, but some soldiers walking nearby stopped expectantly, eager to see who was on the sharp end of his tongue.

Another careful read of the message brought forth a further string of invectives as he re-rolled the messages.

"Crispus!"

His secretary hastened his way out from the tent. "General?"

Agricola stared at his secretary of so many years standing, realising the temper he was in and the mistake he had been about to make. This was one missive he would not, and could not, share immediately. Instead, he modulated his tone and indicated the *allectus*. "Ensure Marcius Rufinus is fed and is quartered for the night."

The short nod from his secretary was followed by Crispus reaching for the recently delivered scroll.

"Not yet, Crispus," he declared, holding on to the scroll, and to his rage. His conciliatory smile probably did not work, but at least Crispus would know what he intended. "I am not nearly finished with it."

His secretary knew better than to do anything but acquiesce.

Crispus signalled one of the nearby sentries, naming the *contubernium* tent that the special messenger should be taken to.

"Marcius? Rest now, but make sure you get what you need to clean up before you return to me tomorrow." Agricola knew his request was an impossible one. Not even he had had the luxury of proper bathing for weeks, his last being in the small bath-house at Corstopitum.

Without proper roads being laid everyone was continually wading knee deep in muck, including him. He paced around the *carbonarius* drawing his cloak in tight to his chest, the scroll scrunched underneath in his fist. Creating permanent roads for the transportation of goods and personnel was routine on conquering an area. It kept the men busy, and the physical labour tended to prevent petty quarrels from erupting, but the creation of stone roads was only worth the immense effort if there was anything useful to send south and thence across to the rest of the empire.

The slush underfoot got slicker with every new step he took.

"No roads, no bloodied barbarians, and no goods to send on them!" he grunted as he swivelled round to once again face his junior *tribune*, who still hung around like a clinging limpet on a tide-washed rock. It was a personal bone of contention that the slave count already sent south from the campaign was pathetically low.

"Sir?" Flavus' response was tentative, not knowing what to answer.

Agricola felt the goddess *Fortuna* was definitely not favouring him, because he presently had nothing at all that was worth transporting anywhere. He had better find something soon, though, or his ever-demanding Emperor would be insisting on even more. From the tone of this latest missive, he was extremely doubtful of any future assistance at all from Domitian.

It was more than the winter weather that was bleak, his future was in the balance, and the divine *Aequitas* was tipping the scales towards the emperor's favour.

"He wants five *cohorts*!" he raged, again to no one in particular.

"Sir?" Flavus stepped back a pace to avoid his wrath, alarm spreading along with confusion.

"Pay no heed."

He did not even try to suppress the sour downturn to his mouth. He had no aspirations of his capricious Emperor Domitian ever giving recognition to, or even showing appreciation of anything he did in Britannia.

Studying the flustered Flavus, he reminded himself of why the junior *tribune* was always scuttling around at his heels. His outstretched palm denied further stutters.

Turning round to his tent, he bawled, "Crispus! Fetch me the latest recruits to our *speculatores* unit! And find out why I am still waiting for today's second update from the *Legio II Adiutrix centurions*."

On demand, his secretary scuttled out of the tent.

"The newest Taexali *speculatores*?"

Agricola was glad to see that at least Crispus was always attuned to his needs.

"Yes, Crispus. I want to speak especially to anyone who used to live where Flavus' disaster took place."

He sent heartfelt thanks to *Jupiter* when Crispus drew the hapless junior *tribune* aside to ask some questions: away and out of his vision.

During his first Britannia campaigns Agricola knew his temper was never riled so easily, but these local Caledon and Taexali tribesmen were the most unpredictable and spineless he had ever encountered. Though, he also had never had such an aggravating junior *tribune* to thole either.

Chapter Thirteen

*Ceann Druimin, Caledon Territory
– Chief Lulach's Roundhouse*

"This building of watch towers at the lower mountain passes in Venicones territory started well before the battle at Beinn na Ciche?" asked Chief Lulach.

The gathering that night was smaller in number. Sleet and snow had made daylight surveillance of Lulach's territory almost impossible, except for the areas closest to the valley that surrounded Ceann Druimin. One consolatory hope was that the Romans encamped at the Ythan, and even those at Moran Dhuirn, had not been patrolling very far either.

"Aye, long before." Nith chewed around a mouthful of the flat bread he had been given with a bowl of watery barley-broth. He lounged by the side wall of the roundhouse, in what had become his habitual place during larger gatherings, though the space near him today was expansive. Enya was propped against the wall on the opposite side of the fire, two rows behind Ineda and slapped right next to Feargus, both of them looking very cosy together.

The chief was given the first choice of the smoked venison strips and pieces of roasted fowl. But one glance at that plate told Nith that each person would only receive a tiny amount, The stored stocks of slain deer were negligible and only smaller animals and game birds had been pursued in the snow for the soup pots that day. He had volunteered to use his sling, but had been told as a warrior-guard he deserved to rest.

Nith paused to pick a bird wing before carrying on the conversation. "They build their forts and towers very quickly. The ironwork supplies arrive soon after they have established a route to their chosen site. The soldiers hew the wood themselves from nearby forests, if suitable straight trunks are available. If not, then timbers are hauled from other woodlands." He hated the Roman turds with all of his heart, but he had never managed to deny that they were skilled, well-organised men. He put a question to Conchar of Finhaven whose departure had been postponed till the weather cleared. "Is their flattened pathway now well into the territory of Venicones?"

Conchar, seated in the front row around the fireside, turned round to face him, using his knuckles to wipe drips of broth free of the hair that drooped down from his upper lip. "It is. They widened our northern path with the tramp of so many feet. But they have also created a new track westwards to their fortress." He paused to point to Ineda. "The one she called Pinnata Castra."

The chief's attention swivelled to Ineda. "This is the fortress you escaped from, Ineda?"

"Aye, I lived in that one, and in other forts on southern Venicones territory. Pinnata Castra is Agricola's special base for the domination of the Taexali, Caledons, and all of the tribes north of them." Ineda bit into her piece of bread and chewed it quickly before adding more information.

While Ineda talked Nith slurped the cooled barley-broth from his bowl. He intended to concentrate on Ineda's words, but it was nigh impossible not to notice how often Enya whispered up to Feargus' ear, her closeness to the lad almost the same as she had been with him the previous eve.

"How different is it?" After wiping his hairy upper lip free of food crumbs with the back of his hand, Lulach reached for his wooden beaker of small-beer.

"Larger granaries and specialist workshops make it unlike an ordinary fortress," she said. "The smithy at Pinnata Castra is very large. It will ensure the troops have all the other metal equipment they need for their kit, if any gets damaged or lost. But the most important thing about the smithy is that it will fashion the nails and brackets needed for the building of every new wooden fort, fortlet and watch tower that Agricola constructs on northern lands when the territory is officially claimed for the Roman Empire."

Nith felt apprehension grip him. He had not appreciated this aspect of it. His question was bad-tempered but that was how he was feeling. "Will Agricola not get these metal goods from his southern bases, Ineda?"

Ineda's sigh reached across the fireside to him, her eyes seeking him out. "He could do, Nith, but his northern supply base is designed to rival the one at Corstopitum. The furthest reaches of his Roman Empire boundaries need to be serviced from somewhere closer than southern Votadini territory."

Nith understood what Ineda was telling them, but he was not sure if everyone else appreciated the significance of such a fortress. "What makes you certain of this, Ineda?"

She swallowed a last mouthful before continuing. "The smithy – one of the first areas to be set up – was underused because the iron bars had not yet arrived from the south. That was why *Tribune* Valerius went out to meet supply wagons on the morning he was ambushed."

Nith felt her keen gaze on him as she continued.

"It is many seasons since I was last there. That smithy will have a large stock of ironwork ready now for the building of forts, right here in Caledon and Taexali territory."

Lulach grunted at Ineda. "Is there anything else we should know about this special fortress?"

Ineda thought for a moment before adding new information. "Apart from the granaries – designed to hold enough to feed troops stationed in the north for a whole year – there is accommodation for the healing of the wounded and the sick. Soldiers on campaign meet more hazards than a Celtic sword. Disease can befall them as well."

"Then Agricola plans to house many men during the winter seasons – sick and healthy?" Lulach looked disgusted with his own question.

Ineda's nod was solemn. "Pinnata Castra will supply the needs of a continued northern campaign; winter through summer, till the whole of Britannia is conquered, every single pace of it, and afterwards when the province is well-settled."

"Will Agricola continue northwards with his troops, even if this coming winter bites hard?" Lulach probed.

There was a catch in Ineda's voice. "Good weather or poor, Agricola will use every possible tactic to ensure Rome knows that he has conquered the whole of Britannia, and that every single tribe kneels at his feet."

Curses and other dissent grumbled around the room.

"Regardless of how many battles he has to fight to ensure that it happens, and regardless of what falls from the realm of the sky god?" Lulach sounded as though someone had just gutted his entrails.

Nith decided it was time to intervene again. "Agricola will use the dominating strength of his amassed forces where possible. But, Lulach, he can only engage in battle if his enemies gather together again, and confront him."

Enya mumbled around a mouthful of hazelnuts. "What of the tribes north of the Vacomagi? Would they rally together and face Agricola's mighty army?"

Garth of Culbeuchly grunted, setting down his emptied bowl with one hand, the other wiping off his drooping whiskers. "The Decantae and the Lugi might assist each other in local skirmishes, but I doubt they would ally themselves with other tribes north of here. They dwell scattered across the hills and valleys, and many of their villages are more distant from each other than ours are."

"How many tribes lie north of the Vacomagi?" Enya asked.

Nith was not sure why he had never asked that question himself, but it could be vitally important regarding Agricola's intentions.

Lulach's face squirmed as he scratched his ear, while pondering the answer. "At least six tribes live north of the Caledon lochs, and a few more to the west. No encouragement made them join us at Beinn na Ciche, so I doubt they would raise their swords at another place of battle."

"Would they make treaties with the Romans without blood being shed?" Nith asked.

The chief huffed at the blaze in front of him. "I suspect their resistance will be minimal."

"We need to know what those tribes will do just as much as we need to know what Agricola plans!" Enya's words were a demand.

Nith felt the force of Enya's glare from across the crackling fire. He felt her anger was for him alone, because he still sat discussing the Romans, rather than doing something active about them. It took only moments before she broke eye contact with him.

Garth of Culbeuchly tossed a small bone onto the burning logs, contempt oozing from his snorting. "Lugi, Decantae and Cornavii tribal lands can be seen on the far side of our firth, when the day is really clear. If even one of Agricola's ships disgorges a half-century of those auxiliary soldiers of the fleet, then none of those coastal villages will resist. Though, what Rome could steal from them is likely to be a disappointment because their mountains leave them little good land for farming."

"Do your Vacomagi shore-line crops grow the best hereabouts?" Nith was frustrated that he still knew so little of those further north.

Garth's laugh was mirthless. "Our gods do not favour all Vacomagi equally. Between the Abhainn Caelis and the Abhainn Tuesis, the sandy soils produce a good barley crop. On the far side of the Abhainn Tuesis there are fertile fields across to the mouth of An Cuan Moireach that give better yields of barley and spelt when the goddess favours them. The Cabrach, on the other hand, is bleak damp-moorland which defies any kind of crop farming and is barely fit for the sheep that graze it."

Nith spoke across the central fire. "Ineda? What does Agricola intend the fleet to do at An Cuan Moireach?"

Ineda shrugged her shoulders. "*Tribune* Valerius boasted that Agricola had two aims for his fleet. The first was to sail all the way around Britannia and learn of its entire coastline." She paused to address Chief Lulach.

"His other aim is?" Lulach barked at her.

Ineda ignored the chief's rudeness. "He uses his fleet to terrorise locals who dwell near the shoreline. His auxiliaries of the *Legio II Adiutrix* are battle-ready the moment they lay down their oars. Watching armour-clad columns of them marching towards you is like the thunder claps, and lightning bolts, of *Taranis*. I tell you, their clamour is a frightening experience!"

Lulach's tones were more conciliatory. "Aye. Before battle at Beinn na Ciche, plenty of coastal tribespeople fled in fear, but I had not heard of this plan to sail around the shoreline of every one of our Celtic brothers."

The elder who spoke was one Nith knew to be blunt. "How can you call them your brothers, Lulach. Of old, those northerners have been enemies of the Caledons. They are nothing like us in their ways, or in their dealings."

"Maybe so, but they are more akin to us than the Romans usurpers are."

Nith sought to soothe some tempers. "Agricola used mariners of the fleet at Beinn na Ciche. Even if they returned to their ships immediately after the battle, those ships will not have had time yet to sail all around the coastline and get back to him to report their findings."

Brennus held forward his palm to interrupt. "Troops of Batavians came from the *Classis* to join the confrontation but many of them have sailed off southwards from Baile Mheadhain, their ships full of our snatched tribespeople."

"Where will they take those captives, Ineda?" Lulach asked.

Nith noted that Lulach now sought Ineda's opinion before any other.

She thought for a moment before answering. "Agricola's *Classis Britannica* were beached at Celurca in Venicones territory, a wide sheltered bay that the locals named the great sea-loch, where only the narrowest of channels leads out to sea. It was a walk of more than a day to reach Obar Dheathain from it. Roman ships may have gone there first since the shortest day approaches."

Ineda halted to address Aila of Finhaven. "Does he put more of his ships ashore between that large bay and the Abhainn Tatha, near Trune's Hillfort?"

"Ships have been using the inlet at Celurca, but they are also visible on the sands across the Tatha estuary from Trune's hillfort. There are sure to be even more places used all the way to Votadini lands…" Aila's words tailed off.

Ineda continued. "Aye, when I was there, the fleet was based on the Votadini coastline near Dunpendyr, on the Uisge For. From there, captives were marched to the slave markets in the fortress at Eboracum, in southern Brigantia. Some of those unfortunates were bought by Britannia-based Romans, but most were not."

Lulach's anger erupted. "Then where will Agricola send our tribespeople?"

"Men are conscripted into the auxiliary units under tribal settlements with Rome and are stationed across the empire. Ruthless slave merchants buy the women and children that Agricola sends southwards. They are shipped off to markets across the empire that will pay a good price for them." Ineda looked to the rafters, blinking back tears, before Nith felt her water-lashed gaze seek him out. "Higher-ranking captives have been dragged all the way to Rome, as proof of a mighty battle. Like the one fought at Beinn na Ciche."

Across from him, Nith was drawn to silent tears streaking Enya's cheeks, her gaze fixed across the fire to where he stood, but she was seeing nothing but her loss. Her brother and cousin might be among those Ineda last spoke of. He wanted to tuck Enya into his chest to absorb some of her pain, and feel his calloused caresses inadvertently snag in her tuggy braids, but she was not beside him. His insides roiled when Feargus' bent head sought to soothe her. Her clutch at the lad's outstretched hands for support made his own fingers turn into frustrated fists.

"By *Taranis*!" The plea was inside his head but his vow to find out the fate of Ruoridh and Beathan was doubly renewed as he forced his attention away from Enya and Feargus.

"We must know more of what that scum Agricola does every which way!" Lulach turned to Conchar of Finhaven, his determination building. "Do you have more news from your territory that we have not yet heard?"

Conchar seemed unaware of Lulach's sarcasm, or perhaps was unaffected by it. "A good-sized detachment of the *Legio XX* arrived at Pinnata Castra a few days ago. They have resumed pace with their building programme within their wooden fort walls, and Agricola has strengthened the guard at all of his established towers and fortlets along the mountain fringes."

Nith was intrigued when Brennus padded towards Garth of Culbeuchly, his lofty height a brooding threat. "Have troops from Agricola's fleet been sent to block your mountain passes?"

Garth shrugged, unable to immediately face Brennus eye to eye. "I only know of those who dominate our coastal plains."

There was a pause while Brennus waited for more information.

Nith watched as Garth eventually looked up towards Brennus. "Roman ships are berthed at different places along our coastline, all the way west to An Cuan Moireach. It is a shorter trek to reach the Vacomagi hills from the estuary than it is from my village near the Taexali border."

"How many ships are on that coastline?" Lulach's ire was not yet spent, his penetrating glare focused on Garth. "How many troops are they spewing out onto your Vacomagi soil?"

"I have no idea." Garth's expression was changing to one of frustration.

Nith knew that the only way to tell was to count the amount of ships, and see the size of their encampments, because that was the best way to estimate the number of units. "We cannot only defend your territory, Lulach. We must know everything about Agricola's actions."

He watched as Enya shrugged away from Feargus before stepping towards Lulach. "I agree. And we must discover the fate of our captured tribespeople."

Chief Lulach's mouth twisted. "Aye. I selfishly want my territory safe, but knowing where those damned Roman soldiers are skulking about is crucial to that, though we must remain unseen by his troops and avoid confrontations with them."

Brennus' sudden burst of deep chortles echoed around the room. Nith thought they were almost of delight. Regardless, it heartened the mood of the room.

"Not quite." Brennus' tone sobered as he sat down again. "We should not seek to begin skirmishes that we cannot win, but that is different from avoiding every opportunity to strike at his forces."

Nith was glad to join in. "Well-planned ambushes, as happened near the ancient stones of Upper Ord, will keep our blades honed."

"Then let us make plans!" Lulach was motivated, but not all around him had the same liveliness.

His hearth-wife tugged at his sleeve to gain his attention. "The night is well advanced. Look around you at the exhausted faces, Lulach."

The chief struggled to his feet, sending her a defiant glare. "Leave now, if you will, but I intend to make some attack strategies!"

Nith stared as Enya sidled out after Feargus, the pair of them grinning at some amusement. The roundhouse continued to empty as his gaze fixed on the entryway. His sigh was deep. Heading off to bed seemed like a good idea. He debated with himself whether he should do that, too, and give his nagging wounds more chance to heal, but the prospect of wondering where Enya's bed might be that night turned his feet to stone. Feeling strangely bereft, he stared at the glowing embers and allowed the last general farewells to wash over him.

He did not understand what Agricola was doing in northern territories, but in some respects he understood Agricola's motives a lot better than his own.

"Nith! Come sit with us." Lulach's shout blinked him back. Noting that the male warriors of Garrigill still remained spurred him into action. Even though he moved closer to the fireside, and to the heat of the burning logs, a forlorn cold was his cloak. His hand strayed to rub his chest wounds, but the strange ache was somewhere else.

Chapter Fourteen

Ceann Druimin, Caledon Territory
– Garrigill Roundhouse

"Keep that poultice on!" Ineda sounded irritated, but Enya knew she was not the cause of it.

Enya sat at the central fire with her mother, Fionnah, who had missed all of the talk in Lulach's house, Fionnah having remained with the youngest children of the Garrigill brood.

Ineda had cleaned her wound again, but it was too dim in the small roundhouse to ensure there were no slivers of wood in it. She did as Ineda bid her, and cradled the plantain and comfrey wrapping tight to her jaw, to reduce the newest swelling, and to draw out anything that might remain in the gash. The smell of the mashed leaves was strong, redolent of the midden. It almost made her retch, but she tolerated it because she knew of its benefits.

She spoke quietly so as not to waken the little ones who were already asleep in a huddle, like a litter of puppies, but her tone was determined. "I have to search for Ruoridh and Beathan. I know the dangers that might befall me, but I must find out what has happened to them."

Fionnah's words were strained. "I want to know what has happened to them as much as you do, Enya, but I cannot feel happy about you putting yourself in such danger."

Ineda responded before Enya could reassure her mother. "Danger surrounds us all. Even if we remain here with Lulach for the coming seasons, can we be sure of safety? Can we be sure that Agricola will not attack the settlement? I think not, and yet I have no wish for any other young Celtic female to be taken as the slave of a Roman soldier. I survived to tell my tale because it was *Tribune* Gaius Livanus Valerius who claimed me. I am loath to say it," Ineda's words were regretful, as she continued, "but the *tribune* was an honourable man, even though a despised Roman. Most female captives taken as personal slaves did not survive their treatment."

Enya would not be swayed from her decision. "*Mathair*. My warrior training is as good as it will ever be. You know that." She sought her mother's full attention. "*Athair* knows that, too. You heard what I did some days ago. I do not fear putting my knife against a Roman neck. We need people out there gathering information, and I want to be one of them. I have to be one of them. Ineda proves how it is possible to survive in Roman held territory."

"Do not forget that I had good reason to be moving around with Bran." Enya heard Ineda's chuckle, the woman's head shakes just able to be seen in the faint firelight. "Ah! Forgive me. I will always think of Brennus as being my Bran. Let me start again. With Brennus, I was bartering goods with Celt and Roman alike. That gave us credibility for journeying in Roman held territory. You will not have that kind of justification if a Roman patrol finds you."

Fionnah cleared her throat. Loudly. "Enya…"

She wondered what was coming. Her mother was not one to take her to task, except when her domestic duties had been lax. This was the same sort of tone.

"Enya." Fionnah repeated. "You have entered the childbearing state. You should already have chosen a warrior to beget a child with. Your goddess will forgive your haste: she knows our times are far too troubled to wait for your *Beltane* Rites, but will you not consider this?"

Ineda was almost as persuasive. "You know that we need to replace our people, as much as we need to rear a new stock of horses."

Her mother was persistent. "Are you forging more than a friendship with young Feargus? At times, I have thought so."

"Nay, I am not." Though she hotly denied it, she did not really know how she felt about Feargus, or any other warrior. Dallying over mating rituals had not been a priority.

"Are you certain leaving to search for Ruoridh and Beathan is your best choice?" Fionnah asked.

"*Mathair*, I have no desire to bed a warrior for pleasure, or to breed with just now. I will not be tempted to change my decision while the whereabouts of my brother and cousin are unknown." She was resolute. "Brennus and Ineda have been information gatherers. I know I can be that, too!"

"What is this I hear, Enya?" Gabrond's voice was muffled as he hobbled into the communal roundhouse, the wattled entry way being low, and needing tall people to stoop down.

In behind her father trailed the rest of the Garrigill clan, with the exception of Nith. He had slept every night in their roundhouse since his arrival after the blood-letting at Beinn na Ciche, so his absence was notable. Though Enya remembered that had not always been the case during their long trek northwards. She might not yet be ready to lie with a man herself, but she had long known that Nith, with his quiet steady ways, had won the favour of many women. On those occasions, he had found shelter elsewhere: sometimes only for one night, and at others perhaps longer.

A sudden chill had her reach her hands to the low flickering flames, blaming her father for allowing in the draughts. She looked up and faced Gabrond as he drew near. "*Athair*. I am leaving as soon as the weather clears, to seek news of Ruoridh and Beathan. Someone needs to find them." She allowed no weakness in her words, even if they set a challenge and sounded as though she was blaming others for not already doing what was mentioned.

The Garrigill brothers, along with Nara, joined those already around the hearthside.

"I agree. Someone does." Gabrond lowered himself carefully onto a stool, ensuring his injured leg stretched out in front of him as he gave it a soothing rub.

Enya gulped into her poultice and stared at him. She had expected resistance from her father.

Gabrond's tone was matter of fact, his expression candid. "We do need to gather more information, but not just about our missing sons. We must establish reliable communication chains to ensure we know all of Agricola's troop movements. However, that does not mean it has to be you who ventures forth."

His change of stance irked her anew. It would not be the first time she had been at odds with her father. "Why should it not be me? You have made me the warrior I am. Let me prove it! I do not have the strength, or the stupidity, to confront a whole legion but I can worm my way around them to seek information, as well as anyone."

Lorcan's placid tones and gentle arm pats she knew were intended to sooth her ruffled emotions, but they annoyed her even more.

"Did your father say it would definitely not be you? Perhaps you are too quick to judge him, Enya?"

Looking from one Garrigill brother to the next she could see that she may have been a bit hasty. "Have I missed important plan-making?"

The sound of Nith dropping his spear in the weapon stack drew her attention to the door. She jerked her palms away from the flames, shocked at the sudden warmth that flushed through her.

"Aye." Her father dipped his head, his tone now one she could not judge at all. When she turned back to him there was none of the teasing in his words, yet his small smirk was confusing. "We have made some plans."

She looked to Lorcan to answer. He would not tease her in the same way as her father. "Do they include me?"

"Enya, you do not have to do this." She was surprised at Nith's interruption. He slipped down onto a nearby stool, his gaze pleading. "Your father and uncles may be convinced, but I am not."

"What are you talking about?"

Nith sighed and shoved wayward strands of hair back from his forehead. "Can this wait until the morn? Till after I have rested?"

She looked at her Aunt Nara's somewhat odd expression. Was it vexation because Nith was delaying? Whatever it was, her anger bubbled and would not be contained.

"Nay. I want to know now. I have been on patrol again, as you have, Nith, though our day was less onerous compared to recent ones. I will make my own decisions, despite what my father, or you, may deem is good for me."

Gabrond chuckled as he turned to his brothers, nudging the nearest one with an open palm. "See there. I told you she is of a fine temper."

Enya had had enough of their amusement and dropped her gaze to the fire. She laid bare her own plans. "Regardless of what all of you have planned, I am leaving as soon as the weather clears. Feargus will help me start my search."

"And after that, what then?" Lorcan was well known for making simple words mean a lot.

She lifted her gaze again, hesitant at the expectant looks on the faces around her. None spoke, though she knew all were listening, even Nith who toyed with a sling-stone, dropping it from one palm to the other. "I will find a new guide to take me to the next place, and the next, till I get news of my brother and cousin. I can do this!"

Even after her little tirade, Lorcan's voice was calm. "Where is your first destination?"

She looked not at Lorcan but at her father, her answer resolute. "I am going to Baile Mheadhain with Feargus."

The sound of Nith's round pebble pinging off the edging stones of the fireside drew everyone's silent awareness.

Brennus broke the hush. "Enya, we have already had communication from there, only a few nights ago."

Turning her full attention on him, she persisted. "Aye, we had some news, but nothing that clarified the fate of Feargus' mother's clan who are from Baile Mheadhain. He needs to know if there are any of his mother's kin left. He will help me find out if Beathan and Ruoridh have been amongst the slaves sent southwards from there."

Brennus nodded as though contemplating her plans. "Feargus is a lad of many talents, but Taexali lands are flooded with Roman scum."

"Is there anyone better who shelters here at Lulach's village who know of byways to avoid Roman patrols in that area?" She had no qualms about Feargus' ability to get her there, but she supposed that it would not hurt to hear the plans she had missed.

"Perhaps the Taexali warriors from Dunnideer would be the ones to lead them to the coast?" Gabrond asked Brennus.

Enya now regretted leaving the chief's roundhouse early. Perhaps, she had missed too much. "If you believe they will be better guides, then I would be happy to go with them, though Feargus may feel differently. He is keen to leave as soon as possible."

Alongside her, aggravation laced Nith's tone. "How much of this plan have you arranged with Feargus?"

Her answer came out more belligerent than she intended. Her plans with Feargus were no concern of Nith. "Feargus knows how to trek around the Moran Dhuirn area, avoiding the machair monitored by the Romans."

"And after that?" Nith still seemed unconvinced and insisted on more details. "Where is this machair that Feargus refers to?"

Enya huffed, already depleted by the questioning. "It lies between the many fisted Roman camp at Moran Dhuirn and the coast. The barrenness of the machair, and the dangers of its deep-sucking bogs, mean we will have to take a long diversion to avoid the Roman patrols, because we could be detected too easily from afar. But if any villagers remain hidden anywhere near our route, we might gain news of where the troops are, since Agricola moved on to the Ythan well. You do not know how many of his soldiers still shelter at Moran Dhuirn, or even why they linger. That in itself is a good enough reason to venture there. New information might prove useful for us to plan attacks on them."

Brennus nodded to Lorcan. "She speaks of the flat wetland plains, the place we avoided when we sought news before the battle."

Lorcan agreed. "Aye, I remember our detour to avoid it. Perhaps it will be possible for Enya and Feargus to establish contacts for us?"

Enya was jolted when Nith's vehemence shone clear.

"Nay! Feargus is too new to Roman ways and the responsibility too great for such a young warrior. Enya would be in the most dangerous of areas and too vulnerable."

She was furious at Nith's offhand suggestion that she was too young to look after herself, Feargus, too. Jumping to her feet, she towered over Nith, her smelly poultice plopping onto the rushes. "If my brother and cousin were taken aboard one of those Roman slave ships, I want to know. I will not be swayed from finding out!"

Nith stared up at her for long moments before he turned away. She could see the tension in his clenched fists, before he heaved in a huge breath through his nose. His expression was as rigid as her face now felt. Her mouth was pursed so tight her swollen jaw ached.

Rising up to be nose to nose with her, Nith's words were low through his clenched teeth. "So be it. If you must tread in that direction know that I will be with you and Feargus, every step of the way."

It now seemed as though she and Nith were the only two people in the room. The silence was profound, apart from some soft snores from a child.

Not willing to be the butt of Nith's anger any longer, she countered with some of her own questions. "What do you not trust about Feargus?" The merest flicker blazed before he blinked it away. When no answer came immediately from him, she continued. "Or is it me you do not trust to gain the information?"

"Enya." Nith's scoffs were muffled as he padded away. "You are a fine warrior, but you are still young and…untried." His fingers shoved his side braids behind his neck before he contemplated the roof beams.

Her anger boiled over. "Untried? What exactly does that mean? Did I not just kill one of the Roman scum in Glenlaff Woods? Were my warrior skills lacking then? Could I have tracked the forest any better than you these last few days, given the awful weather conditions?"

Nith swivelled back, but addressed the Garrigill brothers, his tone grim. "She did a very fine job, as did Feargus. There is nothing wrong with how the lad handles his spear, yet I would still go with them."

Enya watched as the Garrigill men shared a serious nod. Her father and her uncles still felt that they ruled over her, but she was not sure that their judgement was sound. She loved them dearly yet she was tired of their dictates. She tried for a mollified tone, suppressing the bitter anger that her skills and judgements were doubted.

"*Athair*? Too many nights have passed since my brother was in our sight. You need Nith far more than you need me for other duties that you and my uncles cannot do yourselves. Feargus and I do not have the experience for those tasks, so let us do what we can in our own way. Or are there other plans afoot that I do not yet know about?"

"Aye, Enya. There are. Sit down." Her father's tone brooked no disobedience.

She was not sure whether to gloat, or not, when Nith also sat down though on the opposite side of the fire.

Gabrond went on to tell her more plans she had missed after leaving Chief Lulach's roundhouse.

From her position on a low stool she studied her father's careworn face realising for the first time that he and her uncles were all showing signs of their age. Streaks of grey peppered Gabrond's braids and hoodie crow's feet lined his eye sockets. Most of all, she had not noticed how gaunt her father's face had become. The knowledge that her father and uncles had lost some of their former strength made her pay more attention to the newest plans, though it did not make her better disposed to Nith. She kept her temper in check as she listened, but it was not the easiest task.

Brennus had been charged with establishing communication with the eastern shoreline, but he was happy for Nith to head that way instead, and do it for him. He, in turn, would ensure contact was made with the southern Taexali.

Jumping to her feet, she faced Brennus. "You are forcing Nith to shadow my every step! He can do this task for you, Uncle Brennus, but he does not need me to be with him!" The anger would not subside, yet she no longer understood why it had become such a large confrontation.

"Enya!" Nith's equally heated response drew her reluctant attention. "Three will be a much safer band than two."

Padding around to Nith she scoffed, her height above him adding even more heat to her words. "Have you lost your courage, then? Do you need us to guard your back? If so, you are not the Nith I used to know and recognise."

Having delivered her barb, she huffed away from the fireside.

The soft reply was possibly not for her ears, but she heard it anyway.

"I do not recognise myself either."

Enya was not sure that she had won any kind of battle with her family when the talk ended and they eventually settled down for sleep. Every single warrior had to play their part whether in the areas flooded by Roman presence, or elsewhere. And not get caught. But what had she gained by having Nith shadow her every move?

She had intercepted many glowering looks from Nith, and other strange ones that had been directed her way while her father and uncles shared the plans, but she had no idea why he had become someone unfamiliar. For many, many seasons, he had been like an older brother. His wounds still bothered him, but that irritant did not account for his changed attitude. Plenty of people at Ceann Druimin still sported equally bothersome healing wounds although they were not bad tempered all the time.

She fingered her jaw to find that Ineda's poultice had indeed reduced some of the swelling.

The effort to think about Nith was too great as she settled in beside one of the younger children on the raised platform that ran along the inner wall of the roundhouse. Finding the most comfortable place on the thick straw and bracken, lined with a rough blanket, she snaked herself under the top woollen cover.

Where Nith slept did not interest her at all.

Chapter Fifteen

Ceann Druimin, Caledon Territory

Enya wakened when the first hint of light crept under the rough woollen cloth that kept draughts from seeping into the roundhouse. Since no one else moved around her, she guessed she might be the first to be up and about, not too unusual since rising before dawn in the winter season rarely served any purpose. Her first thought, as she crept past her sleeping relatives and her hosts in the feeble light of the low-maintaining fire embers, was to seek out Feargus.

She popped her head outside the roundhouse entryway to see what the pre-dawn had brought. The sleet of the previous day had gone in the mercurial way that happened often in northern Britannia. The morn was nipping-cold, but it was heartily cheering to see *Taranis'* deepest-blue cloak stretching endlessly above her.

Feeling lighter in spirit, a sensation that often came with the lack of woolly-grey skies, she retreated back inside the roundhouse to gather what she would need for a long trek. She had two sharpened spears ready, but generally found carrying both hampered her pace. After replacing one near the weapons rack alongside the entry passage, she sheathed her well-honed long knife into its leather pouch. Groping around, she grabbed her water skin, her small knife and the threadbare tunic she had been given to give her extra warmth during her surveillance duties. After stuffing her collection into her leather bag, she slung it across her chest, tied her foot bindings securely and yanked her bratt from the hook where it had been hung up to dry. She whipped it around her shoulders and slipped past her relatives a second time.

"Does Feargus of Monymusk sleep within?" Her question was put to the woman who had just exited the roundhouse that lay furthest off from her own at Ceann Druimin, a woman she had seen but had never talked to.

Three other people hovering near entryways had given her negative responses, not even sure of whom she referred to. Guilt hopped onto Enya's shoulder. She had been on guard duty with Feargus for days, yet had never asked which roundhouse he crept off to for shelter at the end of the long monitoring, or after being in Lulach's roundhouse like the evening just gone. Her Garrigill clan, which included Nith, were all squashed into the roundhouse of a family who had lost most of its members during the conflict at Beinn na Ciche. She realised, belatedly, that the security of being with her family was something she had not really appreciated enough. Feargus, and maybe others sheltering at Ceann Druimin, had none of that extra blanket of sanctuary.

"Nay." The woman spoke tersely, her focus on placing a small fire-brand into the metal bracket that sat next to a quern stone, sufficient illumination till more of dawn's pink streaks lightened *Taranis'* realm. As the woman emptied a meagre pile of grain into the bottom quern stone, from a poorly shaped clay pot, Enya felt keen eyes assess her.

Her spirits plummeted again. There were not all that many roundhouses in Lulach's village, though Enya knew it to be a lot larger than some in Taexali territory.

"You are one of the Brigantes?" The question was curious.

"Aye. I am Enya. I have been on patrol with Feargus these past two days, and need to talk to him."

Her words brought a nod from the woman who sifted and lifted the ground oats back to the stone indent for further working. "Feargus does lie inside here at night, but he has already risen and left. He goes elsewhere to break his fast, but I do not know where that would be."

"He shelters with you, yet does not eat here?" Enya was puzzled.

"Nay. He gives me brief thanks for his safe harbour, though most days he takes off before first light."

"Most days?" Enya's curiosity was stirred further.

"He is a proud young warrior. On the one time he brought something for the pot, he ate with us that night and the following morn. Otherwise? I do not know if he eats at all."

A memory stirred of Feargus slurping appreciatively of the thin broth given to them the night before. It pained her that he could feel so alone. While she traipsed around the hamlet, she wondered if a tiny space could be found for him in the roundhouse her family shared with old Torquil.

Seeing a shadow bending down by the burn that lay beyond the distant roundhouses, she darted off in that direction. It took a moment to gain her breath when she caught up with him. Water dripped from his stubbly whiskers and from the hair around his cheeks as he threaded his water skin onto his waistband.

"Are you ready to leave, Feargus?" she asked. "Since the skies of *Taranis* are much kinder to us?"

Feargus finished securing the ties before he looked at her, a penetrating solemn stare. "Aye. I am leaving, but I go on my own. You must wait for Nith."

Enya erupted. "I need wait for no one – and especially not Nith!"

Realising his haste when he reached for his spear and a small tied-up bundle, she dumped down her own weapon and untied her water skin. Bending to fill it, her words tumbled forth like the rippling water that bubbled over the smooth stones beneath her knees. "I choose to go with you, Feargus, as we already planned."

Feargus gave her no reply.

When she raised her head her water bag overfilled. Squeezing it gently, the skin bag oozed fresh water as she lifted it from the flow. Tightening its leather tie, she confronted him, having just realised something that puzzled her.

"How do you know I must wait for Nith?"

Something between a grunt and a huff passed his lips, one corner of which turned up just the smallest bit. "Nith told me himself."

"When did he do this? I only found out when my kin came back to our roundhouse."

"Nith made sure to seek me out and tell me last night." His smile was strained but his declaration firm. "I have no objection to showing you the way to Baile Mheadhain, Enya. Nith is another matter. I do not dislike his company, but I would rather not have him clucking at my heels like a bird training her brood, and keeping them in line."

"Feargus, please think again about this." Her request fell on deaf ears when the young warrior stepped away from her. Lightly grasping his arm, she begged some more. "I truly understand how you feel about Nith. I, too, find his brotherly protection cloying, though be assured that he would protect us with his life." Enya clutched her fingers gently at his elbow to stall him as he set into motion again, turning him around a little to make full eye contact with him. "I really do want you to lead me to Baile Mheadhain, Feargus, but first I must let my people know I am leaving with you. Otherwise, they may think I have headed off alone, and that would distress them unnecessarily."

The sheer loneliness that flickered from his eyes almost floored her. Her next appeal was heartfelt. "Will you wait here for just a few moments, or come with me?"

When Feargus gave no answer and turned away to stare into the distance, she doubted if he would wait at all for her, but she had to bid farewell to her mother. Grabbing up her spear, she sped back to her own roundhouse to find that Fionnah was lifting up the water bucket, before heading to the burn for a refill. Wrapping her arms around both woman and wooden container, she fiercely hugged, effectively trapping her mother in the process. Looking directly into Fionnah's eyes, she conveyed how important her words were.

"Feargus and I are leaving now. I do not want him to leave alone. He will get me to Baile Mheadhain safely. I know this. I will try to get news back to you as soon as possible about my progress."

Fionnah made no attempt to free herself, the smile she returned filled with pride though her expression was also tinged with worry. "Nith is already awake though has not broken his fast. You will not put him off so easily, Enya. His mind is made up to go with you, and I believe Feargus will come to see the good of it."

After Fergus' brief conversation Enya heartily doubted it, but wanted to linger no longer. She released Fionnah after another tender squeeze. "I must go now." She turned to look back to where she had last talked to the young Taexali warrior. He was well across the burn and heading for the nearby forest. "Look where he is already. I need to run to catch up with him."

Her mother's fingers snagged her cloak as she turned to go. "You must wait, Enya. You have not yet eaten anything. Please. I will only be a moment." Fionnah dumped the bucket on the ground before darting into the roundhouse.

Enya swithered about lingering or leaving straight away but found her mother's plea too compelling. She had no notion of when they would stop to eat or, indeed, would have anything to put in their mouths.

Fionnah scurried back out juggling to hold a bundle of dried meat, a piece of cloth holding a pile of oats, and a handful of other seeds and hazelnuts which she pressed into Enya's hands. "I will pray to my goddess that she will guide you and protect you. I wish I had more food to send with you, but you know too well how we all rely on the goodness of Lulach's people."

"We will eat when we can." Enya reassured her mother as she stuffed the food into her waist pouch. "My water skin is already filled this morning. Do not fret. Feargus would not be so foolish as to light a fire in a place of danger." After one further loving look at Fionnah, she turned away and loped towards the burn, hoping that Feargus would not be too far ahead.

She managed no more than a handful of strides before the one voice she would rather not have heard interrupted her progress.

"Is Feargus gone already?" Nith's call from behind her was matter of fact. Not commanding, nor annoyed – just bland.

Though she wanted to ignore him, Enya found she was unable to do that. If he had been angry, she would have railed back at him. She inhaled a deep breath through her nostrils, determined to keep her temper before she half-turned her head to answer him. His spear in hand meant he was all set to go. "You do not need to do this, Nith. Feargus and I can manage on our own." Sending back his own words to him gave her only a little satisfaction.

"Enya. You probably can. But if you go, then I will be with you every step of the way." His face was grim, riddled with crushing guilt in his eyes. "Your grandfather set me a task at Tarras before we left there. I have not fulfilled that successfully so far, but I vow that I will not fail to look after you in the future."

She had no idea what he was talking about, but he had been her friend for so long. She could not bear that he had grown into such sorrow, and found she could not argue. "I must catch up with Feargus."

Nith's lengthy paces brought him quickly alongside. "Then why do we tarry? I am as eager to get to Baile Mheadhain as you are."

Enya was not sure exactly how she felt as she crossed the stepping stones of the burn with Nith at her heels, after a last wave to Fionnah. Nith had always been a steady presence, one to be relied on, but she wondered if he intended to stifle every initiative she might make as they journeyed.

Ignoring his very presence, she sprinted forward to reach Feargus.

Chapter Sixteen

Votadini Territory

The heaving bile rose to Beathan's mouth yet again.

He had been sick so many times that what came up now only trickled out as a thin slime which dribbled down his chin. He had no strength left to heave it away or even to aim it sideward.

"Pull!" A short lull followed, and then the bellow 'Pull' came again.

Wiping away the bitter taste was not possible, because his hands were curved around his bent legs. Chained to his neighbour, they were wedged in between two oarsmen in a space that was probably not meant to be filled by anyone at all – Roman mariner, or slave. The call of the *centurion* kept the pace. Beathan had already gleaned it was a dire mistake for any of the oarsmen to fail with the rowing pull, whether his eyes were shut or open. The rhythmic pull, rest, pull was unending, yet the strong oarsmen kept rowing regardless.

The flail in the hand of the *centurion* had left stinging weals across more backs than his own when someone failed to adhere to the issued orders, or when a captive slumped too close to the feet, or hands, of the rower next to them. The salt water made the cuts smart even more when the unrelenting waves crashed up the sides of the ship, and sent a mist of stinging moisture to cascade over him. He felt so wretched, tired of wondering how much longer the agony of being aboard the ship could last.

Opening his eyes the tiniest bit, he braced himself for the ache that came to them from the seawater. He peered at the sight beyond the rhythmic rise and fall of the oars. Faint pinpricks of light appeared, and disappeared, in the growing dim, weak moonlight intermittently appearing between wafting darkest-grey cloud cover. Could the lights be the place the helmsman was aiming for?

Beathan wondered how long the Roman ship would hug the coast this time. On his last voyage, the rowers had rested and pulled from the point of the sun being high in the sky to the coming dusk before they had put in to shore, the sails used infrequently to speed them on. The light of day had almost gone on this journey, but they had not yet sidled in to shore.

"Beathan."

He barely heard the thready whisper alongside him.

"I swear to the god *Morimaru* that if he sees fit to let me survive this journey, I will avenge those who have been tossed overboard. Do you hear me?"

"Aye," Beathan returned, equally quietly. "I hear you, Derwi, and vow to do more than that, if the gods will that I live to become a man."

The weak nudge and chuckle next to him heartened Beathan more than the following words ever could.

"You are alive, Beathan. Many of those fully grown captured tribesmen, who were dragged along with us from Agricola's Moran Dhuirn camp, have not borne their chains as well as you have. Some had more physical strength than you to start with and yet, they are long gone to the otherworld. It is the inner strength that matters, my Brigante friend."

Beathan looked askance at Derwi who had not been nearly as sick as he had been. "I am not so sure of that. One more sea voyage may make me tip myself over the boat edge."

"You will tolerate what you have to. Your father has instilled that into you."

Beathan almost grinned. "It was more that my mother did. Nara of the Selgovae is a warrior princess who slackened no rope during my training."

Derwi lifted his head to look him full in the face. "Your father is Brigante and your mother Selgovae? In days of old they were sworn enemies. You have many tales to tell, young Beathan."

The rapid slashing of the whip at Derwi's shoulders put paid to any further talk.

The words shouted by the *centurion* were immaterial, the meaning was clear, but Derwi barely flinched at the new weals bleeding through his shredded *leine.* His whisper was a deadly oath. "When we disembark on that shore, that is looming closer, if I have the opportunity, I will kill those *Ceigean Ròmanach!"*

Beathan dared a quick glance, a deep groan rumbling free. "That is a very small bit of land, Derwi. We are surely not landing on that?"

"Pull! Rest! Pull!" The *centurion*'s renewed bellows followed other cries from the helmsman, words that Beathan did not understand, but their effect was easy to appreciate when the vessel heeled well away from what Beathan could see was not much larger than a rock surface sticking up out of the water.

What territory he was in he had no notion of, but any landfall at all would be preferable to being out on the endless water. His head dipped, his eyes closing tight.

Struggling awake he realised that he must have nodded off for a few moments. Looking around, it seemed as though some of his earlier prayers were bearing fruit. The god *Morimaru* must now be appeased, since the earlier high swells were now a gentle buffeting.

"Hold!" The *centurion*'s order was repeated for those rowers slow to act. More commands rattled out as the hull turned enough to sidle towards the shore against the river flow, flaring torches on the shoreline guiding the boat in.

Beathan raised his shoulders to look all around him. The sight of other Roman vessels beached on the sands made his breath hitch, and what was behind them made the blood inside him truly surge. What lay ahead was no temporary camp. The wooden walls of a substantial fort loomed above the dunes, the higher watchtowers at the corners manned by shadowy figures near the flickering torches.

A gut feeling told Beathan that he was a lot further south than Venicones territory.

The oarsmen pulled in their oars and flipped them up before forcing a space for them down the sides of the boat, heedless of whether they clunked on wood, or the captives.

Beathan dreaded what might happen when he was dragged off the vessel, but those thoughts were fast overtaken by the scene near the prow, some five or six slaves ahead of him. Two of the mariners were shaking and prodding the tribesman that the *centurion* pointed to.

Not satisfied with their responses the *centurion* whipped out his *gladius* and dealt a swift series of stabs at the man's bent back designed to put paid to the issue.

"Dump him overboard! There is no question now about him still being alive."

Chapter Seventeen

Well of Ythan Roman Camp, Taexali Territory

"Your detachment was sent to patrol the northernmost Taexali territory?" Agricola asked the *decurion* of the Second Tungrian mounted unit.

"It was, sir." Manius Helva's nod was deferential, but the tone was confident.

When *Tribune* Flavus made to drift off, Agricola growled, "Stay and make sure you learn something useful!" He was still having to thole the *tribune* close to heel.

Turning back to Helva, he gestured the Tungrian to speak.

"Due north of here there is one river flowing to the northern Taexali coastline, and out into the Oceanus Germanicus."

"You found no other rivers?"

Helva's eyebrows twitched. The man carefully formed his reply, as though the question was a trick one. "No larger rivers in Taexali territory open out onto the northern coastline. We have been told there are more rivers to the west, but they are in Vacomagi territory."

"Your unit has not explored these?"

Again there was the tiniest flicker in the man's expression. "No, sir. My unit was dispatched to investigate the extent of northern Taexali lands, and was bidden to report back as quickly as possible."

Agricola brushed off the wispy white fall from his cloak before it seeped in and soaked the wool even more than it was already. He ignored the stinging chill at his cheeks, and stared at Helva who appeared unaffected. As well he may do, since the lands of his origin were probably not so different from

Taexali territory. "Your unit has been on patrol for days. What took you so long?"

A trickle of melted sleet slid off the Tungrian's nose, though the man's stance remained firm. "We established the route of the river that we found close to here, till it reached its estuary to the sea. From locals, we confirmed that the river forms the western border of Taexali territory."

"The natives were friendly?"

"Not exactly, sir. However, it is not difficult to extract information from the weak and the elderly who have no one around to fight for them."

Agricola's mood dipped. "That sounds like a dearth of captives to send south?"

Helva's lips quirked, his gaze impenetrable as stone. "Those left are hobbling and too old to lift a laden platter."

"You did not kill them?" He awaited the man's answer knowing full well that his command to kill only those who challenged might have been disregarded.

The Tungrian's eyes lost focus and were not quite on him as he answered. "They have little time left before they move on to the otherworld. They are beyond feeble."

"Why do you think the Taexali warriors abandoned them?"

Helva stared at him fully this time. "The Taexali do not dishonour their elders. Their gods will see them to the otherworld when it is their time."

Agricola dipped an acknowledgement. Helva probably worshipped similar gods.

A flurry of movement down the *Via Praetoria* momentarily preoccupied him, but there were now too many gathering there to see who was arriving. As he peered a bit longer, he continued his distracted inquiry of Helva. "And what did you learn from those who remain?"

Another of his reconnaissance patrols had returned and it was for exactly this reason that he stayed out of doors in this infernal awful weather.

Helva gave answer. "The old ones told us nothing we would not have found out for ourselves. There is a long Taexali coastline that heads eastwards. We trekked in that direction till we reached a promontory where the land turns south."

"How far a distance?" His eyes flicked back to the Tungrian, now satisfied that he could give the man better concentration.

Helva continued. "One full day's ride, though at least two days for infantry to cover the dunes and the rough grasses. Prickly whins and brackens grow freely. In other places, difficult boggy terrain persists, interspersed with clumps of ground elder and coarse clinging scrubland grasses. All of that means a slow tramp."

Agricola absorbed the information unable to fight the lure of the brazier's heat, the wood recently added now well aflame and tempting. Stretching forward to warm his hands, he invited Helva to do likewise. "Apart from this river mouth, are there other landing points for the fleet to safely offload supplies on this northern coast? Where they can take on fresh water?"

Helva inched closer but did not seem to need the heat as much as he did, the man's hands remaining tucked by his sides. "There are many treacherous low cliff areas, but some smaller streams disgorge into the northern sands where some of the fleet could beach, though not good for all of our vessels at the same time.

Catching the eye of his nearest guard, Agricola bawled, "Where are those senior officers and the *speculatores* that I sent for?"

The salute was swift before the soldier scuttled off.

Crispus appeared at his side. "Some of the *centurions* of the *Legio II Adiutrix* are not in the camp."

He felt his temper rise again, although taking it out on Crispus was counterproductive. After a quick reflection, he rattled off *cohort* numbers.

Crispus set off with a nod as though the conversation had been harmonious.

Agricola turned back to Manius Helva. "Your knowledge gathering took you three days?"

"Sir. The weather... It slowed us down considerably."

"Be easy." Agricola sought to soothe the man's ruffled feathers, realising the soldier was exhausted. "That is what you were sent to do. Do these Taexali farm most of this land you speak of?"

"Here and there, sir, it is laid to crops – barley and oats where the land has been drained. Some grazing for sheep, but much of the rest is uncultivated blanket-bog."

"Not Rome's favourite cereals crops, Helva."

The Tungrian's answering grimace was of the wry variety. "Not really, sir."

"How do the Taexali tribes exist?" His question was not a fair one. Many tribes across the empire survived on much less. The deliberate clearing of Helva's throat made him turn to the man. The hint of a smirk was as fleeting as it was unexpected.

"Coastal Vacomagi territory supposedly has spelt field-strips."

"For some reason you are not inspired, Helva? Am I to assume they have limited spelt?"

The short nod was succinct. "If the land resembles the Taexali territory we have ridden on."

He paced away a short distance. He should have sufficient basic supplies arriving soon via the *Classis Britannica* to feed his soldiers for a new half-moon, if the weather improved. But before then, he needed to find alternative food stocks.

"Horses?"

Helva's head shake dashed those hopes. "We saw evidence of domestic livestock, though the beasts are gone. The locals must have taken them with them when they mustered at Beinn na Ciche."

"So in the area you have patrolled, Helva, we will gain little of immediate use to us?"

"Virtually nothing, sir."

"These northern tribes are so unpredictable!"

His exasperation was profound. He padded around the *carbonarius* as he gathered his thoughts. His report to Emperor Domitian would have to be delayed as long as possible. Rome's coffers had to be filled from Caledonia, but with what?

The hurried approach of the huddle of *centurions* from the *Legio II Adiutrix* halted his musings. After acknowledging them, he issued general orders to be undertaken by nightfall, making sure he did not miss deliberate eye contact with Rubrius Mucius. Close by, he was gratified to see that Flavus looked terrified. Before he dismissed the *centurions*, his parting words were barbed.

"Tighten up your discipline. Careless attitudes are not tolerated in any legion."

As the men filed away, he turned back to Flavus who looked like he was about to be heave up his guts. He could not bear to have the irritant in his vicinity any longer.

"You are temporarily dismissed, Flavus," he ordered. "But do not think to head in that direction." He indicated the route taken by the stiff-backed *centurions* of the *Legio II Adiutrix*.

When the junior *tribune* tripped off, he added, "And come back directly."

The latrines would no doubt be the *tribune*'s first port of call.

He paced back and forth in front of his tent. His ambition to tramp the whole of Britannia was looking increasingly threatened. "In the name of *Ceres*! Could more of the Taexali wedge to the north of here be farmed?"

The Tungrian contemplated the question before answering. "Productive soil could be reclaimed from the wetlands and rough moorland but the draining and tilling of it would take the efforts of a lot of men. It would be a good few seasons' work before any decent crops would be yielded, and thereafter it would take a lot of sweat to keep the new areas adequately drained. Not impossible, but hard going."

"Native labour we do not currently have our hands on!"

Helva was circumspect. "No, sir."

The update was unfavourable, but he planned a dispatch to Emperor Domitian. He could indicate future grain stocks for the Empire, though only if sufficient workers were available. Delegating his Britannic troops for such a lengthy secondment would be impossible, especially since a *cohort* from each of his four permanent *legions* in Britannia had recently been clawed away by Domitian. Those soldiers were now in a hostile situation in Germania, and from the reports he was receiving they were unlikely to survive. Their return to Britannia could not be counted on, but if slave labour could be found for other reasons across the empire then it should not be impossible to obtain more slaves for Taexali territory – once the new western boundary of the Roman Empire was officially established.

Unfortunately, this kind of contemplation always soured his mood. The *Legio IX* was even more undermanned than his other *legions* after Domitian's removal of two *cohorts* worth at the beginning of his sixth campaign season. He could never risk putting the *Legio IX* in such a vulnerable position again, like it had been in Venicones territory. They had almost been annihilated by the northern barbarians.

Domitian might readily suggest that troops raised from southern Britannic tribes should be deployed for such a task, but he was not sure he could trust them in such circumstances to give longer-term allegiance to Rome. The wily Caledon and allied neighbours might just be too persuasive, and might foist rebellion.

Like a mangy cur worrying at an already-stripped bone, he could not move his thoughts on.

"The river you encountered is a natural border between Taexali and Vacomagi territories?"

"Yes, sir. They call it the Caelis." Helva's last word was hesitant as though only vaguely sure of its pronunciation.

"Is the Caelis water navigable?"

A swift nod confirmed this, but by the look on the *decurion's* face Agricola could tell there were limitations.

"Our smallest vessels could travel a short distance inland from the river mouth, but the banks narrow very quickly. Barges could be used, but the width and depth of the water varies and there are many tight bends to negotiate around. It is not a large river flow and parts are very exposed."

Agricola digested the information. Rivers were more convenient than roads for the transportation of both goods and men, but that possibility was not looking likely, either, in these barbarian lands. His teeth clamped together more from frustration now than cold, his bottom lip curving up over his top teeth.

He continued to question Helva about the reconnaissance gained, his concentration just sharp enough to absorb the new details, since exhaustion was creeping in again. It was the numbing cold wind around him: it froze his body and his mind. Padding a little way down the *Via Principalis,* he bid Helva follow him, his toes so frozen, the nipping and tingling was almost impossible to bear. He berated *Vertumnus,* and all the associated gods he could think of, for bringing on the early winter.

He now had enough information to choose the locations of his next forward camps. Though, how many men to keep permanently in the north was a major question still to be answered. Overwintering in these inhospitable barbarian territories could only be done with advance planning. He could send the bulk of his men down to the nearest legionary supply fortress at Corstopitum in lower Votadini territory to overwinter, even if it was a march that might take from one ides to the next in poor weather. On the other hand, he needed his troops to explore beyond the Varar Aestuarium, the waters to the north of Vacomagi territory, at the beginning of the next campaign season – as early in the coming year as possible. Though Domitian's recent demand for more of his troops was making that highly unlikely.

The thoughts set him to pace around. He trod heavily to get rid of the last numbness at his toes, nagging himself to remember to find better foot coverings for inside his leather boots. Vulnerable toes made vulnerable men. Splitting up his armies had been inevitable during these Caledonian campaigns, and it would continue to happen, but he was disinclined to have his *legions* so susceptible ever again.

Currently, the Caledon allies who skulked in the mountains were too wily and fickle to march any of his men away from.

"You said few of those Taexali tribespeople had returned to their farms, Helva?"

"We saw little evidence of that, sir."

"Why are these barbarians so unpredictable?"

"Northern men can be thrawn, sir." Helva's slight shrug mirrored his own feelings.

Agricola screwed his eyelids tight to dispel the annoying sleet, wishing he could banish all of his misgivings as easily. It was not only the natives who were erratic. Emperor Domitian's reputation for being fickle was increasing according to official correspondence recently received from Eboracum. The letters from his wife gave her views of what was going on in Rome, though they had to be officially verified. It was not for the first time that he regretted his strained relations with Domitian. Commands from the previous two emperors had been so much easier for him to execute, his strategies in Britannia more in tune with their demands. Domitian, however, was very different from his father, Vespasian.

A feeling of extreme unease crept up Agricola's spine. He needed to have his augur read some entrails immediately. Speeding up the conquest of northern Britannia seemed more essential than ever.

He had no idea about surviving native numbers because, so far, none of his *exploratores* had come back with useful information. Caledonian dead after the battle outnumbered those of Rome, but how many living ones remained was vague. Attack from them was still a possibility since no treaties had been agreed. That meant retaining troops in strategic passes over the winter to hem them in, regardless of how disgruntled his men might feel about it. Dissention of any kind from within his ranks was not to be contemplated. He knew the men of the *Legio IX,* and *Legio XX* well enough and never doubted their loyalty, but a niggling unease existed over the *vexillationes* that had been drafted in for this Caledonian campaign. Even the allegiance of the *Legio II Adiutrix* had yet to be undeniably proven.

He paced back and forth his mind an unending swell of unanswered questions before he focused on the Tungrian who had stepped away from the brazier, seemingly unaware of the deeper nip the increasing darkness brought.

"Monitoring the northern Taexali territory will require only a small resident force, in your opinion?"

"Yes."

Agricola's small smile of agreement was echoed by a gap-toothed one from Helva. The thought of little resistance from the Taexali was a more enticing prospect than how to contain rampaging warrior-bands of the hill tribes.

A feeling he had not experienced for days gripped him. After complete subjugation of the Taexali and Vacomagi, he would deal with the tribes north of the Varar Aestuarium. If reports from the *Classis* were favourable, perhaps only one of his *legions*, or even a few auxiliary *cohorts*, would complete the task? Though when? Before the weather deteriorated?

But it already had!

His pacing ceased. He stared at Helva, who waited patiently, and Flavus, who had just returned looking a mite relieved. The shiver that ran down Agricola's back was discounted as the chill from a damp and miserable day. He had no time to fret about the possible failure of the patrols he had already sent to check that the interior of Vacomagi territory was not a roiling hot-blooded cauldron.

In amidst the huddle of senior officers who now approached him was a distinct group, the native dress indicating their infiltration function. The leader he had spoken to many times before, and now had utter confidence in the man's abilities, but the recent additions to his group had yet to prove themselves.

Trust was more than just words and deeds. Drawing the band of *speculatores* away from the front of his tent, Agricola bid them follow him towards the eastern gate where he spaced them out to see them better.

"Apart from Quintus Laterensus, name yourselves!"

He took note of any flinching, or inability to look him in the eye, as they declared who they were and where they had come from. Two of them claimed to have originally been Taexali warriors who had given allegiance to the Roman Army during his sixth summer campaign. Men like these he intrinsically detested, yet pragmatism meant he needed their intelligence reports. He took note of the way they stood to attention, sensing their natural arrogance had not yet been beaten out of them, which might not necessarily be a bad thing. A few direct questions established they had been giving his *speculatores* unit valuable information, from well before the confrontation with Calgacus' warriors at Beinn na Ciche. Still, he was suspicious by nature. The men may have proved useful already, but their allegiance to Rome would take more than one campaign season. Turning to Quintus Laterensus, he gave precise instructions before dismissing them all.

"Have you any others who are due to report back soon?"

Laterensus nodded. "At least two are in Caledon territory, and one other is more likely now to be with the Vacomagi."

He studied the man who had been a *speculator* for many years. "Do you trust them to work individually?"

Laterensus' jaw twitched but the man otherwise showed no signs of affront. "Undoubtedly, sir."

"I want their information the instant they return."

Absolute allegiance was paramount.

Chapter Eighteen

Well of Ythan Roman Camp, Taexali Territory

"Come in!"

Agricola's command was for his senior officers, after Crispus alerted him that those who were in camp were assembled and waiting outside for the day's routine instructions.

It was a squeeze around his central table, the reason he more often than not had them gather outside. He acknowledged each one in turn, then realised someone was missing.

"Crispus!" His secretary was already at his elbow. Though loath to issue the order, it had to be done. "Send for *Tribune* Flavus."

"I am here, sir." The jingle of new metal-plated lorica clanking together signalled the late entry of Flavus.

"Unpunctuality is inexcusable!" His bark produced a string of apologies from Flavus which he halted with an outstretched palm. "Observe. And learn."

His next order was for Crispus as he moved to the back of the table. "Fetch my itinerary of these northern lands."

A quick rustle amongst a pile laid on a trestle near the back of the tent produced the large boards requested. Crispus' tight smile flashed across firm cheeks as he laid out the thin panels, two by two, on the central table having checked their sequence. The wooden mounts were dovetailed to fit together with minimal intrusion of the waxed surface.

When assured Crispus was ready to record the details of the meeting on his own tablet, Agricola began. Bending over the rudimentary wax itinerary, he bid the assembled company to pay heed. Framing the irregular shape covering the two bottom boards, his fingers pointed to match his words. "This is the territory settled during previous campaign seasons. The main tribes subdued here are Votadini, Selgovae and Novantae – those who dwell between the Brigantes, and the narrow stretch of land that joins the Rivers Clota and Bodotria.

The senior officers who had seen the itinerary before nodded an acknowledgement, and those new to it he ensured came closest to the boards. He focused his attention on Manius Helva who indicated his understanding. Then, he sketched out the large wedge that covered the four central boards with his forefinger. "This represents the territory we have campaigned on from the Clota and Bodotria to where we presently are camped. We now know that Caledonia is mainly covered by mountains apart from this eastern fringe of Venicones, Taexali and Vacomagi lands."

There was nothing at all on the top two boards, the wax having been recently cleaned of previous markings. "This top section has been cleared for a redraw of the unknown territory that lies north of the Varar Aestuarium, which lies here." His finger pointed out the wide estuary. "Early *Classis* reports indicate the stretch of land to the north of the estuary is smaller than Caledonia though it is also mountainous, except for a narrow eastern coastal fringe with flatter plains near its northern coast. The *Classis* is currently establishing if there are any north-western coastal flatlands."

Helva, he was glad to see, was concentrating on the centre section of four boards.

Agricola carried on. "This itinerary needs to become more accurate and our present experience on the land should improve that."

Helva peered at the boards. After a few moments thought the man's lips pursed, questions flashing across his expression. The Tungrian was familiar with his methods of detailing the landscape, and had already been invited to view itineraries of southern Britannia during earlier meetings, but he could see that something bothered the *decurion*.

Agricola pointed to a small metal eagle that was impressed into the wax about half way up the middle section and much closer to the eastern coast than the west. "This is the new legionary fortress, Pinnata Castra, in Venicones territory."

He waited for them all to nod their understanding before he reached forward to place his finger near the top of the middle section. "The wide-notched line here," his speech slowed while his finger dragged along it, "is the northern sea coast of the Vacomagi and the Taexali." Again a dip of the chin from Helva had him continue, though the man's expression was still hesitant. He pointed to another metal eagle that was pressed into the wax. "This is where we are now, named the Well of Ythan by the locals."

The Tungrian looked to the west of the eagle where clusters of tiny etched-in scratches indicated the Caledon Mountains. Then Agricola watched the man's focus turn to the line which represented the east coastline of Taexali lands.

"These marks indicate our previous camps?" Helva asked. The Tungrian's fingernail traced a line drawn through the dots, the line roughly mirroring the outline of the displayed mountain area.

"They do. How far is it from this present camp to the northern coast?"

Helva's answer was immediate. "Fifteen *mille passus*, so marching due north, it would take two days if there was poor visibility like today, or one with some double-pacing on a good day, on the most negotiable route."

Agricola acknowledged the reply and then referred to his senior officers, to verify their findings of the territory closer to the present camp. Others shared updates on the progress of patrols that had been sent to scour Taexali territory. All the while, Crispus and Lentulus scribbled down the information which would be added to the itinerary, and to the general campaign plans.

Agricola moved on to future intentions for the *legions'* deployment. "If you have recently taken up your duties, you may not know this." He was at pains to focus his attention on his newest officers. "My *trierarchi*, those captaining the fleet during my fifth and sixth summer campaigns, indicated that this northern coastline of the Taexali and Vacomagi tribes is about a four-day march from the most easterly point here to the furthest west." Using his finger to indicate the shoreline on his itinerary he drew it to the furthest west point. "This is where the sands round into a river at the western end of the Varar Aestuarium."

He then waved his hand to the topmost empty boards.

"I, for one, am gratified to know that Pytheas the Greek seafarer was correct when he wrote about Britannia being an island and that there is a triangular wedge of land that lies to the north of Vacomagi and Taexali territory." He stopped to make sure his officers were listening carefully, and stabbed at the centre of the empty top boards to prepare them for what was to come. "If the interior of this wedge is flat land, it may be much more productive than Taexali territory. A further campaign north of here will establish that."

"Do we have any confirmation of that from our current fleet?"

It was a pertinent question from the officer who pointed to the empty wedge, but one that frustrated him.

"Reports are due." His *trierarchi* reports were overdue, in fact, but he would not presently share that with his *tribunes*.

His terse answer prevented any more discussion. He moved on to present matters, his finger back to indicating the areas occupied by the Caledons, Taexali and Vacomagi. "Our immediate priority is to block up all routes into the mountains of the Caledons and completely hem the barbarians in from the Taexali and Vacomagi flatlands." He pointed out the curved line of mountain edges on his itinerary that went from Pinnata Castra all the way north eastwards and then arched north westwards to the Varar Aestuarium.

Now irritated, Agricola pointed to the shoreline due north of the eagle that indicated the present camp at the Well of Ythan. His index finger settled on a spot before he addressed Helva. "This is where this River Caelis disgorges into the waters of the Oceanus Germanicus? And the northern Taexali dwell here?"

"No, sir." The Tungrian sounded very sure.

Surprised by the negative response, Agricola waited for further explanation, and from the intakes of breath around him others in the company thought likewise.

"The river mouth of the Caelis does lie almost due north of here, but there is much more coastline to the east that is not yet marked on your itinerary." The Tungrian bent over the wax and used his thumb and forefinger to judge the distance to the corner indicating the promontory at which point the land curved south. "What you have here would only represent a one-day march along this shoreline from the Caelis to the promontory. The reality would be more like two short day marches."

Agricola gave Helva a tiny metal eagle. "Place this where you believe this promontory should be."

Helva used his thumb to gauge the spot, then he impressed the eagle into the wax.

Turning to officers of the *Legio XX,* Agricola questioned them. "Does this meet with information from your scouts who have patrolled this area? Are the indigenous tribes here all Taexali?" He pointed to the new wedge that was created by the insertion of the tiny symbol. After a brief discussion between the men of the *Legio XX* and some of the *Legio II Adiutrix,* who had patrols working across the southern part of the wedge, an agreement was reached that clarified Helva's judgement.

Agricola flicked a finger to his junior clerk. "Change this to represent the new line and record this point here as the Taexalorum Promontorium."

Helva continued when prompted. "When we stood on the low cliffs near the River Caelis, the shoreline lies fairly true from east to west, but the river mouth below us would not bite into your coastline as much as it does on your itinerary. The estuary is not so extensive."

"How does that match the report you got from your *exploratores* in Vacomagi territory?" Agricola asked the legate of the *Legio IX,* and then barked out more questions to the other officers.

Satisfied with their responses he turned back to Lentulus. "See to all of those changes and additions."

Before the stylus touched the wax, his junior clerk clarified what was needed. "Do you want the promontory to match up to here beside the River Bodotria, sir?" The clerk's finger pointed to the bottom right of the central section of the itinerary.

Agricola thought first of the implications of the recent changes before responding. The new line would make no difference to his marked forts and signal towers in Venicones territory.

"I do."

He waited till the junior clerk erased the original and carefully drew a new coastal boundary line.

In the interim, Crispus, ever efficient, took the opportunity to intervene. "These are ready for your approval, sir."

Agricola scanned the communication to ensure all was in order before adding his signature.

Handing them over to Crispus, he turned back to the Tungrian who stood deep in contemplation, the junior clerk having stepped back from the newly scaled itinerary. "Is this more accurate now, Helva?"

"It is, sir."

Helva's small smile assured him: the man had done well for him across previous territory. He trusted the Tungrian's judgement, but it would be further verified when he himself was on the move with his full armies. He ran his finger due west from the newly shaped Caelis river mouth to that of the Varar Aestuarium. "It would then be a six, or seven, day trek to this west end of the shoreline?"

Helva gauged the distance before he answered, shaking his head. "I would think it a much shorter march, but there was no hill high enough to confirm that from Taexali territory."

"It will soon be established by the *Legio IX*." Agricola's right index finger went back to the eagle marking his present camp at the Well of Ythan and slowly slid north, stopping at the half way point between the eagle and the coast. "Is there fresh water available here?"

The Tungrian was definite. "The Caelis would lie a little to the west. There are small streams to the east of your finger, but the only larger river in this Taexali wedge is the one which starts here at the Well of Ythan and flows to the eastern coastline."

Agricola turned to Lentulus. "Was there not a mention of two rivers that flow out onto the east coast in my information from the fleet? One that the *trierarchus* said is north of this Ythan?"

His junior clerk looked flustered, apology dripping from him. "Yes, sir, but you agreed to leave the river mouths off the itinerary till they are corroborated by the mounted *exploratores*, who are currently on a northerly trek of the beaches. Their start point is where our ships are berthed at the place the locals name Baile Mheadhain, just north of Obar Dheathain."

"They confirmed this other one yesterday!"

"I will ensure it is added, sir."

Lentulus' obsequious bending and apologetic tones grated on him when he remembered he had not shared the information from those scouts with anyone yet. It had arrived at the same time as a bundle of other important correspondence which had taken priority.

He hastened to his littered desk and ruffled through the scrolls, tablets and blocks of wood. "Ah! I have not yet told you that." Finding the errant wax tablet among the mess, he scanned it first before passing it to his junior scribe. "The locals name it Ugie."

A hasty discussion between Helva, a *tribune* of the *Legio XX*, and Lentulus took place as details of the new rivers were marked onto his itinerary. Till they were done, Agricola padded around the confined space, accepting more communication from Crispus. After his usual check of the correspondence he gave instructions for replies, before turning back to the Tungrian.

"Helva? Will this Caelis River supply water to all my soldiers that are currently here, if I site my next camp in its vicinity?"

"It would, sir. The streams to the north-east are sufficient for a smaller camp of a few *cohorts*, but aren't sufficient for even one legion."

"How much resistance can we expect from the natives near the river banks on the Taexali border?"

He noted the Tungrian pondering his response before replying.

"Presently, none at all on the Taexali side and, from the stretches I've patrolled, I doubt there would be any on the Vacomagi side, either. But that may not be the case further upstream."

Agricola extracted more information from the officers of the *Legio IX* who had men assessing the territory. Dwellings near the riverbanks came next, Helva supplying details for Crispus and Lentulus to frantically record.

He set Helva another question. "The surviving Taexali warriors could be a definite threat, if they creep back from the mountains. Can you tell how many that might be?"

Helva bent down and produced a wax tablet from his canvas pack that lay at his feet.

Agricola admired the man's efficiency as it was passed over to him. While he scanned the numbers, the Tungrian explained.

"Those are my estimates of the Taexali who lived in the north-easterly triangle from the Caelis river mouth to the Taexalorum Promontorium and south to where our ships are berthed at Baile Mheadhain. That number is based on how many roundhouses we found ourselves, added to the number of other clusters named by the elders. We will not have got all of their habitation, but it may serve as a rough assessment across the territory we patrolled." Helva looked to those assembled around the table for confirmation.

Another hasty conference was started between his officers of the *Legio XX* who had information to add when they studied Helva's account.

Agricola passed the tablet over to Crispus whose small cough after reading was well known to him. It indicated his clerk's approval.

"More reports compiled just like this will be very welcome!"

Helva beamed.

Agricola listened to Crispus thanking Helva profusely, but knew the comment was intended to be heard by all present since it would make the recording much easier for the scribes involved. Helva returned Crispus' smile before bending to retrieve his emptied bag.

"I am not done with you yet, Helva. I have more questions." Agricola referred to the estimated number of inhabitants. "Why do you think the Taexali wedge is so sparsely populated?"

Helva did not even hesitate. "Much of the soil is marshy."

"The land is not profitable, then, because there is too much surface water?"

Helva nodded, though there was a wry tilt to his lips. "Yet contrarily, there is not enough drinkable water for high numbers of humans and domestic animals either."

"Is there evidence of bog-iron being used in metal work?" His question was a general one and put to all of his officers who had scoured the land.

The positive chorus was the most cheering aspect of the whole meeting.

"Well, at least we will have something to add to Rome's coffers!" His sarcasm was not really appreciated. His officers were never enthusiastic about ordering their men to engage in the more tedious work.

Agricola turned to one of the *tribunes* of the *Legio XX.* "Did you locate any *carbo* deposits like your units found in the territory of the Votadini, and the southernmost Venicones?"

The officer shook his head. "No, sir, my units saw no evidence of quarrying. Not *carbo* at ground level, and not stone either."

The habitable Taexali buildings they had encountered were all of wooden construction. Except for a few long-abandoned ceremonial enclosures, on some of the higher reaches, stone was not a material used for building in the area. The consensus amongst his knowledgeable officers was that the local granite must have been deemed too hard a stone for the local population to expend effort on. Some field strips were separated by low stone dykes but the undressed stone used for the walls had been gathered during the land clearance for farming and had never been quarried.

Agricola put more questions to all of his senior officers about the extent of the woodlands they had penetrated in their foray: the results of even that being disheartening. He stomped around mulling it over. If he was to overwinter men in this inhospitable north then he needed huge supplies of trees for fort building, timber for charcoal production, and wood for thousands of cooking fires and ovens.

Further questions on the availability of suitable trees were answered by Helva and the men of the *Legio XX*, though their answers were not exactly what he wanted to hear either. Good straight trunks of wood, of solid types that did not quickly deteriorate in the ground, were needed, but it did not sound as though enough could be extracted from the north-eastern wedge.

He addressed the Legate of the *Legio IX*. "What do we know of rivers in Vacomagi territory?"

Answers to that question were limited till reports came back from the *cohorts* that he had already dispatched to assist the fleet along the Vacomagi and Taexali coastline. Agricola stared down at his itinerary and sent a swift prayer to *Bellona* asking her to care for his *Legio IX*. The minimal new information given was added to the itinerary by Lentulus, while Crispus scribbled down more instructions.

Issuing duties for the next stages of the campaign came next.

"*Legio IX* – you task will be to subdue Vacomagi territory, supported by our Batavian *Cohorts* on land and assisted by our fleet beached in the area." The legate accepted the order with a nod.

"*Legio XX* – your task is to maintain control of Taexali territory." The senior *tribune*'s scowl was quickly replaced by a bland expression before he gave his acknowledgement.

The reaction was as Agricola expected, though it was still annoying. The troop numbers of the *Legio XX* were currently higher than those of the *Legio IX*, making it better suited to being used for front-line operations during the campaign. The *tribune* of the *Legio XX* was justifiably disenchanted, but presently Agricola had no intention of telling the officer that Emperor Domitian's commands would soon decimate the twentieth legion's roll call.

He did not, in the least, look forward to that conversation.

He broke off to allow those involved to absorb the orders, resolutely ignoring the qualms the recent correspondence from the emperor had given him. He was not ready to send *cohorts* from the *Legio XX* anywhere yet, except around Taexali territory. His grasping emperor would soon have news of their current deployment.

Agricola turned to the officers of the *Legio II Adiutrix*. "Your men will hem the Caledon allies into every mountain pass you can find. Where necessary, your *cohort*s will support the other *legions* from the Varar Aestuarium all the way south to the Venicones and Taexali borders."

Not a flicker of doubt crossed the countenances of the officers of the *Legio II Adiutrix,* even though they had lost men in the most recent skirmishes with the local rebels.

"All additional *vexillationes* will take commands directly from me." After a snatched look around the room, he was almost done.

He paused to let the instructions be absorbed, then added, "I want effective plans at dawn tomorrow after discussions with your *centurions*. Report back with assessments of where best to place your legion bases."

The legate of *Legio IX* raised an important issue. "Will we move into fortlet building as soon as possible?"

Agricola put his finger back onto the waxed boards. "We will make a temporary camp here by the River Caelis. From there two further temporary camps will be built at a day's march apart. By that time, the units already dispatched into Vacomagi territory will have assessed the best sites. The fleet already have orders to create two fortlets closer to the Varar

Aestuarium. If the coastal Vacomagi capitulate quickly, and agree treaties as expected, then a few resident *cohorts* will be sufficient to maintain order." He stopped to look around, sensing the mood had subtly altered now that plans had been voiced. "We will strike camp after our dawn meeting, tomorrow."

After issuing a few more general commands – about the order of exiting the present camp, and to the *tribune* in charge of the additional *vexillationes* about the number of men who would remain to guard the surrounding area – he dismissed everyone. Some of the auxiliary legionary *cohorts* were more than ready to move on though he knew others would bicker amongst themselves over who would be left in the area to ensure the vicinity remained subdued. They always did.

He stared at his itinerary. "Grumble, grumble."

"Sir?"

He realised his ruminations were being acknowledged by Flavus who was the only one left still hovering at the tent flap, like an unsuccessful carrion crow after the feast had been devoured.

Crispus and Lentulus knew better to ignore his musing, and had already retreated to the rear of his tent.

"I hope you learned from that meeting, Flavus?" Agricola could see the young man was startled to be asked, since he had been a silent observer for such a long time.

"I did, sir. It adds to what you have already told me."

"Good! I share with you for a very good reason. Now go away and absorb the implications of all that was discussed. Most of all, speak to the *Tribunus Angusticlavius* since he knows what his *vexillatio* is capable of, and to your *centurions*. Listen to all of them, since you lack a senior *tribune*. Your *centurions* have all the experience you will need to guide your next movements."

One glare was sufficient. He was confident he did not need any further words to warn Flavus about who would give the best advice.

A red-faced Flavus saluted and wheeled about, bumping into the tent door flap in his haste to get away.

Though he had felt the need to issue the orders, Agricola prayed that the bumbling idiot steered clear of *Centurion* Rubrius Mucius.

Once again, he went outside to pace about in front of his tent, his insides grumbling from lack of food and other inner more-bothersome sensations. Instinct nipped at him, insisting that the subjugation and control of all of the northern tribes had to be done without delay, regardless of the season. Yet, caution also sat on his shoulder. Marching into fresh territory appealed greatly, but starving his troops or getting them massacred could play no part.

"*Jupiter*'s balls! Those Caledon Mountains will be a bugger to control."

Chapter Nineteen

Baile Mheadhain, Taexali Territory

Enya strained to see what was happening. From her position, she knew where she expected Nith and Feargus to be as they crept nearer the top of the dune, a short distance from the ditch of the Roman camp. Below the encampment, the dark masts of Roman vessels were just visible, the almost-full moonlight twinkling clear across the water, her companions as close as they could get to count the vessels. A vague idea of how many were pulled up, higher than the mark of the tide, was not good enough. It was crucial that they sent back an accurate account to Brennus of Garrigill.

The excitement of the young lad who was crouched down alongside her, and also his terror, was evident in his slight fidgeting and erratic breathing.

She had encountered few locals during their last two days of trekking towards Baile Mheadhain. No Taexali dared live openly in the roundhouse villages that they had passed along their route, though she had seen more than enough dead ones. The emptiness of the habitation was eerily unnatural. The sight of the already-rotting, animal-nibbled Taexali, who had in some way defied the Roman Army, was a distressing memory that she knew would linger in her head for many moons to come. That there was no one left in the villages to honour those struck down with the rites to the otherworld, was a second thrust of the Roman *spatha*. From the slashing wounds on the mangled bodies, she guessed it was the longer swords that had been wielded freely on the poor Taexali victims – *spathae* that she had seen used by the Tungrian mounted forces during the confrontation at Beinn na Ciche.

As promised, Feargus had taken great care to avoid detection. When they had got closer to the Roman Camp at Moran Dhuirn, they used the earliest daybreak and the deepest dusk to cover some distance quickly across the valley floors and low rises to reach the machair. Once on the flat marshes of the machair, their progress had been extremely slow and cautious, the need to be constantly alert exhausting since bush cover was scarce. The sucking mire seemed to be everywhere. She hated slithering over the less-deadly squishy ground, elbow over knee, unable to even crouch since they could have easily been spotted had there been any Roman patrols anywhere near.

It had been a feeling of sheer relief when they had eventually reached the gentle slope on the far side of the machair, their route becoming one of rush and pause behind the low blaeberry and gorse bushes that dotted the hillside. During the endlessly long day, they had caught glimpses of Roman patrols a couple of times, but, thankfully, those had been at quite a distance. Her inner anger had made her want to confront them, and wipe her blade clean afterwards, but such yearnings were far from practical. They had instead curled up and bided their time, afterwards moving on when the area was clear.

They were almost at the coast before they encountered any living Taexali.

Those who had not fled west to the mountains, before and after the battle at Beinn na Ciche, were finding places to shelter that the marauding Roman patrols had been unable to detect. It was one such warrior who had made himself known, and had led her and her companions to some of his surviving kin.

The lad now alongside her was that warrior's son, his whisper at her ear increasingly panicked. "I no longer see Nith and Feargus crouching. Where are they?"

Enya wished she knew, because she had no sight of them either. "Stay calm, Donnachadh. We will spy them when they make a move."

"I fear some mishap, Enya. Should we go closer to check?"

She was up with spear at the ready before Donnachadh had finished talking. A black form was now visible, heading towards Nith and Feargus who had just begun to crest the dune. Praying to the goddess *Scathach* that she was in range, she hurled her spear at the third figure, the moon glinting off the soldier's helmet.

"Run!" Grabbing Donnachadh by the elbow, she propelled him into motion and scampered away from the Roman camp.

She did not stop for breath till she had covered two handfuls of dune crests. Flinging herself into a natural sandy hollow, she flopped back onto the soft bed, her chest heaving. Donnachadh was likewise crumpled alongside. There was still enough room for Nith and Feargus when they plopped in alongside them, their longer legs having covered the distance faster than she had.

The contentment she felt when Feargus heaved a huge breath alongside her was overshadowed by sheer exhilaration when Nith's open palm patted her leg.

Nith's raspy words were full of praise, though whispered low since sounds travel further in the night dark. "That was a throw very well done, Enya. You have my heartfelt gratitude." What she felt next was not a pat at her leg but a deliberate gentle rub, the kind a mother would make to assure that all was well with her child.

"A perfect hurl, indeed, but it is a pity she lost her one and only spear," Feargus sniggered in sheer relief at having escaped detection by the Roman patrols.

Enya's breath was still erratic after their hasty retreat, but the feelings that were coursing through her were causing her a different alarm, and a strange confusion.

Though it was too dark for them to see her grin, her laughter was evident when she replied. "Aye, Feargus, I have lost my favoured spear, but you can spare me one of yours since now you both know I can defend your backs, even in the dark of night."

There was a short lull while all recovered, then Enya spoke again. "If it was so perfect a throw, then you had an easy task in dispatching that guard?"

Nith reached over to squeeze her hand. "No need for our knives. Your spear went straight into his neck. No time for him to shout an alarm before he keeled over. It was the noise of his armour clattering against his pilum that roused our attention. Till then we had not realised that he was so close by."

Another gentle tapping to her hand she found soothing, yet even more disturbing, since all of her senses were on full alert.

Nith continued, "Why he was outside the ditch in the dark of night has to have been unusual, but whatever the reason it will not be long before he is missed. Before then, we need to a put a good distance between us and that camp."

Enya calmed her strange emotions and gathered breath for the next scamper.

"Donnachadh? Where do you suggest we go for shelter till the morn?" asked Nith.

Enya was pleased that Nith intended to use the local lad's knowledge, because her Selgovae friend could be stubbornly dismissive of help.

The boy was definite. "The Romans will trot the sands quickly if the sky remains clear of clouds and the moon full and shining-bright, as it is just now. They could easily reach the Abhainn Ythan in no time at all. Those Romans pace well."

"We know that from experience, Donnachadh, but the coastal plains, and the dunes, will surely slow them down?" Enya asked, propping up onto her elbows and then knees to peer over their hollow. Seeing no one approach, she let them know.

"Aye," he answered. "They will tramp less quickly over the dunes, but by daylight their best trackers will note our flattened grasses and know our route. Due north of here is the Foveran burn. They will track us to it, but if we pick our way up its waters, it will slow down their progress, and hopefully stop them following us further. My father and some of my kin intend to hide at the Fiodhais, and that is not so far from the burn of Foveran."

"Is this copse of trees on a hill?" Nith wanted to know.

"There is a slight rise there," Donnachadh's high-pitched chuckle was full of regret, "but there are no high hills nearby. Come morn's light, and if the day is still clear, we might be able to see if any ships leaving their base sail northwards."

"Should we wait till dawn to head to this spot?" Enya was exhausted, but being even more tired was preferable to being caught.

"Nay." The lad was firm. "We should move now. If any of the Romans head inland in the dark, they are likely to be caught in the tussocky grasses and the bogs that I know how to avoid. But we should not risk them coming after us."

"That seems a very good plan, lad."

Enya heard the praise in Nith's answer as he pushed to a sitting position.

"Lead us, then, though I do not believe they will send out any patrols till day dawns."

Donnachadh's youthful voice squeaked as he, too, sat up. "Did you get close enough to count the vessels?"

Feargus answered from his still prone position, sounding reluctant to move anywhere. "I counted nine of them, two larger but most of the rest of a fairly small size."

"Aye, that matches my tally." Before saying any more Nith popped up his head to view down the length of the beach. "I see no one coming this way. We should ready ourselves."

Stretching her length and wriggling hard to get rid of the kinks in her muscles, Enya yawned. She purposely shook her head quickly, her eyes tight shut. Sleep was too inclined to sneak upon her when she rested. "Was the moonlight sufficient to make an estimate of troop numbers?"

"I counted enough tents to shelter several *centuries*." Nith looked to Feargus for agreement with his assessment.

"It was hard to tell with the amount of horses tethered there. My guess would be that there is a whole *ala* of mounted auxiliaries."

"Aye, maybe so. That makes sense since they are patrolling a large stretch of sands." Nith agreed.

Enya noted the respect in Nith's voice at Feargus' estimation though could not prevent smirking. She knew too well how difficult Nith found it to be less than accurate about something.

Donnachadh piped up. "Every day since the battle at Beinn na Ciche we have watched mounted patrols ride in both directions along the sands, some going further north to monitor beyond the Abhainn Ythan. Our wide, flat sands are perfect for fast covering of the distances."

Nith was up on his feet, fisting his spears as he turned to Donnachadh. "Lead us now to your safety."

When Enya was standing, she accepted the spear Feargus passed over to her.

"It is as well that I carried two of them. I hope that you can use this weapon as well as your own one." His grin showed his confidence that she could do exactly that.

Enya grunted an acknowledgement. "Not before daylight. One throw was enough in the moonlight."

It seemed an age before she was sitting around the dying embers of a small fire, near the top of the Fiodhais. There was a natural dip on the northern side of the crest that was unable to be seen from Baile Mheadhain and the south.

"Welcome. Find yourselves a spot." Donnachadh's uncle was the one who had taken the lead role of those sheltering there, and was the one currently on guard. Most of the other people around the fireside were sleeping restlessly, shifting and shuddering at the least hint of noise.

It was hard for Enya to tell in the dimness around her, but the Taexali in hiding seemed precious few considering the amount of people who must have populated the local villages before the invasion of Agricola.

It took only a short, whispered conversation for Enya to find out that a number of captives, taken after the battle at Beinn na Ciche, had sailed off in the Roman ships. Unfortunately, Donnachadh's uncle had no knowledge of who the tribespeople might be. What he had seen from a distance indicated it was only a small selection of those who were fit enough, after the chained trek from the Roman camp at Moran Dhuirn. Sick, weakened prisoners had been executed on the sands, their corpses dragged free of the area where the vessels were beached. What she had not expected to hear was that some of those not thrust onto the ships were marched southwards by groups of auxiliary soldiers. Why that should be, she could not even begin to reason.

Their hushed voices were enough to waken the others around the fireside. One by one, they stretched legs and wriggled the kinks from their sore bones before sitting up, not willing to miss the news from strangers.

"You definitely know that those prisoners were marched to the sands from the many fisted camp at Moran Dhuirn?" Nith asked.

Donnachadh's uncle was convinced. "Aye. We had warriors watching that camp. They warned us of local people being driven like sheep to the shore, but there were too few of us to do anything about rescuing our wretched Celtic brothers and sisters. They were prodded and poked down the hillside that lies to the coastal side of the machair, three or four times as many soldiers around them as there were captives. Many of those small lines arrived, day by day, after the battle. And their ships sailed off one by one, their bellies full of tribesmen."

Feargus' voice was hushed, his gaze glazed over when she looked at him. "How many locals were sent away?"

Donnachadh's uncle stroked his whiskers. "Perhaps five, or maybe six, twenties of Roman soldiers manned the larger vessels, their oars poking out one above the other." When his friend nodded agreement he continued. "The bellies each of those held at least twenty of our tribespeople."

His friend added more. "And smaller ones carried off ten, or maybe as many as fifteen slaves."

Donnachadh's uncle agreed. "True, and those arriving and departing now are the flat bottomed ships, oared by fourteen or fifteen men, on each side. They sometimes carry horses."

"How many horses?" Enya asked.

The men looked to each other for guidance, doubt on many expressions, till one answered. "Five or six?"

Enya felt her eyebrows rise as she sought Nith's assessment of the amount. She had seen how many mounted

Tungrian*s* had been sent to crush her fellow warriors during the turmoil at Beinn na Ciche. "It would take at least five of those vessels to ferry a single *ala* northwards."

Nith's agreement was certain. "Aye, it would."

She watched him turn to Donnachadh's uncle. "Did your men see a lot of the smallest kind of ships beach at Baile Mheadhain before the battle?"

One of the warriors answered, clearly rattled by the events. "Those damned ships went back and forth all day long for two days before our clash with Agricola."

More information came from others around the low burning fire.

"For the last couple of days, they have disgorged packs of supplies that have been swarmed on by eager troops and carted off in a blink."

Another man finished off his tirade. "And they have filled them up with ten, and more, of our stolen people."

Enya felt Nith's gaze swing to her his expression questioning.

"I hate the thought of any of our fellow Celts being shipped off, but that is still not a large slave count. Perhaps Lorcan was wrong? Maybe fewer warriors than he guessed were taken as slaves after the conflict on the slopes of The Mither Tap?"

Donnachadh's uncle interrupted. "Nay! This Lorcan you speak of was not wrong. Though the ships took away only what they could cram in, I have had reports that the Romans have marched much longer lines of captives from the Moran Dhuirn camp. Many more have tramped southwards into Venicones territory."

Enya could see the frustration gathering over Nith's brows even in the dimness of the campfire. "Did any of your warriors get close enough to see how they chose those who would be thrust into the bellies of those vessels?"

The man shook his head. "The selection had already been made. By the time the lines reached the shore the only decision was about their fitness to survive a sea journey."

A short lull in the discussion sent Enya into a gloom of despair.

Feargus sounded just as doleful. "I had hoped coming here would give you more positive news of your brother and cousin, Enya, but it seems our trip was in vain."

She hastened to assure the Taexali lad whose own family information was even direr. Gently patting his arm that rested alongside, she waited till he made proper eye contact with her. "Thinking like that is unworthy, Feargus. Our trek has been valuable. All of this news is useful to send back to Ceann Druimin. It is all part of us knowing what Agricola might still do."

The coastal Taexali warriors continued to share all they knew of the ship movements, and the Roman activity at their Baile Mheadhain camp.

"Did the Roman *Classis* choose your Baile Mheadhain shores because your village was as large as the one at Obar Dheathain?" Nith asked.

"Nay, lad," one of the older warriors interrupted.

Enya grinned at Nith being termed as lad since her friend sometimes told her he already, at a little over twenty summers, carried a great age on his shoulders.

The elder sounded grouchy, but determined to play a part in the conversation. "Those Roman usurpers chose the beach at Baile Mheadhain days before the confrontation led by Calgach. Their ships had terrorised the villagers along our long coastline on many occasions since late summer. They have plenty more vessels beached to the south of Obar Dheathain in a perfect bay that shelters them from the summer storms. They give our Venicones brothers down there no peace."

Nith caught her gaze. "We already know of that shoreline bay from our trek north to Calgach's mustering point."

Enya had some questions of her own. "Can we talk about just before our confrontation with Agricola? What happened after the vessels arrived at Baile Mheadhain? Did the crews all remain on their ships?"

The guttural laugh was bitter, the man's face an image of disgust. "Some of them stayed aboard to guard the vessels, but most of the oarsmen stepped off fully-armoured and ready to do battle. On the eve before the combat, the bulk of them marched to Agricola's camp opposite Beinn na Ciche. We were also heading that way to join Calgach, and had to steer clear to avoid them catching sight of us. We had a miserably longer northwards-trek around the machair to reach the back of The Mither Tap."

The frustration and humiliation of the recent fight made further talk of the battle undesirable. Enya sensed that their Celtic resilience was re-emerging, but was careful with her words. "Did you all return to your roundhouse villages after the bloodshed?"

The mocking answer was much as she expected. "By the time we did, the Roman scourge had massacred anyone who had stayed here. Our possessions may still be in our houses, but their constant patrolling makes it impossible to inhabit them."

"Are these patrols made up from the troops of the fleet?"

"Nay. Agricola sends out large patrols from the Moran Dhuirn camp, but they are not the ones who sail the ships."

"Could Agricola have left so many of his troops at the Moran Dhuirn camp because they will still need to be ferried back by ship to southern Britannia?" Though Enya asked the question, it did not seem like a normal Roman strategy to her. "Or, could it be because they are sending special captives, taken after the battle, in a slow trickle to the sands at Baile Mheadhain, and those prisoners need a heavy guard in case there is an attack on the way?"

She could see that Nith only looked partly assured by that reasoning, his response full of head shakes. "The numbers of captives who sailed off would not need the amount of *cohorts* left at Moran Dhuirn."

Something niggled that had not yet been explained. Enya's question was put to all of those around her. "Did the Roman escorts of the prisoners return the way they had come?"

The warrior who answered shook his head. "Perhaps a few of those escorting soldiers went south in the ships, but so many of them are camped at Baile Mheadhain it is difficult for us to tell what happens to anyone – Roman or Celt – once they are behind the camp ramparts. Maybe a number of them have tramped southward, and we have not had news of that, yet? We have had no contact with the Taexali who dwelled south of Obar Dheathain. We fear that not many of them survived, if they returned to their homes."

Enya listened with dread as Nith updated their hosts on what they knew of Agricola's movements from Moran Dhuirn to his next camp at the Ythan Well.

She shivered violently all the while, as a desperate plea wordlessly escaped her lips. Her brother and her cousin were strong young men. If they had been taken by Agricola's forces, they would have survived a trek from Moran Dhuirn. Her insides lurched so restlessly she feared she might empty her stomach of its meagre contents. Her brother and her cousin must have survived, they must, but that would also mean they were lost to her family, if they had been captured. They could be taken to any of the slave markets of the empire.

"Have Taexali warriors of the sands to the north of Baile Mheadhain returned to their homes?" Fergal asked.

The answering words vaguely washed over Enya.

"Nay. None who dwell between Baile Mheadhain and the Abhainn Ythan would be so foolish." Donnachadh's uncle was dismissive. "The Romans patrol the whole coastline. I have heard of no regular beaching of boats north of Baile Mheadhain, but that does not mean they will not do so in the days to come."

Enya's mind drifted. As a young girl, she had watched line after line of Brigantes fleeing her home hillfort of Garrigill. For a short time, she was back in her own snaking line of utter dejection as her displaced kinfolk made their way north to the territory of the Selgovae. She remembered trekking for days, up the bleak and barren hills and down through the ferny valleys, to reach the hillfort at Tarras, the birthplace of her Aunt Nara.

Nith's nudge at her elbow made her realise she had missed some of the conversation.

"You definitely heard about these warriors?" Nith asked.

"Aye, but I have not set eyes on them."

Enya jolted to attention when Nith's hand clutched her own and gripped hard.

"Enya? Did you hear this man? Survivors of the battle have joined the warriors at Tap O'Noth. They are the ones monitoring the area closest to Moran Dhuirn."

She stirred the weariness from her heart, though it was not easy to banish it completely. "Forgive me. What did you hear?"

Lurching from despair that her brother and cousin might have been sent to southern slave markets, she felt elation that instead they might have ended up at Tap O'Noth. Could that have happened? The Tap O'Noth warriors who had visited Lulach at Ceann Druimin had mentioned a number of them watching the surrounding territory, but they had not said that some of those warriors were new to the area. Was that so unusual an omission? She thought not since Lulach's village was crawling with people who had not been brought up there. People like her clan.

The earlier thoughts returned. Her brother and cousin could not have died.

Her attention drifted again, her inner feelings fluctuating like the dips and rises of a summer swift in flight. The surge of excitement dissipated into a mass of exhausted worry.

She had to get to Tap O'Noth when daylight next came, to find out if Ruoridh and Beathan were there. But part of the arrangement with those back at Ceann Druimin was that she and Nith would monitor where Agricola's ships were along the coastline, and send back regular information. Feargus was also tasked with this, unless he decided to make his own arrangements. Lulach and her kin needed reliable updates, but did they need to be from her? Maybe Nith could stay near the coast, and she could go to Tap O'Noth on her own?

It was so hard to make decisions. Her eyes closed. Her shoulder slumped into Nith, her head dipping into his neck. The murmurs around her slipped into silence. The secure feeling of a strong arm snaking around to cuddle her close to a warm body made her feel protected. Her customary warrior alertness drifted away.

Chapter Twenty

Burn Field Roman Camp, Taexali Territory

"Monitoring the Caledon passes is more difficult than in Venicones territory, sir. Many of the lower hilltops are currently occupied by Taexali and Caledon warriors. They watch our movements; though show no signs of challenging us."

Agricola grunted. The man was stating the obvious, though at least the *tribune* of the *Legio II Adiutrix* spoke from experience. One local valley merged into the next one, with no distinct line edging the entry points into the Caledon mountains. He would only maintain good communication, if he took control of all of the peaks, and every low hill. He discussed plans for this with his *Legio II Adiutrix* senior officers.

It could be done, and had been done in other parts of Britannia, but not quickly and not without positioning a lot of isolated troops in potentially vulnerable situations, till all bases were secured. Frustration gnawed. Winter season or not, he had to ensure that the natives knew he held the upper hand – even if the control had to be handed over to someone else.

His answer was terse. "These natives need to be wedged in as firmly as the tightest *testudo*, from all directions, and at every high pass!"

When he swivelled round, his gaze fell on Flavus who looked compelled to answer, even though he would rather the gormless young man did not even try.

"How can we do that, sir?"

Though clearly rattled by his vehemence, he conceded that the junior officer had at least responded. There was some hope that Flavus would learn, eventually. Agricola was mildly surprised when Flavus took more initiative in the conversation.

"Can we not discount the southerly direction, sir, since we have control of all of the mountain entrances in Venicones territory?"

He could not resist a glower, and a quick prayer to *Jupiter*.

"Flavus!" He pointed to his itinerary that had been newly spread out on the central table, after his move to the present camp on the banks of the River Caelis. "Have you personal experience of our watchtowers and fortlets in the Venicones territory you speak of?" He knew full well that was not true, since Flavus had journeyed straight to Pinnata Castra from the *Legio II Adiutrix* base at Deva, many days' ride away.

"No. Only what you have told me, sir, but I thought they are all secured." The *tribune*'s tone was chastened, though marginally less frightened than of late.

Agricola pointed to his itinerary, outlining as he proceeded. "We monitor these Venicones eastern fringes of this huge swathe of mountains, but we do not control the interior. These peaks to the west pile in upon each other, and the valleys and passes are tight and snaking. It can take days to go from east to west even by the easiest routes. That I know from previous scout patrols." He stabbed at the numerous peaks. "Soon we will control the Taexali foothill passes, as we currently do in Venicones territory, but we are not in command of that interior – are we, *Tribune* Flavus?"

The pointed demand had Flavus flushing.

Agricola continued to rant. "We do not yet monitor, or control, the mountain accesses from Vacomagi territory, either. But we will, Flavus. We will!"

"Yes, sir."

He was glad of the *tribune*'s bare response. He had had enough talk. It was time to plan some more.

"Crispus! What is taking those Batavian scouts so long?" His bark had his secretary whip his head up to face him, but Crispus' expression was controlled, as was the deliberately slow answer when it came.

"I imagine the same as what delayed the Tungrians, sir."

Agricola grunted as he strode around again, Flavus almost tripping him up as the young man scurried free of the tent door flaps. Crispus' droll nature could be amusing; sometimes.

"Never ask Crispus a vague question, Flavus. The man will parry with twenty more while you await an answer to your first one."

His words made him remember exactly why Flavus was still dogging his heels. By all twelve of the *dei consentes*! He still had a skilled engineer to replace. More men had been scythed down by marauding Taexali tribesmen in the interim, yet there still was not a hint of a treaty signed yet with the Taexali, or the Caledons!

For some unfathomable reason it reminded him of news he had received from his wife, Domitia, about the Chatti in Germania who were already breaching the terms of their recent surrender to Emperor Domitian. She sent on gossip from Rome, though her news came to him via Londinium where he had intended to join her for the winter. With no formal capitulation of the northern tribes, even a short stay at the newly built governor's house was never going to happen.

He stamped his feet to get the blood flowing properly. The day was cold, but at least it was clear and crisp.

He missed Domitia's happy chatter…and a few other things besides.

The crushing of the revolt of the Chatti tribes, some twelve months past, had been overseen by the emperor, but it now appeared that those tribes were again staging minor insurrections. That news was not pleasing, not pleasing at all. Trouble elsewhere in the empire generally meant Domitian demanded more of his Britannic troops to mop up the mess, and left him to rummage up raw recruits from Britannic tribes that were not wholly trustworthy. He needed every single man of the four *legions* in Britannia that he had left under his present command, including all of his auxiliary *cohorts* and *vexillationes*, to carry out his Caledonian expansion plans.

He could not afford to have men slain by the tribal allies who still skulked in the mountains, like brooding wildcats.

Keeping composed was a sore trial, but he refused to let his staff detect any slip of his control when he turned attention back to the awaiting junior *tribune*. One look at Flavus' puppy expression changed his mind: other needs took priority.

"Wait here!" Striding off, he headed for the latrines acknowledging those who crossed his path. Not inclined to chatter overlong to the current occupants alongside him, when finished he hurried back realising he was starving. On re-entry to his tent, he bawled at Crispus to fetch him some food.

Flavus was next. "You lost eleven men not so long ago. Remind me of the incident." He had not forgotten the details, but wanted to see if Flavus had learned anything useful in the interim.

"Yes, sir. The patrol accompanied the Ligurian mineral expert who was assigned to the *Legio II Adiutrix*."

"Do you have another specialist now to replace Vibius Malleollus Ligustus?"

He watched the young man squirm, feeling little sympathy for his situation.

"No, sir."

"What of the *Legio XX*? Do they have a similar minerals expert?"

"I…I do not think so, sir."

"Did you seek one out after you reported to me?"

Now the *tribune* really was discomfited. Agitation and hesitation oozed from his skin. "No. I did not think of that."

"In future, investigate all possibilities before you report to me again about this kind of situation. If something untoward occurs, then you work out a way to compensate. You ask questions of anyone who can get you another expert. If that means communicating with our southern fortresses, then that is what you do. Do you understand me, Flavus? You have much to learn as a *tribune*."

Agricola realised that a talk to all of his troops must be fitted in soon; he could not afford to have them careless, slipshod and half-hearted. "Where did you believe that ambush would have happened? My best scouts are not usually so inept."

As expected, Titus Sicinia Flavus had only a vague answer for him.

Stomping to the groaning table at the back of his tent, he reined in his irritation. Scrolls tumbled around as he tossed and turned the pile hither and thither.

Crispus, hastened forward from his own corner desk to restore some order to the mess just created. "What can I help you with, General Agricola?"

"No need." He was in no mind to be held up. "I have it here, Crispus, but in future make sure this desk is kept orderly." The reprimand rankled even as he mouthed it. Every little thing about this campaign in the lands of the Caledons now infuriated.

Victorious. He should feel victorious, but that was far from how he actually felt in the aftermath of a battle that had no decisive end.

He strode to the torch now lighting up the centre table. Unrolling the selected scroll, he squinted at it, desperate to clarify just one thing, cursing his occasional forgetfulness. He turned back to *Tribune* Flavus tapping the re-rolled scroll between fist grip and his other palm. "What do you know of beyond the Varar Aestuarium?

"One of the tribes is believed to favour the god *Lugh*..." Flavus' answer tailed off with the arrival of someone at the tent flaps.

Agricola inwardly groaned when he saw who awaited his attention. The senior surgeon of the *Legio XX* was not known for his humour, yet an ingratiating smile displayed his large teeth.

"Please forgive the intrusion, General Agricola." Rubrius' expression was full of self-praise. "I thought you would be delighted to know that one of my slaves has located some large calvatia today."

"Indeed, Rubrius." He waited till the surgeon explained further.

"Not the largest ever seen, but sizeable. Our stocks of the puffball mushroom ran out a long while ago. They are one of my best ingredients for the staunching of blood."

Agricola's stomach rumbled again, very loudly. "And I am partial to the taste of any edible mushrooms, freshly sliced and cooked in whatever my cook makes to coat them. Are your finds edible, and are there enough to eat as well as store, Rubrius?"

"Well," the surgeon stuttered. "We did not gather all that many, sir, but they are edible and there will be some to spare for your...special digestive needs."

Agricola made sure his smile was appreciative. "You have my grateful thanks, Rubrius. Send them to my cook immediately." His tone altered appropriately for his next words. "I take it that you have eliminated whatever it was that caused the excrement of so many of my men to overflow the latrines in our camp at Durno?"

"The water was contaminated, sir."

"Yes, Rubrius. I guessed that. Tell me in *Jupiter*'s name how they were drinking water that was fouled enough to affect a quarter of my troops?"

Rubrius trotted slowly after him as he paced around the central table to ward off his hunger pangs.

"A decomposed sheep's stomach was found upstream of the area where the horses were watered, and the troops fetched drinking water."

He stopped short and faced Rubrius. The surgeon had been mending the *Legio XX* for more than a decade. The man was a pompous ass, at times, but he never normally doubted Rubrius' competence.

"Animals often fall into rivers and drown, but their carcasses do not cause hundreds of troops to fall prey to prolonged vomiting and vacation of their rear ends at the same time. Those men were weak as new born babes, and smelled a whole lot worse!"

Rubrius sounded calm but Agricola realised the man held back unleashed fury. "The animal gut had been filled with a mix of noxious herbs which poisoned the water."

"When did this sabotage happen?"

Rubrius shook his head. "I cannot say exactly. The herbs would have disintegrated to sludge after a day or so, and after that the contamination would have begun. We did not have many options for water retrieval around Durno, sir."

"Someone added the plants before fleeing to the Caledon hills, knowing that water supply would have to be used by us?"

Rubrius agreed it was possible. The *legions* were drawing water downstream from where the Caledonian allies had fled to after the battle. The *medicus* slunk away on his dismissal, a lot less cheerfully than he had come.

"Crispus!" he roared. "Get me the camp prefect!"

He vowed his men would never be vulnerable again.

"And Crispus!" he bawled to his secretary's retreating back. "He can wait here. I will be praying at the *aedes* for a short while."

His men had been neglected: he would not neglect the gods as well.

Striding round the *principia* area, he waved back his personal guards to their posts, informing them that no one was to disturb him in the sanctuary tent.

He had no desire to be in the presence of the likeness of Domitian in the shelter, but it was possible to get to the altar he wanted without laying eyes on the emperor, who seemed to be thwarting his every turn. Only a substantial offering to *Averruncus,* to avert further calamity, would appease. And perhaps more for the sake of his troops – a short propitiation to the *Lymphae* to ensure their water was always pure.

Chapter Twenty-One

Fiodhais, Taexali Territory

Enya peered at the two vessels out on *Morimaru*'s waters as dawn's first tinges surged into a blending of orangey-blues the following morning. The boats were close enough to the shoreline for her to see the tiny shapes of the oarsmen alternately pulling and resting. One large, and one of the smaller vessels were heading north. Unfortunately, her vantage point was not good enough to count how many vessels may have sailed south. No sails were visible on the endless stretch of water since the morn was utterly calm. Man power alone moved the ships that she could see.

"My pleas go to both *Morimaru* of the waters and to *Taranis* of the skies. Keep your breath still. Slow down the progress of the Romans. Make the usurpers exhaust themselves hauling on their oars to monitor our coastline." Enya heard her prayer echoed by those around her.

Donnachadh's kin stood within the watching group as Feargus' questions were answered.

The most senior warrior of the group was speaking. "We are not from your aunt's village near Baile Mheadhain, but it is unlikely she still lives. Well before Agricola forded the Abhainn Dhè with his *legions*, the coastal tribespeople felt his wrath."

Feargus was stricken, his words stilted. "Were there no warriors at all to aid them?"

The man hastened his explanation on seeing Feargus' appalled expression. "The attacks happened after the village warriors had gone off to join Calgach at Beinn na Ciche, leaving only elders and the young mothers with the smallest children. Those left were no match for battle-thirsty Romans. The few younger women who were still there felt a final sting of the *gladius* after their bodies had been repeatedly abused. And after the tribespeople were slaughtered, the roundhouses were set aflame."

Enya found it hard to ask any questions, the grief around her palpable, but she needed to know. "We heard that is what also happened at Obar Dheathain."

The man nodded. "Aye, but the ships and crews were different."

Enya watched Feargus' awkward swallows before his question came. "Did they take any of the coastal Taexali as slaves and send them off in the ships?"

The man shook his head, his tone angered. "Their frenzy was so heightened on landing that we fear none of those local to Baile Mheadhain survived. If any did, we have seen no sight of them."

One of the others added more. "What he says is true about the Taexali of Baile Mheadhain and Obar Dheathain but after the confrontation at Beinn na Ciche, we watched lines of prisoners being marched along the sands into their encampment at Baile Mheadhain."

The first warrior spoke again. "But they did not come from the battlegrounds. They were survivors of raids on coastal villages to the north of here. Files of those captives arrived for days after the battle. They came near dusk and sailed off after dawn."

"By which time, they were piled onto the ships?" Feargus wanted to learn everything the men could tell him.

"Each ship that sailed off had a line of prisoners squeezed in between the oarsmen, though none seemed compelled to man the oars."

Nith intervened. "Rome only allows its own mariners to power their ships. That way they can ensure the handling of the vessel is good on the water. The Roman oarsmen are controlled by their…" His words faltered for a moment. "Men like the *centurions* who command a part of an infantry legion."

"Lorcan calls them *centurions* as well."

Enya felt Nith's smile fall on her. "Does he? Then perhaps the name I forget is for the one who is in charge of the *centurion*."

His light green eyes twinkled, teasing for sure as she responded. "*Gubernator* or *trierarchus*? Which have you forgotten?"

A peal of his laughter rang forth. It gave her such a happy feeling. It was so long since she had shared true mirth with him.

"I had forgotten both of those names. You remember as well as your spear flies." Nith smiled again before turning away to speak to their company.

She basked in his praise as Nith thanked the men for the information given to them, and for the shelter of the previous night, adding his wishes that they remain safe and able to continue their observations. "You will make it easier for me to fulfil my task about spreading word of Roman movements to our fellow Celts in places of safety." His low rumble of laughter exposed the normally-hidden lighter side of his nature. "Though, I do not know where to base myself along your coastline for best advantage."

"You have no need to remain here, Nith. We have sufficient men in hiding near our coast to continue our watch. We will gladly organise links to send regular word across our familiar Taexali territory, and on further to Lulach at Ceann Druimin. Anything that will rid us of this Roman dominance will be done while we still draw breath." Donnachadh's uncle was adamant about that as he named a number of places that he knew warriors kept a watch from.

With the promise of new information being relayed regularly back to Brennus, via a series of messengers from the Fiodhais, the feelings that came to Enya were as unsettling as they were welcome. Nith did not need to stay, which meant he would be free to dog her heels again. She would miss him if he was not with her, but she was not at all sure she wanted him to be her only companion when she journeyed on. The excitement she now felt at being alone with him was too confusing. Her feelings for Nith were deepening in a way that no longer seemed brotherly. She trusted Nith with her life, but she was not so sure she could now trust herself to focus only on finding her brother.

Desperate to be on her way, she bid the tribespeople farewell.

"We can guide you for part of your journey back to Caledon territory to get you past the machair more quickly."

The local warrior's offer was kind but she made a polite rejection. "Nay. I am heading to Tap O'Noth."

She looked towards Feargus. "Thank you for bringing me here safely, Feargus. If you do not find any of your kin alive, know that my Garrigill kin will welcome you as one of their own."

The initial look on Feargus face was a mixture of embarrassment and surprise but it was quickly followed by one of wry humour, the twitch at the corner of his lip almost a smile. "It seems I will find no encouraging answers here, Enya, so I may take up your offer sooner than you expect me to."

Turning her attention to Nith, her tongue snaked out to wet very dry lips. Though it was painful, she made sure to fully confront him. "I cannot stay here, Nith, when there is a chance that I may find my brother and cousin. But I will share what I find at Tap O'Noth with you as soon as I am able."

The intensity of his silent gaze was too much. Feeling her courage deserting her, she strode off in the direction she hoped would lead to her destination. A few steps were all she managed before Nith clutched at her cloak.

"Enya. Not so hasty."

Unable to move forward without shrugging him off, she reluctantly turned her chin round to listen, determined that she would not go back to Ceann Druimin no matter what he said. She knew how well Nith could mask his feelings in bland expressions yet when his words tumbled out, they came much more quickly than they usually would.

"What will you gain from going to Tap O'Noth first? Are we not better to do what we set out to do for our kin back at

Ceann Druimin? We agreed to pass on what the Romans do on the shoreline. There is much more of the coast to the north that these good people of the Fiodhais cannot monitor, as well as their own areas."

She stared at him. Perhaps he was not as controlled as he wanted her to believe? The intensity of his gaze displayed some form of desperation, as did the punishing grip on her bratt.

Enya was torn. She wanted to find out what the devious Romans were doing on the whole Taexali coastline but finding her missing brother and cousin had to come first. "While Agricola's soldiers patrol the sands, I could help you relay word of their movements for many moons to come. However, that will establish nothing of the fate of my brother and cousin. We have just heard that Tap O'Noth is a place where warriors have congregated. If I go there first, I can find out what they know of survivors. Either they will have news of my kin which I will follow up, or they will not, in which case I will return to Ceann Druimin. While I am gone, you can establish the messenger chain north of here." From the flash at Nith's eyes, she could see he acknowledged the possibility yet he remained unconvinced. She continued to reassure him. "Donnachadh's kin will keep the lines of communication open between here and Ceann Druimin. They do not need me clipping their heels!"

Gently pulling the material of her cloak, he brought her nose to nose. "Enya. Where you clip, I will also clip."

She could see from Nith's flash of wit that what she had left out of her jibe had not gone amiss. His teasing warm breath was a tickle at her neck, a contrast to the seriousness of his gaze.

"Then Tap O'Noth it will be," he said. "But after that, our duty is to send back news from the Taexali coast to the many survivors in the Caledon hills."

Donnachadh's uncle had listened to the exchange, his words urgent enough to break Enya's absorption of Nith's expression. "I have sufficient men to send a few of my best warriors north of Abhainn Ythan, to find any Taexali who are in hiding up there. They can be trusted to extend our chain of contacts. Ceann Druimin will hear of everything we learn."

That proposal met with Nith's approval, and also of Feargus since he had no wish to linger in the vicinity where his kin had perished. To make sure that Donnachadh's uncle could employ all his warriors for the task of communication, Enya agreed when Nith refused the offer of an escort. The instructions they were given for covering the ground, she was sure, would be just as good.

This time she was truly glad when Feargus asked to go with her to Tap O'Noth, not wanting to think of him being totally alone and abandoned at Baile Mheadhain. He was good company. He was teaching her about his Taexali territory, but mostly she was glad he was accompanying her because she would not be alone with Nith.

Though looking at Feargus' happy grin, her feelings for him were just as puzzling. She was coming to like him very well. The role of a warrior was much simpler than that of a woman.

The trail to Tap O'Noth was as perilous as the route had been from Ceann Druimin to the coast. Each day, Agricola's patrols scoured the countryside in all directions around his former camps at Moran Dhuirn and at the Well of Ythan – which meant long detours. Evading detection by the Roman units became a never ending chore during days that were short in daylight with fluctuating weather conditions, as they headed north-west. Sometimes, it was neither snow nor sleet that fell but a chilling persistent-rain. At other times, it was miserable, murky cloud and haar that dampened Enya's spirits, as well as her clothes. Finding a place to shelter for the night was a problem she did not care to dwell on each coming dusk, till absolutely necessary.

Desperate to end their long trek as daylight faded, Enya was more than grateful when Feargus, leading their small band, halted their progress in the small valley they had just made their way down into. Though no rain had fallen that afternoon, it was a brisk chittering-wind that dulled her senses.

"This should do as well as any other for the night." Feargus thrust his spear down to the ground and pulled off the pouches that were slung across his chest.

Nith looked around at their location. Being in a small valley was not easy to defend, but he was fairly sure that no Roman patrols would come their way now. "I think we can risk a fire tonight." He pulled out his sling. "I'll see if I can get something to feed us."

Enya was sure he would but an anxiety overtook her that was powerful, more than reason dictated. She stretched forward to touch his arm. "Be careful, Nith. Though we have seen no soldiers this last little while does not mean that none are wending their way back to their camp."

Nith's arms enfolding her in a swift and tight hug was unexpected, as were his fingers lightly massaging her back before he released her. After a lingering look that she found difficult to comprehend, he went off to hunt. So many of his stares and gestures were not how they used to be, but she had no time to dwell on whether or not he thought she was confusing, as well.

"Help me over here, Enya?" Feargus' request jolted her back to their present situation.

The partially burned-out roundhouse Feargus had chosen was similar to others they had encountered on their trek. The Romans had no doubt set a torch to it recently but *Taranis* of the skies had seen fit to put out the blaze before the whole dwelling had been consumed. One part of the house still had lower walls, the wattling damaged yet still upright. The roof had fallen in but it was better than the other three in the cluster which really were blackened stunted-remnants.

Feargus pulled and hauled at usable roof beams that showed evidence of burning though had not charred to disintegration. Enya helped to drag them over to the sound part of the wall where they leaned them close together from floor to the top of the low wall, creating a crawl space for them to shelter under overnight. Leaving one end open, Feargus used shorter bits of wood to block off the other end, an attempt to keep out the wind. Knowing heavy rain would pour in between the gaps, Enya set off to look for packing materials around the area.

By the time she returned with damp mosses and brackens to pack the spaces, Feargus had supplies laid out for making a fire. Some partially dry leaves and seed heads lay beside a pile of thin twigs. She doubted he would be able to light them since everything around was sodden but she was proved wrong when sheer persistence with two flat stones and a stringy plant strand eventually brought forth some sparks. Rolling and rolling to heat up the strand, he eventually bent the thin rod till it almost snapped and gently blew on it to encourage a spark. When satisfied it was hot enough, he set the fibrous stick amongst a bundle of the driest seed heads in his pile. Kneeling with his nose almost to the ground, time after time, he blew patiently. Smoke billowed up and around choking him and Enya, as well, till the smoke burst into the tiniest flare.

Stalk after stalk, and twig after twig, was added till a good little fire was burning well, still a very smoky fire but enough to lighten up the growing dim. Feargus' wide grin and whoop was compelling. She could not help but return his glee.

"Pay heed!" she cried. "Or it will go out again."

"If it does, then I will light another."

Feargus had already been designated the fire-maker since he was more skilled than she was. Nith was good, but Feargus created fire much quicker than anyone she knew of, the flat stones he carried in his pouch something he was proud of. She knew by now that he also carried a small stock of plant strands which he regularly replenished as they journeyed through woods and moorland.

The fire was set just at the end of their shelter, not the best place to avoid smoke from wafting back into the crawl space but it was the best situation given their circumstances. Since Feargus was in charge of keeping the fire going, she set off to search the area for anything useful that had survived the Roman raid.

In the furthest-off roundhouse, she scoured around. Shoving charred bits of roof beams aside, the dull clunk of metal was encouraging. Peeling away more of the charred timbers, a tarnished-hue was a thrilling glimmer, but extracting it from the debris became a heartbreaking task. The burned remains of a young child lay under the pot.

Had the child, not much more than a baby, been thrown onto the fire by a Roman soldier? The thought appalled!

Enya turned aside, the contents of her stomach emptying onto the blackened mess below her feet. She had seen fresh blood being shed, had created some of that blood-letting herself with her own weapons, but this was vastly different. The child's kin would never have used their life-giving hearth to send it to the otherworld. She was sure of that, but how did the babe come to be on the roundhouse fire?

Putting aside the battered pot, Enya prayed to the goddess *Brighid* whose hearth had been violated, and muttered fervently her hope that the child had passed over safely to the otherworld. Further raking around proved a waste of time, there was nothing else that could be used.

When she returned with the rinsed-out pot full of water from the nearby burn, she was relieved to see that Feargus' fire was blazing better than before: crackling and sparking but well lit. He had already found strong branches for spitting the pair of grouse that Nith was gutting, his knife flashing in a curved arc to clean out the birds, the feathers having been plucked and set near the fire to dry off.

"Do you still have some dried oats, Nith?" she asked, sure that they had not yet used the small supply they had been given by Donnachadh's uncle.

Their fare that night was better than the previous one. It did not matter that the charred grouse flesh was still half raw in the inside, or that the oatmeal was a thin brochan.

"Aww!"

Nith's grunt of pain halted her chew of her piece of grouse meat.

"Are your wounds bothering you again," she asked, after swallowing over her mouthful.

Nith delved into his mouth and produced a tiny bone. "Nay. Just this. My hunger was greater than my caution."

Feargus guffawed. "Then you will not want any more of this?" He held up the half stripped cooked grouse.

A moment or two of happy banter followed which brought gladness to Enya's heart. Both men were the best company she could ever have.

While the thin brose cooled, they made plans, and when it was able to be drunk from the pot, they each took a turn to sip from it. The warmth in her belly was comforting, even if she could have eaten more.

When drizzly rain began to fall Feargus' fire guttered to a smoky sizzle, their illumination gone. There was no point in staying awake.

Snuggled between the two men in their cramped and makeshift shelter Enya could not sleep even though it had retained some heat from the fire. Facing Nith's back it was tempting to wrap her arm around his middle and burrow against him, to share his heat, but the time had passed for that kind of sisterly comfort. Moving slightly backwards into the cradle of Feargus' body was not yet something she was ready for either. Her mother's recent words came back to her. Coupling with a man to beget a child of her own was something to think about after she had found her brother, not yet, though she had to come to terms with the fact that her body was stirring in some deeply disturbing ways.

The tiniest of smiles curved her lips. Her Aunt Nara had told her that it was pleasurable to lie with a man whether or not a child resulted from the coupling. But she had also encountered many women who seemed dissatisfied with their hearth-warrior. Not every choice of mate meant lasting contentment like that shared by Nara and Lorcan. She knew her mother and father had a deep affection for each other, but she was not convinced their bond was as strong.

Soft snores from behind meant that Feargus would be rested come the morrow. Nith she was not sure of. His breathing was controlled and low, but his body seemed unnaturally stretched next to her.

Her head was too full of everything to slip into sleep. Thoughts of the dead child intruded, though she tried to banish them. When the children of her ancestors died, their remains had been set out for nature to wear down, the bones afterwards collected and put in to join other loved ones in the stone long barrows. Her own immediate clan dealt with the passing of their loved ones differently.

The Garrigill clan had been lucky. Her mother, Fionnah, had only lost one young child to the harsh breathing sickness. Enya's memories of her younger sister were so vague, the baby being only a summer younger than she had been. She had not even reached four summer seasons when her sister had taken ill at Imbolc. The cough had gradually got worse and by Beltane the child had ceased to breathe. A waking dream came to Enya of her mother's heartbreaking grief for the lost daughter. They had set out her sister on a small pyre at the hillfort of Garrigill and had invoked the full rites for her passage to the otherworld, where all would be happy for her.

Nara. She remembered that Aunt Nara had conducted the rites since their druid was rarely seen, hounded into obscurity as most of his kind were by the Roman scourge.

Images of the bodies she had encountered on this trek with Nith and Feargus kept her awake even longer. Those tribespeople still lay where they had been slaughtered.

The *Ceigean Ròmanach* had ruined so many of the normal traditions of her clan. And Agricola was still ruining them. All thoughts of men, coupling, and children fled.

They were replaced with a despairing vengeance.

Chapter Twenty-Two

Votadini Territory

Come the new dawn, Beathan wished he was back on the ship going to unknown destinations. The instructions issued to his new set of captors were clear enough. He understood where his slave line was headed, on foot.

Corstopitum.

Brennus and Ineda had told him about the large supply fortress in southern Votadini territory. He stared ahead. It was going to be a long march. The physical trudge south did not daunt him nearly as much as the fact that he remembered his father, Lorcan, telling him never to trust the Votadini. A flash of camp-fire talk made him picture Brennus' hearth-woman Ineda as she spoke of her ordeal whilst a slave of a Roman *tribune* of the *Legio XX*. She claimed she would rather die than trust the Votadini.

During his family's trek northwards to Taexali territory they had avoided being in Votadini lands, so he had no prior knowledge of the route he was currently being forced to go along. Reasons he remembered for distrusting the Votadini were that his Aunt Nara's Selgovae tribe had always been territorial enemies of the Votadini.

But the more salutary one was that his wily Selgovae grandfather, Callan, had been sure that the Votadini were surreptitiously making treaties with the Roman Empire. Something they keep hidden from their nearest Celtic neighbours.

Beathan soon found that one method of transport was no worse than another. Sick to the innards on the open sea water was just as dreadful as the relentless tedious march. Food was scarce and watering only done when a water source was nearby, many of the slave-line almost collapsing by then.

"I vow anew to kill the Roman scum who drag us to some unknown place, if I ever have the strength and am free of these cursed shackles," Derwi groaned from behind.

Derwi was still chained to Beathan but the man in front was different, the line being a few shorter since they had begun the trek from the Roman ship.

"Where can they be hauling us to?"

Beathan did not think Derwi expected an answer, yet he gave him one. "Corstopitum."

"And where would that be?" Derwi's disgusted response showed he had no knowledge of the place.

Though talking drained him, there was no Roman guard near them. Beathan was pleased to be able to tell Derwi what he knew of their destination.

All around him, day after day of the long tramp, there was physical evidence of Roman influence. The stone roadway under his tattered foot-bindings was an unyielding one. The wooden forts and guard towers spattered regularly along its route were unmistakable as were the soldiers guarding the installations. Unlike Taexali territory, the Votadini had embraced Roman domination. From what he could see of the locals they passed by, they were either happy to be subsumed or were bearing their grudges in deep-secret. The route they travelled was a busy one with non-military use of the land nearby.

Though he made no mention of it to his fellow-captives, except Derwi, he was glad that his father had taught him some Latin.

His slave line was frequently halted and forced off the camber edging of the stones to allow other traffic to pass by. Swift horses would thunder past, the legionary messenger's horse burdened by both soldier and laden bags of correspondence. Scroll tops sometimes poked out of the leather ties, the satchels so stuffed-full.

Laden wagons also passed by – sometimes heading south – but the most heavily-burdened ones were going northwards.

Often these were guarded by a small patrol, a half-century or less. Others had only a *contubernium* group clustered around them.

When these temporary halts occurred, Beathan strained to see what filled the wagons and carts. Timbers were easy to spot since these tended to be on low vehicles with the burdens open to the elements. Driven by legionaries urging the mules to keep a steady pace, they were rarely accompanied by more than a couple of soldiers on foot. Sometimes he saw higher-sided carts hauling black rocks, but he had no idea what those shiny shipments were. The cloth covers on others could not hide the shapes of the Roman jars he knew were called amphorae and which held wine and oil. Plenty of them were going northwards, those carts strongly-smelling of herbs and fragrances he could not put a name to. Their food use only served to make his empty-innards growl even louder. During his time at the hillfort of Tarras, his grandfather, Callan, had been so proud of himself when he had made raids on Roman transport which resulted in such spoils.

He knew from Brennus that the heavily-guarded wagons would be carrying the most precious consignments of raw metals, replacements of soldier equipment and perhaps even the coin that the soldiers were paid. Though his father, Lorcan, had said that the legionaries and auxiliaries of the Roman Army had to wait a long time to receive their dues from the Roman Empire's coffers.

"Move over!"

Yet again, the bawl came for the slave line to shuffle off the edge of the road onto the slippery mud that bordered the stones. To hurry the process, the auxiliary guards at the front whirled around and flicked their whips against the stones creating resounding cracks and sparks and not caring when the whip tips ricocheted to sting those who were too slow in their side-stepping. No longer needing to peer to see over the heads of fellow prisoners, Beathan watched the approach of a number of low wagons trundling quickly over the middle of the stone surface, each one stacked high with sacks. The considerable auxiliary escort flanking along both sides of the vehicles gave him an idea that the goods were important and probably in high demand.

As the convoy passed his captive-column, the orderly formation of the Roman army descended into chaos. The driver of the second wagon howled a warning when the vehicle made a sudden lurch to its right side, one wheel having sheered off from the shaft. Rolling into the legs of the nearest horse, the ensuing panic made the rider lose his grip on the rearing beast. The soldier's sidelong plunge crashed him into the slaves at the front of the line. The mules were all yanked to a halt, but it was too late to avoid the beasts that pulled the third vehicle from crashing into the disabled wagon, which had slumped towards the camber of the road. The impact forced the wrecked vehicle to shunt off the road completely and into the slave line.

The resulting shriek of horses and mules was in competition with horrendous human-squealing, and Beathan could do nothing to prevent the onslaught of filled sacks from pounding him into the ground.

Half buried by sacks of grain, he took stock of himself. He could move his feet. One arm was flattened and stretched out more than the other but he was able to wiggle his hands and fingers. A sack covered his head, almost suffocating him, but he was sure there was no lasting damage. Groping with one hand, he jostled aside a sack to free his arm so that he could thrust off the one coving his head. The chain linking him to the man in front only gave him a little leverage, but it was enough to dislodge himself and turn onto his side.

His wish then was that he had stayed flat. The sightless eyes of his neighbour stared up at him, the man's chest and groin area impaled by jagged timbers of the shattered wagon bed and spear tips from Roman *pila*.

"Derwi!"

Beathan shoved off more sacks from his legs, and made enough room for him to sit up, his groans now over the new bruising that made its presence felt all over him, though his complaints made no impact on the horrendous noise around him. Howls of agony were in competition with the bellowing of the guards, some of them attempting to bring the braying mules and squealing horses to order, others issuing commands to the captives who were unhurt to stand at peace. His belly ached when he leaned forward to check his legs and feet, but he was convinced nothing was badly hurt inside him.

He looked around at the devastation caused by the runaway wagon. On the far side of the dead neighbour, who had been in front of him, a captive groaned, praying to a god who was not responding. One leg was a mangled mess with so much spouting blood it was difficult to tell if the man had other injuries.

He steeled himself to look to his other side, the side where his normally talkative friend Derwi lay immobile. A clay amphora of wine lay shattered all over him, shards piercing the skin around Derwi's forehead, his head having taken the impact. It was impossible to tell how much blood had been lost, the colour of it mingling with that of the red wine. The reek of the vinegary-wine around was only surpassed by the smell of fresh blood and the emptied innards that came from more than the dead man next to him.

With one arm still shackled to his unfortunate neighbour it was difficult to shunt close enough but, by over-stretching his arm almost out of its natural place, he managed to clear some of the pieces from Derwi's face. As he awkwardly moved his palm across Derwi's mouth to clear off the wine and bits of broken clay, he felt a whiff of breath.

Relief flooded him. He prayed to *Aarfen*. She had seen fit to spare him and his friend. Or perhaps it was still the goddess *Rhianna* who saw to his welfare? No matter. He sent prayers of gratitude to as many gods and goddesses as he could squeeze in, thanking them in advance for Derwi's recovery as well.

Working himself up onto his knees, he looked at the Roman guards up on the roadway in front of him. Two of them pulled away one of the uncoupled mules, the terrified creature resisting being moved. He looked down the road to where all of the other animals were being tethered, just beyond the front of the slave line.

Another auxiliary led the equestrian who had tumbled off his horse, the senior soldier looking dazed but only limping from probably no more than a broken foot.

"Get up!"

He turned around to see if he was the one who was being spoken to.

He knew he was when the soldier scrambled off the camber of the road wielding a large iron tool. Beathan was thankful that he had seen a similar implement used to open the slave shackles, otherwise he might have been terrified of the result. The man spoke in guttural tones, but it was similar to the language of the tribes.

"Hold out your wrists."

He stared at the soldier and the predicament he was in. Standing was only possible when he was almost bent double since those to either side were prostrate. Thinking the soldier stupid, he realised after the first thump to his jaw of the iron tool that being bent over made him more vulnerable. Not so foolish after all. Before the auxiliary had broken apart the second shackle, another soldier was there to grab him by the shoulder to yank him away.

Beathan looked around him wondering if *Aarfen* would favour him in an escape attempt. Unfortunately, it looked as though only the cavalry officer had been injured, which meant the area was teeming with Roman guards when those of the convoy of wagons were added to those marching the slave line. To both sides of the roadway lay flat uncultivated scrubland: barely any shelter and it was probably too boggy in places to risk running into.

After much shouting, swearing and threats, the dead and the severely injured were uncoupled. Beathan found himself seated in the middle of the road in a huddle of unhurt captives, the ring guarded all around by auxiliaries with drawn swords. He watched as his dead neighbour was tossed further into the shrubs near the edge of the road. A sword to the guts had finished off the warrior with the spouting-wound, though Beathan thought that was perhaps a favour since the man was unlikely to survive such a loss of blood. Of Derwi he was not sure. When he had been forced along the road into his present huddle, a couple of soldiers had been bent over Derwi. Now his friend was nowhere to be seen. He barely knew Derwi, but he felt they had bonded-well in such a short time.

He could do nothing while the Roman soldiers cleared the road, the remains of the broken wagon swiftly bundled to the side. Unbroken amphora were collected and piled upon the sound wagons, along with the sacks that had covered him, making their stacks of goods even higher. Using the captives to help with the clearance would have completed the task more quickly, but Beathan could see that posed too many dangers. Neither he nor his fellow future-slaves were going to escape easily.

It was almost dark when Beathan noticed the flares of torches in the distance. He had been forced to the front of the line after the incident, and made to keep pace with a guard on either side of him. His feet were free of shackles. Only his left wrist was chain-bound to the captive behind him and, thankfully, any oncoming traffic was met without the earlier drama. He found it strange to be at the front of the file, not liberating but curiously empowering as he struggled up low hills and down into narrow densely-wooded valleys. It was easier to imagine he was the fearless warrior leading his people to war in order to achieve freedom, leading his people to a life liberated from Roman domination.

That was a much better prospect than the reality of his situation.

He doubted the fort he was approaching was Corstopitum: did not think he had been shuffling long enough for that. He had no idea where he was, but the shadow of three hills, over where the god *Lugh*'s warmth had sunk right down, were memorable in the otherwise flat terrain

Chapter Twenty-Three

Tap O'Noth, Taexali Territory

Enya was in front, picking her way from bush-to-bush across flat marshy-ground, when she became aware of a shadow in the distance. Her warning crossbill 'choop…choop' sounded strident, even to her, in the relative quiet of the dull day.

The answering bird calls indicated Nith and Feargus awaited her updates.

Slipping down to her haunches she waited, her breath held still.

Nothing moved.

She felt the surge inside, though contained the tendency to be afraid.

After a long pause, Nith's slide in alongside startled her, since she had not called an all-clear. His body tucked in tight to share the small space behind the young blackthorn.

"What do you fear, Enya?"

She had been so focused on what was in front that she had not paid sufficient attention to her rear.

"What do you see?" Nith's repeated whisper at her ear calmed her breathing. But it was only brief. His arm moving across her shoulders set her insides churning once more, though differently.

"There was a shadow over by that standing stone." She half-turned in his arms and faced his concerned gaze. "Perhaps I am too tired. Maybe it was an animal, or just that dusk is closing in…"

His head shook, though his penetrating gaze reassured, his eyes turning from inquisitive to a warm glow. His encouraging smile warmed her just as much as his fingers caressing her shoulder. "Your instincts are sharp, Enya. You would not be leading us if I thought otherwise."

The squeeze of his curled palm and swift peck at her cheek were unmistakable before Nith slipped away and crept forward to the next bush. Before he even got near the monolith a spear whipped through the air, landing just short of his foot.

Enya gasped on its thudding to earth but immediately relief flooded her insides. A Roman soldier would not have aimed at Nith's feet.

"Go no further!" The cry came from an unseen warrior.

"We seek the warriors of Tap O'Noth," Nith answered.

A short but strenuous climb up to the ancient hillfort on the Hill O'Noth followed the simple welcome from the warrior, once he was told of their need to speak to the leader. Though the granite wall was partially tumbled-down, the enclosure still provided protection for those who sheltered there. Following her guide through the unfenced gateway, she could see a few small roundhouses had been hastily repaired. The original thatching and proper roof struts were long gone, but some of the side walls were still sufficiently upright for a temporary-hide covering to be draped over. They were sleeping quarters and nothing more, since there would not be room for standing to full height inside them.

At the centre of the large enclosed space was a roaring fire, the wood burning bright in the almost-dark that now surrounded them. She thought it such an unexpectedly welcome sight as she paid attention to the people clustered around it.

There were more warriors than Enya had imagined: a good number of men and a scattering of females who had tasked themselves with monitoring the Roman movements of the surrounding area. Her gaze lingered on them all but none were her brother, or her cousin. Swallowing the huge lump of disappointment, she accepted the hospitality offered and sat down next to Nith and Feargus, all of them bid to sit alongside a brawny warrior named Gilie, the leader of the group.

She learned that the men sent to Lulach at Ceann Druimin had not yet returned, but that was of no concern at Tap

O'Noth. The task of those messengers was to ensure warriors would be monitoring all of the mountain passes near the Taexali and Vacomagi borders. Gilie told her that such a quest would take them to many Caledon villages along the mountain fringes, not just to Lulach, and their return was not expected for many nights.

While she greedily supped the last of a very welcome bowl of barley-broth that she had been given, Nith made polite inquiries. "Your Tap O'Noth warriors told Lulach about your successful ambush some days past."

Gilie nodded while he finished gnawing off the meat from a roe-deer bone, his portion having been dished out to him before anyone else. After tossing the remains into the well-burning fire, he wiped the juices from his glistening lips with the back of his powerful fist. "Aye, and we will do the same again, if we get the opportunity. We aim to prevent those invaders from marching into Caledon territory, and will kill every last one of them."

Enya accepted a venison rib-bone thickly encrusted with partly-charred meat from the wooden platter offered to her, the warrior circling the fireside to ensure all got a share. She asked a question of her own. "We heard that one of that Roman patrol escaped. Do you think he made it back to the Roman camp at Moran Dhuirn?"

"Nay, he did not survive." A rumbling guffaw followed Gilie's answer. "His well-chewed remains were found the following morning."

Enya could not hide her pleasure. "Was it a just retribution from the *Cailleach Bheur*?" Her words tumbled out before she considered they might offend the local goddess, or even the local worshippers of the deity.

Gilie looked horrified, the mention of the old blue hag not a welcome one. "There were signs of wildcats around the corpse, but I would not recognise those of the *Cailleach Bheur*."

Another answered. "Neither would I, and I would not want to. I care only that the *Cailleach Bheur* favours us over our Roman enemies in her territory."

Enya was quick to reassure her superstitious company. "Then let us give thanks to your local gods and goddesses that we will all have one less Roman to kill the next time we confront them."

A hearty agreement followed from the whole company.

"Do you have warriors monitoring Agricola's columns?" Nith asked dulling the mirth around the fireside, amusement that was welcome since there had been little to smile about.

Gilie lobbed a few more stripped branches onto the now lower-burning fire. "Nay. Each day, Agricola sends out patrols in all directions, but my warriors are not foolhardy. They are careful not to become encircled while those Romans snake around the valley floors. We watch their direction from the peaks and low hilltops. We share news of their movements each day when the weather is favourable for it. As with Lulach of Ceann Druimin, we send word to any Caledon chiefs who might find themselves at risk of being invaded."

Enya congratulated the Tap O'Noth warriors. "You will have the continued gratitude of the Caledons and of my Brigante kin who shelter at Ceann Druimin." It was good to learn of their strategies at Tap O'Noth, but she itched to know more of those who had recently sheltered at the old hillfort. And have news of any visitors. She was pleased when Nith broached the subject.

"You have a good number of warriors here at Tap O'Noth, but by the looks of the repaired roundhouses you do not normally live in this fort." Nith stopped to pick meat from his teeth before continuing, not wanting to waste any of the fine fare. "I had not expected there to be so many of you here."

"Most of us had farms and roundhouses down on the foothills O'Noth. The others limped here for safety after the battle. It is many generations since these walls had celebrations within them. It was well before my grandfather's kin and so long ago only our Taexali *Seaghanachaidh* has the telling of it. The walls are well-enough known that my fellow Taexali were sure it would be the best watching-place for survivors, so long as the *Ceigean Ròmanach* had not settled behind them."

"Did they try?" Enya was curious about any determined Roman incursions.

"Nay, but that is not to say they will not attempt to come the morrow, or the dawns after that." From his casual pose, Enya could see that Gilie did not seem too alarmed at the prospect.

"Do they know you shelter here?" she asked.

"They would have to be blind not to see our fires at night. We do not care to hide them, but we do it in the knowledge that they do not know exactly how few of us bide here just now."

Nith laughed. "There are more of you than we expected, but I wondered why your fire was big enough for an army!"

Pointing another half-chewed bone at Nith, Gilie joined in the mirth. "It has been a trial to lug the firewood up the hill, but it is best to keep those damned Romans guessing about how many of us keep watch here because our numbers change every day. Some of those who belong elsewhere have left for the Caledon hills and we have sent others, as you have seen, to neighbouring villages with updates."

"Have any of your messengers gone north, or across into Vacomagi territory?"

Gilie flicked his well-gnawed bone at the flames. "Two of the young warriors who were here a few days ago, Fingal and Ruoridh, have gone north to see what Agricola's troops are doing along the stretches of the Caelis."

Enya's insides churned. Words tumbled out. "Ruoridh? Is he one of your Tap O'Noth kin?"

"Nay," Gilie answered after slugging down some small-beer from a wooden bowl. "I have no notion of where the lad originally came from, but he had battle wounds like most of us. Fingal, and those two men at the end of my fireside, dragged Ruoridh from the woods near The Mither Tap on the morn after the battle. They left him up at SrathBogie to be tended by the only local healer who had not fled to the mountains."

Enya could not contain her excitement. "His battle wounds could not have been too severe, if he has already gone north?"

"Many were much worse than young Ruoridh." A raucous belch was followed by Gilie rubbing his belly.

Nith sidled closer, his shoulder a supporting weight against her as though to absorb any pain his next words might cause. "Was the lad around sixteen summers, tall and strong?"

"With hair slightly darker than my own?" Enya rushed her question.

Gilie laughed. "He was only with us for one night. I paid little heed to his hair colour, but he was not red-haired like I am!"

Enya gripped Nith's fingers tight, turning slightly to stare into his eyes. "It has to be my brother. I feel it in here." Using her curled fist she tapped his fingers at her breastbone.

Nith blinked before he broke eye contact, but let his fingers remain trapped in hers while he posed a new question. "Can someone take us to the woman who healed the Ruoridh you speak of?"

"Come the morn, aye, but unless you want to take first guard duty, it is time for us all to sleep. We have no idea what those Roman turds might do when the new day dawns."

Enya spent an agonising night, her sleep on the hard ground constantly disturbed. Not by any threat from their Roman enemies, but by her own fears that the Ruoridh talked of might not, after all, be her brother. Ruoridh was a common enough name.

"Are you cold?" Nith's whisper tickled her chin as he slid his body closer to her. He wrapped his arm around her waist and tucked her in. Though his palm was on top of her clothing a burning-heat transferred all the way through, giving her more reasons for not sleeping. She couldn't rebuff his brotherly gesture. He had often tucked her up beside him when it was his turn to ride during their long journey northwards to Beinn na Ciche. Nith was still the caring kin, he always had been but she was…older now.

"Sleep." His words muffled into her bundled up bratt. "Or you will be too tired for our trek, come the morrow."

The low-burning fire that they slept around was now only maintained to give the warriors on watch enough light to warn those who slept. She itched to leave for SrathBogie at daybreak. Relaxing in the cradle of Nith's safe and coddling arms, her last thoughts were of times past when Nith and her brother Ruoridh had been in a teasing mood, and she had borne the brunt of it.

***

"Rouse now, Enya." Nith's pats at her shoulder were tentative.

Hardly believing that sleep actually had come to her, she stretched her legs to get rid of the kinks. She rubbed her eyes clear of the stickiness of the night with a loose fist before she looked round at Nith. "Did you not sleep well?" Tiredness bracketed his eyes.

"Well enough." He grunted as he got up to his feet but did not say more.

Warriors bustled around the low fire, one of them using a wooden ladle to fill bowls with a reasonably thick oat-brose. Enya was disturbed by her poor reactions. Some of the people around her had been awake, yet she had not even stirred. Was it because she felt safe in their small community, or was it because Nith had offered her an even better protection that led to complacency? She sat up and hugged her knees, vowing to do better. Feargus was just returning to the fireside: he must have wakened some time before and she had not even felt him move away, either.

"Here. Break your fast."

Enya was humbled when she realised she was amongst the first to be served. She looked up at the tall young man who offered her a bowl and a torn off lump of bannock.

"I cannot take more of your food. We can find something along the way."

His gruff laugh rang out, his gesture more insistent that she take the food. "Our stocks may be low but we can spare you all some." Her suggestion was waved aside as the same warrior handed a bowl of the oatmeal to Nith, and another to Feargus. "Now, if you three empty them quickly we can have our turn." The smile that accompanied the words took away any sting.

Her belly feeling nicely-full, Enya looked forward to the trip ahead knowing the oats would give her sustenance for a good while. She stood outside the main opening to the fort at Tap O'Noth and looked all around her. The morning was fairly-blue with only some grey-white wispy clouds from *Taranis'* bellows scudding above her. She drew in a deep breath. The sight of the valleys below her was awe-inspiring.

"Take it all in just now." Gilie pointed behind them to dark clouds that were forming over the distant mountain summits. "Before long that rain, or sleet, will be falling." He then indicated what was to be seen closer to their perch on the hilltop O'Noth.

Nith asked some questions that she would have asked herself, if she had been less taken by the view. "Is that twinkling over there the sea-waters by Baile Mheadhain?"

Gilie snorted. "Not quite." Following his stretched arm as he moved it slightly, she trailed his pointing finger. "More like there."

It was too far off to see anything like ships on the water, yet it was impressive just how much of the valley floors were able to be seen from the vantage point, the view going all the way to the waters of the god *Morimaru*.

"I see no camp at Moran Dhuirn." Nith was straining to make out features across the landscape.

Again Gilie patiently guided their focus. "Follow the river course that you see down there for three more twists that way."

Enya scanned below, her gaze following his pointing finger as he mentioned a standing stone circle and a single megalith down below. "Can you now see a slightly darkened patch on the hillside above the river?"

It was faint, but she could just make out something.

Gilie continued. "The camp of the many fists lies in a hollow between two rises, and that is why you cannot see all from here."

As more of the vista was identified, Enya felt a slight disappointment when Gilie told them the Roman camp at the Well of Ythan was not able to be seen clearly either, though columns of soldiers had been noticed departing from it, heading towards the Abhainn Caelis.

Nith was generous in his praise of the vantage point. "The Romans will want to wrest this from you as soon as they can. You realise this?"

"Aye, of course, and we will die defending it if necessary. You can see that even if the day is marred with light cloud, we can see approaching armies well before they reach here."

Gilie indicated which route they should take to SrathBogie.

A short time later they approached it.

"We seek information about a warrior who was tended here after the battle. Ruoridh was his name." Nith's question was put to the old man who guarded the area, a sentry too old to see them properly coming from afar, and too late to sound an alarm if they had been enemies. The old man was so worn out he was ready to drop off to sleep again as he sat perched on the log, a short distance from the first visible roundhouse.

"Young Calum is bound to have an answer for you. Try the third dwelling that you come to. That is where his mother bides."

"Is Calum here?" Enya called just short of the roundhouse.

A young boy erupted from the building at her soft inquiry, a short knife held rigidly in front of his chest. On seeing her he squawked loudly, pointing the knife at her face. "You have the same long nose and wide brows as Ruoridh!"

Her gasp was audible, her moth agape.

Calum stared even more. "Your front teeth overlap just like his, as well."

She was too elated to hear news of her brother that she paid no heed to the less than complimentary words and gave even less attention to Nith's chortles.

A few questions later, she learned that Ruoridh had gone north some days earlier.

"Calum? Who are you talking to?" The careworn young woman who exited one of the other roundhouses carried a wooden bowl, the contents of which she discarded beyond the beaten-earth pathway that snaked around the dwellings.

"*Mathair*. These warriors seek Ruoridh."

The woman approached them. Like Calum, Enya felt the woman's stare linger before a nod of recognition was acknowledged. She indicated the roundhouse Calum had come from. "Enter. Please. I have little to offer but come and sup with us."

The smell of a thin fat hen broth emanating from a pot dangling over a low fire made Enya's stomach gurgle.

"Thank you for your care of my brother." Enya accepted the small wooden bowl once she was settled at the fireside, the woman handing a similar portion to Feargus and Nith.

Calum plopped himself to the ground with a wide grin after his mother signalled he should join them.

"But no food for you till a bowl is free." The woman's rebuke was lightened by her wide smile.

One flat freshly-baked bannock was carefully shared around as they were updated on Ruoridh's wounds and his recent plans. Enya was relieved that his injuries had not been too serious. If the god *Arddhu* favoured him, he would regain all of his shoulder movements.

"Aye," Calum gushed after licking his lips free of every morsel. "Ruoridh intends to trek the banks of the Caelis to see what the Romans do now, and after that he plans to head over the river into Vacomagi territory."

His mother's gasp halted the flow of his chatter. "You did not tell me this before. Why does he want to enter Vacomagi lands?"

Enya had an idea but let the boy continue, a lad who seemed to have hung on every word her brother had uttered.

"Ruoridh did not think much of the Vacomagi warriors he met before the battle at Beinn na Ciche. He thought that some would have changed sides in a blink, given a good enough reason." Calum barely drew breath.

Enya could easily see her brother venting such opinions, though it was true that there was some truth in them. There had been a couple of instances before the battle when an argument had broken out between her brother and a few of the young Vacomagi warriors, who were in makeshift shelters near her Brigante clan. The nights of planning before the actual confrontation had seen many frayed nerves amongst the assembled warriors, but Ruoridh had taken particular exception to the comments made that perhaps it would be a better thing to make some sort of peace treaties with Agricola and Rome. The Vacomagi lads had not seemed cowardly, but they had not been hounded out of their hillforts like her Brigante kin had been. In fact, when the almost out-of-hand disagreements had taken place, the Romans had not yet stepped foot on Vacomagi lands.

Nonetheless, those quarrelsome young men had taken their places in the battle lines just like her kin had, but whether they had survived was something to be proven. Their allegiance needed to be put to the test, if they had not fallen on the battlefield.

Enya realised the boy had been wittering on and she had missed some of the conversation.

"And how is Ruoridh to get there?" Calum's mother asked.

"Fingal says he knows the territory well enough to get them to An Cuan Moireach." Calum was regurgitating word for word what he had heard.

"Tch!" Calum's mother spat at the fire. "Fingal of Wichach has never been anywhere near the Vacomagi shores. Who knows where he and Ruoridh will end up! Have I been given the favour of the goddess in healing Ruoridh, only to have him die by the stupidity of that reckless Fingal?"

Enya stopped the boy's rapid answer and his mother's ire with a raised palm. "Wait. Did they say why they want to go to An Cuan Moireach?"

"I wanted to go with them to see the Roman ships, but they would not take me."

Calum's mother clipped her son's ear, but it was a gentle reminder for him to remember his young age and not talk out of turn. "We had word days ago that Roman ships were patrolling the waters of the firth, but there was also a rumour that some of the ships had berthed on the beaches."

Nith was quick with the next question. "Who brought you this news?"

The woman lips pursed, the crossing at her brows indication she was trying to remember. "I cannot recall a name for him, but it was a Vacomagi warrior who was returning home to the firth."

Nith frowned at her before continuing to question Calum's mother. "Was it only one warrior who visited you? Not two of them who were heading south to the Caledon passes?"

The woman's head shook quite definitely. "Nay. Only the one going north."

Enya probed further. "Can you describe him? Was there anything remarkable to remember about him?"

"Ruoridh did not like him," Calum interrupted, eager to be part of the conversation. "He said the warrior was over friendly, and that he asked too many questions about how many warriors were in this area and what they were doing."

Enya caught Nith's gaze. "I do not like the sound of this. He may not be what he seems."

"Asking such questions is no proof that he was an infiltrator, Enya." Nith's answer sounded reasonable, but she knew how he felt about her worries. "We would need a lot more evidence than that." Nith turned back to Calum's mother. "Is there anything that seemed different about him?"

Calum's tongue would not be still. "Remember you told me about how quick the man always was to jump up when you came into the house?" When his mother nodded, he let his memories run on. "You said you had never seen anyone stand up so straight so quickly."

The woman nodded agreement. "Aye. Calum is right about that. I remember nothing else unusual…except about how he startled to his feet so readily."

"Ruoridh wanted to see the ships, to work out what General Agricola plans next," Calum gushed.

Enya could tell that her brother had made a good impression on the young lad.

"Does he intend to return to SrathBogie?" Her question was for the woman, but the boy answered.

"He will not return here." Calum was crestfallen. "Ruoridh told me he wants to do as well as his uncle at setting up a messenger chain. He is determined to send information about the Romans to the Caledons."

Enya turned to Nith. "Do you think he will head back to the Mither Tap area?"

Calum gave Nith no time to answer. "Nay, he said he will not. His cousin was dragged off from there. He never wants to set eyes on that hilltop again."

The youngster then dived into a regurgitation of Ruoridh's last sight of Beathan. After hearing the details, Enya felt frayed. Both her brother and cousin might still be alive, though it seemed unlikely that she would find either of them easily.

Her glance at Nith when she felt his soft squeeze at her shoulder, betrayed her dilemma. "I want to see my brother, and my cousin, back into the Garrigill folds though the task is daunting. Beathan may be in the greater danger now but I must find my brother first. Will Lorcan ever forgive me?"

Nith's arms enfolded her tight in to his chest, his chin resting on her head. His words and caressing fingers quietly reassured. "Aye, in his heart he will. He wants the return of his son, but he is a practical man. It now makes more sense to seek Ruoridh than to go in search of Beathan."

In his embrace, Enya could not say why she felt safe yet very confused when her glance rested momentarily on Feargus whose face reddened before he turned aside to ask young Calum a question.

Chapter Twenty-Four

Abhainn Caelis, Taexali and Vacomagi Border

Enya was no longer surprised that it was the locals who declared themselves first when they moved from one abandoned roundhouse to the next, as they followed the Caelis downstream to the best fording place suggested by Calum's mother. Vague memories returned to her when they entered empty dwellings, some odd trappings of daily-life still strewn around the interiors.

Looking closely, it was evident that the Romans had plundered the buildings they had come upon. Few metal objects were to be found, but shards from broken clay bowls and wicker stubs from torn baskets were hazards under the decaying bracken floor-linings. She had experienced this desertion when she was a very small child. Fleeting recall of her parents' deep anguish, when they found no food stocks to stave off the hunger of their children, caused silent tears to course down her cheeks.

Back then, many Brigantes had found that they were fleeing refugees.

Why could her people not be left alone? What made the Romans believe that they had the right to impose their domination, and their culture, on territory that was not their own? Her whole life had been spent avoiding Rome dragging her by the torque she had yet to wear, to a destiny she did not want, and did not court.

"Enya?"

Feargus' soft call from the roundhouse entryway brought her back to her present predicament.

"You need to hear what this warrior has just told us."

Dashing her face dry with her tunic, she followed him to the last dwelling where Nith stood talking to someone she had not yet met.

"Why did you believe this warrior to be a traitor?" Nith asked.

She had thought herself unhappy just a short while before, but the old man's news was devastating.

"What did you do to this Ruoridh you speak of?" She could not hold back her temper.

"We did nothing to him, but a loyal young warrior could not know as much of the Romans as he seemed to do." The elder was convinced and would not be swayed from his opinion.

"Where is he now?" Nith asked, his tone tempered compared to what she was feeling.

The old man grumbled as he contemplated the ground beneath him. "How can I possibly know that? The lad rested one night here with his Taexali friend and left us on the next dawn. We were just glad to see him leave."

Enya drew breath through her nostrils and forced herself to be calm. She stared into the distrustful gaze when the man eventually raised his head again, after the silence that his words provoked. "If the Ruoridh you speak of is my brother, then he is no traitor. Almost his whole life has been spent avoiding the yolk of the Roman neck-chain. My kin have all experienced more than we wish to of Roman domination. If you want, I will tell you of my own treks to avoid the Roman invaders and you may see if our stories are similar!"

Though the old man was frail, he led them to his place of shelter in a nearby copse. Enya's spirits plummeted. The makeshift dwellings set in a hollow and behind thick blaeberry bushes would be far too scanty for deep-winter survival. The small community of older tribespeople who greeted her seemed resigned to moving on to the otherworld whenever their gods deemed it time. Sympathy for their plight overrode her earlier animosity. She could see why the man's distrust was evident. The little that they had, these elders needed to keep secret from marauding Roman patrols.

"Nith? This would be a good opportunity to show us how cleverly you use your sling."

Nith caught her meaning immediately; the slight rising of one eyebrow accompanied by a glare did not put her off. It was one she had seen recently that warmed rather than repelled. It had become customary for him to snag something for them to eat at the end of a day's trek without needing any prompting, but he was normally only using his expertise for feeding the three of them, rather than a small community.

Feargus grinned at Nith, also in harmony with her. "It is about time you showed me those secret skills that you are famous for hoarding."

They left with some lively banter which Enya hoped would satisfy any independence that the elders still clung to. The old folk clearly needed all the help they could get.

While Enya related her own story and she learned of their plight, Nith and Feargus went hunting. Not Romans, but they returned with sufficient small animals and birds to make a hearty broth for that evening, and for a few nights to come for the old ones.

Before their departure the next morning, they made sure to improve on the shelters as best they could – but all knew that if the god *Arddhu* no longer favoured the old people, then their time in the woods might be very short. Enya had learned the direction that Ruoridh had taken, though no more than that. It was disheartening to think that the initial distrust of her brother, in this small community, might be much the same elsewhere.

Somewhere around the middle of the day, according to the fleeting sight of the sun in the intermittent clouds above, she was surprised when Nith disappeared from her view. The first real feelings of unease of the day crept over her. Always vigilant about maintaining good cover as they crept across the countryside, no alerting birdcalls came from him, yet she and Feargus paused in their trek along the riverbank and sheltered behind tall reeds.

Hunkering down, she waited for Nith to return. They had decided to cluster together if danger was present, believing that their strength would serve them better than being individual targets.

Nith was slightly out of breath when he eventually crouched next to her, his return a cautious one from reed to reed. "Ahead of us, the river course bends sharply."

"Then should we continue that way?" She could see nothing amusing in her question and was annoyed by Nith's answering grim smile.

"We will definitely not go that way. There is at least half a legion's worth of Roman soldiers setting up camp on the southern bank of the Caelis. They are swarming all around the floodplain."

Enya listened to the sounds around her. Natural bird calls and the gentle rushing and sloshing of water over the pebbly river-bed were easy to detect, but there were also distant dull thuds and a faint clinking.

Tramping hobnailed feet and tinkling metal breastplates!

"Does Agricola move his whole army?" Feargus asked, slipping up onto his knees.

"How far away are they?" Before she could ask another question, she was sure the sounds of tramping were increasing.

Enya scrambled to her feet and took to her heels after Nith who had regained his breath and had taken flight along the riverside, to a natural curve in the banking where the reeds gave way to a curve of soil. Skittering down into the freezing water of the river after Nith, flowing reeds tangled around her legs as she sought to find her balance. When Nith's body disappeared up to his chin, she knew the water depth would completely cover her. Turning back to warn Feargus, he was still on the banking.

"Hurry, Feargus. They will be within sight any moment."

Feargus head shivered, his eyes wide in panic. "You must go across without me."

"Nay we will not. What is wrong with you?"

Feargus pleaded, his hands shooing her forwards. "I can not enter the water. I would rather die here on the edge of a Roman *gladius* than have *Caela*, the river goddess claim me."

"Nith, wait!" she hissed before clutching at the banking to pull herself back up out of the river. "Feargus needs help. He fears the water."

Scrambling up the slippery slope, she clutched at Feargus heels to prevent him from running off. "Nith!" Her cry muffled its way into the reeds at the top, though she clung on.

"Ugh!" The weight of Nith clawing over her pushed her even further into the soft ground, but their combined yanks toppled their protesting friend. Between the two of them they dragged Feargus down and into the water, till it covered Enya's shoulders.

"Be quiet!" Nith was not amused by the noise they all made. "Lie on your back, Feargus, and pray to *Taranis* of the skies."

Shoving Feargus around, Enya grabbed one arm.

"Take a deep breath now, Feargus." Her orders did not stop there. "And hold it. Wait till I tell you to breathe again."

The river was not all that wide and was only out of her depth at the very centre, but the current was considerable. Towing across a terrified Feargus was much more difficult than she had imagined it would be. With Nith on his other side, she swam with one arm and tugged the Taexali lad with the other, the flow pulling her downstream, a direction she wanted to avoid.

Around the middle of the river, she surfaced to splutter another demand. "Nith. He has taken in too much water. Pull harder!"

As in battle situations, it was apparent that danger gave an extra surge of strength. Like Nith, she had to ignore that Feargus' head was lolling below water and concentrate on kicking towards the reeds at the other side. Once there, she bolstered up Feargus till Nith scrambled up onto the verge. Once Nith had secured his feet and reached down to grasp Feargus under the armpits, she helped to push Feargus up from beneath. Hauling herself up after him, she was thankful that the experience was quickly over. She doubted she would have survived if the river had been a really wide one.

Her breath heaving, she lay alongside a groaning Feargus.

From the amount of pummelling that Nith was dolling out and the shaking at Feargus' shoulders, she knew her Taexali friend would be bruised all over, but by the amount of spluttering and coughing it would be worthwhile.

Once he was sure that Feargus really was recovering, Nith flung himself down to rest beside her, his glance exhausted but approving. In a weak gesture of comfort, his hand blindly patted at her thighs. "It was a good thing that Nara taught all of your family to swim in the nemeton loch near Tarras."

Intending to give him a gentle nudge of agreement with her back-flapping hand, his yelp of agony told her that she had missed his arm and had pelted his upper chest.

Struggling to her knees, she looked down on his contorted expression. Without permission, she peeled back the sodden cloak and then the neck of his tunic.

Her smile was one of relief tinged with worry. "Nara and Ineda will be very unhappy with you, if that wound starts to leak again."

Nith's palm covered her own: a gentle touch. Just like his expression had turned.

Feargus' coughing ceased enough for his croaking to break her eye contact with Nith.

"You could have left me and made your own escape," he said. "But I thank you both for dragging me across. The river goddess may claim me another time, though clearly not this day."

The sounds of clinking metal, and the pounding of feet coming closer, cut off any further praise from Feargus.

"By *Taranis*' noisy sky-pounding, they are closer than before!" Nith struggled up to his knees. Drawing his sword free, his emptying of his scabbard and knife sheath prompted Enya to do the same.

Their weapons could not be allowed to rust, but now was not the time for proper drying as she swiped her blades across the only thing available: the edge of her wet bratt. Carefully scooping up the squirming fish that had fallen at her feet, she tossed it back into the water. She knew she should say some sort of prayer for the river goddess' tiny creature, but she did not know the words. Instead she turned to berate Feargus who still lay on the ground. "Do any of your Taexali people learn to swim?"

Feargus' answer was blunt as he heaved himself up and readied himself, the experience in the water having taken its toll. His movements looked a bit exaggerated as he shook the water free from his knife pouch. "Maybe some people did, but none where I lived. We had no need to with only shallow streams nearby. The nearest large body of water to my roundhouse village was some distance away. Skene water is south of the place where the Romans camped before they settled for battle at Moran Dhuirn."

Enya remembered passing the loch he referred to on her way north to Beinn na Ciche.

"Cease your gossip and get moving! They are almost within reach." Nith's admonishment shattered any further conversation.

Stepping away from the banking, she looked back across the river. A long column of Roman soldiers was not far off on the opposite side of the river, their progress made at a steady trot.

"Faster, Enya!" Nith urged. "We need to make a good distance between them and ourselves. We have no shelter on this side."

Enya scanned around. The reeds were thick right at the riverside, but the nearest bush and tree cover was a good way across a flat stubbly-floodplain. If they stayed in the reeds, and the Romans continued their way along the opposite bank, they were sure to be easily spitted by their spear tips. If they sprinted across the vulnerable sparse grass, they would also be highly visible. Her hesitation cost them all precious moments.

It was Nith's grasping hand that pulled her out of her dither.

A cry of alarm rang out across the water. They had been spotted. The pounding of feet increased, the pace of the Romans now at full-pelt.

Nith's hand dragging her along, the three of them sprinted towards the cover of the nearest copse of trees, leaking water all the way. The thudding of spears behind her heels made her run all the harder.

The sudden jerk next to her broke her stride when Feargus slumped into her, his cry of agony muffling against her cloak. When she glanced at him, his limping was testimony to an injury.

"Pay it no heed," he gasped trying to right himself.

Grabbing Feargus' elbow, she drew him towards her and clamped him to her side. From that point on it was Nith who dragged their whole line forward, out of range of the Roman attack and into the shelter of the grove. Once he was well in, she felt Nith drop her hand. The relentless lugging at both shoulders stopped.

Feargus slumped to the ground precariously balancing on his left knee.

"I hate those *Ceigean Ròmanach!* His voice grew weaker with each word as he keeled over onto his shoulder, his injured leg askew. "Kill some of them in my name."

"Feargus!" Dropping to her knees, she cradled his head free of the rough ground. "Do not give them the satisfaction of slaying yet another of our numbers. You must be strong."

Looking back to be sure the Romans hadn't yet crossed the river, Nith crouched down beside her and inspected the damage done by the Roman pilum. The metal tip, and a short stretch of the wooden shaft, had gone straight through.

"We need to get it out, Enya, before we can move on. He cannot run otherwise." Nith heaved, still out of breath but determined.

She had seen her Aunt Nara care for many a wound and knew what needed to be done. Pointing to the longer length of shaft, and taking a firmer hold of Feargus, her words were a grim whisper.

"Break it."

Feargus snapped back at her. Agony laced each word. "Waste no more time on me. Make your own escape."

When she wrenched her hands free of his shoulders, the look of despair in his eyes almost made her weep. Fumbling with the clasp of her dripping bratt she swung it free.

Snagging a corner of the material she deftly twisted it into a thin rope. Thrusting the middle of it into Feargus' mouth she pleaded with him. "Breathe through your nose. Do not let the Roman shite have the satisfaction of hearing your pain."

When Feargus bit down on the gag with a suppressed squeal Nith used a small boulder to break off the wooden shaft as close to Feargus' skin as possible. "Pull it out, Enya. Your fingers are defter than mine. I'll steady him."

Changing positions with Nith, she made sure to peel away any rough shards from the broken end, smoothing the wood as quickly as she could. Using her knife, she ripped off the edge of her tunic creating a strip for binding the leg. She had some knowledge of herbs to pack within the binding, but gathering them would need to wait till later. Staunching the blood would be her priority when she freed the spear tip.

Nith settled Feargus' head in his lap and firmly grasped the injured man's shoulders while Enya used her short blade to slit down the cloth of Feargus' braccae. When the material flopped aside, she could see the spear had gone from back to front near the outer edge of his leg. She prayed to her Aunt Nara's favourite goddess *Rhianna* that it had not made too much inner damage, and had missed shattering the bone. She would have prayed to her own favourite goddess, but she could not yet settle on any special one. She could not remember a time when it seemed a particular goddess favoured her with peace and healthy surroundings, so that final choice still eluded her.

After another glance at Nith to ensure he still had a firm clasp of Feargus' shoulders, she gripped the metal tip and slowly prised the remaining shaft free of the wound.

Feargus' muffled howl of pain did not deter her. Feeling his body jerk, she pinioned his leg to the ground with her own weight and ignored his cries while she concentrated on completing her task.

When the stub of wood was fully-out, she was relieved to find the wound seeped rather than spurted blood. That had to be a good sign though she could not be sure. Scrabbling at the pouch around her waist, she extracted a long leather thong before she wrapped her strip of cloth tightly around Feargus' leg. Firmly binding it with the tie, she fell back from his legs.

"Well done." Nith's praise washed through her, a solace that she deeply appreciated. "Can you find a stout piece of trunk he can use as a crutch, while I get him upright? I have not heard them cross the water but we dare not linger."

Much as she would have liked to rest a while, and gather her wits, she knew he was right. They needed to put as long a distance as possible between themselves and the Roman army. There was still time for the enemy to cross the river and stalk them.

Foraging around the thicket, for it really was not much more than that, she spied a suitable forked piece of wood. Trimming it off took only moments before she handed it to Feargus who was balancing on one leg, the other bent and off the ground.

"*An cù!* I hate that Roman," Feargus moaned.

The injury was nasty, but not so severe as to make him lose his senses.

"Aye. So do I, Feargus. So do I."

Chapter Twenty-Five

Vacomagi Territory

It became evident to Nith that the Roman patrol had not crossed to their side of the river, so their painfully slow progress did not matter. Enya's question broke his introspection as they put some distance between themselves and the nearest copse of trees.

"If the Romans were making camp beyond the bend in the river, why did that patrol come our way, Nith?"

"Perhaps they were checking the water source. It is their habit to use the upstream water for their own purposes. Even though the water becomes less clean after thousands of their men have used it, the downstream water is considered good enough to water their mules."

Enya's nod showed her understanding. Her Uncle Brennus had explained such things many times. "Aye, and the horses get the middle area. Maybe they were checking to see if there were any obstructions along the river, though it was easy to see the current was flowing strongly."

Feargus' mocking tones joined in as though he would not give in to the indignity of his injury. "I noticed that!"

His comment made Nith laugh. Finding it was a relief from the tension, he caught Enya's grin.

Feargus was not done. "Maybe they noticed you, Nith, when you were scouting that area?"

The thought had occurred to Nith but he would never have admitted it. Perhaps he was losing his skills, or more likely his continual weariness of spirit was taking its toll?

"Nay! They did not spy Nith. If they had seen him they would not have followed him at that usual trot."

Nith acknowledged Enya's championing of him with a wry smile. "They would have been running after me double-paced in the chase."

Feargus grunted as he repositioned the crook under his armpit, though it was one of agreement. "Whatever their reason, I would rather they had headed to their new camp instead of using me as their target."

Nith watched Feargus' grim hobble as Enya's Taexali friend attempted to move more quickly over the flattish ground they now found themselves on. The lad showed more fortitude than he had first given him credit for. Yet he knew how easily that determined strength would wane. He needed to find some kind of shelter for them all before long since the afternoon was slipping away. Darkness would fall quickly, the deep cloudy-grey changing to the blackness of night. And though not snowy, the winter chill was already biting at them.

The flat banks of a tributary of the Abhainn Caelis nearby were extensive but not too far away he could see a low knoll that would hopefully provide some kind of shelter for them. If nothing else, being behind it would hide them from any Romans wandering the northern riverbank. Travelling deeper into Vacomagi territory was not their intended destination, but it was preferable to finding a Roman patrol at their heels. Their trek to follow in the footsteps of Ruoridh had been interrupted, but Nith was confident he could find a way to pick up the Abhainn Caelis again, though not till the following day at the earliest. And that would only be after he was sure that no Roman patrols were searching for them, because it seemed inevitable that they would.

The new Roman camp was situated only a fast-trot away for a fit and healthy Roman *century*.

He was soon glad he had persisted in dragging them behind the hillock, even though Enya had protested, claiming the damp ground they were travelling over was making it even more difficult for Feargus to keep up. Once they rounded the mound, the sight ahead made him smile. A solitary forsaken roundhouse lay in the middle of strips of land that had reverted to marshy terrain.

Picking his way across the easiest route, Nith reached the dwelling. By then, he was feeling less confident. The farm had obviously been abandoned for a long time, well before the Roman invasion. The thatch on the roof was half gone, the interior stinking-damp, but they needed rest and the driest end had to be better than sleeping under a tree.

Leaving Feargus to propel himself all the way inside to the far end, he pulled Enya back out by the elbow.

"See if you can find enough bracken to make a dry bed for Feargus, while I forage for something to eat. We can take turns to watch, but if he gets some sleep he will cope better on the morrow."

Enya's whispered response was as forbidding as her knotted brows. "Do you not think I know that?"

Sensing her mood was belligerent, he drew out his sling and strode off after a brief nod.

If Enya considered him indifferent to Feargus' condition, it did not matter to him. His priority was making sure she was safe. The likelihood was that later on that night there would not be any marauding Roman patrols blundering around in the dark, but unpredictable wild animals could be a nasty nuisance.

On the far side of the dwelling, a thicket hugged the lower reaches of the nearby hill. He headed that way knowing his chances were greater of bagging a small animal, his fingers rooting in the pouch at his waist to check how many stones he still had. It had been a while since he had added to his collection of specially prepared ones.

As soon as he entered the trees the pervading peaty smell of the marshy ground he had just sludged his way across changed to that of a different sort of decay. The stench of rotting blood was unmistakable, though whether it was animal or human he could not be sure. His senses went on alert in the deepening gloom as he skirted from bush to bush. He wanted to be waylaid by neither man, nor marauding beast. Peeling back a clump of blaeberry the sight was not unexpected. The corpse that lay ahead of him face up had been partially gnawed by small wild creatures, and pecked at by birds.

Nonetheless, there was sufficient left of the leather breast coverings to see that it was not the body of a Roman soldier, but a local female warrior.

His guess, from the state of deterioration, was that the tribeswoman had been dead only a couple of days. Her neck had been sliced open, the cut deep enough to empty the blood from her body. The forest floor around her was a congealed dark-brown mess, spattered with occasional animal excrement, all made even slushier as a result of the inclement weather of the previous days. From the flattened forest-floor around her it looked as though the woman had slithered about before death had claimed her. Or perhaps she had gallantly put up a good fight before succumbing. Not far from her outstretched arm lay a spear.

On his way across to pick up the spear, he bypassed her body. The bone hilt of a small paring knife was still visible in the pouch at her waist. He found that at odds with the violent attack. Whoever had killed her had not bothered to acquire her weapons. Suspicion grew. Nith could think of few reasons for not claiming useful weapons from an attack victim.

Looking more closely at the ground some steps away from her, he could only see minimal disturbance. A single *contubernium* group of eight Romans would have flattened much more of the undergrowth, the damage being even greater from a larger patrol.

Animal scurrying nearby made him think of his purpose in being there. There was little he could do for this poor woman, save saying a prayer to the goddess *Scathach*, but he could ensure Enya was safe and fed.

Moving around the copse in search of the game that had disturbed him, his suspicions increased when he found two more bodies, lying at short distances apart. Both were face down into the undergrowth. Both of these male warriors had suffered a frenzied attack from behind. Slashing wounds to their shoulders and backs had floored them, one of the unfortunates' legs having been almost halved.

Levering up one corpse with his foot, the muffled sound of metal scraping on metal startled him. Jumping back from it, he searched the glade for any enemy that might be around. Satisfied no danger was present, he willed his worn-out senses to calm. Thinking carefully about the source of the noise, he realised it had to have come from under the body and not around the glade.

Annoyed with himself for being inept, he once again set to turning over the remains. It was with a grim smile and a snort of disgust that he acknowledged it was the grip of the man's long knife that had scraped against the spear hilt that lay under the warrior, the spear shaft having snapped. The weight of the body tumbling down would account for that, but the knife being unsheathed needed some thought.

Saying a prayer for the men, the vaguest swish nearby broke into his deep thoughts. His sling was up into place automatically and his arm at length ready to let fly the stone. The plump ptarmigan within his sight had no chance of escaping his deadly aim.

Gathering up the bird, hunger returned with a vengeance of its own, his insides protesting. One bird would presently satisfy him, but was not enough for three. It took a while but his stealthy creep around captured a hare as well. He trudged back to the dilapidated roundhouse still contemplating the dead warriors.

"Are your sling skills rusting? That took you quite a while."

Enya's greeting on his entry to the roundhouse was not as cordial as he would have liked, but he was long used to her occasional sarcasm. She had a small fire going which was more important than giving her a snide answer. Feargus was already stretched out on a low pallet of brackens. The dampness from them and the prickliness would not be comfortable, but was much better than lying on nothing at all. From the slight heaving of Feargus' shoulders, he seemed asleep.

Nith looked closely at Enya before setting down the hunt on the stones at the side of the fledgling blaze. She was as tired as he was; he needed to share his thoughts with her but first, the food needed to be prepared.

Enya looked longingly at the bird. "That would do well cooked in a pot of water to make a nourishing soup for Feargus, but there is nothing left around here that I can use."

Nith nodded. He had seen earlier that the dwelling had been stripped of all cooking utensils and bowls.

"The fire will do well enough." Feargus let free the smallest of moans. Nith looked over towards the lad. "It is a nasty wound, for sure, but Feargus will manage."

Pulling free his paring knife, he set to skinning and gutting the hare. Enya had the bird plucked and cleaned out in half the time it took him, it's carcass onto one of the stout damp rods she had placed at the fireside.

"Let me fill your water pouch," she demanded. "I found a small spring nearby when I went to gather herbs for Feargus' poultice."

By the time she returned, Nith had the hare on another of the sticks and had lashed together a frame to spit both of the carcasses over the flames.

Rising to his feet he whispered, "I have something to show you. We will return before the food is cooked."

He could not miss her glance at the still sleeping Feargus.

"Feargus will do well enough, and the fire will last till we get back."

Lighting a sheaf of reeds, he strode out of the roundhouse and headed for the trees, Enya at his heels. "I took so long foraging for our food because another matter took some of my attention."

Annoyed by his reticence to tell her why they were going into the woods, Enya dunted his shoulder. "Do we have to go just now, Nith?"

He stopped to look down at her pinched face, the skin over her cheekbones more stretched than he would like to see. None of them had been well enough fed for a long time.

"We do. Your warrior skills are as good as mine are, Enya, and I would not drag you out again if I did not value your opinion."

That seemed good enough reason because Enya made no more conversation till they arrived at the first male. She said little as she moved around in the dying dusk, taking note of the surroundings.

"There is more to see." He led her across to the other male, the one with the spear and knife beneath him.

"It looks as though he has been unexpectedly attacked from the rear," she said after a taking a good look around. "I would have expected a more trampled mess around him, if he had been killed by Roman soldiers, though that is hard to see with the shadows in here."

As he had done earlier, Nith used his foot to turn over the body.

"His knife is still sheathed. This one did not foresee the attack at all. If he had been wary, he would at the very least have withdrawn it."

Taking her by the elbow he pulled her away and across to the female warrior. Enya sank to her knees a short way away from the victim and bowed her head. A moment or two later, she stood up and padded around the area also praying for the two men. "They all still have their weapons. Nith. This was not the work of an animal. Nor do I think it was a Roman attack."

Nith nodded agreement, but before he could say any more Enya grasped the lit-rushes and held them to the ground before she continued scanning the undergrowth as best she could. "The men seem not to have been aware of their attacker behind them. The woman may have been suspicious by the amount of undergrowth that was disturbed around her, but I do not see enough disorder for it to have been a group who attacked her."

Bowing her head, he watched Enya's throat muscles clench as she fought with her feelings. Her next words were telling and proved she thought much like he did.

"Had it been even a small patrol of Roman auxiliaries, they would have created much more mess and she would probably not have been left…unmolested."

He had already come to the same conclusion.

Enya's eyes sparkled in the growing moonlight as they sped back to the roundhouse, Nith's torch now useful to guide their footsteps. "Do you think the weapons were left because the person who killed them could not carry them?" Her pretty eyes turned to a distrustful glitter. "Was it someone they knew but also someone in the pay of the Romans? A *speculator*?"

The answer might come to them, but they had more immediate things to attend to.

Between the two of them they now had two extra spears, two long knives and four small knives that they had removed from the scene. They might come in useful, and he would not leave anything that the Romans could possibly reuse. Not even the sling and drawstring pouch that was filled with well-shaped slingshot that he had removed from one of the bodies and added to his own collection.

Feargus was awake when they entered the roundhouse and was awkwardly adding more fuel to the fire, his odd stance favouring his good leg. The look he threw his way, Nith was not sure how to interpret. The lad's expression questioned, but there was also hurt flickering there as well. Whatever bothered Feargus would have to wait for another time because he had plenty to think on.

"The food is ready. It was the spattering and crackling that woke me. Not to mention the welcome smells." Feargus looked to Enya. A wry humour was not beyond the Taexali lad when he gestured to the fire. "One of you two had better take the meat off the spit, in case I fall over and flatten the food."

As they gnawed the bones free of tenderly roasted flesh, Nith updated Feargus on the bodies in the wood.

"Well, the only good thing I can think of is that none of the men were your brother or cousin, Enya," Feargus said, a yawn sneaking in that he tried unsuccessfully to hide.

"Aye." Nith inhaled a deep breath before wiping his greasy hands on his bratt. He fixed his gaze on Feargus who was drinking from his water pouch. "We will keep looking for Ruoridh come dawn. Will you manage to keep up with us?"

Water dribbled from Feargus' chin as he gulped his expression serious. "No doubt I will be slower than normal but if you two need to go faster than I can, then that is what you must do."

The resignation in his tone disturbed Nith. Till the battle at Beinn na Ciche he had always had his brother Esk to rely on for companionship and support. Feargus was currently as brother-less as he was, but the lad needed to accept that he would not forsake him. Even if it cost him heartache since he could see how much Enya cared for Feargus. He vowed that he would not fail Enya or Feargus.

Enya was much more practical in words and deed when she answered Feargus. "You will come with us, Feargus. Fear not. If you had seen the wounds my father received in battle a long time ago, you would not be worried about your present one. Now lie down on that heather and bracken so that I can repack the wound. Your leg will be as stiff as a tree trunk in the morning, but it will not have dropped off, mark my words."

Nith turned away, unable to prevent the grin. When Enya was like this, it was time to leave. Temporarily refreshed by the food and water he declared. "I'll take the first watch."

Nith returned to the dilapidated roundhouse late the following morning. Sending Enya a warning call from a little distance away, he waited for her reply before entering the decaying dwelling. Regardless of the bad news he had to share with her, he could tell from her concerned expression that Feargus could not travel that day.

"The north bank of the river is crawling with groups of Roman auxiliaries. Enya, I cannot be sure that a patrol will not come this way."

The hint of tears welling in her eyes were dashed aside as she fussed about, adding some more wood to the low-burning fire in the centre of the dilapidated roundhouse. Her words were venomous, grimly delivered to the weak flames she produced with the wooden switch used to poke the embers. "I detest those Roman invaders more and more come every new dawn!"

He looked over to the makeshift bed where Feargus lay sleeping. Placing his spear and sword near to hand, he slipped down onto one of the fallen-logs he had brought in to sit on the previous night.

"We are too near their new encampment to be safe from foraging patrols."

The look she sent him was one of strange satisfaction. "Then they will find as little, or as much, as I did. This farmstead has been abandoned for many seasons. There are no wandering hens or pigs gone wild, and they will find no grain stores either."

Enya passed him a handful of juniper berries and hazelnuts. "I can pick plenty of these when I find them but you, as well as anyone, know that my hunting skills are only good for killing men and not beasts for the spit."

Nith swallowed down a smile before popping some of the berries into his mouth. He understood too well that when hungry Enya could be very snippy. He glanced over to Feargus. "How is he?"

"His leg swelling is much worse this morning. I have re-wrapped it with a different herb poultice and I have prayed, and prayed some more, to the goddess *Rhianna* to ease his pain."

"He has a fever?" Realising he was starving, he grabbed up another handful of berries and nuts from the batch she had piled onto a bit of cloth that lay on a flat stone next to the fireside. It was poor fare, but he knew that those particular berries and hazelnuts were always good for staving off hunger.

"Aye, he has that too, though I managed to get a feverfew infusion into him."

Biting down on some nuts, he mumbled around them. "He looks peaceful enough. Has he been sleeping since I headed out at dawn?"

Enya nodded before she padded over to the cot. "He is peaceful now, but earlier he was very restless, his sleep disturbed."

After a quick spread of her open palms to Feargus' cheeks Enya continued her whispering when she settled back down beside him. "He feels much cooler now."

He looked askance at her. The words made her grey eyes look less anxious as she absently clutched at his arm. A tiny smile curving her lips brought warmth to him that he knew was nothing to do with the flames in front of him. Animation quickened her next words.

"Nith. After you left, I realised Feargus was fevered. Leaving him alone was risky, but I went back to the woods. I remembered trampling around some feverfew plants last night when I walked around those bodies. I picked some of the feverfew this morning. The leaves were past their best now that it is after Samhain, but I think they were worth a try."

"If you know how to use the plant then it will surely help, Enya." He was not in all honesty convinced, knowing very little about which plants the healers used, but Enya clearly needed reassurance.

Her sparkle continued. "I looked again in the daylight and came to the same conclusion as we made last night. Those people were definitely not killed by a Roman enemy. The murderous coward who felled them did not look them in the eye."

"Do you still think it was only one warrior?"

Her eyes glittered and the clutch at his arm intensified. "From the tracks around the area, including our own, I can only think it was one other person who was in that glade."

He curled his palm over hers and returned a gentle squeeze. "Enya. That means he, or she, may not be far away. We must be very careful when we meet strangers."

He hated to see the doubt clouding her soft gray eyes and did not want to make her even more insecure, but he could not hold back his words as he looked over to their friend who was stirring in the corner. His palm slid up to softly cradle her cheek. "We really should move on."

"Aye, we should, but I will not leave him."

Her expression softened while he held her gaze for a few moments and then she rose to check on Feargus.

For as long as he had known her, Enya had always been loyal to those she loved and on this occasion she was no different. He was not sure how that acknowledgement made him feel but regret was part of it. The rest he was not ready to think about. Instead, practicalities were more important. He had a vow to keep.

"I will watch from the crest of the knoll till dusk descends. That should give me ample time to warn you, if they come anywhere near here."

Chapter Twenty-Six

Abhainn Tuesis Estuary, Vacomagi Territory

Ruoridh's soft whistle was only intended for Fingal's ears. He was tucked in behind a smattering of low-growing brambles that clothed the sallows bordering the lochan, his eyes intent on the scene ahead of him. Down on the sands near the *Tuesis* estuary was a long line of Roman soldiers transferring sacks, hands over hands, from their beached vessel which buffeted about in the lapping water close in to shore.

Feelings of sheer hatred erupted. He wanted to rush forward and snatch the supplies out of their firm grips, but nothing would be achieved by one man alone. Or two. Fingal was not far from him, surveying the same scene.

A few moments later Fingal scurried in alongside him almost flattening him in the process.

"That amount of grain would feed a number of our villages all winter long."

Ruoridh whispered agreement. He knew just how important it was to have such supplies be shared amongst hungry people, yet he also knew just how vast the Roman Army needs were. "That is so true, Fingal. Agricola has many soldiers to feed. Two of those sacks will be needed each day to provide rations for one of Agricola's *centuries*."

"How can you be sure of that?" Fingal's eyebrows arched high above enquiring eyes.

Ruoridh hurried to explain. "My Uncle Brennus knows many things about the Roman army. For a time, while he was gathering information for the Brigante King Venutius, Uncle Brennus learned about the needs of the Roman soldiers in a legion. Those ships will have to sail constantly to provide for all of Agricola's troops, if they do not get any local supplies of grain, or from land transports."

Fingal's soft harrumph told him what his new friend thought of that. "Should it concern me if those Romans starve?"

Appreciating the man's humour and assessing the situation were two different things. "I would like to stay and see just how many times those ships can return each day with supplies, but that defeats our plans."

Fingal's head nodded assent, the momentary twinkle gone from his expressive grey eyes, his tone instantly sombre and chastising as he looked towards the east. "We have put a lot of responsibility on those Taexali elders who still dwell near those beaches."

"I know that but what else can we do?" Ruoridh had been shocked at the lack of able tribespeople still inhabiting the northern Taexali villages that they had visited near the Abhainn Caelis. Now, they were well into the Vacomagi flatlands much further west at the Abhainn Tuesis. They had encountered some small villages, but the quagmire around them was not the best farming land.

"Fear not. Those elders will not betray us." Fingal was sure.

"I believe you about the Taexali, but what of those Vacomagi you have mentioned who dwell right down on those shores?" Ruoridh's pointing finger dragged along the shoreline that lay in the distance.

Fingal's expression was resigned, his tone of voice disgusted. "I cannot see how they will do anything but capitulate to the Roman scum. Those shore dwellers are cut off from their own Vacomagi neighbours by these vast areas of scrubby marshes and lochans. They cannot expect anyone to come to their aid quickly, except by sea on small boats. Would any Vacomagi rescuers dare to put to sea along that coastline when there are so many much larger Roman vessels plying along that shore? I think not." Fingal may not have been a natural friend of the Vacomagi, but it was despair for their plight that soured his words.

Ruoridh's insides lurched. The thought of what the Romans might do to those who still lived along the shoreline cut into his insides, his nod full of regret and resignation.

Fingal's whisper tickled his ear as the warrior crept to his feet to move on. "We need to cross the Abhainn Tuesis now and see how those Vacomagi beyond it fare with the Roman presence on their lands."

Slinking back slowly and keeping out of sight, Ruoridh scampered after Fingal who picked a careful way through the reeds around the lochan edge, heading towards the river they could see in the near distance.

The Taexali elders left in the local villages they had already visited would do what they could about sending back messages to Tap O'Noth, and from there the chain would be established to send their updates to the nearest Caledons, though only if they were not claimed by their gods or goddesses first. He was not sure if his Uncle Brennus would be pleased with what he was attempting, yet he hoped so.

However, he had not been so free in making plans with the few Vacomagi they had talked to. Something made him wary, but he had not yet worked out what, since the hospitality tendered to them as strangers had not been lacking. It was not reluctant, either, but it was lukewarm.

"Is there a good place to ford the Tuesis river?"

His question was met with a typical grin from Fingal. "How could I know? I have never been this far north, so it is in the hands of the goddess *Avon*. Should she favour our crossing, we will only dip in a toe and not die in our attempts to cross."

It was not for the first time that Ruoridh wondered if Fingal really appreciated what he attempted. He had no knowledge of the terrain at all: Fingal at least could claim to be relatively local. The Taexali warrior's instincts were good, though, and that was important. It took them only a short time of following the river course till they found a meander that became shallow enough to wade across, mostly just knee deep.

Taking care on the slippery stones of the river bed, Ruoridh ploughed his way across. On the Vacomagi banking, he yanked on the reeds to pull himself free from the clutch of the swirling current. The cloying cold from his sodden braccae made him shiver as he attempted to shake off what he could, before they moved on.

Fingal seemed less concerned about the water dripping from him, instead lifting a finger to point. "I suggest that hillock over there will give us an idea of where the best cover will be."

Ruoridh agreed. The land was very open and generally flat, some of it cultivated in field strips but places to hide behind were sparse. A couple of roundhouses were visible, and the smoke rising from behind a sizeable copse of trees indicated there were more dwellings further on.

From the top of the gentle rise, the land was laid bare. Not high, it was a knoll just sufficient for him to see ahead almost the whole way to the sands. The only parts obscured were hidden behind thickets dotted here and there.

"Which bit of the shore do you want to see first?" Fingal pointed a finger.

Ruoridh watched as his new warrior friend dragged his grubby nail along the sightline of the water's edge. "Over there," Fingal's progress came to an abrupt halt. "Are those the Roman ships we saw earlier?"

"I suppose so," he said. "I can see no others on that side of the Abhainn Tuesis."

Fingal drew his attention away from the small group of ships, his finger travelling along in the other direction. "I see another two groups of ships. There. And there." His finger halted. Almost directly ahead there definitely were some ships, and some further left again.

"Does that tiny twinkling mean a river mouth?" It was so faint he could not be sure.

His Taexali friend's head bobbed. "That would be sensible. They will need fresh water. I had not thought of that before. We will probably find them at all of the river mouths that flow into *Morimaru*'s waters."

Fingal's finger moved on and then stopped, his arm holding a position. "It is more difficult to tell because of those belts of trees between here and the shore, but I think I see ship masts rising up just there."

It took him time to peer further, but eventually he decided Fingal was right. That meant at least four different lots of ships on the shore line, the dark shapes of them just visible in the deepening-blue as the realm of *Taranis* dipped away into the grip of *Morimaru*'s water.

He stared at the last ones again. "Could those be Vacomagi ships?"

Fingal guffawed, his hand slapping his thigh. "I doubt Vacomagi ships have masts like that. Those mean a high sail, according to you earlier."

His stare continued. "Fingal? Have you ever seen any Vacomagi ships?"

His friend strutted away, his hand rising to push away wayward strands of hair that escaped from his braid. "How could I? Till now, I have never travelled this far."

Ruoridh was confused. "But you said you could take me to the Romans on the northern shores?"

Recovered again, Fingal stood in front of him. "And I have got you here, Ruoridh, my friend. But I have only ever heard tell of the sand down there. I have never felt it run through my fingers."

"Ah. The blind leads the blind. My Uncle Brennus would approve of you, Fingal!" He laughed, for what else was there to do.

"Where do we go next?" Fingal sounded hopeful, a cheeky smile beaming from ear to ear.

The question was a good one. He thought about his intentions. He had not planned much beyond travelling to Vacomagi shores to find out what Agricola's troops were doing. He could head straight towards the nearest cove which looked as though it held a few ships. It would mean crossing a number of strip fields that looked productive, but had next to no cover. Or, he could skirt the hillock they were on, find shelter for the night and head towards the larger group of ships that looked to be in a natural bay over to his left come the new dawn. The second possibility provided the best cover of bushes and small woods, even though it was not the shortest route to the shoreline. He had a hankering to understand why the Romans had not beached all of the ships in one area, and that meant getting closer to as many as possible.

"We will go straight ahead." He playfully nudged Fingal. "If they are Vacomagi ships, then it will still be news to my kin who know little or nothing about the Vacomagi. Though we had better get down from this knoll quickly and find shelter before dark descends fully."

Groping his way in the new-moonlight he approached the edge of the belt of trees. Stepping over the lichen-decked tangled remains of a fallen log he froze his position and held his breath. Flicking his hand back and forth a few times behind him, he warned Fingal to come no further. It was as well caution sat permanently on his shoulder.

No more than twenty paces beyond the wood's fringe Roman auxiliaries worked swiftly to take advantage of the weak light that was left to them. The trench of a small Roman camp had been dug, the soil piled up behind to create a wall about the shoulder-height of a man. Some soldiers were piling up the last of the turf that had initially been stripped off, deftly throwing the patches on the top of the mound.

Others scrambled in behind, beating the turves into place with flat tools. A couple of other soldiers were pounding in sharpened stakes lifted from a pile beside a flaring torch. They created a barrier to keep out marauding animals and not only local tribespeople who might dare to attack.

It was as well the Romans were so intent on their work and not looking his way, but Ruoridh knew it would only take a jerky movement from him and he might be detected. Side stepping, bit by bit, he got himself behind the nearest slender tree trunk. It wouldn't cover him but was much better than being totally exposed.

His prayers to *Cernunnos* were that the dimness of the god's surroundings would blend his body with the tree. It seemed an age that he froze there, just watching, reluctantly admiring the efficiency of the soldiers as they completed their fortifications.

One by one, when their task was completed they disappeared through the nearby opening and into the encampment.

His breathing evened out.

He could not see over the barrier, but from the noise of men shouting orders, and the thumping of wood, he guessed they were raising their tents. Flares of new firelight sparked up into the darkness. Ruoridh grunted. Those damned Roman invaders would be having a hot meal, or getting heat from the fire to warm their night. He could not see that in his near future.

His blood leapt, his fingers nipping into the tree trunk when an auxiliary came back through the opening, shouting to the only two men who still worked at the far end of the turf-topped wall. He had no idea what the soldier shouted, but the response petrified him. One of those at a distance slid down the newly packed turf into the ditch below before climbing back out on the side nearest to Fingal. In the growing dusk, the man grubbed around on the soil close to him, calling a reply, though shaking his head. Whatever the auxiliary had lost, it was important enough for all three men to begin searching the ground between the turf wall and the belt of trees, growing ever closer to where he and Fingal hid. One of the soldiers grabbed up the flaming torch to aid the search, fanning it back and forth over the trodden earth below their feet.

No more than two or three paces away from him, so close he could almost count the dark hairs on the nearest man's bent head, a triumphant cry halted the hunt. The dull thud of a heavy iron tool plopped down right at the wood's edge, even closer to him, the shout sounding as though it berated the soldier for being careless, or untidy. Ruoridh could not tell what, but after grasping up the tool that had a flat base attached to the shaft the soldier straightened up, guttural hollers his response. Something not complimentary from the sound of it as the soldier stared into the trees. It seemed the auxiliary had an afterthought when he dropped the tool again and groped aside the tunic material below his chain mail. The auxiliary stepped forward to one-tree-away from where

Ruoridh huddled, willing his body to be even thinner and more merged into the trunk. Unaware that he was there, the man emptied his bladder against the trunk, shouting all the while to his fellow auxiliaries.

Ruoridh closed his eyes, not wanting the man to see any glow in the darkness. He held his breath for longer than he ever thought possible. It was a long tense wait before the soldier finished. Opening his eyes to a slit, he watched as the soldier picked up the turf cutter and eventually turned around before walking back into the fortifications with the other two men. From the way they brandished their own tools, and the sounds of laughter, finding the cutter was likely to be a topic of conversation around the fireside.

He remained motionless for a while longer, to be sure that no one else would come out again, his body stiff from the tension of the episode. A brief recall of something his Uncle Brennus had said reminded him that every Roman soldier had to ensure no loss or damage to their equipment, or it cost them dearly. Turning around, he sought out Fingal. It was much darker looking back into the trees than out towards the moonlight. The merest flicker of Fingal's outstretched fingers indicated his position.

Stepping back to Fingal he whispered, sounds travelling so easily in the dark. "We cannot go forward that way."

"Nay," Fingal agreed. "But which are the worst predators?"

They had already heard movements of night animals stirring, and he was in no mood to do battle with a wolf or a wild boar. "What do you suggest?" He was hoping Fingal had a good idea for keeping them alive.

"We need to keep near the edge of this wood to be sure of getting out quickly, but not so close that any strays who might be returning to that camp are in our vicinity."

Picking his way slowly in Fingal's wake, it was an interminable time before his Taexali friend eventually crept out of the trees. Ahead there was no shelter that he could see, but it seemed that Fingal was a better tracker than he was because even in the weak moonlight, his friend found a successful route to the dunes. Once again Fingal had good instincts, having picked his way around areas of sticky, stinking-bogs that had he slid into he would likely never have got back out of. They were just skirting a shadowy clump of tall brushwood when Fingal's abrupt stop caused a collision.

"Listen." Fingal's warning gave him a jolt.

"I cannot hear anything." There was no tell-tale clanking of Roman metals.

Fingal grunted. "Not Romans. I hear a trickle of water somewhere close, and not the sea surge. Follow me."

He traipsed after Fingal like a faithful pup. Stopping and starting while the young warrior grubbed around, pushing back greenery, all the while swearing and cursing when he became snagged on the spiny bushes.

Eventually, his friend's satisfied tones filtered up to him. "Get your water pouch ready." Bent down, Fingal was already filling his from the tiniest trickle that wended its way down to the shore. Grateful that his water supply was replenished, Ruoridh lapped plenty into his mouth after tightening up his water skin. He had tasted sea water before and knew drinking it was no option.

Straightening up again, he felt a nudge to his shoulder.

"We can feed too, of a sort." Fingal pointed to the tallest bushes that were dotted around. "These have already felt the icy chills of the night, but near the sea they hopefully have not been severe. We will tear our hands to shreds, but the fruits of those sea-buckthorns are sure to be good sustenance."

Ruoridh was not convinced. In the dark, he could not tell what kind of bushes they were.

"Stop doubting me," Fingal chided. "Smell them. I know that smell even in the dark."

Picking the tiny berries that were only a little past their best was excruciatingly prickly, yet he knew that in some ways picking in the dark was faster than it would be by daylight. The nasty jagged thorns remained unseen, but every berry savoured was a triumph worth waiting for. After a first frantic gorging, he slipped as many into a waist pouch as he ate. They would be squashed and more likely tasteless come the morn, but it was always better to have something than nothing.

Traipsing back to the tiny burn, he let his shredded hands lie in the freezing water for as long as he could bear it.

"Not much further." Fingal dried off his palms on his cloak.

At the sea end of the dunes, Fingal found a natural hollow that would afford them some cover. His grins were easier to see in the moonlight reflecting off the water, but his hushed tones still held notes of caution.

To both sides of him, Ruoridh was relieved at not seeing any signs of Roman activity – not ships and not men.

"We will have to move come the first signs of dawn, but I will take first watch."

Ruoridh watched Fingal slide down to his knees after which he scooped out a deep trench in the fine sand, allowing the grains to trickle through his fingers.

"Look. I am here with the sand in my fingers, Ruoridh." Fingal's low-laugh was infectious. "We may sleep still hungry tonight, but come the morn foraging will be easier."

More memories stirred: of his kin being near the sea in the territory of the Venicones. One of the warriors of Trune, the High Chief of the southern Venicones, had shown him how to find little slimy animals of the shore. He could not remember the name given, but he would recognise them. He had learned how to winkle them out with a sharp ended twig and remembered the strong flavour of them on his tongue, though it had taken him time to get used to the slimy feeling as they slipped down his throat. He was sure to know them again. Perhaps they were something new to Fingal? The thought cheered him since he had been feeling very much the follower, than the leader, the last long while.

Ruoridh's last doubts before slipping down to sleep in his own scooped out hollow was about whether the marram grasses that Fingal was stripping out with his long knife would be sufficient to warm him in his little nest as he was showered with handfuls of them. Though in the chill night air, any warmth was going to be welcome. He realised he was frozen, yet strangely elated.

Chapter Twenty-Seven

Votadini Territory

Beathan woke up with a start when the icy water was thrown in his face. Brief prayers were sent to *Andarta* for he was still breathing and in reasonable condition, if his recent bruising was not counted. As he shook the water droplets from his head, he noted the first rays of pink that barely invaded the inky-darkness above. Faint they may be, but he knew the pre-dawn heralded his time of sleep was over. At first, he recognised nothing of his surroundings, but that was not so surprising since he had been led to his tethering place, in the dimness of a spitting-torchlight. He was outside a long wooden building. Still the first in his line, the main differences were that shackles had been renewed around his ankles reducing him to hobbling yet again. As before, he was chained by the wrist to the man next to him, but in addition he now had a long fetter attaching him to a huge iron ring set into the wall behind him.

"Up!" The command was issued along with a furious yanking at the tethers, as though some further down the line needed more awakening.

Preparing himself for another long trudge that he was not ready for, he was surprised when the line was ordered to stand ready. An auxiliary menaced in front of him, pacing back and forth, more auxiliaries covering the length of the slave line as he struggled to his feet, his legs weakened from the creeping cold and the cramped position he had been sleeping in. He almost cried out from the agonising tingling on the undersides of his feet. It was worse when he stamped them, but he knew that would eventually return the life-blood to them. Low groans of his fellow captives sounded along the line, though none dared to be too loud, unlike the other noises he was becoming aware of.

Some were the far-off whinnying of horses and the braying of mules. Others were barked out orders issued nearby and the sharp responses of a lot of men, their noise carrying in the new morning chill. The clanking of metal vied with the stirring of other men. Their laughter and their grumbles were startlingly loud as they spewed forth from the long building on the far side of the roadway just to his right, a path which led towards the fort walls.

He presently stood at the corner where one pathway crossed another. Directly in front of him was a strange building. Strong stout posts of wood held up a sloping roof of deep-red clay tiles behind which was a large empty space and a good walk away behind that were more posts with a roof above. A man could stroll under the overhang and not feel the fall of rain. He could not work out any other purpose for it, save that the strange roof was joined to a building at each end. It was such an odd sight it made Beathan smirk for the first time in days.

When the guard moved down his line, he sneaked a look over his shoulder to squint around the corner.

As in the encampment at Durno, he realised another inspection was underway when a *centurion* marched towards him, vine rod at the ready, though this time the *centurion* was in the company of a higher-ranking legionary soldier, his helmet much more decorative. Another soldier walked in behind them, carrying a board in one hand. Whipping his head round to look straight ahead as ordered, he wondered if the senior officer was a *tribune*. This time he could hear no conference between the senior officers as they approached.

After they rounded the corner, Beathan felt their assessing glances on him from head to toe.

"Name?" the *centurion* barked.

He could not be sure in the growing dawn, but the *centurion* held no familiarity, he did not look like any of the guards who had marched alongside him the day before although they were probably still fast asleep. That thought soured and curled his lip.

Not flinching when the vine rod slapped at his forearm was impossible: his reply had not come quick enough for this particular *centurion*.

The inspection of the whole line was swift. All too soon Beathan found himself unfettered and shoved into a brand new line, a short line of only a handful of captives. Utter dread washed over him.

These Romans forgot nothing! Those wax tablets ensured that every useful detail was passed on and passed on again. He let his chin drop to his chest. He would not allow the detested invaders to see that he was fighting to control the tears that threatened to fall from his stinging eyes.

How could he have let Agricola's soldiers know in the Moran Dhuirn camp that he was not just any Brigante but was the first son of Lorcan of Garrigill? He scarcely believed it but somehow his father's name was still known as an important Brigante, even though it was many seasons since his father had represented the Brigantes in peace treaties with the Roman scum.

He could not ever remember his father having mentioned that he had met Agricola when Agricola had been the *Legate* of the *Legio XX*. Lorcan had been in discussions with Governor Cerialis, that he did remember but not…Agricola.

Chapter Twenty-Eight

Haughs, Vacomagi Territory

Enya was pleased with Feargus' progress. His fever had subsided after she had used the feverfew infusion and his wound areas were not so red-angry by the time she had applied the second moist patch of herbs. She had tried a mixture of knitbone and plantain. She had never seen anyone use the two together, but the leaves of those plants were still fresh enough, given the heavy frosts of winter had sent most other plants near the dilapidated roundhouse into a winter-mush. The important thing was that either they had worked to make the wounds less tender, or it was the haphazard prayers that she had made to Feargus' goddess. When in delirium, he had constantly murmured pleas to *Dheathain*. Holding his hand and echoing his pleas to his local goddess had seemed to comfort him.

Determined to move on after two days of rest, their present journey westwards had been an easy one for her and Nith, though less so for Feargus, especially since they had recently had to use stepping stones to cross a trickling river bed. The woodland Enya was now making her way through had been flat enough, but entangled tree trunks were abundant. She had been leading for some time and had been forging the easiest pathway for Feargus to limp over. When the gloom gradually lightened, the thicker birches making way for reed thin saplings and bushes at the edge of the wood, her steps quickened across the less tangled undergrowth.

"Enya!" Nith's sudden hiss at her back had her hackles rising, but before she had time to prime her spear two warriors launched out from behind dense blackthorns.

"Go no further!" Their crossed spears allowed no pathway forward. "Why do you tread this way?"

Enya was not expecting that question. "We seek my brother who was lost to me after the battlegrounds at Beinn na Ciche."

The questions she expected first now came from the second warrior. "Who are you? And where are you from?"

Nith came abreast of her and between them they gave answer to the warriors' enquiries. When the investigation eventually ceased Nith put forward some questions of his own. "Your vigilance is praiseworthy. Have you halted many travellers who have made you uneasy about their purpose?"

One warrior's retort scathed, though Enya realised it was not really an answer to Nith's question. "Would you not be over cautious if unfamiliar people were wandering around in your territory?"

"Aye," Nith agreed. "You will have to take us at our word. We mean you no harm but do want to find Enya's kin. If you can help us, we will be grateful."

Their spears still a barrier, the larger of the men nodded to Feargus. "I watched you limping here. How came you by your injury?"

Enya saw that Feargus was embarrassed by the question, though he answered honestly. "I found to my cost that a Roman pilum has a longer reach than my running skills."

In his defence Enya jumped in. "We had to swim across the Abhainn Caelis to avoid a Roman patrol, and then found that the far bank had no nearby cover. Feargus did not come out of the Roman attack unscathed."

The men still looked unconvinced, but after a silent agreement they beckoned her to move closer.

"We allow none to freely wander our Vacomagi territory."

Enya could find no real fault in that as they followed one of the men, the other taking up position at the rear.

Out of the wood, she looked across the gently-rolling landscape that spread in front of them. The ground had been cleared to fields to the nearest low foothill, but she could see no roundhouses. That was not too unusual, though, since there were plenty of small copses dotted around which would obscure them. "What name do you give to this place?"

"Towie Mhor, behind that thicket, is our nearest hamlet." The warrior stopped talking then cupped his hands together.

His shriek of a wildcat startled her. It was not so much that he used similar methods to their own to make contact with his fellow warriors, but more that the volume the man achieved was truly deafening.

"Your guards are nearby?" Nith asked with a hint of a smile breaking his stern countenance.

Enya smirked at Nith's droll comment. There were no obvious signs of anyone near them.

The man's expression showed he was not fooled by Nith, his eyebrows an amused question. "Not so close that I could use the melodic trill of a linnet, but they are near enough to see you coming."

Nith's answering chuckle was good to hear. Enya reflected that it had been a while since her friend from Tarras had properly smiled.

"Nith makes good bird calls but the sweetness of the linnet is beyond him," she quipped, feeling her own grin spreading.

The warrior was soon ushering them into what seemed to be a fairly well-concealed and sufficiently defended roundhouse cluster of five small dwellings. At one of them, the warrior indicated they should enter.

Having gone through the low wattled entryway, Enya felt all eyes on her as she straightened up. The conversation of a handful of men and a couple of women, seated around the fireside, ceased till Nith and Feargus joined her.

"Sit and tell me of your purpose in breaching our territory."

The order coming from the man seated facing the doorway held no customary welcome, but Enya guessed him to be the leader of the village.

After some very direct questioning, the man seemed satisfied about their purpose. "My warriors must be overly cautious. We monitor our surroundings thoroughly. Some Vacomagi families have fled to the mountains, though most remain in their homes."

Enya caught Nith's glance. From the warning signs in his intense eye-flare, she knew to be careful with anything she said. If Vacomagi tribespeople were still in their dwellings, they were very different from their Taexali neighbours.

"Have the Romans not been threatening them?" Her question was hesitant, but she felt even more disheartened with the man's answer.

"Vacomagi from the tidal area of the Abhainn Tuesis warned us some moons past about the Roman ships that patrol along their coastline, but it was not till recently that the Roman hordes began to patrol our flatlands by the Haughs."

"How close are the Romans to your village?" Nith asked.

"If the day was clear enough from the Towie rise above us, you would be able to look across the valleys and see their new encampment."

"Do they threaten you and your neighbours?" Nith's question was met with a hoot of derision from the man who claimed leadership.

"What do you think?" He sounded affable enough, but in his eyes was a glimpse of a snared animal.

That was not what Enya wanted to hear. "Have you had other people approaching your dwellings?" she asked.

"One Vacomagi warrior passed through some three nights past on his way to the An Cuan Moireach coastline, but otherwise you are the only ones we have seen coming this way for a half-moon. Wary people do not wander."

Enya felt it time to let the questions rest. She had a gut feeling the answers given were only half-truths, but Feargus was not so cautious.

"We really need to find Enya's brother. Her family are deeply concerned about their missing kin. Are there other villages around these parts where Vacomagi might have sheltered visitors?"

The leader looked across to one of the men sat around the fireside. "Nhiall came to us from the Laich. Ask him."

Nhiall stopped whittling the wood he had been shaping to answer. Enya thought the glint in his eye as acute as the blade that twinkled in the firelight. "My fellow Vacomagi farmers of the flatlands had two choices. Stay and face the commands of the Romans who disgorged from their ships. Or scatter to join our brothers who resist from the old places."

"Do you mean the standing stone circles of the ancients?" Enya found the conversation hard to follow.

The man's twisted smile gave little away. "The old stones might give some comfort to those who sometimes still worship there, but they give no real shelter."

Nith questioned before Enya could voice it. "Are you saying that some of your fellow Vacomagi tribespeople gather at other places?"

"Aye. Some do."

From the bland tone, Enya could not tell whether there was approval or not. While she thought about the possibility that the men around her had already capitulated to the Roman yolk, Nith continued with some further questions, ever hungry to know more about the landscape they might travel across next.

"Does this Laich you speak of have only small hamlets?"

Nhiall scoffed. "Nay, the Laich is the most-favoured ground hereabouts. That is where you will find the largest Vacomagi villages."

"Would visitors like us, who seek the advice of local people, be warned to stay clear of the coastline now that the Romans are occupying it?" Feargus' direct question was a surprise to her since he had been silent for a while.

One of the warriors burst into harsh laughter. "We would advise you to steer clear of all Vacomagi territory till you know if the Romans do more than march into it."

Enya was becoming even more wary and extremely confused. Was she sitting amongst warriors who had already given allegiance to Rome? Spending time with these men of cryptic answers now seemed too hazardous to contemplate further, and finding her brother through them sounded impossible.

The chief's smile was rueful. "We can give you directions to our larger gathering places, but we cannot be sure who might occupy them now."

Enya sat up straighter and addressed Nhiall of the Laich. "Are these places in the Laich?"

Nhiall's head dipped. "What the chief refers to are places like the stone walls on the promontory at Am Broch."

Nith sounded just as confused as she did when he asked more questions. "Are you saying that Am Broch is not an old stone fortress, but something else?"

The Vacomagi leader's smile was rueful. "Aye. Some seek the protection of the round walls of stone that tower up to the skies of *Taranis*."

Enya could tell Nith was not yet convinced of the man's meaning. "Did the ancients dwell behind these walls you speak of?"

The man laughed. "Am Broch may be very old, but I doubt as old as the ancients you speak of. Am Broch harbours many busy people. Some work inside, though perhaps some also sleep there."

Enya was out of patience with evasive answers. "Then we will ask at Am Broch. And if my brother is not there, are there other gathering places we can try in Vacomagi territory?"

Nhiall scratched his whiskers and looked to the village leader for confirmation. "I imagine that Dunrelugas will harbour some warriors. That is an old stone fort near the Abhainn Fionn Èireann."

A short conversation ensued which eventually confirmed that there would probably be some warriors up at Dunrelugas, but with few people moving around Vacomagi land the chief claimed that no one could be sure of anything anymore.

Enya feared she would learn nothing of her brother. Her spirits low, she was glad that Nith took charge of the conversation.

"Do most of your Vacomagi families who fled to the mountains intend to return soon?"

The leader of the hamlet snorted. "Nay. Those who went will remain gone till sure it is safe to return. Why would they leave the security of the hills and return to areas that the Roman army already occupy?"

"Have the Romans confronted you here?" Enya knew the question was a foolish one as soon as she had voiced it, but she was tired. Tired and dispirited with a conversation that went round and round and got no where at all.

The leader stared at her. It made her feel uncomfortable. Deep down it hurt to be under suspicion.

After a pause his words were sombre. "You told me you had been part of the confrontation at Beinn na Ciche."

She hated the feeling of being distrusted, but that was now the fate of any travellers till their reason for being anywhere was proved to be valid. What were her brother, and possibly her cousin, going through every single day?

Her reply was apologetic. "My question was foolish. I do know what a marching legion looks like. I should not have asked such a thing. Of course we would not be here at your hearth if the Romans had come to your village."

Enya wanted to lie down and sleep away the problem but she was a guest in the roundhouse and till bid to rest, she had to remain awake in their company. The warrior was correct about the invidious Roman presence. It seemed yet again she would not hear of her brother…or her cousin.

She was more than glad to have Nith's body curving around her own, his arm relaxed over her middle, when they settled for the night in a small space on the floor near the fire in the very crowded roundhouse. Their hosts seemed more hospitable by the end of the evening but not enough to make her feel really welcome. Feargus was alongside her, though just not quite so close as Nith.

"Try to relax, Enya." Nith's words were the tiniest of whispers at her ear, his lips so close she felt their softness against her skin. "I will let no harm come to you."

She had no doubt that he would look after her but as to relaxing, with him so tantalisingly close? That thought just might keep her awake all night long.

And she did not imagine the stretch of his long fingers burrowing across her bratt to find the edge of it, and when he did, his fingertips rested just inside.

***

"Not another river that I must cross?"

The following day, Feargus' horrified expression made Enya want to smile, but she could not show Feargus her humour.

"It will be much easier this time," Nith cajoled as he strode forward to the water's edge. "This time we will not let you delve too deep. Granted, it is wider than the last one, but I am sure not nearly as deep at this curve."

Feargus pointed to the fast flowing water eddying around the middle. "That would suck anyone down in a blink."

Enya agreed about the strength of the flow, but they had no option. They had no time to go upriver to the source to find a narrower fording place. They had been told that the origin was many days away and high in the mountains. She had to convince Feargus he would survive another wetting.

"Feargus, I am crossing whether or not you do. If you do not want to come with me, go back to Towie Mhor and wait there till I return. Or, perhaps better still, return to Lulach at Ceann Druimin." She made herself sound out of patience with him. "Nith can also do as he pleases, but I am going to the northern coast."

Nith's slither into the shallower water at the river's edge was better than any words.

"I know you fear the water, Feargus, so perhaps it is better that you do not cross with us. I do not want to leave you here, but I must go on to find my brother. So this has to be a farewell." She broke off to glance at Nith's progress across the river before turning back to Feargus. "May the gods go with you. Take care of your wound and do not let it fester. I hope to see you at Ceann Druimin before another moon has passed with news of my brother."

After a swift pat to his shoulders, she turned away and slid into the water. Ahead of her Nith had reached almost the middle. From the slow and deliberate steps he took, she could see how much he battled against the current. But he had been correct about the water's depth. It sloshed around his chest though no deeper than that.

"Wait!" Feargus sounded desperate.

The agitated splashing from behind told her that Feargus had slid down the banking. Barely hip-deep, she reached back to steady him, grabbing his elbow to keep him upright. When Nith came back towards them, she gave him room to reach for Feargus' shoulder. Saying nothing, Nith dragged their tight-lipped Taexali friend across the river while she pushed from behind.

At one point around the curve, the current grew strong enough to knock her off her feet but with Feargus still firmly in Nith's grip still, he was the one who maintained her link to the chain. Drifting away would have been some sort of retribution meted out by the local river goddess, but she was glad to have avoided that.

Apart from a few instances where the water sloshed over Feargus' head, it was a battle easily won. As they again shook themselves and their weapons free of water on the far bank, Feargus' natural optimism broke forth. "Next time, I may pray just as hard for my passage across, but I should fear the task less than before."

Nith punched playfully at Feargus' shoulder. "Should we ever have the opportunity, and a peaceful enough time to do it, Enya and I will make a swimmer of you. But for now, we need to walk at a good pace or the clothes will freeze upon us."

The teasing look Nith sent her way warmed her more than a speedy lope, much more even than the winter heat from *Lugh* above ever could.

After the crossing of the Abhainn Tuesis they crept between the best of the sparse cover they could find as they headed to the coast. The pace was not as fast as Nith would have liked, but it suited Feargus' dragging gait and frequently suppressed agony.

Since Nith was leading, and Feargus was at her rear, Enya had time to reflect on the men who flanked her, and who continued to confuse her. For a time she had felt herself more drawn to Feargus, especially when he needed her tending skills…but now?

She feared her judgement, feared her feelings. Her initiation into the mating processes was becoming more inevitable with each new day, but choosing which man was something she had not anticipated.

Chapter Twenty-Nine

Auchinhove Roman Camp, Vacomagi Territory

"Summon the senior *tribune*s immediately." Agricola turned away from the guard at his tent then had second thoughts. "And also the *Primus Pilus* of *Legio XX*."

Realising that the new arrivals approaching him were from the fleet, he halted the departure of the guard, yet again. He had chosen his guards for their efficiency, and they were proving to have been very good choices. "Terentius! Find out if Manius Helva is back in camp."

He recognised one of the newcomers, but could not remember what the mariner's command was. The others were new faces. It rattled him that his memory for people was slipping: he used to be so good at recall. "Which ship have you come from?"

"*Salve,* General Agricola! I am the *trierarchus* of the *Fides.*"

Agricola's acknowledgement of the captain's salute was prompt before he launched in with impatient questions. "Where is your ship beached?"

"A half day's march from here. We put to shore near the Tuesis estuary a short while ago."

"You sailed from Baile Mheadhain?"

"I did, sir. As requested."

"Have the last of the higher ranking slaves been shipped off southwards to the Vedra from Baile Mheadhain?"

"The ship they were due to travel in had not yet returned."

"Was the line delayed because of that?"

"All I know is that the captives were not in camp on my last night at Baile Mheadhain."

"If that last line left when the Durno camp was abandoned then they made very slow progress." He broke off to speak to Crispus. "Find out why they tarried in transporting that last batch of slaves."

Agricola turned back to the captain. "You have new information for me?"

"All three ships sent to patrol the far northern coast beyond the Varar Aestuarium have now returned and are berthed beside my ship. The *centurions* have full reports of the immediate coastline north of it." The *trierarchus* indicated his companions.

After salutes were exchanged, Agricola was impatient. "Tell me all."

"Daylight being short, we put to shore when we could. We explored the flatlands close to the white sands but the villages of the local tribes were empty, though not abandoned."

"Shy?" Agricola's attempt at humour was poor. He knew it was much more likely that the tramp of thirty of his fully armed mariners had terrified any tribespeople into running for cover.

The *trierachus*' smile was a tight one. "Distrustful, sir, and not inclined to clash with us. There are few villages along that extensive shoreline. Mostly the high hills slope almost down to the sands with limited flat strips to the marram grasses and the dunes."

He fired questions at another of the *centurions*, the answers extremely disheartening.

"Exploring the hills and mountains would take many days, sir. From our questioning of the few locals we did encounter, it seems there are even fewer tribespeople inhabiting their mountain areas than were found in Taexali territory."

Further questions satisfied Agricola. They corroborated the already known findings about the bleak northern coastal land, information gathered from previous voyages of his fleet. He thanked the *centurions* before dismissing them and then turned back to the *trierarchus*.

"A *cohort* of the *Legio IX* is already in place to establish a permanent *castellum* near the mouth of the River Tuesis. Your men of the fleet will support this small fort. An additional *cohort* of the *Legio II Adiutrix* will base themselves at the mouth of the river the locals name the Fionn Èireann. Should we have any resistance from any local Vacomagi, then we will build a smaller *castellum* between those two just mentioned, men of *Legio IX* providing support to the *Legio II Adiutrix* advances into the nearest Caledon mountain passes. Speak to our camp engineer before you return to your ship. He is organising the other *agrimensors* and the necessary ironwork – give him any details that might be of use to him."

"Sir." The *trierarchus* acknowledged the orders but his open mouth indicated he had more to say. "These fortlets are always best situated very close to the shoreline for offloading and loading of supplies but in this territory bogs and marram grasses stretch far-in from the sands. Existing tracks through the bogs would not presently do for heavy wagons, though lighter loads could be dragged over it."

Agricola stifled a grunt. "We can deal with that. The *agrimensors* can build supported pathways."

He thought on the logistics of that plan. It was possible, though likely slow to execute. The hills of the Caledons had plentiful supplies of wood, even if Taexali and Vacomagi territories did not.

It sounded as though it would be worthless sending on the supply wagons too soon, which he now had. "Are the Caledon hills always within sight of the Varar Aestuarium shoreline?"

"No, sir. The land is very flat from the sea for some distance. Then low hills block the skyline with many shallow valleys between. I am told that the major mountain passes that are used as tracks to the south are well behind that."

Agricola switched to future planning rather than the more immediate. Stepping towards the *Porta Praetoria,* he bid the *trierarchus* to accompany him. "Tell me what you saw on your journey to the headland at the end of Britannia."

A lengthy discussion left Agricola feeling elated that his ships had actually rounded the cape, and from the helmsman's description they had come to the many small islands mentioned by his fleet who had sailed the western coastline three summer seasons ago. Though, he was less than cheered that the helmsman described the northernmost terrain as being treeless and bleak, boggy-moorland. He still wanted to proclaim that he had conquered all of northern Britannia, yet he needed more reasons to justify marching his *legions* there. There was no point in Rome subsuming even more countryside that brought no tangible rewards.

He thanked the *trierarchus*. "I may seek more answers from you this evening. Remain in camp till the morning."

Agricola's thirst for knowledge of everything he had not yet conquered was now desperate. To not know everything about Britannia was unthinkable. He had been in Britannia for too long and yet not nearly long enough. It had been such an age since, as a youth in Massalia, he had learned of the voyage of Pytheas. A voyage where the old seafarer had sailed the coast of an island he had named as Pretannica.

It was an experience he so desperately wanted for himself but since Fortuna rarely favoured him now, he had to piece together the whole journey through the eyes of his mariner captains.

"Where have you two come from?" His question was directed to the soldiers who approached him, both pinched-looking and bedraggled.

The first to reach him answered. "Pinnata Castra, sir."

Returning the man's salute he smiled. "How much progress do they make at my newest supply fortress?"

The soldier launched into a series of new developments as he pulled out a thick batch of wooden boards from his pack.

A tingle of satisfaction warmed Agricola. "That fares well. What news of the natives?"

The soldier handed over a scroll that had been tightly clenched in his fist. "There have been skirmishes where the Venicones territory meets that of the Taexali, though all is quiet again now, sir. This report is from Quintus Bassianus, *Tribunus Laticlavius* of the *Legio XX*."

Flicking open the wax seal, he scanned the contents. He allowed himself a moment before replying. "Did you set out before him?"

"I did, sir. He had some issues to deal with, but did not expect them to take long. He intends to be with you by mid-day tomorrow."

"Then he will likely have a longer ride than he anticipates." Agricola's quick grin took away any barb. He knew just how attached his *tribune* was to being in residence in the supply fortress. "But no matter, he will find me, eventually." Briefly thanking the soldier before dismissing him, Agricola turned his attention to the other one.

"Sir, I am assigned to the staff of *Legatus* Salvius Liberalis."

Agricola's smile widened further and stretched his cold cheeks. Asking the man a couple of simple welcoming questions, designed to ensure the soldier was who he claimed to be, Agricola was satisfied. "Your dispatches are well overdue! I hope you have more than just correspondence from Londinium?" His question was an impatient one.

"I do, sir."

When the messenger made to pull out the contents of the over-laden bag slung across his chest, Agricola forestalled him and bid him follow. Once back at his tent, Crispus was at his elbow before he even needed to issue any orders.

On his nod, the soldier held out a first batch. "The *Praefectus Castrorum* of Eboracum asked me to deliver this personal correspondence from him. A courier will follow with routine news."

Accepting a small pile of scrolls, Agricola studied the messenger. Though he had not encountered the man before, he was clearly one of the small group of elite couriers that had been set up to ensure the most sensitive of correspondence never got into the wrong hands.

The man rummaged around and extracted more from the copious bag. "This comes from Deva."

"You were at Deva?" Agricola's abrupt question was quickly denied.

"No, sir. The correspondence I carry has been given to me first at Londinium, and then at Eboracum. The Deva scrolls come to you via Eboracum."

Agricola had to be content with that, but he was not happy if sensitive information had been read by the wrong people in the interim. He handed all of the given scrolls to Crispus to put onto his table at the rear of the tent.

"Your bag is still not empty." Agricola gestured to the bulge at one side of the canvas.

"A few more batches, sir. These are from Viroconium Cornoviorum, again given to me in Eboracum."

The soldier rooted around and pulled forth yet another scroll from a deep pocket. "*Legatus* Salvius Liberalis instructed me to give this one into your own hands, sir."

"Your journey has been a long one." Agricola accepted both bundles, handling the one from his Judicial Legate with some relief.

"Poor weather and early dusk has not hampered my progress, sir."

From the weary lines on the man's face and the dirt on man and clothes, Agricola could see the courier had no need to justify the long days it had taken to travel the hundreds of *mille passus* from the newly constructed Governor's House at Londinium.

Undersized *cohorts* of the *Legio XX* had been left in place at Viroconium Cornoviorum to guard Rome's interests in the area, along with one of the auxiliary *cohorts* newly raised from Gaul, the units that Domitian had reluctantly allowed him to assemble. The bulk of the *Legio XX* was with him in his northern campaign, but it was crucial those left around the fortress in Cornovii territory kept the region stable. He pulled apart a seal from Viroconium Cornoviorum and scanned the contents.

The news was not as good as he hoped, though peace of sorts did prevail. Some of his newest civic arrangements were meeting with some resistance, it seemed, but he was determined to persist with them. He re-read the missive carefully before instructing Crispus they would deal with it soon. His response needed more thought. Some of his predecessors, as Governors of Britannia, had had a much easier job over encouraging the creation of Roman towns in the far-south of Britannia. Those tribes had accepted the structure of Roman rule more readily, recognising the advantages that links with the Roman Empire had already brought them.

To the contrary, the tribes he presently had to deal with continued to demonstrate a reluctance to change their habits. However, he knew that stability only came with good governance and that required consistent perseverance. More obeisances to the goddess *Concordia* would be in order, since he needed her powers of agreement and understanding to be more freely bestowed.

He wiped his brow free of lingering droplets of rain, a huge sigh rumbling right down to his freezing toes. These northern barbarians would accept Rome, too, though domination had to come first.

Rolling the scroll, he tapped it against his palm as he paced away from the courier and down the *Via Principalis*. More soldiers stationed in the Viroconium Cornoviorum area would be a greater threat to those locals, and would bring more effective results, but he needed every last man who was presently around him. He could not expect his men to keep the tribes peaceful with less than they presently had, but he had none to spare to send south. It was yet another logistic to work his way through.

Whirling back to the courier who stood patiently waiting, he again pondered the merits of extending the Empire's boundaries with limited men at his disposal to maintain order. Subduing the stubborn Cornovii and neighbouring Ordovices tribes had been his first priority when he had assumed the governorship of Britannia. It had taken commendable engagement though he was under no illusions as to what could happen if insufficient forces remained to keep the area stabilised, and productive for the empire's coffers.

He gave the scroll into Crispus' competent hands. "On my desk, please."

The written word was too often open to misinterpretation or worse, correspondence sometimes ended up in the wrong hands, or in the hands of the enemy. As Governor of the whole of Britannia it was unthinkable that his authority was questioned, or flouted. He held out his hand for another batch from the courier.

"These come from the Lady Domitia Decidiana."

Agricola accepted the large tightly bound pile with a formal nod. He needed time and leisure before opening those from his wife. He enjoyed her news but concluded that since there was no urgency indicated by the messenger, she must fare well enough. He went off to set the pile on his desk himself then turned around and back to the courier who now held out another large wrapped bundle.

"Also from the *Legatus* Salvius Liberalis, sir." The man's voice dropped to a confidential whisper. "To be put into your hands, or destroyed if that was not possible."

Agricola felt no enthusiasm as he accepted the scroll which was sealed in the name of his second-in-command of Britannia. It was thickly rolled which likely meant there was another scroll embedded within: one that no doubt came from Domitian.

Walking towards the back of the tent, he unrolled it carefully and removed the inner communication. Breaking Domitian's seal, he scanned it quickly.

A cold sweat broke at his temples. Conditions he could not possibly meet. He read on to the end of the missive.

Rome!

In sheer frustration, he fired the rolled scroll sideways, the thwack of it hitting the tent side a thunderbolt crack from *Jove*. He grimaced as it dropped to the moist ground behind his table, thankful that Lentulus, who scurried to retrieve it, could not see how much the devastating missive had twisted his innards.

A sudden hollering outside the tent halted the progress of his desolation. His junior scribe whipped up and laid the scroll on the table before dashing out to investigate the commotion.

Agricola drew a calming breath before he turned around. Lentulus had a bedraggled Batavian *optio* in tow. Blood seeped from an arm-wound so brutal that the limb might never recover from it. While listening to the auxiliary's information, his frustration spiked. These Taexali and Caledon warriors were far too skilled at petty insurrection around the mountain fringes.

"How many men have we lost?"

"Eight are dead, sir, including our *centurion* that they were fighting alongside. Thirteen are wounded, some severely."

Though the soldier stood tall, he could see the *optio* was incredibly strong to be able to ignore his own condition.

Agricola wanted to wipe out every single one of the Caledon bastards but how could he do that and obey these new orders from his deranged emperor?

There was still so much to do in Caledonia!

Chapter Thirty

Well of Buinach, Vacomagi Territory

Feargus' wound healed well, but their pace during the previous days had been slow in order to avoid the increasing numbers of mounted Roman patrols that peppered the vicinity as they scoured the Vacomagi roundhouses for any visitors.

"Aye, this is Well of Buinach." The woman's leathery skin was stretched-tight across her sunken cheeks.

She invited Enya and the other two into her ramshackle roundhouse. Bidding them all join her at the fireside, it took great effort for the old woman to lower her bent frame onto a stool.

"You choose to remain here alone? Even though you know the Roman hordes are likely to descend upon you?" Enya asked, once her host was settled.

"My legs carry me no distance now, and I am ready to go when my goddess *Momu* calls me. As for the Roman scum – they have already been rummaging around me. Next time they will kill me, or will move on. Regardless, my coming summer days will be few."

She sounded so sure Enya believed the woman.

"My kin will return when the Roman shite sail off again." The gob of phlegm spat into the tiny fire was as thickly-yellow as it was accurate.

As in the couple of previous roundhouses, the woman claimed to have had few visitors. "The Vacomagi who stay around these parts hope to reap another hairst, but that may prove to be a hasty decision on their part. It may be that their fields revert to the goddess *Anugh* while their bodies rot in their roundhouses, should the whim of the Romans turn against them. Others, like my kin, stay safe in the mountains. Were I many years younger, that is where I would also be." The old woman broke off to wheeze.

Enya waited till the hacking cough ceased. "If you have already had Roman soldiers marauding around your home, I do not imagine there will have been many other visitors like ourselves?"

The answer was a nod while the woman beat her upper chest with her open palm, the resultant barking intended to ease her speech. "Only two young warriors during this last moon bided who were foolhardy enough to be travelling to An Cuan Moireach."

Enya's spirits lifted at the mention. "Did they give you their names?"

The old woman stared at the fire. "They may have done, but I do not remember. They were not here long enough for me know them well. Their haste to devour my thin broth rivalled their conversation. I learned little of them, save that their plans were muddled." She managed to cackle and pick at her teeth with a well-used twig at the same time before continuing, "The older one claimed they intended to travel as far west along the Vacomagi coastline as they could, and as far north into the lands of the Decantae and the Lugi as they needed to track the progress of the Roman ships. The other one only talked of what a southern Brigantes tribe had done to thwart the Romans. I know nothing of Brigantes."

"Ruoridh!" Enya gasped. "That had to be my brother. Did that one look like me?"

The woman lifted her head and peered at her.

"How can I tell that? I see you through a misty veil, just as I saw those other visitors."

Enya dipped her head. The old eyes were definitely milky and she had not noticed, her own wishes too selfishly prominent. Amends needed to be made. "Whether it was my brother or a stranger, I thank you for your kindness to them and for your welcome to us."

Nith probed for more details after the old woman had given them all some aging barley-beer.

"Where were they headed when they left here?"

The woman sniggered, but it was a bitter one. "I warned them it was not a good idea but they have gone where everyone congregates just now."

"Do Vacomagi warriors intend to confront Agricola's armies?" Enya was flabbergasted.

"Vacomagi? Nay, lass. You will not find any coastal Vacomagi massing together: they would not dare." The old woman's crowing ceased to be replaced by a sarcastic look that would strip a hide. "It is the Roman *legions* from their many ships that have made camp near the sands." Her bony arms waved about restlessly. "Climb the Hill of Buinach and see. For myself, I have to believe the word of others."

Nith rose from the fireside, beckoning to Feargus as he did so. "We will not be long."

Enya knew they were more likely to be bagging something for the old woman's pot than viewing the land from the hilltop. Helping the infirm they encountered, even in a very small way, was a responsibility that Nith took seriously, a trait she was very proud of. No matter their own haste to journey on, there were tribespeople who were far less able. She kept the conversation going for the short while it took for her friends to return, learning of the best paths to take and which marshes to avoid.

"This very fine brace of grouse just flew right up and in front of our sling shot as we climbed Buinach. It is a pity we cannot lug them with us, but I am sure your pot, over there, will not be too small for them." Nith's grin was wide as he laid them down on one of the flat stones that ringed the fire's edge.

The gratitude of the old woman was well worth the delay.

***

Enya soon encountered yet another river flow, the Abhainn Losaidh, but they all crossed it without any drama from Feargus. Dripping from the shoulders down, she tramped westwards flanked by her equally cold and wet companions: their clothes never properly dry even though there was a brisk wind. The landscape was flat and cover was scant as they skirted field-strip after field-strip, using bushes for cover, and scuttling across any exposed areas to the nearest copse of trees.

She was glad it was past the festival of Samhain. The farming folk they spied from a distance only crept out of their roundhouses to quickly tend to their animals, before scuttling back into the warmth. Since speaking to the old woman of Buinach, Enya had agreed that they should avoid being seen by the neighbouring Vacomagi. The chances now seemed too high that the locals would betray them.

When she had crested a particular bald-headed hilltop, Enya gasped. Not too far off, little clusters of roundhouses lay close to field areas which stretched almost all the way down to the waters of An Cuan Moireach. Though that was not what made her breath hitch.

Earlier, she had given thanks to *Taranis* when the day had dawned fine, only an occasional cloud marring the blue above which made it easy to catch glimpses of sun-streaked metal and the dark smudge of the tented camp close to the shoreline.

"Your brother will surely not be down there…" Feargus' question faded away.

Enya stared at the shadowy throng in front of her. The distant Roman camp held nothing like the amount of men in the many fisted camp at Moran Dhuirn across from Beinn na Ciche, but it was still a threatening presence on the landscape. As were the Roman ships that were tiny to her eyes. "Is that three or four ships?"

Feargus shaded his eyes to peer better. "I would say four. From this distance, I would guess they are a mixture of the vessel sizes that we saw at Baile Mheadhain."

"Aye. But that camp is much larger than for mariners from a few ships. The fleet down there has support from an auxiliary *cohort*," Nith snarled, clearly not pleased by the prospect.

Beyond the encampment the water twinkled, a short distance to the land on the far side of the firth. "What territory is that distant shore?" she asked.

Nith grunted at her side. "Not Vacomagi."

"Lugi?" Feargus said. "Someone told me a long time ago that one of the tribes beyond the Vacomagi worshipped the sun god *Lugh*. And I remember something about a Decantae tribe who are said to have come from very distant shores, many ancestors ago."

Enya shared out their meagre pile of dried berries. Chewing a mouthful, she stared at the scene below.

Feargus wiped the drips of water from his wispy whiskers before re-tightening his water skin. "I'll need to fill this ere long but more urgent might be deciding which direction we should take next. It seems to me that we have meandered around."

Nith's smile was not mirrored in his pale-green eyes when he turned to face her. "The sensible route would be to head back to Ceann Druimin, but I fear that will not be what you think, Enya?" He playfully nudged her knee with his own.

What kind of encouragement he indicated she was not sure of. His teasing had become much more physical of late, more personal and...sensual – something she was beginning to like very much.

It was, also, very distracting, yet she had no intention of going back now that she was so close to finding Ruoridh. Instead, she pointed towards the distant Roman camp and turned aside to address Feargus. "My brother is not a coward. If he and his friend have reason to go closer to that camp, they will find a way, though they would be foolish to linger."

Feargus used his grubby nail to pick fragments of dried meat from his front teeth. "I can believe that," he said, "but why would they want to be down there with all of the dangers surrounding them? Those glints flashing in the sunshine are patrols moving in all directions from that natural harbour."

"Aye." Nith turned slightly to get a different view. "And a good number of those glints are headed this way. If we are not careful, we may be in no position to find that brother of yours, Enya."

"My brother is dicing with danger to gather information about those Romans."

Feargus sniffed reflectively. "And what will he expect to do with any information he has gathered?"

Before Enya could answer Nith pointed to the bottom of the hill. "I see no evidence of the Romans putting any of those roundhouse villages to the torch. The spiralling smoke down there is from busy hearths, not from a more sinister firing. I can even make out some of their domestic animals foraging around the hamlets, peacefully and with no haste. Do either of you see any signs of Roman repression?"

She looked below in all directions. There were small clusters here and there, all the way to the sparkling water. "Nay. But they did not burn all of the Taexali roundhouses either."

Feargus got to his feet. "That was because most of the able Taexali had fled to join Calgach or because they had already killed the occupants. The Romans had no need to destroy the roundhouses to deny their owners a shelter."

"You have the right of it, Feargus." Nith stood up. "Those Vacomagi are not like your kinfolk. If the Romans have not burned out those villagers, or massacred resistant tribespeople, then the reason is clear."

Enya jumped to her feet as well. "The Vacomagi have made treaties already! They must have. We must send word to our kin at Ceann Druimin."

Chapter Thirty-One

Millbuie, Vacomagi Territory

"Do you plan to run all the way back to Ceann Druimin? Have you given up all hope of finding your brother?" Nith clutched at Enya's bratt as she stomped her way down the slope, momentarily pulling her from her desperate stride. Whipping in front to confront her and stop her headlong rush, she blasted fury at his face.

"Leave me be, Nith of Tarras. I did not ask you to dog my heels…or my toes."

Refusing to cower beneath her ire, he stared into her furious expression. Since he was now downhill their gazes clashed at an even level. After a few moments the glistening began, but Enya refused to acknowledge any weakness. He changed his tone to reassuring.

"Continuing that way in anger will surely lead to disaster, Enya. Close your eyes. Clear away your wrath. And then look down the hill. Who do you see beyond the distant copse of trees?"

He waited till Enya controlled herself. Knowing it would not take long, he held her in place with a light grip at her shoulders, unable to prevent his thumbs from soothing her trembling. When she opened her eyes and looked over his shoulder and down the hill, the fire went out of her.

But only for a moment.

Bracing herself against his grip, her tone was still determined as she came nose to nose with him. Her words tickled his lips, so quiet as to almost be silent. "Then I will crest the hill behind me and go a different route. With, or without you, daubed to my body."

His innards flared at her blatant change to tantalising though he let his palms drop to his sides. Staring at her expression, now changed to something akin to longing, he moved close enough to whisper against her ear, his lips touching the soft skin around it. "And I will be there every step of the way, Enya. I will not leave you. Whether you believe it yet, or not, you are bound to me as I am to you."

"If you both want to be caught by that Roman patrol that inches closer to us then so be it, but I am heading back over the hill now to find some cover for the night. Dusk is already descending."

Feargus' snippy tones broke the spell Enya had on him. Shelter for the night sounded good but not just to be out of the cold, or away from the dangers of the marauding Roman patrol. Sleep might bring dreams. Though, he knew exactly who was likely to disturb his slumber.

Being daubed next to her body, as she termed it, during recent nights had led to him losing a lot of sleep. She had definitely relaxed under his arm, sleep coming to her fairly quickly, but controlling his feelings…and urges…had been a trial. Though no longer. Enya's responses to him were clearer now. He was sure that Feargus was not the prime subject of her affections. Breaking the barrier of having been a loving foster brother to her for so long was achievable, he just needed to find the best opportunity to assure her that his love for her was a mature one. That of a man and his long-term mate.

After an intensely curious scrutiny of him, Enya whirled around. He followed her up the hill wondering what the strange regard was all about.

They were half way down the other side of the hill when Nith spotted the roundhouse. Smoke seeped out of the conical roof. It also wisped out of the side-walls in places, the low wattling in a poor state. Its inhabitants looked to be unable to renew deteriorating parts that had been too long exposed to the elements. Whatever the truth of it, he urged the other two to caution as he withdrew his sling. A hare for the pot above that fire might be well-received because they had disturbed plenty of them as they descended the hill. A nod to Feargus was sufficient for the lad to head a short way in the opposite direction. They had found success came more swiftly when they shared the task. If one of their sling shots failed to stun or kill, then the other tended to catch the creature as it scurried off in panic through the scrub.

Though dusk was well-drawn, it took no time at all for Feargus to make the first kill. A second frantic hare had no luck in escaping his own slingshot. A good few more of the creatures scurried across to safety but two of them were sufficient for a gift. Loping sideways across the hillside he ensured the hare was dead before slicing the neck to allow the blood to drain. He pulled a cord free from his waist pouch and wound it around the feet before tying the carcass through his belt to dangle and drip.

Raising his gaze to note Enya's direction, he could see there had been another couple of roundhouses in the cluster. Their blackened remains were stark in the gathering-gloom but the deterioration of the wooden posts indicated the damage had not come recently. The burning had not been done by a Roman patrol.

No one guarded the roundhouse as he approached it. Sending the others a cautionary glance, they spread out to check around the habitation. Silent signals were passed back to him, indicating no signs of humans before they all converged close to the dwelling.

"We seek shelter for the night!" he called, when they stood only a few paces away. He freed the hare from his belt, and shook it out. Alongside him Feargus followed suit, Enya positioning herself in between them.

It took a few moments before someone peered out, having groped his way through the low entrance tunnel. The long knife held in front of the man's bony chest showed some caution was still maintained, though against the three of them the warrior would be powerless, if they were intent on harm. Nith felt shrewd eyes assess him before the warrior eventually nodded an acknowledgement of the gifts he and Feargus held out.

The man took both hares into his keeping.

"My hearth is yours to share." The voice rang clear, though the age lines on the forehead were well-advanced.

Once inside the low entry tunnel Nith's eyes adjusted quickly to the dimness, the central fire providing the only illumination. A seated warrior shot up so quickly to his feet that Nith saw the remnants of a bowl cascading onto the rushes that covered the beaten earth floor. He moved in further to allow Enya and Feargus to enter before tendering the traditional greeting to the younger man.

"Ciamar a tha thu?" he asked.

A short nod acknowledged him, the quick smile friendly enough as the warrior returned his greeting and asked how he fared. Having done likewise to Enya and Feargus, the younger man sat down again, placing his now empty bowl on one of the flat hearthstones.

"It is rare now to have visitors walk my Millbuie territory and a while since my hearth has been a busy one." Their host pointed to a pile of furs at the fireside, the flick of his finger as jerky as his cackle. "There used to be extra stools in here. The fire devoured those, but I am sure some of the skins over there will be better than sitting on the hard floor."

Nith could not quite work out the man's mirth. Had the tribesman been too lazy to collect firewood, or was there some other reason for his stools being consumed?

After sharing some of the scraped wolf skins with Enya and Feargus, he sat down at the fireside. Their host was already busying about, expertly skinning the hares. The knife flashing so quickly, and the amount of furs lying around the room in various states of treatment, indicated that even though age was creeping up on him, the man was a dexterous hunter.

A large pot dangled above the flames, the smell of its barley-broth contents highly appealing. It would take some time for the hares to roast but Nith hoped for a bowl of broth before then. The noise he next heard echoed his longings. Enya's growling stomach brought a smile to more than his face.

The older man chuckled. "Has it been a while since that belly had some proper food, lass?"

"So long I hardly remember." Enya's smile was irresistible. "We have journeyed for many nights."

Nith nudged her enthusiastically, so much so she almost toppled over. "Not that long," he smirked, steadying her again. He tucked her into his chest and left his palm cradling her elbow, glad to note she did not shrug him off. In fact, she even sidled a shade closer to him and returned some teasing eye contact. "Our slingshots bagged some birds the other evening. Perhaps not as filling as those hares," he broke off to point to the now gutted animals, "but they staved off some of your hunger."

He turned away from Enya's too appealing amusement and addressed his host again. "She is always as slender as a twig, yet she has the appetite of two grown men."

Further banter ensued as they introduced themselves.

Nith's vigilance resurfaced when his host declared that the younger man, Seaghan, was also a traveller. He had thought them to be related.

Seaghan explained. "My Vacomagi kin bide near An Cuan Moireach."

"I have not yet seen An Cuan Moireach, but I have heard the firth is a narrow one."

Feargus' statement showed a general interest, but Nith knew the Taexali lad just long enough to know there was more to his words when he continued. "Someone told me that a coracle can cross to the lands of the Lugi in a few shorts pulls." Feargus' laugh was disbelieving, "But surely that cannot be true."

Seaghan guffawed. "Someone has been teasing you, though it would almost be possible near the headland where my kin live."

The older man sneered. "A coracle would have some rivalry on those waters just now! I would not advise anyone to try it."

The talk sobered, their host happy to disclose all he knew. Roman vessels were beached on the south shore of An Cuan Moireach with enough soldiers marching around to prevent any kind of movement on both north and south shores.

"I have not been there myself, but they say the Romans are well-enough settled now along Vacomagi shorelines to be cutting trees from the nearest woods."

Their host did not seem bothered by the information, no sense of a threat evident in his words or expression. Nith's hackles rose. He understood that the present place, named Millbuie after the hill nearby, was a reasonable distance from the Vacomagi shoreline but displaying no sense of danger did not seem credible in an area infiltrated by the Roman armies. "Have these soldiers bothered you here?" he asked.

The tiniest pause gave Nith some more room for disquiet.

"Our Vacomagi territory is now riddled with Romans but, nay, they have not bothered me."

It was not the answer Nith was looking for. Being so evasive confirmed nothing. Yet, he was not sure success would be gained by pressing for answers.

Enya changed the conversation. "I seek news of my brother. He has been lost to my kin since the battlegrounds of Beinn na Ciche. Have you had young warriors visiting you recently?"

Their host looked towards his other visitor of the night. "Only Seaghan has recently darkened my door. Since my hearth-wife went to her goddess some seasons ago, I have been alone."

"Is it also a while since you had neighbours? We saw the shells of two dwellings outside. It is a heart break when fire engulfs," Enya said.

Nith watched the man bathe in Enya's sympathy, his concentration upon her alone.

"After the fires, my sons chose to rebuild on more fertile land. The fields here are spent, the yields were poor. Had fire-tragedy not struck, we could not have bided in these parts much longer, at any rate. My surviving kin now work better land that lies closer to the firth."

"You lost family in these fires?" Nith asked.

The warrior nodded. "My hearth-wife, a daughter, and three of the younger children succumbed to the flames."

"Yet you chose to remain here afterwards?"

"Those who survived dwell close enough. If I need their help, I will ask. I prefer to bide alone now."

The stiff pride in the warrior's talk was commendable. Nith could appreciate that, yet something continued to make him uneasy.

While the hares roasted, Nith was glad when a single bowl was passed from person to person. Refilled with barley-broth, each time, was just perfect for staving off some hunger.

Both Seaghan and the old man seemed friendly as they chatted about the peril around them. Seaghan spoke of being in battle at Beinn na Ciche, and knew enough details to satisfy. He then claimed to have lingered for a while afterwards in the hills of the Caledons. Not at Ceann Druimin, but with another Caledon chief that Nith had heard of though had never met.

The Vacomagi's words seemed genuine enough, but there was an occasional veiled look to his eye when the lad scanned around the roundhouse that fed Nith's suspicion.

Seaghan claimed to have met some other warriors during his trek home but the names he gave were neither of Ruoridh, nor Fingal. "People wandering Taexali and Vacomagi territory have been rare."

"Aye." Nith snorted, finding and holding Enya's gaze, willing her not to show any of her disquiet. "It is only people like us who dare to wander the lands, anxious for news of our kin."

"You should try other Caledon villages for survivors. Plenty of our loyal brothers who did not die with a Roman *gladius* stuck in their bellies fled to the hills, and still remain there." Seaghan sounded sure, but Nith needed to be convinced. All the words were correct, yet there was a tinge of contempt in the tiniest twitch of Seaghan's lip.

"And some of our loyal brothers and sisters have been slain well after the battlefield-blood was spilled." Enya's words spouted forth, breaking her long silence.

Nith noticed he was not the only one surprised by her venom. A flicker in Seaghan's expression was quickly masked as the young warrior bent to add wood to the fire.

"We have come across a number of dead tribespeople on our journey across Taexali and Vacomagi valleys…and in the woodlands as well," he added. "Have you seen any, Seaghan?"

The man's head bobbed in assent. "Too many corpses lie around these parts. The wolves will have their fill before long."

Nith felt too much was left out of that answer.

General talk about the Roman threat continued till it was clear their host wanted to rest his head. When Enya made to go outside before sleep, Nith stood up in her wake.

"Wait! Take this. This area is not short of animal predators." Their host indicated the piles of pelts that hung from his roof beams. He reached for a bundle of fat-dipped rushes and lit it in the deep-red embers.

With one flaming brand between them, Nith led Enya out.

The night air was bitter-cold and damp. He was not inclined to be out for too long, just long enough for Enya to confirm his suspicions after she had made herself ready for sleep.

Her general distrust of travellers was not new. "We asked Seaghan many questions, yet I fear not the right ones. His being friendly is good. He has been helpful about giving us directions, but we have to be sure they are not misleading."

He felt Enya grasp his arm that held the brand, careful to avoid the flames. In the flickering light her beautiful eyes were troubled, as anxious as the fingers that gripped him.

"Nith, I fear there are things he does not tell us. I sense a danger in him though I do not know why."

The intensity of her plea broke down any lingering resistance to her attraction.

Gently prising off her tense fingers, he extended the arm holding the torchlight and gathered her in close to him with his free arm. Looking down at her anxiety, he sought only to drive it away when his lips touched gently down on hers. Meaning it to be a fleeting solace, he was staggered when Enya's response was as immediate as it was fervent. Her arms gripped tight around his waist as she burrowed even closer and stole the breath from him. The kiss deepened and continued to the point where he did not know who began the next. Or the others that followed. Low moans grew around him.

The first yelp of the wolf jolted him.

He withdrew his lips and stared down at Enya's bereft expression. He wanted the kisses to grow into much more, but it was neither the time nor the place for it. Reluctantly drawing away from her, his vow was profound.

"Know that was not a mistake, Enya. I would have much more from you as a mature woman with her chosen mate, I hope you are certain of that now, but that wolf reminds me about trust. We should not leave Feargus too long. We do not know what those two Vacomagi are capable of."

Enya's expression was stricken. It was clear that she had completely forgotten they had abandoned the third member of their band.

"I will feign sleep but will take first watch," he told her, gripping her hand tightly as he led her back to the roundhouse. Regardless of the undoubted personal discomfort it was bound to cause, he was not going to let her lie anywhere that was not daubed right next to him.

***

"Where are you headed next?" The casual inquiry came from Seaghan the following morning as they were saying their farewells, their night having been uneventful.

Nith was still not inclined to trust the younger Vacomagi, but he would be able to guide them part of the way on the next stage of their search. It also meant they could keep him close, if he really was a *speculator*.

Enya answered, though her words were directed more to their host. "It sounds sensible to try Dunrelugas, if you think there might be tribespeople sheltering there."

The ancient fort had come up in their discussions the previous evening.

"Aye. It lies in a fine position where the Abhainn Fionn Èireann meets a smaller river." Their host agreed, though his raucous laugh was strange. "Some tribespeople have bided there for generations but they are an odd lot. They cannot agree on whether they are Vacomagi, Caledon, or something else!"

"Will they be hospitable to us?" Enya wanted to know.

More laughing cackles were her answer. "Perhaps. Or maybe not."

Skirting the foothills after they left Millbuie was easy enough. Seaghan knew where to avoid the marshiest parts and told them what he knew of the terrain across to the Vacomagi coastline. "Gentle rises in places, but it is mostly flat."

When asked about the locals, Seaghan confirmed that plenty of able farmers stayed to tend their harvests instead of joining Calgach. "Good crops and better grazing on the Laich draws our farmers to cluster in these parts, and they will not give that up easily."

Enya wormed out more answers as an effortless climb took them to the crest of a knoll, one that was just high enough to see all the way to An Cuan Moireach. They stopped for a while to take in the breathtaking scene.

The water was still too far distant to see the detail of the ships on it but Seaghan's pointing finger gave them the direction to look for his coastal village. "Our promontory is as close as it can be to the territory of the Lugi Raven People directly across the firth."

"Yet, the water out that way seems endless." He pointed to the opposite end of the waterline.

Seaghan's explanation helped him to understand better. "An Cuan Moireach is a very special estuary, not just because it is very long but more that it almost shelters an inland loch. The outcrop where my village lies and the opposite Lugi headland are only a short distance apart. They narrow down the water flow before it goes out to sea."

Seaghan turned to Feargus. "That is why you heard about it only taking a few strokes to carry a small boat across."

After giving more answers, Seaghan was brisk. "If you wish to go to Dunrelugas, you need to head through the woods over there." He indicated a route the south-west. "I, on the other hand, need to be out in the open as I cross that moorland."

"Will you reach it by nightfall?" Feargus asked.

"I could easily do it at Beltane, but now that the daylight is short, I may not. There may also be Roman patrols I need to avoid."

"You will be an easy target for those deadly *pila* if you do not find sufficient cover," Enya warned. Feargus' recent injury had been mentioned at the fireside the night before.

"Do not fear. I know how to avoid the eyes of enemy patrols. I am familiar with the iron-laced bogs that are plentiful around here, but I hope those Roman invaders are not."

Nith followed Seaghan's' directions into the woods, ever vigilant of roaming Roman patrols and glad not to encounter any, because the trees presently around them were predominantly of slender-trunked silver birches with scatterings of wider-girthed oaks and rowans. It was when those gave way to plentiful elms, and the sound of rushing water was just discernible, that Feargus' snorts broke their silence.

"Had I known there were so many rivers to cross on this journey, I might not have volunteered to come."

Enya's laughs echoed around. "If Seaghan speaks the truth then the Abhainn Fionn Èireann has many good fording places."

Nith nudged the lad. "You should only need to jump the stones, according to our Vacomagi friend, if he was that. Or, in your case, I should perhaps say hirple across." His suspicion had diminished since leaving Millbuie, but it was not wise to discard all caution.

Leading up a very gradual rise, he plodded on to the fringes of the wood where he abruptly came to a halt.

Not far off, through the patchy branch cover, he saw a sight he had not seen for many seasons. It was not made of timber as at Tarras, the hillfort that he had grown up in. The walls of the hillfort in front of him had been created from impressive blocks of grey stone. Behind the high wall, smoke billowed up from a number of roundhouse roofs, a lot more than he had expected.

In no more than a blink Nith was surrounded by a band of warriors, too many for him to tackle had they been bent on attack.

"Why did you tarry so long?" one of them bawled. "Your slow meander through our woodlands almost had us falling asleep. State your business."

It was clear that Feargus had never been in such a large dwelling place before. Though he said nothing, Nith watched the lad take in everything around them, once they had gone through the entry gate. Unlike the partially ruined Tap O'Noth, Dunrelugas was a thriving hive of activity. People moved from roundhouse to roundhouse, some of them men though plenty of them were women. Children, hounds and fowl darted here and there – playing, scavenging and pecking at the hard-packed ground for dropped seeds.

"Wait here." The guard halted them at a larger roundhouse. Nith had no plan to go anywhere else since it was not only their escorts from the woods who were watchful. He and the other two drew the gazes of most of the tribespeople.

Chapter Thirty-Two

Dunrelugas, Vacomagi Territory

"Aye, we have had a Ruoridh visit us here, but he left us some days past."

Enya felt her insides churn. She had just missed him. Clutching at Nith's arm, she took some deep breaths to steady herself. How could the goddesses have been so unkind? Stricken, she feared it was because she had yet to choose her own particular goddess.

Forcing down the crushing disappointment, she listened more carefully to Torquil, chief of Dunrelugas.

"Ruoridh and Fingal of Wichach left us to get a better idea of how many Roman vessels lie near the narrowest part of An Cuan Moireach. Those spirited young warriors would not listen to the caution of an old man like me."

Over the best fare she had tasted for a long time, Enya heard about her brother's plans.

"Aye." Torquil smiled as though a memory had prompted it. "Your brother almost got himself caught a couple of times when they surveyed along the shores. Even more hazardous for them was to venture up to Am Broch, which teems with Roman soldiers." Torquil pointed a well-chewed wing bone at her. "That was not news to me, but it made young Ruoridh feel his task was worthwhile."

She felt the old man's keen stare linger on her while he picked his teeth free of food remains. He eventually nodded her way. "You and your brother share a likeness. Do you favour your father, or mother?"

Enya gulped, not sure if it was a compliment or otherwise, though remained polite. She had never been asked that question before. "I am not sure." She turned to Nith. "What would your answer be?"

After a thoughtful pause and a gaze that made her feel over-heated inside, Nith answered. "She favours her mother. Fionnah is a fine-looking woman." Enya held her breath. His next words seemed to have nothing to do with the look she shared with him. "Though Ruoridh might prefer to be told he looks like his father Gabrond."

Enya was glad when Torquil broke the tense silence with a guttural chuckle. "Mother or father makes no difference. Nith's regard tells me he would appreciate you either way. You have the sparkle of youth in your beautiful eyes, Enya, and more besides. And your Ruoridh is a young warrior any man would be proud to claim. He had other news to tell me that was far more important and worth the wounds Fingal received."

She gasped. "Was my brother hurt again?"

Torquil sobered. "Nay, he came out of the incident unscathed." The chief described the escapade that had made Fingal and Ruoridh's escape from the headland a very dangerous one, a number of Roman *pila* firing their way as they had scampered down the cliff after being detected hovering around the village smithy. "The gouges to his hands and knees were not from Roman weapons but from his slithering down onto the rocks below." Torquil wiped his mouth with the back of his hand after a long draught of the small-beer from his horn cup. "They had to scamper down the cliff opposite the Roman boats that were beached in the bay, because they had not accounted for so many of them patrolling the whole cliff top. The god *Sucellus* is surely looking after him, protecting him from those Roman turds."

One of the elders who sat nearby joined the conversation. "Those brave lands brought us some valuable information about the size of the Roman vessels, and how many men they could hold. We can prepare better for any skirmishes when we get such information."

"Aye, good knowledge is invaluable," Nith said. "Did Ruoridh share his next plans with you?"

When the chief mentioned having sent her brother and Fingal on their way with a good-sized escort of four of the best warriors from Dunrelugas, Enya thanked him for his thoughtfulness. The chief waved off her gesture, though not unkindly, working at a chunk of roasted venison, his yellowed-teeth aided by his grubby nails. Muttering between chews he went on, "I want no surprise attack from those *Ceigean Ròmanach!* Your brother just made me make the decision a little sooner."

She could see that Nith and Feargus were too eager to eat to pose useful questions, so she did the asking. "If they escaped from this coastal village named Am Broch, why did they come so far inland to you here at Dunrelugas? If they aim to go to the shortest stretch between the Vacomagi and the Lugi coastlines, why did they not hug the beach?"

Torquil scratched the remnants of food from his grey-white whiskers, a brighter smile clearer when he brushed the top lip hair aside. "Not all of the Vacomagi at Am Broch are accepting of the domination of the Romans. There are some who resist in their own way without a shining *gladius* blade being thrust at their innards. Your brother made some good contacts, and through them he learned about us biding here at Dunrelugas."

Enya wondered if her brother was perhaps being too adventurous.

"Moving around the bay from Am Broch would have been foolhardy. Your brother knows well to avoid that." Torquil beckoned one of his serving women, though continued to speak. "Roman vessels are beached below Am Broch, and Fingal mentioned that larger ones have come ashore further west in the natural harbour at the mouth of the Abhainn Fionn Èireann. The whole sea coastline swarms with Roman patrols that march in and out of their nearby encampment."

"The tribesman at Millbuie told us that Dunrelugas is good for seeing down towards the coastline," she said.

"You will find nothing better. The ancestors chose well when they erected my stone walls. After you eat, there will still be enough light for you to be of the same mind."

Accepting a piece of bannock and a small wooden beaker of barley-beer from the serving woman, she agreed it would be very useful to understand more of the landscape. Swallowing down the slightly bitter brew, she told of Seaghan taking them to the top of the small knoll to see the landscape better.

The chief's snorts denied her words. "Dunrelugas is higher. From here, you will see even better. Though now I think on it, we should wait till dusk is almost done for the day."

She could not see how being it almost dark would help with good viewing though would never dare to challenge her host.

Their food half-digested, and after a lengthy conversation with Torquil and his elders, she was standing outside the hillfort wall looking out towards the sea. Her first thoughts were that she would definitely see much more by day. The land between the hillfort and the sea was in dark shadow, so deep she could make out few features.

When she looked further ahead, the distant water was the deepest-blue against fading orange rays as the god *Lugh* made way for the black of night.

Nith was so close at her shoulder, his breath whispered at her ear. "The chief made a good decision. Can you see those tiny flickering glows?"

Mesmerised by the far-off water, she had not paid attention to the faint radiances.

"Roman torchlight at their camps," he said, his arm snuggling around her middle, giving tiny squeezes just enough to stir her anticipation anew, though she had been well-aware of his lure all day long.

She was not willing to spoil the arousing contact, but she was not convinced his assessment of the scene ahead was correct. "Nith, they could be brands set outside Vacomagi roundhouses."

"Any flames that lie close to Dunrelugas probably are Vacomagi, but those are not what we can see out there." Releasing his cosy arm, he used both of his hands to lift her wrist. Curving his palms sensually around her hand he pointed her finger. Holding the pose, he told her to think about what it pointed to as the darkness deepened.

"Are the lights out on the water, or are they by the sea edge?" he asked.

The chief of Dunrelugas joined them, his hearty bellow a disturbance in the nipping-cold night air.

"You see why I thought the darkness a better time? The last clear night we had, some nights ago, I was called by the guards on the wall. What you point to is what they wanted me to see. That glow means a lot of torchlight in one place. At that distance, firebrands from villages of five or six roundhouses are never seen from here. Now I see at least," the man broke off to count, "three different glows."

"Can you tell where they are?" Feargus asked.

The chief was definite about the direction. "The brightest of all is at Am Broch. The one I mentioned while we ate and where your brother's friend almost broke his legs. Am Broch is the smithy where my weapons and metal tools are usually fashioned, though I doubt I shall be sending warriors there just now, unless they are to use the weapons against the Roman scourge."

Nith allowed her arm to drop, though his head bent close in to her, to peer into the gloom.

"And where do the other two lie?" She could now make out all three tiny glows, the darkness having properly descended.

Torquil answered. "The one directly ahead is by the mouth of the Abhainn Fionn Èireann. That smallest glare is off to the east on the Laich, though I did not see that one a few nights ago."

"Those damned Romans have built another new camp down there." Grabbing Nith's arm, she scrunched up the cloth of his bratt. "Agricola will never stop. What can we do? Two camps are by his beached boats and the other on the fertile parts of Vacomagi land."

"Nay, lass," the chief said. "He has a third camp out there by Am Broch."

"Did you not say that was a Vacomagi village?"

"The village is a large one by Vacomagi standards, but it makes no glow like that at night. What you see there must also be a Roman camp."

"Have you sent word of this to any Caledon chiefs? To let them know how the Roman threat closes in on them?" The urgency she felt was almost overwhelming.

The chief's laugh was amused but it was Nith he spoke to. "Your lass is a fiery one, Nith, but that is a good thing."

Enya next snared the chief's attention, his gaze solemn but not stern. "I am Torquil of Dunrelugas. I am Vacomagi, but not of the coastal Vacomagi. Their ancestors differ from mine. My hearth-wife is Caledon. The way I see it is that my sons may choose to call themselves what they will, if a time ever comes that makes them need to. My nearest Caledon neighbours up in the hills are kin to me and we regularly share our knowledge. If the Romans attack and Dunrelugas falls then those conquerors would carry on marching on up the mountain passes. None of us want that: not me, and not my Caledon neighbours who will support me if needed."

Chapter Thirty-Three

Auchinhove Roman Camp, Vacomagi Territory

"*Salvete!*"

Agricola faced his senior officers around his central table, again spread with his itinerary boards. He looked down at the campaign details recorded there, deciding which reports to receive first. The easiest one was not always the best use of his time, but he needed the boost to his spirits that one would surely bring.

First, though, he made a silent prayer to thank *Consus*, protector of grains, that his men were now better fed.

"*Legio XX.*"

The senior *tribune* of the *Legio XX* was clearly pleased to inform the assembled company that the Taexali wedge, from the Rivers Deva and Devana to the Taexalorum Promontorium, and westwards to the River Caelis, was under control. Agricola peered at his *tribune*, a career officer of more years than was usual, and normally a man he respected for his loyalty and honesty.

"Under full control?"

The *tribune*'s head dipped. "Yes, until such times as local warriors return to engage with, though they may not do that until the winter season is over."

"Good. Keep it like that. Leave units at the Well of Ythan encampment, if you think that the best place to monitor from?"

"My patrols can cover the northern part from the Well of Ythan, but it would also be more effective for some units to return to the camp of the Deer's Den on the River Devana. Should the natives make any moves from the southern Taexali passes we would be close enough to lend support to the *Legio II Adiutrix*."

Agricola pondered the suggestion. It was a reasonable one, though it stretched his troops even further. Nonetheless, an advantage could be gained by not needing to spend time moving men if an attack proved imminent. His *speculatores* still indicated this was unlikely, but the damned uncivilised Caledonians were not predictable. It might also provide more security for his supplies coming north.

"Organise it."

He moved on to the *Legio II Adiutrix* reports, though he suspected he would learn little from the routine update.

"The natives maintain a relatively stable presence on the highest peaks around our patrolling area, their numbers not changing much from day to day."

"Relatively stable?" He latched onto that one word.

The *tribune* of the *Legio II Adiutrix* continued, unfazed over his use of the words. "While my orders remain as they presently stand, we do not yet control all of the Taexali accesses into the mountains."

The officer confirmed that regular patrolling of the territory indicated no significant return of the Taexali tribespeople to their own homes, but there had been plenty of evidence of the enemy at some of the mountain passes. "We will eventually subdue the natives, sir, but those warriors of the mountains are only cowed when confronted by whole *cohorts*. We made advances into some passes where the enemy were ranged across the top of the drumlins, though well out-of-range of our pila. When my *cohort* moved through and into the next valley, we found the same warriors had shadowed us and were atop another rise, still surveying our every move. There are only so many of these valleys that we can enter in one day and return to our base before nightfall. At the moment those monitoring us are small enough groups though soon they may do more than watch, and if larger Caledon forces choose to engage with us, only a sizeable fort built and established in each pass will keep them at bay." The *tribune* paused his jaw tense as he made direct eye contact.

Agricola nodded for the *tribune* to continue, sensing the man was not finished.

"Sir, my legion does not have sufficient soldiers to build, and operate, a fort at every Taexali entry to the mountains to maintain control. And so far, we have been unable to firmly identify which locations to start with, ones which would serve us best in the long term."

Agricola padded around his table, the men stepping back a pace to give him room on his approach. It was as he feared, even though he had prayed to *Fortuna* for a better response from the craven Caledons. Another pitched battle and his *legions* would decimate the lily-livered cowards, but they would not confront him.

He reined in his temper, his response through gritted teeth. "That news is no different from when we were encamped at the place the natives called Durno. Where are those many fists of ours? Tell me!"

The *Legio XX tribune* dared an answer. "Already spread too thin, sir."

He knew it. His officers knew it. Even the lowliest of his recruit-milites knew it, but Emperor Domitian still refused to acknowledge it. The emperor's correspondence continued to demand that more and more of the Britannic troops be transferred to Germania, to rescue Domitian's inept attempts to subdue the native unrest there. Domitian being victorious in Germania was much more essential than creating a new western boundary for the empire.

Not for the first time, Agricola wished that Emperor Vespasian was still alive.

The routine update from the *Legio IX* was mainly for continued co-ordination with other legionary commanders. He was kept well up to date, being close by at his present camp.

"Yes, sir. The two camps at the Rivers Tuesis and Loxa are progressing well. Timbers for the fortlets are being felled from the Caledon forest fringes and we already have all of the ironwork delivered to our temporary camp site. There have been petty attacks from the mountain Vacomagi, but our losses have been manageable."

Agricola stared between the lorica clad shoulders of two of this officers and out through the tent opening. "Manageable. I only call something manageable when we do not lose any men at all. I want no more losses of my soldiers to Celtic spears." He brought his focus back around the table. "Or blades. It seems they are very handy with their spear throws, but I also want those blades out of their grips well before they get anywhere near my tree fellers!"

He faced the junior *tribune* of the *Legio IX*. "What of the last treaties with coastal Vacomagi?"

"Those village leaders will be with you tomorrow, sir."

"What is the status of the outstanding ones who dwell nearer the mouth of the Varar Aestuarium?"

"They will give no resistance, sir. They are aware of our capability to quell them with force from our ships, even though they initially believed themselves invincible with help from their mountain neighbours."

"So, their friends from the hills are not so supportive after all?" Agricola grunted.

The *Legate of Legio IX* was less amused. "It is not that at all, sir. They have been persuaded that peaceable dealing with Rome will be in their favour. They are not averse to the sounds of Roman silver coming their way, if they comply and trade with our fleet."

Agricola snorted, though there was little humour. It was just as well those Vacomagi were unaware that his *Classis Britannica* would have a lot fewer ships plying the *Oceanus Germanicus* in the coming months. Damn Emperor Domitian for starving him on land and sea at this crucial time! There were so many things he could not yet share with his officers – those who had been loyal to him during many summer campaigns and those yet to prove themselves.

He concluded the meeting and dismissed them all, even Flavus who had responded better when questioned about the aspects he had been delegated. Thanks were given to *Clementia* for that. Perhaps by the time he no longer needed to mould the hapless Flavus, the boy would have matured? He hoped so, though with little conviction.

He slumped onto the wooden stool that was well-positioned to see outside the tent, his forearms resting on his thighs and his hands hanging limp between his knees. He contemplated his mud-streaked leather boots that had seen better days, boots that had walked across a great deal of Britannia. His ever capable Crispus needed to be told of the most recent developments he had been concealing, but he was reluctant to voice them to anyone.

A despairing tiredness washed over him, draining him so much that he could not even work out how to ignore Domitian's demands for a few more days.

If only *Fortuna* would change her mind. If she bestowed some of her favours, it might be possible?

Instinct denied it.

And it seemed that even his time for quiet contemplation was being shattered.

The approach of clinking lorica, worn by more than one soldier, could not be ignored. Raising his head, he had no words at all for how he felt when he watched the determined approach of the most unlikely of all soldiers who had come to visit him.

"*Salut*, General Agricola! The Emperor Domitian sends his regards."

Agricola stood up to formally acknowledge the newcomer's arrival, ending his salute with a flat palm of friendship to the man's shoulder. "If that really were the case, Gaius, I would be a happy man. Are you sent as my personal escort, instead of his Praetorian Guard?"

Liberalis' rumbling laughter filled the tent. "Not at all, though I am here to urge you to rethink your plans. You have not properly answered my many messages, sir, but I know full-well that you have received them."

Agricola's open-palm gesture indicated that his second-in-command should exit the tent with him, the inevitable discussion not yet for the ears of his secretarial staff. A few paces away he stopped to fully face the man who had not only been his competent administrator but also his best confidant in Britannia.

"I am not ready to leave. There are still so many tribes to quell and territories to conquer."

The sober mien of Gaius Salvius Liberalis exuded understanding. "I know that, but *Fortuna* does not favour you, Iulius. And neither does our unbalanced emperor. My duty has always been to support you but the point of no return has come. I am not presently recalled to Rome, but you of all people know that may also be only a matter of time. Domitian barely knows I exist just now, but when he realises what I will continue to do in your stead during the coming months, you can imagine how soon my orders will change."

Agricola's smile was bitter. "My long governorship of Britannia has exceeded that of any other. Though I may not quite be ready to leave, Domitian wields the clout."

Chapter Thirty-Four

An Cuan Moireach, Vacomagi Territory

"Nay! I will be the one to look after Nith." Enya's laughter rang free.

Nith watched as Enya gave thanks to Torquil of Dunrelugas. He had agreed that they should head for the same coastal village as her brother at the narrowest part of An Cuan Moireach. When Torquil described it, he was sure it was the same place that Seaghan returned to. He desperately wanted Enya to find her brother, though confidence still did not sing in his veins. Torquil had made it very clear that once down the slopes from where his hillfort was situated, the Vacomagi allegiances differed.

"I claim no kinship at all with those down there who have the gall to name themselves Vacomagi – Men of the Open Plains. Their flat fields are undeniable, but their loyalties are nothing like the Vacomagi ones I am proud to bear!" Torquil's ire was easily detected.

Torquil had that very morning been told that many of the small village leaders had capitulated and had sworn a commitment to Rome. In exchange for their lives, a chance to continue to work on their farms and an opportunity to trade with the Roman Empire, they also boasted fistfuls of Roman coin.

"It pains me to say it, but you must trust none of them. If those silver-grasping betrayers have turned traitorous, you must be ever vigilant."

Till Torquil had explained it, he had not fully realised just how many tribespeople lived on the Laich compared to the mountain slopes and the hills and valleys they had travelled over. There were many more people down there to lose their lives, and livelihoods, if they resisted Roman control. Torquil had confirmed there was no overall chief of the coastal Vacomagi to speak for them all. The tribespeople near the sea only bore loyalty to their kin and the neighbours who shared their small farms but they had all capitulated – largely without loss of blood.

"Nith of Tarras!" His thoughts were interrupted by Torquil's loud and gusty farewell, the man's beam one of confidence, his arm hanging loosely around Enya's shoulder. "You make sure to look after this brave warrior-woman. Visit me on your return journey with young Ruoridh and Fingal in tow. I want their news personally delivered."

They were not alone when they scrambled down the tree-clad hillside, Torquil having insisted on them having a guide. Nith was all in favour of that. It seemed a long while since he had been in Lulach's roundhouse realising he knew nothing about Vacomagi territory, but that was constantly changing.

Only half of the morning was gone when Dhoughall stopped talking, abruptly halting to cock his head to listen. Ahead the trees petered out, the alder wood not being a large one, though they were not yet at the fringe. Nith realised his guide's hearing was more acute than his own, a surprise because Dhoughall had kept up a low conversation, delighted to explain everything around. Sounds of activity were faint, but they were not the normal sounds of a working winter day. Shouts and answering calls could be heard, drowning out feeble cries for mercy. The latter was in the language of the tribes, the other unknown.

Dhoughall motioned them all to take cover. "Wait here. I will see what is amiss."

Nith disagreed. "Nay! We will stay together." Having no idea where they were, and aware of the Roman threat, he had no urgency to lose his guide.

Dhoughall's dipped head approved before his finger pointed off to the side. "Then we will head that way."

Nith would have chosen the same since the sounds still came from directly ahead. Picking his way after Dhoughall to the edge of the tree line, he took in the dreadful sight that lay ahead.

Not far off, a cluster of three roundhouses was a hive of activity. A swarm of Romans dragged tribespeople outside, lining them up and issuing orders: commands the terrified women and children probably had no idea of their meaning. A child howled and cowered against its mother's chequered skirts. An old woman was forced to move more quickly than her bones were capable of – her chest heaving, her back bowed and her feet shuffling and stumbling. Nith watched two of the Roman auxiliaries as they forced a small group of men and young boys to stand separately from the other family members, their pila tips jabbing and stabbing them into position.

He heard Enya gasp alongside him when another pair of Roman auxiliaries dragged a body feet-first from the nearest roundhouse, the chin and head bobbing with every single step they took. They hauled it in front of the line of men before letting the feet drop.

Even from the distance he observed from, Nith could see that the man's front had been ripped open, the innards spilling free.

Shouts continued, this time in the tongue of the tribespeople. Denial rippled along the line as each was confronted by the soldier who had taken charge of the interrogation.

Enya nudged him before the merest whisper tickled his ear. "This is surely no normal raid, Nith. They would have killed more of those poor people."

Nith had no reply, yet. It was a strange situation to watch.

When the correct answers were not forthcoming, the *decanus* in charge issued orders for all of the people to move off. The line of men was forced to lead followed by the rest, all closely guarded by what he counted as a double-*contubernium* of soldiers.

They were barely past the roundhouses, and only a short way along the first field-strip when the old woman collapsed, unable to continue any further. Shouts and prods of pilum and pugio forced the miserable, wailing line onwards, forcing them to abandon the female elder.

He had to restrain Enya from rushing forward. "Wait. We will check when they are well-gone."

It was a long tense wait, Enya within his grip, her back to his chest. In other circumstances the hold could have been a much more loving one, but it served a different purpose. Gradually, he could feel her relaxing against him, though he knew she still held her temper in check.

"What will they do to those people, Nith?"

When he looked into her anxious expression, she knew what he was going to say. There was likely to be no other conclusion. He was heartily relieved when Dhoughall was the one to spit a quiet reply.

"When those Vacomagi of the Laich are dragging around their slave chains, I wonder if they will regret being so accommodating of Roman domination!"

When he was sure the Romans were well away, he let his grip of Enya loosen. Bypassing the warrior's body, they sprinted on to the old woman though getting there earlier would have made little difference, for the old woman was almost spent. Bending down on the opposite side from Enya, he heard the woman gasp low prayers to her goddess.

"Can you tell us why the Romans killed that warrior?" he asked.

He saw inevitability in the woman's gaze and no point in holding back truths. Hesitantly, her breathing getting fainter, she whispered, "My grandson was loyal to my family…before he went to…Beinn na Ciche."

"There is no rush." He urged the woman to take her time, though knew time was not in her favour. "I do not think the Romans will return. We will help you back to your home, if you tell us which one."

The agony in the fading eyes was so acute that Nith felt such hatred for her tormentors.

"Too late. *Momu* calls me." Nith watched impotently as her eyes closed.

Difficult-to-make coughs were followed by a silent pause.

He snagged Enya's attention, her small headshakes and finger over her lips indicating she did not yet think the old woman gone.

A few moments later the old woman's eyelids flickered, the stuttered words hard-won. "Few Vacomagi warriors went to battle. We called him valiant."

Enya soothed the old woman's forehead when a rattling began. Nith gave her room to sidle round, to cradle the wrinkled-face between her knees. "Rest," Enya urged. "We can talk later."

In between weakened shallow-coughs, the woman managed a small headshake. Nith felt her imploring stare. "Nay. My time is nigh." Tears ran in rivulets down the cracks of the careworn cheeks. "Traitor!"

The word came out stronger, as was the gnarled grip at his fingers before the old one subsided again.

"Changed...after returning...we thought it the death and destruction...but was more."

Nith had a bad feeling about the outcome. "Did he remain with you?"

The headshake denied it, the old woman having regained a little strength. "He went back to Caledon chiefs. Admirable...was what we all thought." Her tired old eyes implored. "My son was dubious. He followed my grandson. Today, my son heard his talk with Romans, from nearby the ships at Abhainn Fionn Èireann."

Nith felt Enya's revulsion when his eyes met hers over the old woman.

"We confronted him. He denied it..." The coughing started again. The woman's upper-body heaved up with its force, her words almost inaudible, her life force exhausted. "We forced a confession."

Nith watched the plea in the old woman's gaze transfer from Enya to himself as though begging for forgiveness.

"A traitor must die." This time there were no tears, the old eyes losing sight bit by bit. "He was my kin...no...longer."

Sensing her passing was looming Nith finished the story. "The Romans suspected this might happen?" The vague eyes barely blinked, just enough for him to know the truth. "When they came to check, it was too late for their informer?"

The 'Aye' from the old woman was a death sigh.

When he was sure the elder was gone to her goddess, he and Enya laid the woman flat on the stubble of recently-cut barley. He watched Enya rise, her despair obvious. Stepping around the body, he folded her into his arms and held her securely while she sobbed. When the tears receded, he felt her breath at his chest.

"This is another reason why I hate what Agricola and his Roman scum do to our people. These people may be Vacomagi, forced to capitulate, but these Roman bastards turn one member against another within a family. I hate them! Why can they not leave us be?"

It was Feargus' shout that broke the moment. "Come and look."

Nith turned her around and led her from the field, back to the roundhouse, her hand still snuggled in his grip.

Enya was incensed when she glimpsed the face of the Roman spy. "I knew it! That traitor had the nerve to sit in Lulach's roundhouse and pretend to be our friend."

She broke free and dropped down to her knees. Gripping her hands around the man's neck she lifted and bashed the head repeatedly to the ground, as though throttling the infiltrator, before she stood up again and aimed a vicious kick at the body.

It only hurt Enya's toes, though Nith well-understood her anger. This particular *speculator*, Nathrach, had definitely sat amongst them in Lulach's roundhouse. Now, he wondered how many other visitors had been spies and exactly how much General Agricola knew of the intentions of the Caledon allies. Enya had been right to be so wary. Perhaps this traitor was the one who had executed the female and male warriors they had found in the woods? Or had it been the other one named Garth? Where was that infiltrator now?

Enya continued to rant. "I will see the grandmother properly to her goddess, but I welcome the wolves to feast on this scum!"

Nith understood what Enya would prefer to do for the old woman, though a funeral pyre was out of the question. A few prayers said over the body had to suffice before Dhoughall led them away westwards and on to the white sands of An Cuan Moireach.

They avoided the deep bogs and dense scrub land along the way, avoided being seen by the few tribespeople who ventured out from their roundhouses. It was not as cold a day as some had been lately and, for sure, the constant flow of clouds prevented the heat of *Lugh* from warming him, but it was the lingering distaste of the traitor which also chilled.

Dhoughall bid them sit down to rest on the dune sand when they reached a wide-curving bay unhindered by Roman presence, and declared it a good time to eat their meagre food since Torquil had not sent them away empty-handed.

Nith drew forward his water bag and took a deep draught before opening his waist pouch. The oat bannocks he had were soon devoured, as were the dried berries and nuts as he looked out at An Cuan Moireach. The water was currently not far from the shore but he could tell from the ridged stretch of smooth pebbles, and the situation of the low dunes behind him, where the water was likely to reach by dusk. Across the substantial stretch of water, he could just make out the wispy smoke of habitation not far from the shoreline on the far side, higher hills behind darkening the view.

The lack of any movement on the water was startling. Neither Roman ships, nor smaller tribal vessels were within sight, and he could see no evidence of Roman ships beached on the far shore.

Enya was peering eastwards her words in awe. "The water out that way is endless. I cannot see Roman ships anywhere, Dhoughall. Are you sure they have made an encampment further along the beach?"

Dhoughall grunted. "They are not on this part of the coast. There are large shoreline bends and coves along that way." He indicated an easterly direction out to the open waters of *Morimaru*. "That headland, Am Broch, hides them from your sight."

"Am Broch?" Enya sounded amazed. "My brother was there yet it looks so far away."

Nith chewed on some hazelnuts as he took in the details in the opposite direction to where Dhoughall had pointed. "Does the water narrow down beyond the bluff along that way, to the west?" He used his own finger to point to the target. "And lead us around to this village that we seek?"

"The village you want is on yet another headland even further around. We can walk on these sands to reach it, or cut across the dune grasses which might be quicker. One way is as exposed as the other," Dhoughall explained. "There are two small hamlets, one on each side of the jutting point. The smaller, the one that you seek is on this side and lies lower and more open to the wildness of the waters of *Morimaru*. The other village is larger but looks to the enclosed part of An Cuan Moireach."

Feargus finished his water skin with a flourish as though keen to get on with the next part of their quest. "This will need filled soon but since I am not over fond of walking across rivers, I will forgo the pleasure of filling it in the waters of *Morimaru*. I will remain thirsty."

Nith felt the laugh bubble from his toes. It was so long since he had really and properly laughed. One glimpse at Enya's mischievous glint sealed Feargus' fate.

Jumping up at the same time as Enya, he grabbed the opposite elbow from her and lurched off with the stricken Feargus protesting violently. They hoisted the lad over the piles of pebbles and down onto the wet sands, a wind from the sea whipping at their side braids.

It was as well that the water was not far away since he could not have yanked the grown man any further, though Enya did her fair share. A few more steps towards the water he relented, his gaze merging with the woman he knew he definitely wanted to share a hearth with.

"Ah, Fergus." She giggled. "You are so lucky this is not the summer season. Then we would have you properly under the waves. We will come back and you will learn to keep your self afloat!"

Dhoughall was ready to move on when he staggered back, the guide's inquiring look indicating he wanted to know what created such mirth.

To slaps and guffaws from Feargus about retaliations, he entertained their guide with stories of Feargus' river exploits as they picked their way along the deserted pebble-strewn sands until a Roman ship came into view as it rounded the nearest headland. The abrupt sight of it sent him scurrying up to the sand dunes, the others in his wake.

When a second ship followed on and skirted closer to the shoreline, Dhoughall barked an order. "Burrow into the dune grasses as much as possible. They are too close. They may put to shore if they spot us."

Lying face down between the spiky grasses that topped the dunes, he pulled his dull-brown cloak tight across his back. The position was as good a way as any to watch the Roman ships propel along the water. When the bite of a winter-wind nipped he expected to feel chilled, but he had not realised that the sandy dunes under his front would make him cold after only a short while. Though, regardless of the discomfort, he had to remain still because any jerky movement of the marram grasses might be enough to rouse curiosity.

The first vessel bobbed across the waves as the oarsmen pulled and then halted. In some ways it was an incredible sight, one he was sure he would never forget. The rhythmic order impressed him as the vessel glided eastwards, now close enough to shore for him to count the oarsmen.

The second approached soon after, but the interest Nith felt waned when the officer in charge's call sounded different. Worried they had been spotted, he caught Enya's glance.

"That sounded like he said 'halt'."

Enya knew more Latin words than he did but she looked unsure. Almost immediately snatched words of a song rose up over the emptiness of the water, a chant that was taken up by the men so melodically repetitive they no longer needed the pull and rest calls of the *centurion*. Fighting against the incoming tide – and stronger sea breezes – from forcing them ashore, the mariners hauled their way along the wide bay, their oars lifting high as they sang before splashing back down into the foam, the ship heading for the promontory at Am Broch.

Alongside him, Enya was lying flat and snorting onto her knuckles, trying hard to suppress the shaking of her shoulders.

He squirmed around to peer at her. "What amuses you so?"

Enya wriggled one hand up to cover her mouth, stifling her chortles before she rolled onto her side. "I think they are singing of what they will do to a willing woman."

Nith caught and held her gaze. He had no need to tell her what he would do to her given suitable circumstances. Still flat on his front, he stretched forward to grasp her hand.

After the second ship had passed by and was well into the distance, he waited immobile till he was sure there were no others.

"They must have been surveying all the way along the stretch of sea that reaches into the land beyond the headland you want to visit." Dhoughall sounded sure as he rolled up to his knees. He shook off the sand from his clothes and stood up, ready to lead them on. "Do you still want to walk along the sand?"

Nith's answer took little thought.

Picking their way along the beach now sounded too big a risk to take, though the other option was on such flat ground that they would be also be easily noticed from afar.

Some time later Enya was out in front, skirting her way around clumps of gorse that bordered a cleared field area, her hissed warning coming almost too late. "There is someone just up ahead."

"Show yourselves! Stand free of the bushes." The warrior's call sounded loud, not far from the cluster of roundhouses that sat a short walk in from the shoreline.

Edging closer to Enya, Nith watched as more warriors popped up into sight, their places of cover low bushes that surrounded the hamlet.

"Who are you?" One man asked as he approached them, his gaze firmly fixed on Enya, a puzzled frown appearing across his brows.

"We are searching for her brother," Nith answered.

"Enya!" The cry which came from the entrance of one of the roundhouses was followed by the pounding of feet as a young warrior launched himself across the space, the familiar face of Seaghan slowly following in his wake.

Nith could feel the excitement that burst from Enya as she flew into Ruoridh's arms, their hugs and jumps of glee fit to break each others bones.

"I knew I would find you alive!" Enya's gasps of happiness mingled with cries of sheer relief as tears coursed down her cheeks, tears from eyes that looked so similar to Ruoridh's.

Detaching herself only slightly from her brother's clutch, Nith felt her gaze seek him.

"Do you know that of all the warriors in these northern lands, you are the two men that I cannot do without?"

As he felt a huge grin spreading, Nith chose not to answer Ruoridh's chuckled question. "Has my little sister eventually declared her feelings for you, Nith?

***

The stories of the Garrigill clan will continue in Book 5 of the Celtic Fervour Series **Beathan the Brigante***, where we learn more of the fate of Beathan and of General Gnaeus Iulius Agricola.*

Tribal Map – Agricola's Bane

Glossary

Celtic
<u>Gods</u> – Araun (of the dead/ war/revenge and terror); Arddhu (forest); Cernunnos (green man/forest); Lugh (sun); Morimaru ('north' sea); Sucellus (hammer carrying); Taranis (sky)
<u>Goddesses</u> – Aarfen (fate); Andarta (overcoming enemies); Anugh (earth); Avon (River goddess A'an a tributary of the Abhainn Tuesis); Brighid (hearth); Caela (River goddess Abhainn Caelis); Cailleach Bheur (blue hag); Dheathain (River goddess Abhainn Dheathain); Momu (wells and hillsides); Rhianna (queen/horse); Scathach (of warrior women)

Roman
<u>Gods</u> – Aesculapius (medicine); Averruncus (averting calamity); Bonus Eventus (good outcome); Consus (protector of grains); dei consentes (12 main deities) ; Jove (alternative for Jupiter); Jupiter (supreme god); Mercurius (trickery/ transport/ travel); Vertumnus (seasons/gardens/ fruit trees)
<u>Goddesses</u> – Annonaria (grain supply); Bellona (war); Ceres (harvest/earth); Chione (snow); Clementia (forgiveness and mercy); Concordia (agreement); Epona (horse); Felicitas (good luck/success); Fortuna (fortune); Lymphae (water); Pax (peace); Tempestas (storms/sudden weather changes)

Celtic/Gaelic/Scots
Ard Righ – High King
Athair – father
A mhic an uilc! – You evil bastard!
bannock – round unleavened bread
braccae – trousers
bratt – cloak
brochan/brose – thin oatmeal porridge
carnyx – Celtic battle horn
Ceigean Ròmanach – Roman turds!
Ciamar a tha thu? – How are you?
clarsach – small harp

Diùbhadh! – Scum!
haar – low mist
hairst – harvest
leine – tunic
machair – marshes
Mathair – mother
Ròmanach buachar each! – Roman horse shit
seaghanachaidh – bard
small beer – low alcohol content

Latin and Roman Army terms used in Agricola's Bane

A – allectus (special courier); ala [s] alae [pl] (elite mounted regiment approx. 480 cavalry); auxiliary (soldier with no Roman citizenship status)

B – Batavian (units raised from Dutch Rhine area)

C – capsarius (medical assistant); carbonarius (charcoal/wood burner); castellum (small fort/tower); civitas (rules for civic/social structure); clipeus (round/oval shield); cohort (480 + grouping of soldiers); contubernium (basic unit in Roman army of 8 soldiers-ideally + two slaves); cornu (Roman G-shaped battle horn)

D – decanus (in charge of contubernium group); decurion (in charge of a turma of c. 30 mounted soldiers)

E – eques (senior army officer); exploratores (scout)

F – Forum Vespasiani (Vespasian's newly built Roman forum)

G – gladius (short stabbing sword); gubernator (helmsman or pilot)

I – ides (middle day of Roman month)

L – legatus (legion commander/ high ranking officer); lorica (chest armour-chain/plate/scale mail)

M – medicus (doctor); milles passsus (Roman mile)

O – optio (in charge of half of a century)

P – pilum [s] pila [pl] (spear/javelin); Praefectus Castrorum (camp prefect); Primus Pilus (senior centurion of a legion)

S – Salve! /Salvete! (welcome greeting to one person/ more than one); Senate (advisory council in Rome/ political institution); spatha [s] spathae [pl] (double-edged long sword); speculatores (spies/ infiltrators)

T –Templum Pacis (Temple of Peace in Rome); testudo (defensive tortoise shell for a contubernium group created from curved scuta/ shields); tironis (raw recruit to 6 months training); trierarchus [s] trierarchi [pl](ship's captain); tribunus [s] tribunii[pl] (senior officer of a legion - tribunus laticlavius more senior than a tribunus angusticlavius/ broad stripe and narrow stripe); tali (knucklebones); Tungrian (unit raised in 'Belgium'); turma (unit of mounted soldiers approx 30)

V – valetudinarium (hospital); venators (hunters)

Roman Legions in Agricola's Bane

Legio II Adiutrix; Legio IX; Legio XX; vexillationes (additional auxiliary units raised for a particular purpose or campaign)

Roman Navy

Classis Britannica

Roman Camp Locations

Aedes (shrine/place of worship); Porta Praetoria (gate leading to Praetoria); Praetorium (command staff accommodation); Principia (headquarters); Via Praetoria (street alongside Praetorium); Via Principalis (main street); vallum (rampart/wall) - intervallum (area left empty/ bare for defensive distance between rampart and tents/storage / livestock but not horses)

Celtic Dating terms

Imbolc – (evening before and into) Feb 1st
Beltane – (evening before and into) May 1st
Lughnasadh – (evening before and into) Aug 1st
Samhain – (evening before and into) Nov 1st

Summer Solstice – 21st June
Winter Solstice - 21st December (actual event can vary by a day or so astronomically)

Historical Context
Historically speaking, there is no attested written evidence of what actually happened in northern Britannia in A.D. 83 or 84. We mainly have the words of the ancient Roman writer *Cornelius Tacitus* to refer to about the campaigns of General Gnaeus Iulius Agricola in 'Scotland'. The campaign dates are highly debatable and (I believe) there is no proof that Tacitus witnessed any of the details he gave about Agricola's exploits. A few later writers, like Cassius Dio and Suetonius, make brief mentions about Agricola, though none are eyewitness accounts and are also from second hand information.

Tacitus wrote that his father-in-law, Agricola, aimed to invade and dominate the whole of Britannia and was (almost) successful. He stated that Agricola conquered Caledonia but then almost immediately 'let it go'. The answer to why that happened has not passed down to us in the translations of the *Agricola* which are available to us for study today.

According to Tacitus, a battle – *Mons Graupius* – took place late in the campaign season which was generally thought to be April to September/October. After the successful battle, Tacitus wrote that Agricola moved on to the territory of the 'Boresti' where he took some hostages and ordered the prefect of the fleet to sail around Britannia. Then Agricola, having marched slowly southwards in order to inspire fear in new nations by his very lack of hurry, placed his infantry and cavalry in winter quarters. Again these details are not specified and can only be speculated upon.

No Ancient Roman against Caledon Allies battle site has ever been identified north of the Central Belt area of Scotland (Clyde/Forth line). There have been a number of sites put forward as possibilities, but no particular one has been conclusively proven. These range from sites in Fife all the way to the north-east Moray coast near Elgin. Some historians are of the opinion that there never was a battle at all and the account in the *Agricola* was a figment of the imagination of

Tacitus, added in order to bolster the achievements of his father-in-law Agricola.

Tacitus wrote that Agricola was recalled to Rome, possibly in late A.D. 84 or early A.D. 85. Agricola, having been accorded a 'triumph' of sorts on his return to Rome, then retired to his Narbonensis estates and never held a position of authority again across the Roman Empire. Differences of opinion between Agricola and Emperor Domitian are alluded to by Tacitus, though are unspecified.

Since the written historical record is virtually non-existent, it falls to the keen historian to take into account the archaeological record. The study of archaeological remains is a vibrant and organic process as I write this note. I'm always delighted to hear, day after day, of a new excavation taking place somewhere across Britain. Recent discoveries continue to clarify the Roman invasions of northern Britain and I live in hope that some day the words of Tacitus can be proved, or conclusively disproved.

Evidence on the ground in northern Scotland is scant, but the progress of Agricola's northern campaigns – as evident in the trail of forts, fortlets and watchtowers on the Gask Ridge and 'Glen blocker' areas, and temporary marching camps – lead all the way north to the Moray coast. Till new exploration is conducted of sites where limited archaeological 'digs' took place, during the last decades of the twentieth century, we can only speculate what Agricola did and did not do in north-east Scotland after a pitched battle.

Evidence found at Inchtuthil Roman Fort in Perthshire (I name this Pinnata Castra in Book 4) indicates that this huge Roman supply fort was officially abandoned, after partial dismantling, in approximately A.D. 86. If Agricola was recalled to Rome in early A.D. 85, then his successor, or some other senior officer, possibly maintained the fort for a short time afterwards before the complete withdrawal of Roman troops.

The Roman presence continued further south, in the central belt of Scotland and the borders area, for some years after the withdrawal from the north – evidence for this found at forts like Trimontium, near Melrose.

Author's Note

It has taken me some time to put together *Agricola's Bane*, Book 4 of my Celtic Fervour Series. I could say that there were many reasons for it taking so long and that would definitely be the case, but what is very truthful is that I cannot stop researching this utterly fascinating era of late first century Roman Scotland/ Roman Britain.

During the past few years, I've delved into research books that were new to me, and have devoured fresh information that's been uncovered during archaeological excavations – especially relating to the Roman dominated south of Scotland and the border areas between Scotland and England. I've taken some excellent courses on Hadrian's Wall and on general Roman Empire history, my knowledge broadening along the way. My shelves of research books are groaning, as are my computer files of information gleaned from the internet – too many to give justice to specific ones here.

However, very little of my recent studies have been directly related to what happened in Roman invaded north-east Scotland in A.D. 84, yet there has been sufficient information for me to chew over what might have happened after a large pitched battle between the Agricolan forces and those of the Caledon Allies.

Having decided on my battle site being at Beinn na Ciche (Book 3 of the Series), I have thought long and hard about what my surviving 'Iron Age tribal Celts' did after fleeing to the hills (according to Tacitus). Agricola had northern Britannia in his grip but almost immediately 'let Scotland go' which doesn't indicate that treaties were arranged, or the land settled according to usual Roman fashion after a capitulation of the tribes. There was no mention by Tacitus that a new Roman Empire boundary was settled upon, but after being in the as-yet-unidentified Boresti territory, Agricola's forces marched south. We have no written evidence of where the Roman forces went to overwinter, or what the surviving tribes did after the Romans left their territory.

I debated many times with myself about what Agricola was going to get out of his newly invaded northern territory to add to the Roman coffers. Absorbing new land into an extended Roman Empire was only worth the effort of subduing and maintaining a settled *civitas,* if riches were to be had from it.

When Julius Caesar sailed from Gaul to southern Britannia in 55 B.C., he expected to gain material resources like gold, having been told that Britannia had lots of precious metals for the taking. Emperor Claudius probably made the same assumptions of riches he could purloin before his A.D. 43 invasion. Extending the Roman Empire for Claudius was worth some of the huge effort because, for a time, there were profits to be had from southern Britannia. The Claudian coffers weren't boosted by as much gold and silver as was perhaps hoped for, but Rome extracted plenty of tin and other ores as well as a nice regular supply of grain from southern farms – to mention only a few items.

The far north, on the other hand, doesn't seem to have yielded up similar riches as easily for Agricola. What Agricola might have gained through domination of the north has been a large preoccupation of mine. He was a seasoned soldier in Britannia, having spent the bulk of his military career in different parts of the island while attached to different legions. And all of that was before he became Commander of all Britannic troops and Governor of Britannia in c. A.D. 77/78. I think he must have known how little he was going to extract without regularly topped-up legions to ensure stability of the new addition to the province. Emperor Domitian seems to have starved him of soldiers towards the end of his governorship, so reaping valuable rewards must have looked impossible.

Getting inside the head of my Agricola as he anguishes his way through his problems has been a pleasure and one that I hope you can share.

As in the previous books in the series, I've added a few Gaelic words to give a sense of the auditory environment my 'Celtic' characters inhabit. Again, as in the earlier books I use the word 'Celtic' in the broad sense that I am writing about the native Iron Age tribes whose actual names are lost to us. I've continued, as before, to use the names of local tribes as recorded by Claudius Ptolemaeus on his map of Britannia that was created some fifty years after the events of A.D. 84, copies of which have come down to us over the centuries. This time, though, I can write here that I really do believe that the names Ptolemy used must have in some way have been influenced by information sent back to Rome by Agricola/ and or Agricola's support staff. (Read more of my reasoning for the above in the Author's Note of earlier books)

Also as before, I've had great fun choosing specific names for my characters the meanings of which display some sense of their personal traits. More details of my naming processes can be accessed on my blog (https://nancyjardine.blogspot.com). You'll also find articles on my blog of other aspects which have intrigued, or even concerned me, during my researches – such as the question of when the ancient hillforts at Bennachie, Tap O'Noth and Dunrelugas were first constructed. Beinn na Ciche being the hill of 'Ce' has also been troublesome. If, as is thought, the hill range is named after a leader named 'Ce' of around A.D. 500/600, I'd dearly love to know what the hill range was named back in A.D. 84! I use the names in Aberdeenshire, Moray and Banff and Buchan as they presently are on an ordinance survey map, to give my readers a sense of the geographical locations.

Having been starved of written historical facts to base my story on, yet armed with adequate archaeological data, I've thoroughly enjoyed writing my fictitious account of what my Garrigill characters do during the aftermath of the Battle of Beinn na Ciche. I hope you enjoy reading about them as much as I enjoy writing about them. The series continues in Book 5 which develops the story of Beathan the Brigante. If you've enjoyed my Agricola, then you'll also find a little bit more of his story in Book 5.

Celtic Fervour Series

Book 1 The Beltane Choice
Book 2 After Whorl: Bran Reborn
Book 3 After Whorl: Donning Double Cloaks
Book 4 Agricola's Bane

Nominations

After Whorl: Bran Reborn, Book 2 of the Celtic Fervour Series, was accepted for THE WALTER SCOTT PRIZE FOR HISTORICAL FICTION 2014.

The Taexali Game, a time travel novel set in Roman 'Aberdeenshire' AD 210 achieved Second Place for Best Self Published Book in the SCOTTISH ASSOCIATION OF WRITERS—Barbara Hammond Competition 2017. and an *indieBRAG* Medallion, January 2018.

Topaz Eyes, an ancestral based mystery thriller, was a Finalist for THE PEOPLE'S BOOK PRIZE FICTION 2014

The novels in the *Celtic Fervour Series* have Discovered Diamond Status from the prestigious Discovering Diamond Reviews.

Ocelot Press

Ocelot Press

Thank you for reading this Ocelot Press book. If you enjoyed it, we'd greatly appreciate it if you could take a moment to write a short review on the website where you bought the book (e.g. Amazon), and/or on Goodreads, or recommend it to a friend. Sharing your thoughts helps other readers to choose good books, and authors to keep writing.

You might like to try books by other Ocelot Press authors. We cover a range of genres, with a focus on historical fiction (including historical mystery and paranormal), romance and fantasy. To find out more, please don't hesitate to connect with us on:

Website: https://ocelotpress.wordpress.com/
Email: ocelotpress@gmail.com
Twitter: @OcelotPress
Facebook**:** https://www.facebook.com/OcelotPress/

Other novels by Nancy Jardine

Ancestral/ family tree based Mystery/Thrillers:
Monogamy Twist
Topaz Eyes
Romantic Comedy Mystery
Take Me Now
Time Travel Historical Adventure (Annaril Publishing)
The Taexali Game (suitable from age 10)

The story of my Garrigill warriors continues
…in Book 5 ***Beathan the Brigante*** (the following is unedited)

Trimontium Roman Fort A.D. 84

"Your mother is a Brigante?"

The words were in the tongue of the tribes but were hesitant and came slowly.

Beathan stared at the smooth wooden planking beneath his feet and forced himself to stay alert, though could not prevent himself from swaying towards the edge of the wooden table in front of him.

"Answer me!"

When the tip of the *centurion's* vine rod stabbed under his chin, Beathan managed to gather enough strength to raise his head, fully expecting another jaw slap but it did not come. Weary of the *tribune's* repeated questions and the pummelling he had already received, his answer was a faint croak.

"Nay, I told you already that my mother is the daughter of Callan of Tarras of the Selgovae."

"Then you are Selgovae."

"Nay. I am Brigante." Many times during his long journey to this place they named *Trimontium,* he had been gut wrenchingly repentant over having revealed his kinship at the Moran Dhuirn Roman Camp but now that was replaced by a deep anger.

Tribune Secundus stared up at him from his seated position behind the table, the man's brawny forearms placed flat and supporting his weight. Beathan watched the grimy right-hand fingernails tap a short rhythm against the polished wood before the Roman officer finished a calculating inspection.

He had lost count of how many times the man had asked the same questions

A swift conversation in Latin followed between Tribune Secundus and Centurion Atticus, only some of which Beathan understood. They discussed something about the Selgovae tribe though exactly what Beathan could not be sure. Even if he understood all of the words, he was not certain he would know what they referred to since it had been many long seasons since he had spent some time at the Selgovae hillfort of Tarras. A fleeting memory of his grandfather's roundhouse came to him and the irascible old Callan telling him to never ever trust the Votadini.

"Where is this place you name Tarras?"

You can buy the books of the *Celtic Fervour Series* in ebook, or in paperback versions, from suppliers like Amazon https://www.amazon.co.uk/Nancy-Jardine/e/B005IDBIYG/ and other websites across the internet.

Alternatively, buy paperback versions directly from the author (contact via email or website), and locally at various venues across Aberdeenshire, Scotland – mainly at FOCUS Craft Fair Events.

"I have read all three of Celtic Fervour Series books by Nancy Jardine and could not put them down! Thoroughly enjoyed the story telling that had such vivid and believable characters that came to life in their Celtic ways and culture. Well done Nancy, you make it feel so real! Can't wait to read the fourth book (Agricola's Bane)!"
Graeme T Smith, History Blog 'alba-gu-brath.com'

Printed in Poland
by Amazon Fulfillment
Poland Sp. z o.o., Wrocław